DON'T FORGET YOUR SPACESUIT, Dear

EDITED BY
JODY
LYNN NYE

BAEN

DON'T FORGET YOUR SPACESUIT, DEAR

Copyright © 1996 by Jody Lynn Nye.

All material is original to this volume and is copyright © 1996 by the individual authors.

A Baen Books Original

Baen Publishing Enterprises
P.O. Box 1403
Riverdale, N.Y. 10471

ISBN: 0-671-87732-1

Cover art by David Mattingly

First printing, July 1996

Distributed by
SIMON & SCHUSTER
1230 Avenue of the Americas
New York, N.Y. 10020

Printed in the United States of America

THE VOICE OF COMMAND

The two fleets maneuvered subtly as they drew ominously closer. On the bridge of the Terran flagship, the crew waited in nervous silence. Steely-eyed, with his jaw set in stern determination, the commander glanced at the screen showing the opposing fleet. He hardened his tones to the firm voice of command.

"Pass the word! Battle stations!"

"Sir!" It was his communications officer. "There's a call coming in on subspace."

"Patch it through," the commander said, trying to sound unruffled.

There was a moment's silence, then a tentative voice came from the speakers. "Raymie? Is that you?"

The crew exchanged startled glances, then looked at their commander who was staring at the speakers in what could only be described as frozen horror.

"Mom?" he said, at last.

"There you are, Raymie." The unseen voice was now confident. "I was just calling to see if everything was all right with you."

"Nothing's wrong, Mom. I'm fine. Really. It's just been a very busy day…and it's about to get busier in a few minutes."

"I knew it had to be something important. I knew that you wouldn't let Mother's Day go by without calling unless something life or death came up."

"As a matter of fact, it is a matter of life or death, Mom," the commander said. "We're about to go into battle in a few minutes, so if there's nothing else…"

"You're what? Going into battle? On Mother's Day?"

"Come on, Mom. It's not like I planned it this way. It's just how it happened. Okay?"

"No, it's not okay! And don't take that tone with me, Raymond!"

"But Mom…"

"'But Mom' nothing!"

—from "You Never Call"

BAEN BOOKS by JODY LYNN NYE

The Death of Sleep
(with Anne McCaffrey)

The Ship Who Won
(with Anne McCaffrey)

The Ship Errant
(forthcoming)

To Mom, who always made me put on a
sweater when *she* was cold, with love
— JLN
To my mom and in memory of my
boibe — EG
For Mam — MS
To Mom — RLA
In memory of my mother — JRC
To my mother, who taught me — ML
To my Mom — EAS
For my mother — WRF
For Mom, Mother, and my grandmothers
— EF
To Mom —BF
To Anne Dorothy McElroy McCaffrey
— AM
To Mom, for, you know,
all that stuff — GAE
To Mom, who knew I could — LAG
Tell the mothers of Sparta that we stand
here, obedient to their will — ES & CS
Because you both knew we'd make you
proud — TB & CVP
To Mother, who really *does* know best — JS
To Ma: I'll look for a real job tomorrow
— MR
Mom, with all my love — LR
In loving memory of my mother — ENM
To Peter's Mum — DED

CONTENTS

From Your Mouth to God's Ear

Ellen Guon

The morning started out quietly enough. Another mainshift, with me signing on as Johnson signed off. She annotated a few last entries in the log, handing me the lightpen and the clipboard on her way down the walkway. Then it was the start of my shift, and I slid into the seat in front of all the monitors and lit circuit boards. Taking the Chair, as it was called.

From this spot, you can see everything that's going on in the station, in a literal and figurative sense. Central, the command center of Transient Station #4, is a series of unpainted metal walkways, open and stacked like the racks inside an oven. The walkways are lined with chairs and consoles, the boards of which control all of the functions of the station.

And then there's the Chair, which is the post for the shift supervisor. That's me. From the Chair, I can direct my teams in an emergency, and take over control of any system in the station if I have to. It's a lot of responsibility.

When everything's going well, Central is still busy, but routine. The boards currently showed the flawless automated procedure as a shuttle docked, offloading cargo and colonists. The navigational systems worked with the colony ship's computer to plot the correct course outsystem, taking the colonists off to their new homes. And the day-to-day life of the station is monitored here: the environmental and power systems, everything that keeps the station going all the time. We've been the stopover point for colonists heading outsystem for the last fifty years, and we're proud of it. But usually, it's a pretty boring job.

Except for today. Ten minutes into my shift, it happened. A single light flashed yellow twice on the main boards, surrounded by a sea of bright green lights. Then it went to red. Solid, unblinking red.

I slapped the Panic Button on the wall a split-second later. "Depressurization emergency in Section 12! The locks aren't engaging! Immediate evacuation, get everyone out of there! Move it, guys, this one's for real!"

The sirens went off, and I could hear the thundering sound of boots on the metal walkways above and below me. I activated a board that showed the environmental team's position—closing in on the failing airlock system—and pounded my fist on the chair arm in frustration. "Damn it, why aren't the autolocks engaging? We're still losing air in those compartments!"

There were lights indicating the five people inside the compartment, now moving quickly to the next section, where, hopefully, the autolocks would seal off behind them. If not, the team would manually seal the locks after themselves. If they reached there in time.

I stayed where I was. That's my job, as mainshift supervisor, to stay put and coordinate everything while the juniors head for the emergency site, carrying the gear we hope never to need to use: emergency suits, medical supplies, torches for cutting through the automatically-sealing compartments to free the people trapped inside. And the body bags, in case the system fails.

It's not supposed to fail. Why weren't the locks engaging?

I sat there, watching the boards and listening to the radio chatter. That's a super's job, to supervise, not to be there helping them. More than anything, I wanted to vault out of the Chair, grab a suit and head down to Section 12 to help. But I sat there, doing my job, feeling more and more angry and frustrated as the seconds ticked past.

Then Harris's voice on the comm. "It's all right, boss. We've sealed it. Everyone's out, no one got hurt. It's okay."

For a moment I felt dizzy with relief, and leaned back in the Chair. One thought kept going through my mind: the system didn't work. The locks should have sealed themselves. Why didn't they work?

Why?

According to the brochures, Transient Station #4 is critical to the space colonization effort. Thousands of colonists pass through here every week, entering from one of the many shuttles that cart them up from Earth to the station in lunar orbit; then the colonists exit on one of the large colony ships that cart them onward to their new homes.

It's also a little tin can, floating in cold space. There's very little here that's keeping us alive.

No one ever thinks about that, just how fragile this place really is. That there's empty space surrounding us, and that if a critical system should fail, everyone on the station would die. You can't think about that, or you'd go nuts. It would be like wondering if you're going to choke to death every time you eat a bite of food.

Besides, the station has been in operation for fifty years, with no system failures. Ever. Oh sure, little things went wrong all the time. But not *systems*. Transient Station #4 was one of the first stations built with the self-updating computer systems, which everyone takes for granted now but was apparently a Big Thing when the station was built.

Except now, fifty years later, it wasn't working right.

My appointment with the station Director was at 11:45 maintime. Just as well it was before lunch; I

sure wouldn't have been able to eat anything. Garner
had shown me the bent metal fittings of the airlock
seal. I couldn't banish the image from my mind, the
quarter inch of space that had nearly meant death for
five colonists. We were lucky; there's no other way to
describe it.

Walking on the plush carpeting that led to the
Director's office, I wondered what system could go
next. The artificial gravity? That'd be one of the worst,
slowing down the emergency crews to a crawl as they
raced to whatever disaster happened next. What about
the air circulation pumps? Another set of airlock seals,
or maybe an overload in the power generators?

I thought about when I was a kid, growing up
downside and learning how to drive. That's how this
felt; it was like driving a groundcar with no brakes and
no idea what was awaiting us at the end of the road.

I stepped into the Director's office, and waited for
her to notice me. She was intent on the flatscreen in
front of her. Probably reading out the logbooks on
how we nearly blew open part of the station.

Some of the less reverent officers refer to the
Director as the Old Lady. True, she's older than all
of us, probably close to forty. Space exploration is a
job for the young, as the saying goes. But when she
turns those intense dark brown eyes on you, phrases
like the "Old Lady" just don't seem to apply. She's
the Director, with a capital D. A tall, muscular woman
with the first streaks of silver showing in her long dark
hair and that no-nonsense gaze that felt intense
enough to melt steel bulkheads. I'd sometimes
thought about how I'd like to grow up and be the
Director: not the job, but the woman. I'd like to
inherit that calm, controlled way of looking at the
world, and knowing exactly what your place was in it.
And the way she is so comfortable and relaxed with
people. I wouldn't mind being a person like that.

"I've read the reports, Forrester. Your comments?"

I took a deep breath, and started. "It was definitely a computer systems failure. The hatch opened too quickly, denting the exterior lock. Then we'd had the secondary failure, with the emergency seals system not engaging. Fortunately, it was a only tiny gap leaking air, and we could evacuate everyone before we lost pressure in the entire section. If you'll read the report, you'll see—"

"I have," the Director said dryly. "Including Harris's verbal commentary about how we're all going to die because the computer system is so messed up. What do you think?"

"The computer system's very old, ma'am. Fifty years old. It was installed before any of us were born. It's written in the self-updating version of C Triple. It was one of the first programming languages that literally wrote itself; if it found a bug, it would write a fix for it automatically. It's been like ... like a toaster or an oven; no one has ever needed to do anything to it at all. Even when we've had a power surge or drop, it has automated systems that kick in and keep everything going. It's been as reliable as a door hinge, all these years. Until now."

The Director surveyed me calmly as I paused to take a breath. How could she be so calm? Didn't she understand what was happening? "There isn't any documentation on the computer system language. There was once, but someone threw it out years ago," I continued. "We don't even have anyone here who knows the language. Harris has tried to figure it out, but he says it's just a mass of patches now, totally garbaged. No one's looked at it for at least twenty years, and it's been updating itself the whole time, unsupervised. It's a real mess. Spaghetti doesn't even begin to describe it. And it runs everything ... the emergency systems, the life support routines, the docking systems. Everything."

"So next time we have a computer system failure,

it might be the automated docking system crashing a shuttle into the side of the station?" the Director asked.

"Uh, yes, ma'am. Or the system shutting down life support because it's misreading the oxygen ratio data collectors."

"And this horrific situation has been building, unnoticed, for how many years?"

Here it comes. Now I'd get to learn how it feels to be fired. I'd never lost a job yet. Then again, I'd never had another job. I took the position working for the systems super here immediately after getting my engineering degree at MIT. Which had taught me *nothing* about C Triple or any other ancient programming language.

I'd been promoted only two months ago, after the super had headed off to the colonies. I'd thought I could handle his job, no problem. Right.

And now I was going to get fired. What would happen to me after this? Where would I go? And what would happen to the station after I left? How long until the next disaster? And how many people would die?

I was ready to do the right thing. The envelope was in my pocket, ready to hand to the director. I realized she'd repeated her question, and snapped back to the present.

"No excuses, ma'am. None." I reached into my pocket for the envelope that I'd placed there, just before leaving Central for this meeting. I wasn't certain what you were supposed to say in a resignation letter, but I'd improvised something that sounded formal enough. "It's my fault for not realizing what could happen earlier. The system had run flawlessly for so many years, no one thought ... well, it's my fault, and I want to ... I want to do the right thing. I'll resign my position here."

The Director gestured impatiently at the envelope

in my hand. "If that's a resignation letter, you can put that away away. Forrester, you're not getting off the hook that easily."

"I'm not?" I felt a rush of relief, followed instantly by pure terror. If I wasn't going to be fired, I was going to have to *fix* this mess?

"No, you're not. I want a list of recommendations for solving this on my desk by the end of shift today. We have ten thousand colonists come through this station on their way outsystem every month. We have to fix this so there's no loss of life. I don't have much in the way of discretionary funds, but I'll scrape together everything we've got to pay for computer renovations. We can't risk anything less." She leaned forward, elbows on the desk. "Forrester, you're the best supervisor I have on this station. I know what you're capable of. I'm going to give you everything I can, stand behind you one hundred percent on this, and you're going to deliver. You understand?"

I realized I was standing there with my mouth open, and quickly shut it. "Right," I said, feigning a briskness and self-confidence that I didn't feel. She believed I could handle this disaster. Right then, I vowed I wouldn't fail her. "Well, first we'll need a top systems analyst. The software has been so patched over the years, it's probably in need of a complete overhaul. The problem will be finding someone who knows the system language, which hasn't been taught in schools for twenty years, at least."

"So find an older programmer," the Director said, a little impatiently. "There's got to be one out there somewhere, right? Take care of it, Forrester." The Director gave me one last piercing look, then turned back to the papers on her desk. After standing there stupidly for a couple seconds, I realized that I'd been dismissed. I left the office, the crumpled envelope still clutched in my hand.

So this is what it feels like, to have the welfare of the entire station resting on your shoulders.

The first thing I did was call a staff meeting. The conference room, with its old scratched rectangular table, was the only place that could hold the entire systems team staff in privacy. We definitely didn't want to hold this meeting anyplace where we could be overheard, such as the main cafeteria. Harris was sitting next to Johnson, my two best people and worst troublemakers at the closest corner of the table, Smitty, Hargrave, Pointer, Lackland, and the rest beyond them. I sat on the edge of the conference room table, my usual perch, and looked out at the sea of faces in front of me, the twenty engineers who reported to me, and realized that there wasn't a single one who was older than thirty in the bunch.

Damn.

We needed an older programmer. Someone who was not only fluent in a programming language that hadn't been taught for twenty years, but was an expert in it. Where was I going to find someone like that?

I remembered the guy from college ... what was his name? McCauley? He'd been in the programming classes with me, and was a collector of old programming documentation. What I wouldn't give to have him around right now! I'd worked with this team for years now, and knew that none of them had that kind of hobby.

"You know what's going on with the computer system," I began bluntly. "We need a top programmer with C Triple experience, and lots of it. Someone with a great track record, since all of our lives will be depending on this person. I have no idea how we're going to find this person, but within twenty-four hours, we're going to do it. Everyone's going to be working overtime on this problem until it's solved."

Smitty raised his hand. "Should we try the employment

agencies on the ground, ma'am? We could have someone on a shuttle on their way up here tomorrow morning."

"Good idea."

Harris had that puckered expression, like he was drinking lemonade, that he gets when he thinks we're in big trouble. From a real sour lemon, not the sickly sweet reconstituted powder they ship to us here. "How long until the system fails completely, supe?"

"Why, you want to transfer out?" I asked, and got a laugh from some of the other engineers. It was bad, but it wasn't that bad. Yet.

"Well, I've been looking at the job list for the colonies that need system engineers ..." he began.

"Yeah, right," I said, standing up and stretching. "No transfers until this is over, folks. One-and-a-half time shifts from here on, going over every computer-controlled system to make sure that they're in top condition. I want everyone spending today coming up with a list of where we can find programmers who can solve this for us, searching for any old documentation that wasn't thrown out, any reference material on C Triple, *anything*."

I looked at the crowd, and saw Johnson, absently toying with a lock of her long bright red hair, off to one side. Johnson had that look in her eyes that I remembered really well, from all the shifts we'd worked together before my promotion to super. The last time I'd seen that look, she was patching a faulty vacuum pipe with the wrapper off her peanut butter sandwich. It had been hell to pry it out afterwards, but it had worked. "Johnson, what are you thinking?" I asked suspiciously.

"Nothing, boss," she said, giving me that wide-eyed innocent look that I never trusted. "Nothing at all."

"Okay, team," I said, giving Johnson another look. "We'll meet at the end of shift and see if anyone's made any progress."

*   *   *

I didn't expect anything at the endshift meeting. I'd spent all day calling the employment agencies downside, and talking to the supers on the other orbital stations. I chased down the chief engineers on a couple colony ships, hoping that maybe I could find someone with the skills we needed and talk them into staying for another few weeks to solve this.

No luck at all. No one knew C Triple coding. No one.

The team straggled into the meeting, one by one. No one had the "I solved it!" look that I was hoping for. Damn.

Then Johnson walked in, with a little old lady following closely behind her. A very short, very wrinkled little old lady, wearing a prim long-sleeved dress, square antique eyeglasses, with her white hair covered under a colored scarf.

You could've heard a pin drop in that conference room.

"You said to get creative, boss," Johnson said into the sudden silence. "So I did. Folks, this is Dr. Rina Garfinkle. She's a retired computer systems analyst. She was on her way to the Lubavitch colony on Faraway with her family, but I convinced her to stay here and help us, and then take a later ship to Faraway. She's willing to help."

"She's a colonist?" Harris said in a disbelieving whisper. "You brought in a *colonist*?"

"She's not a programmer, she's a geriatric case!" I heard someone whisper behind me, almost but not quite too soft to be heard.

The old woman stood there silently, very dignified, completely ignoring the murmurs through the room as Johnson continued. "She's got over fifteen years experience in programming C Triple, plus a half dozen other, uh, really old languages," Johnson said, a little defensively. "Like C++. She even knows Microsoft C++! Can you believe it?"

"Nobody's used that language in, what, fifty years or something, right?" Smitty asked.

"Fifty-five years, to be exact," the old woman said. Her voice was clear, but frail. "The last time it was used for the operating systems of the European space shuttle program, back in '15. I was senior systems engineer for that project."

"Isn't that something!" Johnson said, her eyes shining.

I knew that look in her eyes. It was going to be impossible to dissuade her of this idea, no matter how crazy it was. And this was crazy. Johnson might be infatuated with this walking historical relic, but to risk the lives of everyone on the station on her elderly shoulders? It was insane.

I stood up slowly. "Johnson, can we talk for a minute?"

Johnson nodded, and followed me out into the hallway. "Is something wrong, boss?"

"Johnson, I know you think this old lady is terrific, but we have to think whether this is the right decision or not."

"She's living history, boss," Johnson said exuberantly. "She's worked on programs that are in the textbooks! She's just amazing!"

"She doesn't have Alzheimer's or anything like that, does she?" I asked. "I mean we're risking a lot here."

"You're being ageist, boss." Johnson frowned at me.

"What?" I said, surprised.

"Just because she's old doesn't mean that she doesn't have the stuff, you know? She's great. I spent the last couple hours interviewing her, with her grandchildren all running around underfoot. She kept them under control the whole time she was answering a lot of really technical questions, no problem. You'll see boss, she's the answer to our prayers. And besides,"

Johnson continued in a practical tone, "What alternative do we have?"

She was right about that. I hadn't come up with another solution, nor had anyone else on the team. God, my head hurt! I rubbed at my eyes. "All right, all right. Let's get her signed up."

We walked into the room. The old woman was still standing in the same spot, silent. I couldn't interpret the look in her eyes. Doubt? Concern?

No, she was just watching me. And the look in her eyes . . . I recognized it now, the same look that the Director had. That same calmness, but even more so, magnified by more years and experience. It was the look of someone who knew who she was, and what she could do. Suddenly, I began to feel a little better about this whole idea. Not much better, but a little.

"Dr. Garfinkle, pending review of your credentials, I think we'll be able to start you on the systems work in the next couple hours. Welcome aboard," I added, and reached out my hand to her.

Her hand was very thin, the skin dry and papery, but her handshake was strong.

God help us if I'm wrong on this one, I thought.

By the start of the next mainshift, Johnson had Dr. Garfinkle set up in a spare office. I stopped by to look in the door, but the old woman caught sight of me and gestured for me to join her.

She had four systems running an automated check of some kind, plus a handful of old, dog-eared reference books piled on the table next to her. "Good morning, Miss Forrester," she said, in her soft voice.

"Everyone calls me Forrester," I said. "You don't have to call me Miss Forrester."

"Why not?" she said, and smiled. "A little formality can be a good thing." She turned back to the monitors, typing in some instructions in a programming language I couldn't read.

"Right. So, how's it going?" I asked, looking at the incomprehensible code instructions scrolling past on the monitors.

"It is quite a problem," she admitted. "But I know I can make your systems behave. I dealt with something like this with another C Triple system, about twenty years ago. It had turned itself into something that looked more like Irish lace than logic, because the self-coding mechanism had gotten completely out of control. But I fixed it."

"Twenty years ago!" I shook my head in disbelief. "I was still in kindergarten then."

"Yes, it was a long time ago." She surveyed me with those calm, clear eyes. "You don't like me, do you, Miss Forrester?"

Startled by the question, it was a long moment before I answered. "I don't know you well enough to like you or not, ma'am," I replied. "I just hope you can do the job for us. All of our lives are depending on that. Your life, too," I added.

"But you are concerned that I can't," she said, nodding. "As am I. If I fail at this, many people could die, including you and me. So you are worried."

"I'd be lying if I said otherwise, ma'am."

She smiled. "An honest answer is always a good one. You're concerned about my competency. As well you should be. I retired from my position with RocketOps fifteen years ago. The technological world had passed me by, young woman, but I was ready for that. This is something you should be careful of . . . never let them make you obsolete." She idly patted one of the computer monitors. "Like these are obsolete. But I had my grandchildren, and the plans for the new colony, and that was enough for me. I'll probably do more systems work, if they need me. They'll need everyone at first. But I expect to spend most of my time with my grandchildren. That's how it is in our culture: the old take care of the very young. Are you a mother yet, Miss Forrester?"

I blinked. "I'm not even partnered yet, ma'am! I don't plan on being a parent for a long time. Maybe never."

"Ah. That would be unfortunate." She turned back to the monitors for another moment, checking for something. I couldn't tell what. "My daughter was born in 2004, and my husband and I decided that while she was very young would be a good time for me to go back to school for my doctorate. So I raised a young child and helped build the first crystalline AI at the same time. It gave me an interesting perspective on computer programming and crystalline AI. And children."

"Do you think they're alike? Computers and children, I mean?"

"Oh, no!" She laughed, a warm sound among the quiet hum and whir of the machines. "They're completely different. A computer is designed for specific tasks, while a child . . . a child can become anything. But a program can be more like a parent, or at least, one can learn to think in the same way as a parent does. I'm always thinking about how to keep my children and grandchildren safe, how to make sure a child grows up to be the kind of person it should. That's what I do."

"They don't teach anything like that in college these days," I said, shaking my head. "I studied two years of systems design. They just teach us how to build a system, or, really, how to tell the system to build itself."

She gave me an odd look. "You're a nice girl. My grandnephew, Ephraim, he's like you. Always in the books, reading, studying. Never taking time for anything else."

"Is he a programmer too?" I asked, curious.

"He's a geneticist. He works in one of the research

parks. He jokes about making his fortune by engineering kosher shrimp, but he's a good boy." She glanced at the wall clock, and smiled back at me. "It's mainshift lunch. Would you like to join me for a sandwich, Miss Forrester?"

I thought about it briefly. Usually I just ate a sandwich at my desk, or with the systems team. Sometimes with a super from another division. But not a colonist, never with a colonist. Then again, this lady wasn't really a colonist, she was now part of the team. I nodded. "Sure, why not?"

I told Harris about Dr. Garfinkle's work over breakfast before one shift, two weeks later. "No way to know if it's going to work, whatever it is she's doing to the system. But she's working hard."

Johnson slid down into the seat across from us, her breakfast tray clattering on the tabletop. "So, how's it going? I haven't had much time to stop in on Dr. Garfinkle and see how she's doing."

"She's ... she's really a find," I said. "She's been working double shifts every day since she started on this. I wish I could get the rest of you to work that hard," I added.

I watched the grin widen across Johnson's face. Harris gave me a dirty look. "What, we don't work hard enough for you? I'm appalled, boss!" he said in mock horror.

"I bet you are," Johnson said with a laugh.

Harris glared at her. "You haven't heard it all. Forrester says that the old lady is treating the computer like she's raising a child. What kind of kid is she going to raise, outdated and half senile?"

"She's not senile, she's just different," I said, more than a little annoyed.

"Weird, you mean." He took a bite of his sweet roll.

"No, just different. Maybe we've really needed someone like her. She looks at things differently.

Takes the long view," I said. "That's not a bad thing, to think more about the future."

"She's had, what, eighty years to get the long view?" Harris asked.

"She's making me think about things, too. I realized that I don't really believe in anything. I'm not really headed anywhere. And I'm not even twenty-five years old. Dr. Garfinkle's got to be, what, in her eighties, and she's headed someplace." I took another sip of my coffee. "I just hope the system won't be too hard to fix. We can't keep her here forever, working on the system, and we sure can't afford any more accidents."

"From your mouth to God's ear, child," Dr. Garfinkle said, standing above us. I hadn't even noticed her walking past with the tray of breakfast food in her hand, but there she was. "May I join you?"

"Excuse me, I have to get back to Central," Harris said, and stood up abruptly. Johnson glared at him as he walked away.

"Please, join us," I said, as Johnson slid over to make room for the elderly woman.

"Thank you," Dr. Garfinkle said. She sat down with the tray, and sipped her orange juice. "So, Miss Forrester, I was hoping you'd continue your description of how they're teaching computer science in the colleges now."

"Well," I began, "we did have an overview of the history of programming, starting back with Ada and Babbage, but after that we immediately got into some of the newer AI languages."

"Which ones?" Dr. Garfinkle asked. She seemed genuinely curious, not just making small talk.

"What, do you want to learn some new languages?" Johnson asked.

"You should never stop learning, Miss Johnson," Dr. Garfinkle said gently. "Not ever."

There was an odd silence before I continued. "So, let's see. I started out learning Alpha Plus, which is the system they're using for space navigation now on the newer ships. The artificial intelligence on that one is really clever, probably smarter than most of the people who program it. Then there's Pascal Composite . . ."

Two weeks with no system failures. Two weeks biting my nails, waiting for the worst to happen.

Two weeks of lunch breaks with Dr. Garfinkle. After lunch that first day, I just happened to be walking by her temporary office close to mainshift lunch break on the next day. Then it became a habit.

We talked about everything during those lunches. Or, rather at first, she talked and I listened. She talked about her work with our antique system, projects she'd worked on in the past, her children, her grandchildren, the new colony, her plans for the future.

Then she started asking me questions. About my family, college, life on the station. Eventually, I started answering some of the questions, talking about stuff that I hadn't talked about in years. About how my family had wanted me to go with them to a colony, but I'd refused. About the years in college, where the intellectual challenges were the best, but it still seemed like something was missing. And about life on the station, which had been very boring, until just a few weeks ago.

But mostly I listened to her talk. She would talk about what her life would be like on the new colony, and how she missed her children and her grandchildren. Impulsively, one lunch while she was talking about the voyage to her new home, I said, "I'll miss you, you know."

"Will you now?" she asked, looking down at me from over the top of those antique eyeglasses.

"From what Johnson and Smitty say, the system is already running better. Fewer yellow light emergencies than we've had for months, years!" I said. "Now my biggest worry is what'll happen when you leave! You've done such good work."

"I've taught the system to look to the future," she said, pushing a stray strand of gray hair back under the scarf. "To think of what might go wrong, and to be ready for that. And when the system updates itself, it will keep you informed, and also tell you about any long-term changes. That way, the situation you had before, with so many quick fixes that combined to ruin the system, should never happen again." She smiled. "Another few days of observation, then I believe the work will be finished," she said.

"Really?" I said, amazed. "I thought it was going to take a lot longer. Months and months." I shook my head. "I really will miss you, Dr. Garfinkle. Not just because you've done such an astounding job, but because I've really enjoyed the time we've spent talking together. I don't get to meet many new people."

"But what about all the colonists that travel through here?" Dr. Garfinkle asked. "Aren't there thousands of colonists staying here every week? Don't you get to meet any of them?"

"Not really," I said, thinking about the faceless crowds. I'd never bothered to get to know any of them. "All I've ever done here is watch people leave," I added, a little wistfully. My pager flashed, and I touched it for the voice messenger. "Forrester here."

"Boss, this is Johnson. There's something weird showing up on the boards, you'd better come look at it."

I stood up. "Excuse me, I'd better get back to Central."

"I'll come with you," Dr. Garfinkle said firmly, rising to her feet. She followed me through the warren of tunnels to the noisy room of Central. We stopped in front of the Chair, where Johnson was stationed for the alternative shift, looking down at the spread of monitors surrounding her. I glanced up involuntarily at the Panic button, the bright red plastic circle on the wall nearby.

"Check this out, boss," Johnson said. "The system has been doing this all morning. Building up the CO_2 pressure in this tank right next to the airlock in Section 15. Doesn't make any sense."

"Anything else going on around there?"

Johnson shook her head. "Nothing, really. Oh, there was a report from some of the transients in Section 15, something about their ears popping all morning, a slow pressure increase in the whole section."

"How high?"

"Not much higher than usual. I didn't think anything of it, it's nowhere near any dangerous levels. Just a little higher air pressure." She pointed at the screen. "This tank, though, is a totally different story. It's definitely going beyond the usual parameters. Not dangerous, but very strange. It must be another computer error . . ." She glanced at Dr. Garfinkle standing behind me, and stopped.

"No. I can't bet on that." I thought about it for a moment, and then felt something cold run down my back. "That tank and airlock are next to the main solvent tanks. Has anyone been working on those tanks in the last couple days?"

"Harris was checking the seals on those tanks, but he didn't find anything wrong . . ."

"Get him up here, right now." I turned to Johnson. "What's on the other side of those seals?"

Smitty spoke without looking up from his monitors. "Transient classrooms. Fifteen colonists preschoolers and their teachers in each compartment."

After a moment, I heard Harris's voice from across the room. "The solvent tanks are fine, supe. It must be a computer error."

"Like hell it is, Harris. I want someone suited up and out there, right now." The light on the main boards flickered yellow one more time. "Team, we've got a potential systems failure, Section 15. Prep for emergency evacuation of all nearby areas, possible pressurization emergency."

"Stay calm, child," Dr. Garfinkle murmured next to me. "Panic will serve nothing."

"Right, right," I muttered, my hands moving quickly over the boards. "What's the pressure in that CO_2 tank, Johnson?"

"Still building, but not dangerous yet."

"Right. Let's get those kids out of there."

Suddenly, a single light on the board flashed, yellow once, and then went to bright red. *No, not again!*

"We just lost the exterior seal on that airlock!" I reached out and slapped the Panic Button. "Johnson, get out of the Chair!"

She was already moving as the sirens began to wail. "I'll take the secondary environmental boards, boss," she said, sliding into the next console station. "The emergency team is on the way."

Would the inner seal hold? There was no way anyone could get out there fast enough to manually flush the airlock, get the solvent off those fragile seals. No way the teachers could get all the kids out of the transient classrooms before the inner seal went as well . . .

"Oh my god, oh my god . . ." Harris whispered from his station.

"Shh," Dr. Garfinkle said calmly. "Don't speak that way about God. He might be listening."

"I sure hope he is," Harris muttered. "From *your* mouth to *His* ear, lady."

I had set the teams in motion, triggered the right alarms, and now had a readout of the pressure gauges on one monitor, the life readings in the compartment on the next. I couldn't breathe, couldn't do anything but stare at the board, waiting to see what would happen next.

"The system is screwed," Harris whispered. I

glanced up and saw him glaring at Dr. Garfinkle. "What did you do to the systems, lady? This is worse than it was before! At least then, nobody died!"

"The system will work, young man," Dr. Garfinkle said, as calm as I'd ever seen her. "Believe me, it will."

The computerized voice was emotionless, as always. "Detecting airlock exterior seal failure in Section 15." If the inner seal failed, that would be it. The entire compartment with those kids would instantly depressurize!

My fingers clenched on the edge of the console. *Come on, system, make it work! Work!*

The computer voice spoke again. "All autolocks engaged throughout entire section. Lifeform detection in airlock: negative. Switching to emergency carbon dioxide blow, to be followed by full venting. Damage report is as follows . . ."

"What in the hell is it doing?" Johnson breathed. She was standing behind me now, staring at the boards over my shoulder, staring at the pressure readings.

"It's using the pressure in that CO_2 tank to flush the solvent out of the airlock," I said slowly. "I can't believe it. The system knew Harris was out working on the tanks. It knew there was a chance that he could damage the solvent lines. It knew that if anything happened to the solvent lines, it'd spray solvent all over the airlock and damage the seals. So it took precautionary measures. It built up the CO_2 in that tank just in case, and now it's blowing the CO_2 to get rid of the solvent." I glanced up at Johnson. "What's the CO_2 levels in the Section 15 compartments?"

She tapped in the query, then looked up from her board, eyes wide with disbelief. "It's perfectly normal. But it shouldn't be. It's the overpressure in those compartments, it kept the CO_2 level down. It's amazing. It set everything up perfectly, just in case something went wrong!"

We listened to the computerized voice detailing out

the individual sections of the seals that had failed, and
corroborate one more time that the remaining seals
were holding. "Supervisor report on airlock seal incident," the computer continued. "Recommend install-
ing additional pressure sensors on lines to prevent
such future incidents. Now updating and debugging
the following code routines . . ."

"Well, I'll be damned," Harris said in the long
silence after the computer finished speaking.

"Yeah, Harris, you probably will be," I agreed. "All
right, team, let's get to it. It's a real mess in there.
Let's get it cleaned up by the end of shift, hey?"

I waited for the team to get up and head out, but
no one moved. Johnson, Harris, Smitty, and the rest
of the Central crew were just standing there, looking
at Dr. Garfinkle. Then Harris spoke.

"Let's hear it for Dr. Garfinkle!" Harris said, and
began to clap his hands.

The thunderous cheers and applause echoed
through the walkways of Central. Dr. Garfinkle stood
silently, as though she wasn't quite certain how to
react. Then she smiled at me, and left Central.

I stood at the entrance to the transient docks. Dr.
Garfinkle, her small valise in hand, those antique
glasses perched on her nose and her hair neatly
wrapped in the perennial scarf, stood watching as the
small groups of adults and children filed past us, heading toward the airlock entrance and the colony ship
awaiting them beyond it. Five years on the station,
and I'd never even looked closely at the colonists.
They had always just been background noise, people
that I ignored while I was doing my job. Faceless
transients. Like the station itself. I'd lived here for
five years, and it had never felt like home.

"You should come visit me and my grandchildren
on Faraway, Miss Forrester," Dr. Garfinkle said. "It's

a beautiful place, green fields and small towns. You'd be welcome there."

"I'll never get out to the colonies," I said wistfully. "I'm probably going to stay here the rest of my life. Guarding the gate for the people like you, on their way out to build new worlds."

"Gates are meant to be walked through," Dr. Garfinkle said. "You should think about it. A nice girl like you would do well in the colonies." She smiled suddenly, impishly. "And you should meet my grandnephew."

I'm sure that's a bad idea, I thought, then reconsidered. Maybe it was a bad idea, maybe it wasn't. I wouldn't know unless I took the chance, right? Maybe I'd like him. Maybe I wouldn't. But wouldn't it be terrific to find out, one way or the other?

I held out my hand, and she took it. "Goodbye and good luck, ma'am," I said. "And thank you. For everything."

Dr. Garfinkle smiled, and pulled me by the handshake into a close hug. "Good luck to you, Miss Forrester," she said, releasing me. A featherlight kiss on my cheek, and then she was walking away.

I watched her leave through the airlock and into the ship, then headed back to Central and sat down at my desk. Around me I could hear people talking, the clatter of footsteps on the metal decks.

"You got that look in your eyes, boss," Johnson said, sliding into the chair for the next console.

"What look?"

"You know. That faraway look. Daydreaming again?"

"Yeah, daydreaming," I said wistfully. Then I stood up abruptly. "Or maybe I'm waking up." I headed down the walkway to where Harris was at his desk, about ten feet away. "Hey, Harris!"

He looked up at me. "Yeah, what?"

"You still got that list of colonies looking for systems engineers?"

I Told You So

Michael Scott

We are the daughters of Palu.

Great is our responsibility as the children of a goddess. At all times we must do her honor, and behave in such a way that will bring her honor and make her proud of us.

But this is not always easy.

Palu—all praise to her name—is demanding, and we are sadly fallible. She sets us tasks beyond our poor ability to perform, orders we cannot fulfill no matter how hard we try, and her advice is often incomprehensible.

When we fail, we go to her and offer abject apologies. Sometimes she is forgiving. Sometimes she is capricious and cruel. But whatever her mood, we know that her actions are always for our own good. If we are forgiven, it is because she loves us in spite of our shortcomings. If we are chastised, it is to prevent us from coming to harm in the future. These things she tells us.

All wise is Palu. And very beautiful, with her pale hair and her azure eyes. Throughout my life, just watching her has given me great delight.

Would that I could grow into half the beauty she is.

But alas, I cannot. There is only one Palu. But I am honored to be counted amongst her daughters.

Behind her exquisitely formed, fine-boned face is a magnificent mind, quite the most important part of her being. She gladly shares her wisdom as a goddess should. From earliest childhood, my sisters and I loved to sit at her feet and listen to her teachings.

"Beware the many enemies of our race," she warned us, long before we had ever seen an enemy, nor yet fully comprehended the term. "You are my children, and therefore clever. But there are others who are almost as clever, and who would delight in doing you harm." Her voice, slow and deep and sensual, gave her words added power. "The Great Dragon, for example, will blind you with evil magic long before you hear his terrible roaring, or smell the stink of his breath. While you stand, paralyzed and unmoving, he will crush you like soft fruit, leave you for the carrion eaters. Look not into his lambent eyes, my children."

When we were very small we shivered with fright at such words. Then great Palu would bend to us and comfort us, spreading the warmth and power of her presence over us like benevolent light until we felt as bold and brave as the goddess herself. With Palu to guide and protect us, we need not tremble at the mention of the Great Dragon. And when we heard the dragons roar and do battle in the night, great Palu would draw us away from the noise and stink of death and foulness and lead us into one of the Secret Places she had prepared with her own blessed hands. Drawing us close to her, wrapping her soft arms around us, she would lull us asleep with a gentle lullaby and the solid beating of her strong heart.

My sisters Tinka and Tenya were both older than I, though we were all brought forth at the one birthing. Tenya, Second-Born, in particular was Palu's pride and joy. She had something of our mother's grace and a great deal of her spirit, and many times I caught Palu watching her with an especial fondness. Tinka and I were jealous, though we loved our sister dearly.

But Tenya had a touch of the outlaw about her. She was more and more often in trouble. She ignored every rule, broke every prohibition—and of course she ran into difficulties that only grew worse as she grew older. How many times did I hear great Palu cry out to her, "You were warned, Tenya! I told you so!" And sometimes, if our mother's anger was great, she would strike out at Tenya, send her tumbling into the dust at her feet.

Tinka and I would look at one another, embarrassed, and then drop our eyes. But Tenya seemed to glory in being contrary. Our home, once a place of sanctuary and learning, rang with the quarrelling voices of great Palu—all glory to her name—and her rebellious second daughter. She seemed set to defy our mother's advice on all things.

Take the matter of Longtooth Demons, for example. Palu had instructed us very thoroughly as to our conduct when confronted with these evil beings. The smaller beasts were cowards, but when they ran in packs they could be deadly, and occasionally attacked our people. There were, however, giants amongst the demons—beasts who stood nearly as tall as the goddess. Few could stand against them. Palu, however, taught us special prayers to say and magical signs and gestures and ritual movements that would put fear into the foul hearts of the Demons, and make them flee from us.

But Tenya refused to do as she was told. She would walk right up to a Demon and laugh in his face, mimicking him when he bared his fangs, standing tall when he hissed at her. It was very frightening to see, and more than once Palu—O Magnificent!—had to intervene at the last moment, to save her favorite child from irreparable harm. I could never understand why Tenya would not listen; our mother's advice was for our own benefit. The Longtooth Demons were said to delight in the flesh of our people.

For though our mother is a goddess, we can be hurt and even slain. And when the Great Dark has overtaken us, there will be no Light again. The Once-

Secret of our race, the power to return to the Light
thrice three times has long been lost to our people.
It is said—though even I do not believe it—that Palu
is the last of her kind, the Many-Living Ones.

My foolish sister was even more careless in the
matter of They Who Smell.

Of all the enemies of our people—and such marvel-
lous, magical people have many enemies—They Who
Smell were the most disgusting. Appalling creatures
of fur and flabby flesh, everything about them was
an abomination. They were bad tempered, brutal and
brutish. They hunted for sport and only occasionally
for meat. The worst aspect of They Who Smell, however was their ignorance. They had no understanding
of elegance or cleanliness, and as for etiquette and
simple modesty ... Well, if I told you some of the
things I personally have seen them do, you would
hardly believe me. I have seen them foul where they
stood and rut in the open, howling out their passion
like base beasts.

One would never expect that a child of Palu would
consort with such beings. Yet Tenya actually sought
out their company. The first time it happened it might
have been an accident, I suppose. Tinka and I were
accompanying our mother on a stroll through the
woods when we saw movement in the undergrowth.
Palu—bow down at the mention of her name!—froze
in her tracks. We followed her example, of course.
Then as silently as a shadow she glided forward again,
with us right behind her, until we came within sight
of a sunlit glade where our Tenya and one of They
Who Smell were lolling on the grass together, their
flesh actually touching, their heads bent together.

Our mother was shocked beyond description. I
thought her eyes would leap from her head. Forgetting her dignity, she shrieked Tenya's name in a voice
I had never heard her use before, a voice that turned
the marrow in my bones to liquid. The sound sent

the beast-creature leaping into the bushes without a backwards glance, leaving Tenya alone in a puddle of sunlight.

She did not even have the grace to look embarrassed, but I knew by the defiant look in her eye that she knew that she had done wrong. That night the goddess and Tenya had a terrible fight. Tinka and I hid our heads under our bedclothes, we were so frightened, but their words were clearly audible. "How could you? To openly consort with such a . . . such a . . ." Palu sputtered, at a rare loss for words. "I fear that there is no crime you might not commit!"

"You exaggerate," Tinka drawled, and I clearly heard her yawn. Raising my head above, I squinted my eyes closed to concentrate the light and peered across the room. Palu and Tinka were standing on either side of the open door. Beyond them the night was silver and black with moonlight.

"Oh, I think not. You have no idea of the risks you run, my girl. I can protect you as long as you stay with me, but there is a wider world beyond this where nothing can protect you but your own wits—which seem to be sadly lacking."

Tinka yawned again, making her boredom with lectures obvious. "You are always warning us about something," she told Palu, "but none of the menaces have ever proved as dangerous as you claimed. Many times I have come face to face with the Great Dragon, but he is awkward and cumbersome. I can dance to one side and be gone quicker than his eye can follow. We are so small that I think we are beneath his contempt; certainly I have never seen one pursue any of our people.

"As for the Longtoothed Demons, when you first warned us about them you said they were giants. But none I have seen are as big as you, or even as big as I am now. What is there to fear in such pigmies?

"And although you have told us that They Who

Smell are a murderous clan, that has never been my experience. I think they fear us more than we fear them. I do not fear them, nor do I run from them and give them reason to pursue me, thinking me weak and afraid. I do not threaten them with arcane gestures, nor spit the old words of power at them. I treat them like anyone else and they respond in kind. Could it be, Mother, that you are blinded by your own prejudice?"

Hearing these words, Palu lost her temper completely. She lashed out at Tinka with all the strength she possessed, knocking her daughter down, drawing blood high on her cheek. Had it been me, I would have wept and pleaded for mercy, but Tinka just got to her feet again and glared at our mother.

"You will be sorry you ever did that," she said in a low, deadly tone, wiping the blood away with a deliberately casual movement, then bringing her hand to her mouth to lick at the pink liquid.

The goddess was visibly trembling with rage. "You are the one who will be sorry, my girl. Continue the way you are going now and you will come to a terrible end. But I will take no further responsibility for one so headstrong and foolish. Just remember, when worse comes to worst and you cry out to me for help . . . I told you so!"

To my stunned amazement, Tenya promptly turned back on Palu.

Decency forbids me to repeat what happened then. Suffice it to say that the goddess—long may she reign!—was beside herself with rage. She rained blows down upon Tenya, and for a while I feared that she would kill her . . . and it would be hard to blame her if she did. No one can insult a goddess with impunity, even her own daughter.

In the end, however, she allowed Tenya to escape with her life. My last glimpse of my sister was of her fleeing into the night, bruised and bloody. But she ran silently, refusing to allow my mother the pleasure of hearing her cry out.

The following morning, Palu simply said that Tenya had gone away and for a long time afterward she refused to let either Tinka or myself say our sister's name in Palu's presence.

But our mother is, in addition to all her other wonderful qualities, a compassionate goddess. At last she relented, and began to speak wistfully of her exiled daughter. "I hear she may have come to real harm," said Palu, eyes glistening with tears she was too proud to shed. "I did my best to teach her, to lead her in the paths of righteousness, but to no avail. Yet even now I cannot abandon her to outer darkness. No."

She set her chin—O Great Goddess!—and gazed into dimensions lesser beings such as Tinka and myself could not see.

"We shall undertake an odyssey," Palu announced at last, returning from her reverie. "A quest in search of she who has gone astray. Wide is the world and very dangerous, but for the sake of my daughter I am prepared to venture into the very depths if need be."

Her courage shone from her glowing eyes, and we, her other daughters, knelt and offered worship. Had there ever been a goddess so gallant as Palu the Perfect?

The preparations necessary before we could actually set forth on our quest were many and demanding. The journey could prove arduous, so Palu insisted we train like athletes. We ate, we slept, we did exercises to build up our strength and stamina. There were sacrifices to be offered as well, and meditations required. We had to spend whole days without moving, opening ourselves up to the spirits of our ancestors and imploring their guidance. Even great Palu would not undertake such a journey without all the assistance she could command.

But at last all was in readiness. Through magical

means our mother never vouchsafed, Palu had located Tenya's trail and knew the direction she had taken. The news obviously disturbed her.

"That wicked, foolish child has gone straight toward our most deadly enemies," she told us sorrowfully. "Had she searched the entire world she would have found no worse a path to take."

At these words Tinka gave a shudder of apprehension. "Which way did she go, Mother?" she asked tentatively.

"Across the River of Stone," replied Palu somberly.

This was grave news indeed. The River of Stone was the boundary separating Palu's world from a land where she had much less power, and one of our earliest prohibitions had been against crossing that petrified river. Even Tenya had not dared it—until now.

But Palu would not be shaken in her resolve. And so, when all possible preparations were made, we set off toward that terrible borderland. I confess I had many misgivings and am sure my sister Tinka felt the same.

If Palu was afraid, however, she did not let it show. O splendid is the goddess!

Inspired by her courage, we warily approached the River of Stone. Its surface had an evil glint in the light of a pallid sun and the shimmering heat waves dancing in the air above it were tainted bitter and foul. "Many of our people have died here over the years," our mother reminded us. "If you are to survive, you must do exactly as I say."

I had no intention of doing otherwise.

I stayed as close to her as I could, and when she set foot on the river, I followed her instructions so precisely that my own footprints covered hers.

I did not sink into the depths as I had feared, nor was I swallowed up and turned to stone as I had imagined. Instead I negotiated that fearsome place safely, though my heart was pounding in my breast every step of the way.

Tinka came right behind me. She too survived the perilous crossing, and Palu congratulated us both afterwards. "You did as I told you," she pointed out. "That is why you are alive."

The lesson was not lost on us. Would that Tenya had been so wise! Before we left the vicinity of the River of Stone I turned back for one last look, just to savour my success. Then it was that I observed the river was not very wide, nor did I see anything on it that could hurt me. Nothing at all.

But soon a new danger waited us. The gentle, rolling landscape we knew, with its lush woods and pools of sweet water, gave way almost at once to a barren desert. The smell of the desert made our nostrils burn. "Poison land," Palu informed us. "I know spells to counteract the worst of the poison, but we must not linger here for very long. No matter what you see, do not fall behind."

Her advice was sound. No sooner had we entered the desert than one wonder after another appeared, exciting our curiosity. So exotic were the features of this unfamiliar landscape that we surely would have succumbed to their entrenchment, had not Palu warned us. "Do not stay any longer than you must," she kept repeating. "One moment too many and you will be bound to this place, unable to leave; the poison in your lungs will chain you here, because you will not be able to breathe anywhere else, not ever again."

And so, with resolute tread, we strode past the flowers of fire and the bridges of light, the silver spires and the golden globes. We did not pause to admire the miniature whirlwinds that danced toward us, nor did we turn aside to investigate the velvet caverns that exhaled an almost irresistible perfume. Nothing could tempt us, not with the words of the goddess singing in our ears.

When we finally left the desert my nose was still burning, and my eyes felt gritty and sore. But I had no real trouble breathing, in spite of what Palu had said. The stench of the place had done me no harm after all.

The first night we made our camp on a hill over looking a valley filled with stars. We were weary, but Palu was tireless. While we slept she kept watch with all her weapons at the ready—many and terrible are the weapons of Palu!—and when we awoke shortly before dawn we found her sitting just as we had seen her in the last light of evening, with her head erect and her eyes unblinking. I had no doubts but that she had watched over us through the dangerous night.

Before we set out again, Palu provided us with a most sumptuous meal. After the manner of goddesses, she could conjure up food where none seemed to exist, and we heartily enjoyed the repast, which she had caught and killed and prepared herself. "Eat every bite," she commanded us. "Listen to what I tell you: you will need your strength."

Each day of our lives, in accordance with the ritual our mother had taught us, we had a period set aside for prayer. It was not always the same time of day, but was always of the same duration, an interlude of calm when we closed our eyes and bowed our heads and spoke with Palu in our inmost hearts. Even on this dangerous journey, we kept the faith and observed the ritual.

But for the first time, I found myself wondering with whom Palu spoke during prayertime. If we prayed to the goddess ... who then did the goddess pray to?

Once we were under way again, I ventured to broach this subject with your mother. Palu halted abruptly and looked at me in astonishment. "You question me?"

"Not at all," I hastily assured her. "I was merely

curious. Is there another deity even greater than your-self? If so, should we not pray to it as well as . . ."

"There is no deity greater than I!" our goddess exclaimed in outrage. "Who told you to ask such questions?"

"This is a thought I had on my own," I replied, then added contritely, "and I am sorry if it offended you."

"So you should be, talking heresy like that." Palu gave a delicate sniff. "Oh, I know there are some misguided folk who claim Tall Ones are gods, but I can assure you they are not. They are worse than the Longtooth Demons, fouler than They Who Smell, who can even command the Great Dragon at their will."

"Tall Ones?" said Tinka curiously. "Who are they? You never mentioned them before."

"And for a good reason, my daughter. I did not want to discuss Tall ones until you were mature enough to understand. They are not nursery terrors, but the worst of our enemies, cruel giants who have deliberately murdered many of our people. Yet strange to relate, in spite of their terrible record some of our folks continue to fall under the influence of Tall Ones and defend them, even worship them."

My sister gave a shudder of horror. "Are there any Tall Ones around here?"

"They are everywhere," replied Palu. "I have kept you well away from them so far, but we are in their territory now and going deeper with each step. If my worst fears are confirmed, your foolish sister has wandered into their very heart."

I gave a gasp. "How are we to rescue her if they are as bad as you say? Is this land not outside your sphere of magic, Mother?"

She gave me that wise knowing little smile of hers. "No land is ever entirely beyond my magic. If we find your sister, I feel confident we can rescue her. If she is still alive."

Those last words chilled me.

Step by step, we advanced. I observed a change in our mother's demeanor, now that we were so close to Tall Ones. Always graceful, she seemed to glide when she walked with a movement so delicate and sinuous that she melted into the shadows. Unless you know exactly where she was, you would not notice her.

Tinka and I did our best to imitate her, but we are not goddesses. Compared to Palu, I fear we were clumsy.

Tall Ones may have seen us.

The land of Tall Ones was a most peculiar place. Until I actually saw it with my own eyes I would not have thought any beings would choose to live as they did. They had an addiction to noise which I found frightening; they dwelt in a constant cacophony. Surely they could not hear the birds sing, nor the rustling of the trees' dance; I doubt they could hear their own thoughts, if they had any.

Because Palu had warned us, I was not unprepared for my first glimpse of Tall Ones . . . but even so the sight of them repulsed me. I found them singularly ugly and repellent, extremely awkward and they stank of a thousand bitter odors. Their gestures were abrupt and brittle, and they breathed with a great roaring noise. I think they could not have been very healthy.

They were strong, however, as a result of their hulking size. "Whatever you do, never get within reach of one," our mother warned us in her most severe tone. "They can seize you and break you almost without effort. They like to break things; they are monsters."

They were indeed monsters. I watched from the shadows as they went about their incomprehensible affairs, scurrying here and there for no reason, baying and screeching at one another, their ugliness equalled only by their clumsiness.

"How can anyone mistake them for gods?" I asked our mother.

"There are those," Palu replied sadly, "who are overwhelmed by their sheer size and assume that anything so large must be magnificent. I have also heard that Tall Ones employ traps baited with seductive luxuries. Some of our people mistake this bribery for generosity and give their fealty to Tall Ones in return. To justify this greed on their part they try to pretend Tall Ones are noble and fine, worthy of their loyalty. But it is a pathetic self-delusion.

"Tall Ones have no appreciation for our ancient culture. They use our people for their own amusement, as if we were clowns or court jesters. They mock our manners and degrade our dignity, and any form of relationship with them is a debasement.

"Never be fooled by Tall Ones," Palu concluded. "They are no good. I tell you this."

Trying to be as inconspicuous as possible, we drifted through the kingdom of Tall Ones. They tend to live in clusters, in hives, which makes the noise they create even louder and more disturbing. Indeed, I do not recall seeing a single one of them alone in meditation, simply enjoying Being.

Palu has taught all her followers that To Be is the first imperative.

We searched for a number of days for our missing Tenya. Palu kept an optimistic attitude, at least for our sakes, but I suspect she was beginning to lose hope. I noticed that her appetite faded and the light in her eyes was less brilliant than of old. Her very step seemed duller and heavier. In my heart I wept, for the diminution of a goddess is a terrible thing. Great Palu, queen of goddesses!

For fear of Tall Ones, our mother did most of her searching at night. Tall Ones are blind in addition to their other faults, and night rendered us all but invisible to them, whereas our night vision is legendary amongst the lesser races.

Our mother always tried to find us a place to hide up during the hours of sunlight, but sometimes however, the dawn caught us still going about our rounds. It was on one such occasion that we got our first clue to Tenya's whereabouts.

We were skirting a conglomeration of hives—noisome, odoriferous dwellings—from whence issued the awful roaring which Tall Ones make in sleep. I could see from the tension in Palu's face muscles that she was fighting back her revulsion, nostrils pinched tight, eyes almost closed. But she was determined to search every quarter for Tenya.

And then it was that she caught that first, delicate wisp of sound which could have issued from no Tall One's throat.

It came again, soft, plaintive ... unmistakably the sound of one of our race, undeniably the sound of our sister. In spite of herself our mother gave a glad cry. Emotion washed through her, leaving her quivering all over, great tremors running the length of her body.

I pressed forward audaciously and kissed her. "It's all right, Mother," I whispered. "We are with you."

She relaxed then. "My good and dutiful daughters, I did not doubt it for a moment. We share this joyous discovery. I tell you, she who was lost is found!" She returned the happy caresses Tinka and I were showering upon her, kissing our faces, our eyes, our lips. Great is the affection of Palu, and honored its recipients!

With my mother's sweet breath in my nostrils, I regretted my earlier disloyalty. Obviously there could be no questioning of her wisdom; had she not found Tenya?

For there was now no doubt it was Tenya's voice we heard. Clear and pure as crystal, it rose above the ugly noise which marked the habitat of Tall Ones. She was calling from somewhere nearby.

But where? We looked at one another in puzzlement. Although the voice sounded quite close, it was curiously muffled and gave no indication of direction.

Palu narrowed her eyes. "They have her trapped," she said bitterly. "Tall Ones have captured my daughter, my daughter, and are holding her a prisoner inside one of their filthy cells."

I looked past our mother to the grotesque and massive hives of Tall Ones. The structures presented a solid face to the outside world, with no obvious way to get in—or get anyone out. The goddess read my mind.

"There are always entrances . . . and if Tenya cannot get out, then we must get in to her."

I bowed my head and nodded, unwilling to even think the blasphemous thought . . . that perhaps Tenya might not want to escape!

She had now been a captive of Tall Ones for some days. And Tenya was intelligent, there was no denying it. Surely she had managed to learn something of her captors, to discover their weakness and formulate some plan for her own escape? Surely, she had made a bid for freedom.

Led by Palu—the wise and wondrous!—we made our cautious way around and around the clustered hives, seeking an opening. Tenya's voice appeared to follow us, moving around the inside as we circled the outside.

At last Palu took a chance. After first glancing warily to the left and the right, she darted forward and flattened herself in an angle of one of the walls of the hives. There she began calling Tenya by name, using a low but penetrating tone her daughter must surely recognize.

Within moments she was rewarded by Tenya's voice answering from just on the other side of the wall.

Palu looked toward us. "This is the place! Come!"

We ran forward eagerly and added our voices to our mother's. "Tenya! Where are you, how are you? Can you get out?"

"I am here," our sister replied. To my surprise, she did not sound as glad as we were. "What are you doing here?" she asked rather peevishly.

"We have come to rescue you," Palu replied.

"Rescue me? From what?"

"Tall Ones, of course! You are in terrible danger, my daughter."

"Danger! You must be joking. I am with friends. Friends," she added rather spitefully, "who appreciate me as you did not."

Palu reeled from shock. "What are you saying?"

"I'm saying it was quite unnecessary for you to come after me. I am doing very well on my own, thank you."

"But . . . but we heard you calling for help . . ."

"Calling for help? No, you were mistaken. I was singing. My new friends enjoy my singing."

Palu's jaw dropped. "This is even worse than I feared," she whispered to us. "Your sister has gone mad."

"What can you do, O great goddess?" Tinka asked. Her own eyes were wide with alarm.

Our mother was growing increasingly frantic. "Something," she muttered almost inaudibly. "I must do something . . . She began to run around the wall of the hive. We followed her with our hearts in our throats, afraid that at any moment we would be discovered by Tall Ones.

But it was ourselves who made the discovery.

Rounding a corner of the hive, we found ourselves facing what appeared to be a huge opening. And Tenya could be clearly seen on the other side! Abandoning caution, Palu ran toward her daughter . . only to smash against some invisible barrier that sent her staggering backward. She shook her head to clear it and approached again, more slowly. We crept after her unwilling to let our goddess face any danger alone.

On the other side of the barrier Tenya watched us with cold amusement. I hated her in that moment.

Once again Palu touched the transparent wall. "What is this?" I heard her ask softly.

Muffled by the material, Tenya's voice replied. "A door, Mother."

"A door? Then come out."

"I do not come outside any more."

"What?" Palu asked in disbelief.

"Everything I need is in here, furnished by my friends," our sister replied. She sounded so smug and superior I longed to slap her face. "Look." She gestured toward a bed piled high with soft cushions. Beside it a table was laden with quantities of food and drink. She lifted her sleek throat to display a collar with a tiny bell set into it. "These are mine," Tenya said proudly, her slave bell ringing softly. "You have nothing so fine, living as you do by your wits."

Palu gazed for a measureless time upon the luxuries Tenya boasted. Fine they were, and tempting; even I could see that. But I could also see the sorrow in our mother's eyes. They were filled with grief, as if she presided over the funeral of her beloved daughter.

At last she made one more plea to Tenya. "If we can find a way to get you out, will you not come with us? Leave now, come home, before you are completely corrupted?"

Our foolish sister replied defiantly, "I shall never leave!"

"Then we must," said Palu. "You think you have everything, my daughter, but I tell you this. You have surrendered your freedom, and so you have nothing." Her voice turned bitter and contemptuous. "You have dishonored the race of Caat. You have become a pet."

To Tinka and me, she commanded, "Come, my daughters."

Resolutely, Palu stalked away. We followed her, shaken by what we had seen. When we were a safe distance from the hive of Tall Ones, Palu paused and turned back one last time, calling her farewell to the cat who watched us from behind her glass door.

"You have nothing," my mother reiterated, "and someday you will realize it. Remember then: I told you so."

You Never Call

Robert Lynn Asprin

The two fleets maneuvered subtly as they drew ominously closer. The crowd would have held its breath in anticipation . . . if there had been a crowd to witness the spectacle . . . or if there were breath for it to hold in the vacuum of outer space.

On the bridge of the Terran flagship, the crew waited in nervous silence. Steely-eyed, with his jaw set in stern determination, the human commander's authoritative pose would have sent any artist scrambling for his or her sketch pad. Without unclenching his teeth, he nodded to his communications officer to open the hailing frequency.

An annoying shrill whistle sounded as the enemy's image swam into focus on the main view screen. While to the untutored human eye, it might look like just another huge reptile in a uniform, the commander was a seasoned space veteran and could readily recognize the individual differences of several alien races.

"Well, Zoltron?" he said harshly. "Have you reconsidered your position? This is your last chance to avoid needless bloodshed. Will you relinquish your claim on this sector and withdraw your forces?"

His rival's response was a sharp bark of laughter.

"Really, Raymond. I thought you knew us better, or at least that you knew me. Did you really expect me to back down from a threat?"

"That's 'Commander Stone,' under the circumstances," the commander spat back. "And I thought you knew us better, Zoltron. Did you think I was

42

bluffing? You have five minutes to begin your with-drawal. Then we open fire."

On the screen, Zoltron stared back for several sec-onds in silence before speaking.

"We've been friends for a long time, Raymond," he said softly, his voice heavy with regret.

The Terran commander hesitated as years of mem-ories flashed through his mind. Memories of happier days before the alliance fell apart ... of shared holi-days and family outings ... of how he was first sur-prised, the friendship with this non-human counterpart.

Then the moment passed.

"Times change, Zoltron," he said firmly. "We aren't the first friends that politics have set against each other, nor will we be the last. We used to kid about what would happen if someday we found ourselves on opposite sides. Well, it would seem that day has come. You have five minutes."

Another curt nod and the screen reverted to its original display showing the opposing fleet hanging motionless in space.

"Well, that's that," the commander said, almost to himself. Then he hardened his tones to the firm voice of command.

"Pass the word! Battle stations!"

"Battle stations aye, sir!"

"Sir!" It was his communications officer again. "There's a call coming in on subspace."

A frown flashed across the commander's face as he both felt and hid his irritation at this unexpected interruption.

What in heaven's name could that be? A late change in orders from Command Central?

"Patch it through," he said, trying to sound calm and unruffled.

Again came the annoying whistle.

"Commander Stone here," he said, knowing that

subspace communications did not allow visual exchanges.

There was a moment's silence, then a tentative voice came from the speakers.

"Raymie? Is that you?"

The crew exchanged startled glances, then looked at their commander who was staring at the speakers in what could only be described as frozen horror.

"Mom?" he said, at last.

"There you are, Raymie." The unseen voice was now confident. "I was just calling to see if everything was all right with you."

"Mom, what are you doing calling me here?" The commander shot an uncomfortable look at his crew, who were now steadfastly ignoring the exchange. "It must be costing you a fortune to call me direct."

"It's not cheap, but I'll manage." The vast void of space was not sufficient to mask the martyrdom in his mother's tones. "It's worth it just to hear from you."

"What do you want, Mom? I'm kind of busy right now."

"I know, I know. My son, the big shot fleet commander. I could grow old and die before you found time to call me on your own."

"That's right. I'm busy," the commander grumbled. "And right now is a very bad time for me. So if you can just tell me what it is you want?"

"I just wanted to check to see if you were all right," his mother said. "I mean, it's Mother's Day and I hadn't heard from you. So I thought there might be something wrong."

"Nothing's wrong, Mom. I'm fine. Really. It's just been a very busy day . . . and it's about to get busier in a few minutes."

"I knew it had to be something important. I mean, after you didn't call on my birthday . . . and couldn't find time to come home for Christmas, I knew that you wouldn't let Mother's Day go by without calling unless something life or death came up."

"As a matter of fact, it is a matter of life or death, Mom," the commander said. "We're about to go into battle in a few minutes, and I have a lot to do before we start. So if there's nothing else . . ."

"You're what? Going into battle?"

"That's right, Mom. So . . ."

"On Mother's Day??"

"Come on, Mom. It's not like I planned it this way. It's just how it happened. Okay?"

"No, it's not okay! And don't take that tone with me, Raymond!"

"But Mom . . ."

" 'But Mom' nothing! You listen to me, Raymond. I've accepted that you're working in the fleet now, and that on any day you could get blown up or shot down or whatever it is that you do to each other. I haven't liked it, but I've accepted it. A mother has to let her children make their own choices, however painful it may be."

"Mom . . ."

"Now you tell me that you're going into battle, maybe get yourself killed, on the one day of the year set aside for mothers? I've never heard of anything so inconsiderate or heartless. You want me to spend the rest of my life remembering Mother's Day as the day my son got himself killed? I won't hear of it!"

"So what am I supposed to do? Call it off? Because it would make my mother unhappy?"

"Is that so much to ask? Oh, I suppose if making your mother happy isn't enough of a reason, you can say that you ran out of fuel or something. Just promise me that you'll postpone this war or whatever of yours until tomorrow or next week."

"But Mom . . ."

"I don't ask you for much, Raymie, but I'm asking

for this. I want your solemn promise ... and I'll sit right here on this communicator until I get it."

"I ... I'll see what I can do."

"PROMISE!"

"ALL RIGHT, ALL RIGHT. I PROMISE!"

"There. Now that wasn't so hard, was it? Well, I've got to go now myself. Wish your mother a happy Mother's Day!"

"Happy Mother's day, Mom."

The commander's voice and face were expressionless for this salutation, and remained so after the shrill whistle signaled the end of the exchange.

After a long silence, he turned to his communications officer.

"Get me Zoltron on the hailing frequency."

Again, the enemy commander's face swam into focus on the main screen.

"Commander Zoltron. I don't know how to say this, but ..."

"Let me help you, Commander Stone," Zoltron said. "Your mother has made you promise to postpone our engagement for at least one day."

Raymond joined his crew in staring at the screen in shock.

"How ... how did you know that?" he managed at last.

"Simple, commander. I just received a similar call from my mother. It seems your mother called her to find out your ship code so that she could call you. To further shorten our exchange, allow me to inform you that my own mother exacted a similar promise from me."

"Really? I didn't know your empire celebrated Mother's Day at all, much less that the days were identical."

"We don't," Zoltron grimaced. "Apparently after your mother explained to my mother the reason for her call, my mother thought it was such a good idea that she's adopting the holiday personally."

"Gee. I'm sorry about that."

"It could be worse. I'm only afraid that she'll pass it along to other mothers in the Empire. By this time next year, it could be a legitimate Empire holiday. In case you didn't know it, our mothers hold no less sway than yours do."

"Hmmm. Tell you what, Zollie. Did you and your ships have anything planned for the rest of the day . . . except this battle, I mean?"

"Not really. We had kind of figured this would be it. In fact, we left our schedules open in case it ran long."

"Tell you what. There's a neutral refueling station not far from here, and I know the bar never closes. What say you and your crews join us in hoisting a few?"

"Sounds good to me. Just be sure everyone on your side joins you in swearing to the Mother's Day truce, and I'll do the same with mine."

"No problem . . . but why?"

"Well, I figure if nothing else, it will eliminate the chance of interservice brawls once the drinking gets serious. It will be hard enough to explain to our respective superiors why we don't fight today without also having to explain to our mothers if we did end up squaring off."

"Amen to that!"

A Mother's Lament

Judith R. Conly

I saw you on the spaceport vid,
accepting that silly statue—
Academy Something, I think—
and thanking everyone but me.
You've lots of time to go on stage,
and prance around in those strange clothes,
making noise you claim is music.
Why can't you find the time to call?

Your brother the doctor is well
and thriving in Mars Colony.
Despite his hectic office hours
he talks to me once every week.
Your sister had her third baby.
She keeps her home immaculate
and cooks the most elaborate meals.
But you—you can't find time to call!

That layover is finally done—
three hours in a low-class lounge
and not a peep from you, my girl,
though you've had my schedule for weeks.
My outbound ship has just left port.
The next stop lasts for five whole days.
It's not like you've real work to do,
so, *nu*, why don't you ever call?

Your Face Will Freeze Like That

Morgan Llywelyn

In our family, Mama was the beauty. When she walked into a room conversation stopped. Mama had red hair and green eyes and a waist Dad's hands could span, and she was so gorgeous other women couldn't hate her, any more than they could hate a painting or a statue.

Mama was a work of art.

I, on the other hand, was not.

Thin, gawky, with stringy dishwater-blonde hair and prominent gums, I was the sort of child who is an embarrassment to handsome parents. Dad seemed unaware of my shortcomings, but mama was forever saying, "Don't slouch, Lucinda, can't you ever stand up straight?" "Stop fiddling with your hair, it's bad enough already." "Keep your lips closed when you smile, for heaven's sake. No one wants to see those gums glistening." "Why are you wearing those filthy jeans, Lucinda? People will think we dress you out of the dumpster."

The more she criticized, the worse I felt. And the worse I looked too.

I was fifteen years old and a straight-A student and I couldn't do anything right; not in mama's eyes. Being smart wasn't good enough. She was constantly reminding me how far short I fell of her perfection. My earliest memories are of her standing me up on a kitchen chair while she tortured my hair into curls, then shaking her head in disgust as they promptly unwound themselves.

I learned to recognize, and dread, the little laugh

she gave when people said in disbelief, "This is *your* daughter, Berenice?"

Upon entering puberty I had set out with grim determination to become as beautiful as my mother. Or at least, pretty enough so that people would accept the idea of kinship between us. Sitting in front of the mirror in the bathroom, I diligently practiced mama's regal, self-assured expression.

On me it looked ridiculous, as if I was about to sneeze.

I ate tubs of butter and gallons of ice cream and mountains of french fries, hoping my insignificant frame would blossom into voluptuous curves.

The rich food only gave me pimples.

Haunting the drugstore, I bought every magazine that promised to divulge the secrets of glamour and beauty. My allowance vanished into the insatiable hands of the cheapest cosmetics manufacturers while my pimples multiplied.

When I brushed my hair a hundred times a night, it just got oilier.

The more I tried, the worse I looked.

Some nights I cried myself to sleep in sheer hopelessness.

Then for my sixteenth birthday, Mama organized a big party. Without consulting with me she arranged through her various friends for all their sons to attend. I doubt if any of them wanted to, but mama could be very persuasive.

Beautiful people are always persuasive. I had learned that years earlier, watching her work.

"The boys will hate being forced to come," I warned her, "and they'll resent me."

"Nonsense," she replied briskly. "They'll have a wonderful time and so will you, if you'll just stop being so negative. Mama knows best."

She took me downtown to buy a special dress for the party. "Something peach-colored," I pleaded.

"That's the only shade that doesn't make me look awful."

We spent an exhaustive afternoon going from shop to shop, each more expensive than the next. Clerks fell all over themselves in their eagerness to wait on Mama, but when they learned we were shopping for me, the ugly duckling, you could see their enthusiasm wither.

I felt pretty withered myself by the time we finally bought a dress. Mama, on the other hand, was delighted with the purchase. That made one of us. Overriding any suggestions from me, she had chosen a ghastly turquoise blue number twenty years out of date, with silly puffed sleeves and a midcalf hemline that made my legs appear shapeless. I would look like an absolute nerd.

Cutting my eyes at her as we drove home, I noticed that she was as smug as a cat in the sun. I began to have a horrible suspicion. Mama knew I would look like a nerd, too. Although she would never admit to herself, that was what she wanted.

A pretty daughter might have given her some unwanted competition.

The event itself was indescribable. I must have been the only girl ever to spend her entire Sweet Sixteen party without having a single boy ask her to dance. Mama, however, danced with almost every boy there. They lined up to ask her. The only dancing I did was with Dad, and most of the time he was watching Mama.

He stepped on my feet.

I must admit, my eyes wandered too. There was one boy—Todd Mamoulian—who was simply gorgeous. He had black curls and black eyes and eyelashes a girl would kill for, and when he glanced in my direction I could feel my insides turn to butter.

That was all I needed, buttery insides.

And sweaty palms. Did I tell you about the sweaty palms?

I'll bet my mother never had sweaty palms in her life.

Todd Mamoulian danced with her more than anybody. After their first dance together he never looked in my direction again.

When at last the party was over I shuffled upstairs to the bathroom and pawed through the medicine cabinet, searching for something that would kill me without causing me any pain; something that would leave me looking absolutely gorgeous in a peach satin-lined coffin.

There were no pills of that description, of course.

But it wasn't in me to accept total defeat. I brooded on my problem for weeks.

How could I possibly compete with mama?

If you can't be beautiful, I finally told myself, might as well try for the other extreme. Be the most of *something*.

So I deliberately set out to be as ugly as I could. Psychologists might be able to tell you why.

I gave up eating hamburgers and french fries and ate nothing but vegetables. Without butter. From being thin, I went to being positively gaunt. I acquired a vegetarian's pallor, red eyelids and a pinched look around the nose. Instead of washing my hair I smeared it with cooking oil when no one was looking until it almost dripped with grease. When new pimples erupted I picked at them until my face was a mass of irritated red blotches.

Night after night I stared into the mirror, finding new ways to distort my features.

One night Mama caught me. She opened the bathroom door unexpectedly—Mama never knocked, she assumed she had the right to go wherever she wanted, whenever she liked—and there I was with my face screwed up like a gargoyle. It was one of my best efforts to date. Every voluntary muscle was contorted. Wrinkles pleated my forehead, my mouth was drawn back in a cadaver's rictus, and my lower lids were raised until my eyes shone with an insane glare.

Mama gave a little gasp. "Lucinda! What if the wind changes? Your face will freeze like that!"

I gave a guilty start and the gargoyle disappeared. But I could still see Mama watching me in the mirror. There was a tiny little frown line above her perfect nose, between her perfect brows.

"What are you trying to do to yourself?" she demanded to know.

"Nothing."

"Well, just stop it. Goodness knows you have enough problems without . . ." She waved her hands helplessly. Her beautiful white hands, with their long and perfectly manicured nails.

I was in the habit of biting my nails to the quick.

June-Bug . . . I haven't mentioned her yet, have I? June-Bug Halliday. If I haven't mentioned her, it's because she wasn't important to the story until now. She was my best friend. She never called me Lucinda, a name which drove me up the wall. And I never called her Harriet, which was just as bad. Since we were in kindergarten we'd done everything together. June-Bug was no beauty either, but she was, well, cute. Pug nose, freckles, big blue eyes with thick dark lashes that made them seem almost beautiful. She even had a boyfriend.

At least, Willy Mason hung around after school trying to walk home with her and carry her books. Willy was almost as thin as I was and had a cowlick that stuck straight up, but he was a boy and he had a crush on June-Bug.

Nobody had a crush on me.

I didn't care. Who wanted a boyfriend anyhow?

"I am going to be so ugly," I informed June-Bug, "that they'll hire me for the circus. They'll put me in a special exhibition and charge money for people to come in and see me and be scared."

"That," said June-Bug, "is the dumbest thing I ever heard, Luce. There are hardly any circuses any more, and the ones there are don't have much money. And nobody has an Ugly Freak. If you looked like an alligator or could swallow swords it'd be different, but you're just skinny and you have zits."

"Just you wait," I promised. Ugly was a lot easier than beautiful.

I redoubled my efforts. In a funny sort of way, June-Bug had challenged me. It was like being ugly was a contest I simply had to win or something would change forever in our friendship. She would have been right and I would have been wrong. I couldn't stand that. We'd always been equal.

Down at the library I found some old books that had grainy gray photographs taken for "medical research" long before my parents were born. Doctors used to let freaks live, not like they do now; now when everyone is supposed to be normal. There were pictures of Siamese twins and two-headed babies and all sorts of malformations. One subject had an eye in the middle of the forehead. Another had just slits for nostrils, and another looked like a turnip on legs. It would serve Mama right if I looked like one of those, I thought.

But the most chilling of all were the pictures in books about World War II, photographs taken in the concentration camps.

There was one that drew me back again and again. It was a living human being, but there was no meat under the skin of its head. It was like a skull, great hollow eyes and sharp cheekbones like boulders. In the black and white photograph it looked as pale as chalk, which added to the impression.

What could be uglier than a death's-head? I thought.

That's what I wanted to look like. I was halfway there already because I was so thin. All I had to do was stop eating altogether and *voila*!

But I really didn't want to die to complete the effect. Being a vegetarian was one thing. Anorexia was another, and despite my sweet sixteen party, I had no intention of going that far.

Still, the more I gazed at my image the more I liked what I saw. It began to look like *me*, the real me I felt inside. And so as women had done throughout the ages—as my own Mama did every day of her life—I undertook to create the look I wanted with cosmetics.

I began collecting paints and powders. If I asked Mama for enough money to buy "a hamburger and a Coke," she would shell out, thinking it meant an end to my vegetarianism. "But you should eat a more balanced diet, Lucinda," she would say with a sigh while forking over a couple of bucks. "You are what you eat, you know."

Mama had a lot of sayings.

Then one day shortly after school was out for the summer, June-Bug Halliday mentioned having noticed a place called The Melrose Theatrical and Costume Shoppe on the corner of Princess Street and Tagg's Lane. "Have you ever been in there?" she asked as we leafed through magazines at the drugstore, trying to find ways to fill the long golden days that yawned before us. "It looks great. I'll bet they've got more cosmetics than the counter here, even. And in the window there's real stage makeup like people wear in the movies."

That was all I needed to hear.

I dropped my magazine with a flutter of pages. "Let's go!"

As we left the drugstore I noticed for the first time that Todd Mamoulian had come in and was standing on the other side of the magazine counter. He was looking at, of all things, one of the fashion magazines—one with an absolutely spectacular model on the cover. "THE FACE OF THE NINETIES!" the big red letters proclaimed.

Of course.

I gave him a glare that would have shrunk him away to nothing if he looked up, but he didn't.

Then I ran after June-Bug.

The Melrose proved to be a treasure house. Every sort of costume hung, glittered, sagged from wire hangers on chrome poles that ran the length of the dingy shop. Dusty glass cabinets were filled to overflowing with greasepaint, spirit gum, false hair, rouge, pencils, powders, Albolene, lipstick as thick and opaque as putty . . .

At first June-Bug was as enchanted as I was. We spent the rest of the morning—and all the money we had on us—at The Melrose.

The shop was presided over by a wizened little man of indeterminate years called Mr. Herbert. He never said if that was his first name or his last. You would think he would have resented a pair of giggling teenage customers who had very little money and yet spent hours trying on costumes and parading back and forth in front of its mirrors. But he tolerated us. More than that, he encouraged us.

Standing behind us as we sat at a littered dressing table and applied items from his extensive assortment of cosmetics, Mr. Herbert gave us the benefit of his professional expertise.

"You really must mix a little gray into that eyeshadow," he assured June-Bug. "You're washing out the color of your own eyes, you see, by rivalling it too closely. That would never do." Taking one of the little pots of cream in his own stained fingers, he proceeded to correct her mistake.

Then June-Bug tired of the game. Summer was outside the shop, ravishing the senses with the smell of sunshine and hot pavement and bubble gum, and she abandoned me in favor of Willy with his cowlick and a trip to the shopping mall.

Forgetting about lunch, I stayed on at The Melrose all afternoon, losing myself amid dreams and visions. That dark, musty-smelling cave seemed . . . comfortable, somehow. Looking back, I realized that I never saw anyone else in the shop. But at the time I thought nothing of it. Children are too self-absorbed to wonder at the absence of people who are not important to them anyway.

I returned the next day and the day after that, and the proprietor always welcomed me with a grave smile and the gift of his time.

Mama never had time for me. She had another life, an adult life.

Mr. Herbert didn't talk to me as if I were a child. He spoke to me as one adult to another, and our conversation ranged over areas I had never thought about before.

While I tried on costumes he spoke knowledgeably of mythology, spinning out wonderful tales. Thus I learned about Diana and Apollo and Dionysius, fauns and satyrs and centaurs. A discourse of his about arms and armor resulted in my acquiring a nodding acquaintance with Richard the Lionhearted and the Crusades. Trying on a Marie Antoinette costume elicited a thumbnail sketch of the French Revolution that stimulated what would become a lifelong interest for me.

But Mr. Herbert spoke of personal things, too. He asked questions about my life, my parents, my hopes for the future. He really seemed to be interested in me. Then one day he concluded some remark or other by saying, ". . . you poor unhappy child."

"I *am* happy!" I snapped, startled.

He shook his head in denial. "No, you aren't. Children are rarely happy, as I know all too well. They are put down and put upon; they are lied to, disappointed and disillusioned. Although adults gild their early years with nostalgia, if they are honest, very few would care to be children again. It can be a miserable time that clouds one's entire life."

I stared at him with my mouth hanging open. I had never heard an adult speak that way before. "This is the best time of your life," my mother all too frequently reminded me. It was one of her favorite sayings, based on absolutely no proof as far as I could see.

But Mr. Herbert was right. And I knew it. He had an instinctive understanding of what I felt inside and I was grateful. So grateful that I haunted The Melrose all that summer.

Within his shadowed domain, Mr. Herbert introduced me to the limitless possibilities of stage makeup. He never remarked on the ghoulishness of the effects I was seeking, but functioned as a sort of male fairy godmother, teaching me to transform my face into anything I chose. In turn I became a Star Trek monster, an ancient crone, and a green-skinned horror that could be mistaken in a dim light for a Ninja Turtle.

But it was the skull face, the death's-head, I really craved.

So he created it for me. One rainy Tuesday afternoon he sat me on a stool in front of the dressing table and patiently worked white greasepaint into my skin, all the way to the hairline, then built up shadowings of palest lavender beneath my cheekbones and on my temples. His hands traced the structure of my head as if he were remolding soft wax instead of following the shape of hard bone. As his skillful fingers pressed and smoothed I watched fascinated in the mirror. Soon I looked as if there were no flesh at all on my face. My cheeks were more than gaunt, they were hollow. My eyes were sunk into dark caverns pits that made them look twice their normal size.

When he was finished, he stood back like a proud parent while I surveyed myself in the glass.

"What do you think?"

"It's . . . wonderful," I replied.

"More than that, my dear," Mr. Herbert assured me, rubbing his hands together with a dry, papery sound. "So much more. Here, try on this black wig to set off the effect." It was as straight as my own hair but long and thick. Sinister-looking, I thought, and reached for it eagerly. The fit was perfect. The wig molded itself to my skull as if made for me.

Transfixed, I gazed at the pallid image in the mirror. Over my head, Mr. Herbert was looking at it too. Then I met his eyes in the glass; piercing eyes, boring into mine as if they were reading the innermost secrets of my soul.

He smiled the strangest smile . . .

Suddenly I realized the shop had grown very dark. It must be awfully late. Mama would be furious. Jumping to my feet so hastily I almost knocked over the stool, I headed for the door.

"Where are you going, dear child?" Mr. Herbert's voice rose querulously. "There is more I can do for you if you'll just . ."

"I have to get home, my folks will skin me alive."

"Do you want your parents to see you like this?" He reached for the jar of Albolene to clean my face but I was already halfway out the door.

Somewhere deep inside I knew I wanted Mama to see me *exactly* like this.

The streets between The Melrose and home were strangely deserted in the summer twilight. Although I was late for dinner I walked, instead of running, to keep sweat from ruining my makeup. As I strode along I amused myself by imagining Mama's horror when she saw me.

But my fondest imaginings were nothing compared to the real thing.

When I got home there was no light in the front room, so I knew Mama and Dad were already in the dining room. She was complaining to him about me, no doubt. Well, I was going to give her something to *really* complain about!

Drawing a deep breath and tossing my head back so the overhead light would catch the full effect. I sauntered into the room.

Mama let out a screech they could have heard in Brazil. *"What have you done to yourself!"*

I smiled my carefully rehearsed death's-head rictus. "Don't you like it?" I inquired with what I fondly thought was cool sophistication. "It's the real me." Then I laughed. Hollow, death's head laughter.

She turned almost as pale as I was. Mama never did have a sense of humor. "Sweet god in heaven, why am I tormented by this child?" she wondered aloud.

Dad was just staring at me, though by the winkle in his eyes I could tell he was trying not to laugh.

"Go to the bathroom, Lucinda," Mama spluttered, "and wash that ... that junk off your face right now, before the wind changes and your face freezes like that!" She could not resist adding the old, childish threat, as if I was still a baby.

"I hope it does!" I shouted at her. I stormed up the stairs and slammed the door.

Once inside, I went straight to the mirror and looked at myself. The effect was every bit as startling as I had hoped. Gazing into my reflected eyes, I practised different facial expressions, concluding that with a very good imitation of mama's most regal, self-assured pose.

At that moment a mighty wind slammed into the house. I could hear the upstairs windows rattling and the curtains over the tub billowed wildly. A moment later the lights flickered, then went out. Crossing to the bathroom window, I looked out.

To my astonishment there was only one light burning anywhere in town. It seemed to be coming from the corner of Princess Street and Tagg's Lane. How, I wondered, could Mr. Herbert keep his lights burning when the entire town was suffering a blackout?

The threatened storm failed to materialize, however, although the wind shrieked and howled. Then the lights came back on.

With a sigh, I went back to the sink to wash my face.

Lots of soap and lather, lots of hot water. But when I raised my head and looked in the mirror, the makeup was still there.

Not a smear; not a smudge.

Desperately I scrubbed again, almost wearing out the washcloth.

Same result.

It wouldn't come off.

Neither would my haughty expression.

And that damned black wig seemed to have grown to my head.

I stood frozen in the middle of the bathroom with water still dripping from my face as I tried to think; to understand. The skeletal face staring back at me from the mirror with its great, haunted eyes was an image of Famine. The image Mr. Herbert had created for me.

What if the wind changes and your face freezes like that?

How could I ever face Mama?

I did, though. With terror clutching my throat like a cold hand, I made my way down the stairs and into the dining room. I thought she was going to have apoplexy when she saw me . . . unchanged. And when I tried to explain, at first she didn't believe me at all.

But Dad kept looking at me in the funniest way.

"What shop on the corner of Princess and Tagg?" he finally asked. "The Academe Chemical Corp. used to be there, but they went bankrupt when I was in grade school. That's been a vacant lot for years."

When repeated efforts to scrub my face clean resulted only in turning my white skin a furious, enflamed crimson, my parents—both of them—accompanied me in search of Mr. Herbert.

But he wasn't there.

Neither was The Melrose.

Only a vacant lot, filled with weeds.

Someone in the neighborhood recalled that the Academe Chemical Corp. had belonged to a family called Herbert, who had great plans for expanding the business. But then it went broke instead, smashing all their dreams. Old man Herbert died penniless and his son hanged himself in his garage, or so the story went. No one was really sure anymore.

Dad wanted to sue but there was no one to sue. Mama went into a kind of blue funk. The explanations she tried to make to her friends fell flat. I had to admit myself that they didn't sound very plausible. And as for my friends—well, the less said about that the better. Even June-Bug didn't want to know me. I was miserable.

But my misery didn't last long—only until the autumn, when a photographer who visited our school for Career Day took one look at me and let out a yip as if he had discovered gold.

Which he had, in a way.

You know this face, you've seen it on hundreds of magazine covers in the last five years. Gaunt, petulant, pale, with prominent gums that are now considered the height of fashion .. it belongs to the highest paid model in the world.

Mine is the image every other girl longs to possess.

As my dear Mama had warned me, my face froze like that.

What's The Magic Word?

Jody Lynn Nye

James Gage dodged around a street lamp, and squeezed past a veiled woman coming out of a shop on a narrow, crowded street of the Casbah. His excellent manners, drummed into him for decades by his mother, demanded that he give room and smile politely as the lady passed, but this time he apologized as he took the right of way. Once, just once, perfect courtesy be damned. He was in terrible danger and running for his life.

Jim hardly knew who was pursuing him, only that they were nearly on his heels. A quick glimpse at the spy detector on his wrist told him that one thug was only twenty feet behind him on this street, and that the other had ducked down a nearby alley to try and cut him off ahead. Thank heaven for the gadgets, or he'd already be floating face down in the unsavory river that rolled by the Casbah, and the precious briefcase secured to his other wrist would be in the hands of the enemy.

The enemy were well prepared, that he knew. They appeared to have obtained information on his mission ahead of time. How could that be? Where was the leak? Or who?

The first suspicion Jim had had that his mission might have been compromised came when he had walked down that first alley just outside of the Scirocco National Airport, and blundered into a fine net of cobwebs. He'd thought nothing of it; he brushed them away and kept walking, thinking ahead toward his journey to Remakand by train and boat to complete his mission for the friendly government there.

It had been an error to dismiss such an event as casual. Someone had known he was going that way, and someone had laced the spiderwebs with confusion spells to throw him off balance. His head had been spinning ever since. Difficult as it was, he had to focus on the facts. His life, and his mission, depended upon it.

The transit through Scirocco to Remakand ought to have been the simplest routine mission. He had the obligatory briefcase—spelled shut at the point of pickup in Whitetower—a Batama tropical hat, and an impeccably Altish, slightly worn, leather suitcase. The customs agents in the airport had passed him through at once. There had been a couple of men and a few women nearby, but no one who even looked twice at him.

That should have aroused his suspicions. He caught a glimpse of himself in the next shop window as he ran past. Yes, hair still perfectly in place, the creases on his trousers still knife-sharp. Why hadn't they been looking? Wasn't he the very picture of a handsome, dashing, wealthy adult male? So he'd been under surveillance from the very beginning of his mission. He hoped it would not cost him too dearly. Mother was counting on him.

Luckily, Jim didn't have to rely upon half-recalled instructions to get him to the part of the Casbah where his first contact was waiting. He'd been in Scirocco hundreds of times. These narrow passages and mysterious doorways were familiar, even friendly, territory. His feet carried him in the right direction on pure instinct.

Whirling swathes of color flashed past his eyes. The Casbah was a kaleidoscope of exotic sights, sounds, and smells. Normally, he would be enjoying his walk. Memories swam up as he passed every doorway. Food vendors offered him chunks of unrecognizable grilled meat on sticks. A tyke with a dirty face followed him for half a block trying to sell him a bunch of ruby-red grapes. They looked like gleaming eyes. He brushed his way underneath a flying carpet laden with tourists, their guide chanting in a hypnotic singsong voice all of the fascinating lies they always told about the Casbah. The reality was far more interesting, but none of the goggle-eyed travelers would ever stray away from their group long enough to find out about it.

Jim wove in between camels, donkeys, and a cluster of modern floating capsules like sedan chairs without visible means of support, some containing beautiful ladies who met his eye for brief, memorable seconds, and some containing important businessmen and women who were too preoccupied to notice a single man out of all the others on the crowded streets. Traffic was heavy in the early evening here. Everyone wanted to get to his or her destination before darkness fell. The Casbah was dangerous at night.

His wrist detector beeped a warning. His befuddled brain had failed to stay vigilant. The enemy was close, so close that the two blips on the small screen had merged into one.

Two shadowy figures had appeared before him, catching him by his upper arms and shoving him back against a stone pillar. His briefcase jammed painfully against his legs. The large man, with a voice like a garbage disposal grinding up stones, addressed him by name.

"Mr. Gage."

Jim squinted up at them in the growing gloom. "I beg your pardon, gentlemen? I don't believe we've had the pleasure."

"Never mind," hissed the smaller man, with a distinctive Remakandan accent. He loomed forward, pressing his face close to Jim's, and poked something into his ribs. Out of the corner of his eye, Jim saw a slim, gleaming, silver object, but at that angle was unable to identify it as gun or wand. "give us the briefcase."

"Ridiculous!" Jim's eyebrows arched into his hairline, causing the eyes of a passing raven-haired maiden to glow with interest. "I'm afraid I must decline to cooperate." He shrugged one shoulder, activating a personal forceshield that could deflect most kinds of attack by fire or light. His perfectly pressed suit was comprised of fibers that could repel most missiles up to iron grapeshot. With his expertise in seven martial arts, there was little that these brutes could do to force him to give up the precious briefcase. It struck Jim as ironic that his inability to create magic left his strength intact for fighting and fleeing. "Do your worst."

"We already have. We have your mother," the first man ground out.

"My mother?" Jim echoed, realizing how doltish he sounded. Of all the things they might have said, that was the most unexpected, and the most absurd. With a deft movement that caused his form to blur in the heavily spiced air, he thrust his way out of their grasp, and stood straightening his tie. It had shifted a quarter inch off center. "You'll pardon me, chaps, if I doubt your word."

"She is our prisoner," the second man stated. "Give me the documents, and we will release her unharmed. Fail to cooperate, and . . ." He left the sentence hanging but he and his companion reached into their jackets for the inevitable shoulder holsters.

"Sorry, chaps," Jim said, with a debonair wave of his free hand. The gesture distracted them long enough for his briefcase-cuffed fingers to dip into his pocket and pull out a smoke egg. He flipped the small object onto the pavement, and jumped for the nearest passage as soon as the explosion came.

He rolled along the ground among rotting cabbages and heaps of stinking offal, and came up on his feet, running. The thug detector showed his two villains standing just where he had left them.

His mother, in the hands of these thugs? What nonsense! he had to admit that their claim had thrown him momentarily off guard. Such a thing could not be true. Could it?

Half a block away he paused, torn between impulses. Ridiculous claims in the world of espionage stood a better chance of being true than those in mundane life. *Was* his mother in the hands of the enemy? But how could they have kidnapped *her*? He must verify the truth of the matter.

This alley would open out into a wider lane in another fifty yards. Should he double back along a different route, and tail the enemy agents back to their lair? His head spun. Jim wished he could sit down until it cleared.

Shouting erupted behind him. A quick peek at the detector told him his ruse only gave him a few seconds' head start. His opponents were right behind him. Well, he'd be a poor excuse for a . . . courier if he couldn't lose them, in spite of his befuddled senses. He dashed toward the end of the passage, and flung himself leftwards, into the Street of Tanners. Among the stinking vats and the racks of stretched hides, there ought to be ample concealment.

The lighter footsteps behind him suddenly doubled in speed, suggesting the use of some magic device. Gage glanced over his shoulder as the smaller man flashed into view. The enemy agent raised his hand. Jim heard a small missile zing past his ear. Ahead, he heard an explosion and a scream, and a man fell to the ground clutching his belly. Jim was fortunate that it was too dark for his enemy to aim. He'd send a card of apology to the injured tanner later.

An escape offered itself on the right: a narrow

passage between two buildings hardly wide enough for a child to walk. The gap could only occur in a city as old as the Casbah, when a new building was put up right next to an existing one. Jim took advantage of the crowd that gathered to attend to the wounded man. If he still had it after that first tussle with his two pursuers, the device concealed in Gage's right sock would slightly alter his body's state so it could squeeze smoothly anywhere his patrician nose could go.

Another magical dart impacted on the wall of the alleyway just as Jim slipped into it. He felt his body compress at once, squeezing between the soiled bricks and a rusted iron ladder; upon the top step a cat contemplated him as he went by. Jim felt his way using the edge of the briefcase. The frustrated villains behind him shouted into the crack, unable to follow.

He had to make time while they ran around the block to intercept him. The gloves that allowed him to climb walls like a spider were back in his luggage at the airport. All he had was what was on his person during the flight, and his befuddled wits. Those would have to do.

Short of the exit, he pulled a mirror from his pocket. He kept moving while glancing occasionally into its surface. Using it, he tried to see past the magical veils that blanketed the Casbah to see if those fiends were telling the truth. One of the devastating effects of the confusion glamour was that he couldn't remember the scrying spell coherently enough to recite it. In the magic game, as in espionage, the wrong words spoken at the wrong place and time could so easily get one killed.

"What's the magic word?" his mother had used to tease him when he was a small boy and wanted a favor. It was a game they'd had between them. "Come on, Jimmy. What is it?"

"Bibbidibobbidiboo!" he would giggle, and the

room filled with soap bubbles. His mother face smiled down at him.

"No . . . try again."

"Mimiximim! Abracadabra! Faropelingo!"

"No dear," she had said patiently, making the enchanted frog, the dove, and the glass of water disappear again. "Those are all good magic words, but which one am I looking for?"

"Please," he would say at last, with a naughty grin.

"Good," she'd say, handing him what he wanted. "Please is the most powerful word there is. It makes people do what you want. Manners are often as strong as magic."

"Wo-ow," he would say, impressed.

"Please," the adult James Gage whispered to himself now. "Let me find her safely."

His father, a senior professor in metaphysical engineering at the university, had been so proud that his son showed such impressive magical acumen.

"You'll be a magical researcher, my boy, or even personal wizard to the king of High Altain!" he had said, putting Jim's latest simulacrum on the food preservation cabinet with an adhesion cantrip.

"No," his mother had said, with the small, secret smile she had, "I think his path lies in another direction."

He hadn't understood at the time. He knew that both his parents worked. He didn't quite know what his mother did, only that her job was very important. She always had time to stop and play with him and to answer his questions.

His mother had gently steered him to learn all he could about magic, which satisfied his curiosity on that subject, but she also saw to it he learned geography and languages, and the etiquette of a hundred different nations. Waving goodbye in Archipelago, for example, was the same gesture as biting your thumb at someone in Rotily. He questioned why she wanted him to know all these things, but she insisted they would all be useful one day.

Jim was still quite a small boy when he heard about the Secret Service. It sounded fascinating and exciting. The Service was responsible for safeguarding High Altain from sneaky enemies who tried to use magic and espionage to undermine the government. No one knew who its agents were, or what methods it used. The Secret Service was known only by its successes. Its head was a mysterious figure known only as M. And one day he discovered M stood for Mother. *His* mother.

Instinctively, Jim knew that he had uncovered the most important fact he had ever known in his life. Though he was dying to tell his friends at school, he didn't. He struggled with the undoubted status of revealing such a secret against the possible sequences, if those wonderful movies at the cinema were anything to go by.

His parents watched him displaying a discretion far beyond his years. They didn't say anything then, but as soon as he had grown up, his mother offered him a job in the department.

He'd had to prove his worth. No matter whose son he was, he had to be able to handle himself in the field, and he did. His own magical talents included a knack for finding things that people had lost or stolen, and an infallible sense of direction. His first job in the Service was as a "courier," according to the royal payroll.

Nepotism notwithstanding, Jim Gage was an excellent choice as an agent. He had wavy black hair, a firm, square chin, a physique that while not overmuscled gave the impression of easy strength and robust good health. His blue-gray eyes were steely yet had a twinkle in them. Women found the combination attractive because he looked dangerous, but at the same time fun to be around, and a perfectly safe escort. And, of course, he was always a proper gentleman. His parents had raised him right. And besides, he never could become too serious with any woman, no matter how tempting. His heart belonged to M.

His responsibilities expanded in later years to include more delicate missions, all of which he executed with panache. It was a good life. His personal transport was filled with all the latest magical toys and equipment. He wore devastatingly well-cut business suits, and on his days off, open-necked polo shirts and trousers that looked crisp even when he was wrestling in alleys with dire criminals. Gadgets of every kind up his sleeves from A in Accessories meant that he could push aside most obstructions, human and otherwise, without so much as ruffling his smooth black hair.

His tails sufficiently far away, Jim thought he could spare a moment to notify HQ of developments. Within the next block he found an etherphone, but it was occupied. A dark-haired woman in a trim summer business suit shook a scolding finger at the screen, on which Jim could see two small children.

"Now, you listen to the baby-sitter. When she says it's time for bed, it's time for bed!"

"Awww!" the children chorused, making faces. The boy had a cap of silky golden hair, and the girl had puffy, red braids.

"I mean it!" their mother exclaimed. "And it's a full moon tonight, so when Gramma turns into a werewolf, I do not want you locking her out of the house. It's rude to make a woman of advanced years spend the night in the garden. Do you understand me?"

"Yes, Mamma," said the children, giggling.

"I beg your pardon for interrupting, madam," Jim said, stepping up to her before she spoke again. "My name is James Gage, and I am a spy. I need to phone headquarters at once. It is an emergency."

The woman's brown eyes went round. She gave him a calculating look, and the results seemed to strike her as favorable. "There, you see?" she admonished the children. "Other people have important business, too. Kiss each other for me. I'll see you tomorrow night, and Daddy will be home Tuesday. Love you. There," she said to Jim as she clicked off the transmission, changing the view on the screen to a swirling haze. "I hope that didn't take too long."

"No, madam," Jim said, with a courtly bow. He held the stance until she went away, although he knew she was curious and would have stayed around to watch if he had allowed it. He slewed his eyes around to make certain no one else was in earshot. The booth's own magic would ensure that his call would be confidential.

He took from his pocket a small card which he thrust into the pay slot of the etherphone. It connected at once, scrambled the line, and paid for his call to HQ. The secretary, Pennyfarthing, appeared on the screen. She peered at him over her half-glasses.

"Cage here, Penny. I am in Scirocco. Have made initial contact, but have run into brutes who spun me an unlikely tale. Is M . . ." he could hardly force out the word, "missing?"

"It's true, Jim," Pennyfarthing said. Her long, thin face was pinched with distress. In all the years he'd known her, back to the days when she'd bounced him on her knee while his mother was in conference with eminent international diplomats, she had shown despair only rarely. "She's gone!"

"But, how?" Jim demanded.

"We don't know how," Pennyfarthing said, throwing up her hands. "She stepped out for a bit of lunch after her morning meetings, and didn't come back.

And she had that appointment with the Poncian ambassador. He waited here for an hour."

"It must have been very important to waste Monsieur Finet's time like that. Do you know what it was to be about, Penny?"

She gave him a sharp look that took him right back to his childhood and stood him in a corner with a duncecap on his head. "Not even over secure line, James."

"I think my ugly friends know where she's being held," Jim said, thoughtfully. "I can try to trace back their paths, if they weren't using trail-mixing spells." His mind was becoming more and more clear as he laid out his plans. He was good in emergencies. They stirred up the old brain cells, and brushed away the cobwebs—literally, this time. "Please alert Intercop and ask them if I may call upon them at their conven—"

"Jimmy!" Pennyfarthing's use of is old nickname squeaked out. "Behind you!"

Jim spun around, just in time to take the coming blow on the front of his head instead of the rear. Waves of crashing pain threatened to drown out the raucous noises of the Casbah, and then it all went silent.

"Jimmy? Jimmy?" his mother's voice said. "Wake up, dear." He knew what the next words were going to be. "You'll be late for school." He started to turn over, preparing to pull the pillow over his head. There was no pillow, and his hands felt surprisingly heavy. They clanked when he lifted them. He peeled open one eye to see the heavy iron chains hanging from each wrist. No, he wasn't in bed. He'd never woken up in chains, no matter *whom* he'd slept with.

A bright magenta spider stared eye to eye with him, then fled toward the crack under an iron-bound wooden door as he stirred, abandoning the webs it had been spinning all over his body. Jim sat up and looked around him. His head was aching. He felt it, careful to keep the chains from bumping into his nose. There was a tremendous goose egg on the top of his forehead. It would be purple by morning.

"Oh, Jimmy, what happened to you?" the familiar voice asked, sympathetically.

"Mother!" he cried.

She *was* here! His mother sat primly in a rough wooden chair a few feet from him. As his eyes grew accustomed to the meager light thrown by the single dim lantern hanging from the ceiling of the dingy cell, he saw that she was tied to her seat. Her wide eyes, the same gray-blue as his own, stared at him with concern, not for her own well being, but for his.

There were times like this when he could not reconcile his mother with the head of the Altish secret service. Wearing a print dress with a lace collar, her graying dark hair coiffed to perfection, she looked as if she was about to host an afternoon tea. Entirely out of place in this dark dungeon. Jim was outraged that someone had treated his mother so discourteously. He sprang to his feet and threw himself against the chains. It was no use; not only were they heavy, but the manacles appeared to have been spelled shut. He knelt down on the floor. He must think!

Jim heard sinister laughter from the shadows. Two forms stood against the walls, arms crossed on their chests. He recognized them as the thugs from the Casbah. He listened carefully. He could hear no ambient noise whatsoever. Either this place was remarkably well soundproofed, or nowhere near the Casbah. He could have been transported after he was knocked unconscious. That took big magic, which spoke of big influence, big money, or both.

The dungeon door creaked open. Jim knew the man as soon as he saw him: Charetin Fou, the most notorious international criminal that the country of

Ponce had ever produced. Glittering, black eyes and hollow cheeks in his long, pointed face gave him the air of an undertaker who lived to solicit business personally. Jim shook his chains, trying hopelessly to remember the spell to free his hands.

Fou stood over him and laughed. "So, Mr. Gage. I've always wanted to meet you."

The chilling voice galvanized Jim. "I cannot say I have entertained a similar wish, sir," he said, in ice-cold tones. "I demand that you release us at once."

"Oh, but you can't leave now," Fou said, inclined to be playful. "I wanted to thank you properly for my gift." He snapped his fingers, and a woman dressed in skin-tight, dark green satin swept into the room, carrying Jim's briefcase. "Such a lovely gift, those documents detailing the secret negotiations between High Altain and Remakand."

"You've opened it?" Jim asked, amazed. The multiple layers of wards on the lock were the work of five magicocrytographers who worked at different ends of the kingdom. It *couldn't* be opened without the codes. Fou waved his hand.

"Oh, not yet, dear sir, but I will be able to soon, and I *do* know what's inside. You see, my dear Natalie," he said, turning to Jim's mother, "I've had a mole in your offices for some time."

M looked grim. "That would explain the tunnels in the floors. I've had them sealed. Permanently."

"Yes," Fou was gleeful, "but plenty of information got out to me before the way was closed. The government of Scirocco will pay me dearly for that briefcase, and for a certain little device that I have designed. Oh, but it is not for *them*. I am sending it as a gift to Remakand, in place of the original briefcase, with an alternate courier, who will look exactly like your James. A small, but very powerful device. It will destroy the entire capital city of Remakand, and start a huge international war. And everyone will blame the great James Gage!" He laughed. "I want you to witness my triumph. Even though you will not be able to share in the glorious aftermath of war, destruction—and power." Jim was chilled by the madness in his eyes.

Behind Fou, he heard the hint of a whisper. He glanced out of the corner of his eye at his mother, who was muttering under her breath. Jim heard a stray word, and knew that she was reciting the spell to free herself from her bonds.

"Shut up!" The green-clad woman strode over and slapped M across the mouth. The interruption caused the half-formed spell to dissipate.

"Leave her alone," Jim thundered. "If you were not a lady .."

"And you were not in chains," the woman said, spinning on a stiletto heel and regarding him coyly from under silky black hair, "we might have an interesting time, no?"

He would make her pay for her disrespect to his mother. Glaring at her, Jim started to chant the spell to unlock his chains. The woman stepped up to him, too, but he ignored the pain.

". . . Gobandala femismob tribba lo!"

The manacles felt heavy, and he looked down at his hands. The woman and Fou stared and burst into laughter.

A rabbit with mottled blue fur had appeared balanced on his wrists. It jumped down to the floor and stood looking up at him, wiggling its small blue nose.

Fou wiped tears of merriment from his eyes.

"Do you like my confusion webs?" he asked. "A mere trifle, but so very rewarding."

Jim gnashed his teeth. Another spell wasted. Each attempt sapped his physical strength. If more failed he would become exhausted, leaving his mother and himself at the mercy of the evil Fou and his associates. A dozen useful devices for extending his power were in the suitcase at the airport. When he did not return to claim it, the case would disappear into the depths of the Casbah. A's wonderful inventions would be sold as souvenirs to tourists, or kept by some of the influential people who lived there. Nobody would ponder what had become of their owner.

"Why?" he asked Fou. "Why are you torturing us this way? Why not kill us and be done?"

The cadaverous face loomed down into his own.

"Why? Didn't your mother ever tell you about me? Natalie, I am hurt. I met her over twenty-six years ago at a Spies and Agents Ball in Fogton. You should have seen her then, Mr. Gage. She was captivating. Everyone who saw her was enchanted. She allowed me one dance—*one*—and then she was gone, like your Cinder woman. I find out who she is, I call upon her. She scorns me, says our countries are enemies." Fou's cultured accent was fading in his fury. "And besides, she has attachments already. And none of them was the man who would be your father," Fou added, bitterly. "It could have been me! Many affairs, and never with me!"

M's face turned pink with chagrin. "You dare to bring that up, after all these years?"

His mother? Jim thought, shocked. Well, no one liked to think of his own mother having . . . liaisons, but after all she was an adult, and she hadn't been married at the time, and it was her own business, certainly not this criminal's.

"How dare you intrude into her private life, you fiend?" Jim said.

"How I dare is that I can," Fou said, with an evil smile, in control once again.

"The Service will be looking for us," said Jim desperately. "HQ knows I was in Scirocco."

"Ah," Fou said, flexing his long fingers. "But where? They can't trace you. My magicians are as good as your magicians. I know! I hired away many of your best people. And those who would not come willingly, I . . . detoured. I have been working many years for this moment, Natalie. I wish to enjoy it." He leaned over to caress M's hair. With great self-control she continued to stare forward as if he was not there. Jim felt himself losing his temper.

"And for the sake of a long-past lost romance you would destroy the Remakand/Altain alliance?" he demanded.

"Of course not, Mr. Gage," the villain said, turning to him with an expression of surprise. "That is for *money*."

Taking advantage of the enemy's momentary lapse of attention, M blurted out the formula for quick release from metal fetters. Jim felt his belt buckle unfasten, and the manacles on his wrists dropped to the floor with a decided clang.

Too late, Fou whirled to point at M, and sputtered out a brief cantrip. A beam of blue light shot from his fingertip. A closefitting gag coalesced around M's mouth.

While Fou's attention was distracted, Jim leaped upon him from behind. They rolled together on the floor. The woman in green stood over them, waving her arms, shrieking a curse. Jim rapped out a counter-spell. And added a knockout charm. The air filled with perfumed soap bubbles and the sound of barking. Another misfire! Jim growled under his breath as Fou knocked his head into the floor. Jim's lucidity had lasted only long enough to defend himself against an imminent threat. He still couldn't piece together a decent spell. Yet his physical skills remained. He thrust a knee and an arm upward and over his head, and sent the master villain flying into a wall. Fou landed on his back, groaning. The woman continued to shriek threats.

Jim heard a bang, followed by a ping. The two thugs by the wall had drawn their weapons, and begun firing at him. The first shot missed him and slammed into the floor near his head. A six-inch crater opened in the stone. Jim shuddered to imagine what would happen if one of those magic bullets struck flesh. He leaped up, spinning in a roundhouse kick that disarmed the smaller thug on the first revolution. With surprising reflexes, the large man backed out of the way, and aimed straight at his head. Jim hit the floor, and came to his feet again with all his weight behind his fist. The big man shook is head as if a fly had landed on his nose, and swayed gently back and forth, his eyes fixed on nothing. He didn't fall over, but he did drop the wand. Jim kicked both weapons out of their reach.

He needed to free his mother. So long as his mind refused to focus on offense magic, he was reduced to mere hand-to-hand combat. Once the gag was removed, M could invoke all the spells they needed. He drove toward the chair where she was bound.

"Ki-ha-yah!"

A shriek from behind told Jim that the woman was attempting some kind of martial arts attack. He whirled, en garde, his hands flattened and ready and she backed off. By now, Fou was back on his feet, growling an enchantment. Jim had to disable the woman quickly, so he could deal with the mastermind himself. By her stance, he judged that she was a master of kyo-do, farensi, and Stepmaster aerobics.

She circled around him, chanting, seeking the best position to begin her attack. Kyo-do was fought mostly with multiple kicks, using magic to stay up in the air. Jim knew all the countermoves and counterspells. He expected her to begin with the mighty aw-faw-dou, a preemptive knockout blow, and braced himself.

"Hya!" She bounded up and flew at him, feet first. Jim ducked out of the way, shouting out the appropriate defense. The woman, caught in a counterspell that used her own strength against her, hurtled toward

the wall. She saved herself just in time, braced against
the wall, flipped right over so her black hair was a
silken blur, and hit the ground in a new defensive
stance.

Jim deflected her next attack with the flair expected
of a Secret Service agent, but he found himself in a
dilemma as to how to defeat her. He could not use
magic against her, because his mind was blurred, nor
could he physically strike a lady. Fou had uncovered
his only weakness. Jim must take her by magic, but
how?

"Persevere, son," his father had always advised him.
"It's the scientist's credo, but it applies to nearly every
walk of life. When in doubt, keep trying until something works." His mother's eyes, over the edge of the
gag, encouraged him.

Jim promised himself he couldn't let either of them
down. He knew a spell that filled the room with small,
infinitely slippery spheres. All he'd have to do was
keep his feet while the others fell down or became
immobilized in the slick mass. That invocation was
easy: all he had to do was repeat the same word over
and over again.

"Aggie, aggie aggie aggie aggie aggie!" Jim cried.
"Aggie! Aggie!" A rain of small glass beads began falling from the ceiling onto everyone's head. The villains
howled with pain, and the woman threw herself under
M's chair for cover. The two henchmen ran to stand
in the door frame, and fell a dozen times in as many
as feet. Jim was pleased that something magical
worked—then he realized he didn't remember how
many times he was supposed to say "aggie," nor how
many times he already had. The wrong number could
cause the spell to backfire. He tried counting back in
his mind while he chanted.

Through the hail of marbles, Fou caught a glimpse
of the expression on Jim's face, and guessed what he
was thinking. Instead of shielding himself, he folded

his arms and waited. Jim tried one more feeble. "Aggie," and Fou grinned.

Instantly, every glass ball vanished in a puff of acrid smoke.

"You cannot defeat us with humor, Mr. Gage," Fou said, laughing evilly. M's eyes flashed with anger for him and then sympathy for her son. Jim, under no compunction to avoid punching men, leaped forward to rain haraki blows upon Fou's head and shoulders.

The henchmen stumbled to their feet and rushed in to save their master. The small Remakandan reached inside his coat for a black, egg-shaped device, and the large man grabbed up another chair to use as a bludgeon. Jim spun expertly to defend himself. He ducked the big man's first pass with the chair, and again so the man would hit his comrade before the small man could use his weapon. No sooner had Jim countered the first attack, then both of them moved swiftly to try again.

They had been well trained, one striking or kicking him when he turned to drive off the other. Jim sustained painful blows to back, legs, ribs, and jaw before he realized he'd been forced to pure defense. Fou leaped back a pace to begin weaving another spell. Across the room, Jim saw the woman crawling out from under M's chair, and heard her chanting loudly as she prepared another kyo-do offensive. Four against one were not normally odds that troubled him, but he'd been hit by confusion spells twice and hit on the head hard enough to knock him out. He swayed slightly, and realized that his strength was flagging.

Quickly, he considered his remaining technical gadgets. There were only three. The device in his right sock would allow him to squeeze thin enough to slip out under the door, but that would leave M in danger. In a closed room, his remaining smoke grenades would do nothing to the villains that it wouldn't also do to him and his mother. The button sewn to his sleeve that allowed him to imitate the calls of over five hundred bird species had no particular application here unless he wanted to use it to sing his swan song. Jim was not ready to die, yet he had only enough reserves left for one last physical effort, one spell of moderate effort.

At most, he could hope only to take out two of his powerful opponents. The others would be left standing, while he would be exhausted. Which two should it be?

Luckily, the effects of the confusion web were fading. His official grimoire was coming back to him. He racked his awakening memory for the strongest spell he knew. It had to be one that would disable a large group of people, but use only a limited amount of power. His inner eye reached the index and started to backtrack through the pages, even as his body reacted to the blows of Fou's thug's.

Only one stood out as a possibility. The Valliamide Incantation would cause his subjects to relax and fall to the ground in a semicomatose state. But could it work, spread out over so many people? It had to. There was no other way out. If he failed it would bring death to thousands, and dishonor to the Altain Secret Service.

Jim assumed a straight-backed posture. No one must know how close he was to utter collapse. The incantation was a long one, and he must get it exactly right.

His entire deliberation had taken only a fraction of a second. Over Fou's mumble, and the woman's ritual chant, he shouted out the first words of the spell.

"Lollabi engudnyt mitaroses beadite . . ."

Fou goggled at him. A soporific charm was not what he had expected. He began to shout a counterspell, but his vocal chords weakened as Jim's magic took hold. Fou cleared his throat and began again, more feebly. His eyes were alert as ever, though. He knew, as Jim did, that it wouldn't be enough to keep him from attacking. He must be wondering what was in the agent's mind. Jim hoped he thought that some further blast was forthcoming, not that the quiver would be empty as soon as this bolt was shot.

Jim forced himself to keep his voice loud, though the heavy, drowsy syllables made him sway on his feet. He had to keep on. The woman started to kick one foot in the air, then dropped it to the floor. She stared at it, as if wondering why it wouldn't do her bidding. The two henchmen's arms fell to their sides, and their eyes looked dull and empty.

Still chanting, Jim looked around at them. He'd stopped them for the moment, but as soon as the spell ended, they'd begin to recover. It was stretched too thin to work fully on all of them. He needed a power boost; where could he get it?

Suddenly, he heard a noise that caused him almost to lose his concentration. M was pounding her bound feet on the floor. Fou, surprised into action, staggered toward her to shut her up. He was weakened, but he could still kill her. Jim caught sight of his mother's face over the villain's shoulder. His mother's eyes flashed.

Remember! they said.

Jim gasped. He *did* remember: the magic word to make people do his bidding. It had been only a childhood game between them—but what if it worked? It *had* to work. Jim took a deep breath and snapped out the remainder of the spell as quickly as he could.

"Fanangalanti parindella woorga woorga somnifent drimidrawzilazi cowntinshiyp yawtabe sawniwud sleep sleep sleep—please!"

He felt a tremendous surge of energy rise up out of the ground, up into his feet, and out his hands as he thrust them toward the villains. There *was* extra magic in the word!

Fou's beefy underlings surged toward him, then their eyes closed, and they fell to the floor, asleep even before they hit. The woman gave Jim one wide, admiring gaze, and sank unconscious in a boneless heap. That left Fou. Jim stumbled toward the man, and clapped a heavy hand on his shoulder. The arch-villain's hands fell to his sides, and his head dropped back. Jim yanked Fou away from his mother, drew back a fist that felt as heavy as lead, and punched the enemy under the angle of his jaw. Fou's body straightened out and dropped like a plank.

Panting, Jim sat down on the larger henchman's body for a moment to regain his strength. As soon as he could, he stood up and untied his mother's bonds.

"My apologies for not doing this first," he said, as he removed her gag.

"Not at all, dear," M said, removing a long, jeweled pin from her hair. "That was quite a fight. Well done! My, my. Who would have guessed that Charetin Fou should have been harboring frustrated jealousy all these years? I thought he'd been happily married to that Sinese woman he seemed so wild about." Shaking her head, she turned to the communication device hidden in the pin. "M to HQ. Home in on this signal, and respond."

In seconds, the room was full of agents, teleporting in from all over the continent. Pennyfarthing was among them. They exclaimed over both M and Jim, giving them revitalizing potions. Penny offered M a magic mirror in which to check on the situation at HQ and elsewhere. Jim accepted the bracing drink with gratitude, and watched the activity around him as he sipped it; he felt his vitality rebuild swiftly. Even the crease returned to his trouser legs. He rose to his feet and went to wait by M's elbow, peering down over her shoulder. The two pairs of blue-gray eyes reflected in the mirror were just exactly alike, he realized with a sensation of mild shock. Jim smoothed his hair, which had become slightly disarranged in the fight. He had a small bruise on his cheek, which only served to make him appear more dashing and dangerous. His mother looked up from her magic overview and smiled at him.

"You look much better, my dear," she said, with an approving nod. "And now, I must get back to the office. The Poncian ambassador will be very cross with me for leaving him sitting like that. This will require very special diplomatic measures." Her eyes twinkled. "I think I may have to employ my holiday fruitcake."

Jim laughed. Even bad temper could not stand long against the combined might of magical ingredients, exotic dried fruit, and choice Kiltish whiskey. M's fruitcake was a legendary mood reviver.

"You may come along and have a slice, too," M offered. She gestured with a cocked finger, and a representative from A Department hurried over to Jim with a clutch of replacement mystical devices, which he began to put into Jim's pockets, socks, and cuffs. "Just as soon as you have delivered that briefcase to the Sciroccan government."

"I would be delighted," Jim said. He squeezed M's hand and leaned down to kiss her on the cheek. "But, I mustn't forget the other magic word before I go. Thank you, Mom."

"I am proud of you, my dear," M said. "Now, off you go! You mustn't keep the Lord High Commissioner waiting."

"Certainly not," Jim said, with a grin, patting the briefcase with a protective hand. "That would be rude."

Don't Go Out in Holy Underwear

Elizabeth Ann Scarborough

Victoria Fredericks, Space Cadet, was just your average titian-haired, emerald-eyed temptress of a time and space traveler, nothing out of the ordinary really. Except that Victoria had a secret. She had an underwear fetish. Long ago, back on earth, even before she began the cadet training program, she had fancied lacy silk underthings in shades to match her eyes and clash with her hair, as well as scanties in purple or black or aquamarine, in tiger stripes or leopard spots or little pink and red hearts. She liked knowing that under her standard issue uniform, she had on something fine, something she wouldn't be ashamed to show in any emergency room.

Her mother had impressed the importance of underwear on her at an early age. "Vicky, baby," she had told her. "I don't want to catch you goin' out to play with holes in your underpants. What if, God forbid, you should fall off your air board or get hit by a low-flying shuttle and have to go to the emergency room? What would the doctors and nurses think to see your holey underwears?"

That was Mom all over. Not well-educated herself, she slaved for hours in a spacer bar saving the money so that young Victoria could have a better education, a broader horizon, than she herself enjoyed. And better underwear too. Mom's job in the spacer bar was such that she particularly appreciated a well-placed piece of lace. In good condition, always. Victoria was brought up to do the same.

However, once Victoria shipped out, she found that

86

her secret satisfaction became her secret sorrow. Her lovely undies wore out, set by set, first the black, which was so basic she wore it for all occasions, followed by the white with the little pink rosettes and bows accenting the lace, then the emerald which went so well with her eyes, followed by all of the other colors until she was in desperate danger of having to wear—ugh—Space Cadet issue underwear. And that was just on her first mission! She sent an urgent dispatch earthward with a supply ship begging her mother to send something suitable from her favorite boutique.

The time thing had entirely slipped her mind. If it seemed like forever until another supply ship brought her special package, it must have seemed longer than that to her mother, who wrote in a shaky hand:

"Vicky, baby, forgive that I don't write so good but for God's sake I'm nearly ninety, so I think I'm doing pretty good, don't you? I hate to tell you, baby, but the port has gone to hell since you left and your favorite boutique closed up. I don't get around so good, but I got my Elderaid to go shopping for me and asked her to buy you something nice. This is what she came back with. It was in a closeout sale at the souvenir shop at the spaceport. Sorry, it was the best I could do. Just remember to change often and don't go out on any missions with holes in your scanties, okay? Take care of yourself. Love, Mom."

Victoria sniffled, ashamed to realize she'd been thinking only of herself in asking her mother to sacrifice precious time, energy and money for her wish, but the Space Corps stuff really rubbed her the wrong way after all those years of silk. So she bravely wiped her eyes and with fingers trembling with anticipation, opened the package to pull out—plain cotton briefs. Her heart sank. They were perfectly respectable, and would surely be more comfortable than the Space Corps ones, but they were so ordinary! And then, examining them closer, she saw that they weren't ordinary at all. The package said, "SPACE PANTIES" but at first, they just seemed to be the sort of typical days-of-the-week panties girls had once worn in school. "Monday, Tuesday, Wednesday, Thursday, Friday." Victoria counted to herself, "Saturday, Sunday . . ." but that was only the first seven. There were thirty-eight more pairs to go, one for every day in a spacer's week! "Shepardsday, Glennsday, Gagaisday, Kristasday . . ." she named them in order, all of the spacer days named for the early astronauts. There was a fresh pair of briefs for each. If she was careful, washing by hand and mending when necessary, she need never be without a special pair! Or so she thought, tears of gratitude, relief and homesickness dampening the white cotton and industrial-strength elastic.

As her time of service lengthened and her data bases became engorged with knowledge as she grew in wisdom, experience and, of course, beauty, her elastic began to give out and her fabric to fray.

A few pairs of her precious undies had become ripped in the line of duty—a couple more, before she came to value them so highly, in the line of other, more pleasurable pursuits. And so the space panties were carefully stowed in her locker to be worn only for good luck on special missions.

Like saving whole entire planets. Such as the one she was saving now, while wearing the Glennsday pair. Not only were they her most especially lucky pair, they were also the only ones left that had no holes, not even the tiniest. She'd cried when she opened her locker to find her entire stack of treasured unmentionables full of bitty little holes. Nobody had told her about space moths or she would have brought along space mothballs.

Only the Glennsday pair had escaped without even the tiniest puncture. Her loins thus girded, Victoria set forth to save the simple, quaint, low-tech inhabitants of

the earthlike planet known in space jargon as Hotel
Whiskey.

"But, commander," she had protested to her gruff,
stern-but-fair commander, when given the assignment. "Why don't the Hotel Whiskonians simply zap
the silly Hasslebads into the next dimension?"

"Because," Commander Helen Highwater replied,
"they have chosen a simple, quaint, spiritual life and
aren't good at fighting. Unfortunately, the Hasslebads
are much more sophisticated technologically and are
very good at fighting. So your mission, Space Cadet
Victoria Fredericks, is to defend the planet from utter
destruction and the domination of the forces of evil
and so forth. Okay?"

"Sure, yeah, okay, fine," Victoria said, with a
snappy salute.

"Here are the keys to the top-secret battle shuttle,
the *Rikki Tikki Tavi*. If, and when, you return with
your mission successfully completed, you will have
passed your final test and will no longer be a Space
Cadet but a full, entire, completely commissioned and
graduated officer of the Space Corps, and in a really
swell ceremony will receive your insignia as *Ensign*
Victoria Fredericks of the Space Corps."

"Just for defending one little planet and destroying
the forces of evil that threaten it? Gee, Commander
Highwater, piece of cake. Send me in there,
commander."

With only a brief stop, so to speak, to don her
special lucky lingerie and her space suit, she had gone
to the shuttle bay and inserted the keys into the igni-
tion of the battle shuttle *Rikki Tikki Tavi* and, pru-
dently waiting for the bay door to iris, had blasted off
into space

What a rush!

It was the first time the commander had let her
take a shuttle out on her own, though of course she
had practiced flying in simulators and under the

supervision of seasoned Space Corps veteran such as Captains Flash Morgan and Chuck Rogers. But this was her premier solo flight *and* fight.

She continued being really thrilled right up until, as she approached the tasteful emerald and purple sphere that was Hotel Whiskey, she saw her enemy sneaking up on her from the far side of one of the planet's pretty lavender moons. She knew it had to be the enemy ship because it was this really ugly, mean-looking black thing with a nose cone flanked by what looked like twin spikes, or fangs, but which were really space-to-dirt missiles. No doubt meant to blow the peaceful, gentle, quaint Hotel Whiskonians to smithereens! The rest of the Hasslebad ship rose like a hood behind the slitted dual view ports on either side of the nose cone.

Mere badly conceived exterior design wasn't about to intimidate Victoria, however. She got right on her com set and opened the preprogrammed Hasslebad hailing frequency and said, "Hey there, you in the cobra ship! Come in. This is Victoria Fredericks, Space Cadet in the Space Corps battle shuttle *Rikki Tikki Tavi* and if you don't stop picking on that poor little planet beneath us *this very instant*, I will open fire and you will be really, really sorry."

"Ha, brave and beautiful but sadly doomed and deluded earth woman, we defy you and your dainty little space shuttle to keep us from enslaving the puny world beneath our jets! Surrender now and you can have a ringside seat as the consort of our emperor while watching us make that world go away."

"Absolutely out of the question!" Victoria replied spunkily. "Your sort are evil, odious, wicked and mean and wish only to dominate others *and* you have a very ugly spaceship. I would never feel comfortable as the consort of an emperor who employs such tacky designers."

"Impudent earthling vixen, we will blow you out of

the cosmos for that! The emperor himself designed this vessel. Prepare to die!"

"Oh, grow up!" Victoria retorted, and opened fire just in time to intercept their volley, which rocked her sideways. Fortunately, since the days when prescient science fiction had predicted ships of her sort, appropriate seat belts had been designed so she was only slightly stirred, not shaken loose from her command console.

But their next volley knocked out her auto controls, her life support systems, her computer, and the communications system. All she had was her viewport, her manual controls, and her wits. She was flying by the seat of her panties!

Fortunately, she also had her laser rockets and they could be fired by manual control.

She sent another volley right into their guts and, since she was a dead shot, with or without computer control, she watched with satisfaction as the ship exploded into many many . . .

Her satisfaction evaporated as a particularly large chunk came flying, despite the lack of atmosphere, toward her viewport, smashing into it.

The last thing she remembered was the jar of the impact, the hiss and sizzle of the control console as it tore apart in sparks, and the feeling of thousands of tiny pricks of fire burning through the cloth of her suit.

Then all she saw was stars and darkness as she descended down, down, ever downward.

To awaken, bruised, burned, in terrible pain, but still apparently intact, in drastically compressed darkness, lit only by the still flickering mini-fires of the *Rikki*'s electrical bits.

Fortunately, the impact of landing had jarred open the shuttle's hatch. Victoria wriggled toward it. Her leg hung at a peculiar angle and she couldn't feel her toes, but she scooted on the bottom of her shredded space suit across the rubble-strewn deck and out the hatch.

What a mess! The shuttle crash had produced a crater many feet deep, with sides so steep she could barely squirm between her vessel and the grave encompassing it.

The ground was also still very hot, though the outside of the shuttle, made of special heat-repelling space ship stuff, was still cool. Her leg was killing her. She ought to have splinted it, but long pieces of anything weren't part of space shuttle design. If only she could climb on top of her shuttle, she might be able to hoist her well-conditioned though still curvily feminine form out of the pit with her strong but shapely arms. She had aced Space Cadet basic training and worked out daily in the ship's gym.

Her leg hurt so badly that she nearly passed out from the effort. She planted her hands on the roof of the shuttle and pushed—and to her surprise boosted herself three feet above the shuttle before coming back down on its roof, rather lightly, and with ample time to protect her injured limb.

That was easy, she thought, and bounced again, with a slight change of direction that landed her beside the crater.

About that time, the press arrived.

That is, a press of robed, girded, masked, painted spear-carrying folk Victoria could only assume were indigenous Hotel Whiskonians arrived.

They didn't look quaint and charming. They looked—well, dangerous.

But of course, Victoria Fredericks. Space Cadet, laughed in the face of danger, or at least giggled nervously. "Hi," she said, twitching her fingers up and down in a little wave she hoped did not have a radically different meaning in their cultural milieu. "I guess you've come to welcome me as a conquering heroine, on account of I just saved your planet and all."

One of them nudged her with the shard of pointed crystal borne on the end of his spear and she yelped. "Please don't do that. My leg is broken, I think. I don't suppose you could call my ship, could you? My communications unit was destroyed in the crash when I was nearly killed defending *your* home world." She paused for a moment with significant glances into each set of masked or painted eyes she could make contact with. Her mother had taught her a thing or two about responsibility, not to mention guilt, a weapon that, like primitive magic, was very effective on those who believed in it. It probably wasn't fair to use psychological warfare on these simple people, but it was nicer than skewering them, as they seemed willing to do to her. She intensified her gaze, mentally projecting the words, "Naughty naughty. This is a nice way to treat a person who gets herself crashed to save you?"

Gradually, first spears and then eyes dropped groundward and toes began describing semicircles in the lush violet petals blanketing the ground.

Two or three of the Whiskonians edged toward the lip of the crater and, looking in, pointed and began speaking in gibberish. They consulted, jabbering among themselves in their simple native tongue. Then suddenly they surrounded her and two of them grabbed her leg. A bolt of agony shot through her and the last thing she thought as they attacked her leg was that if she lived through this, she could never wear her Glennsday panties again.

Sometime later she awakened, still suffering but not so acutely, to find herself floating along atop the shoulders of her erstwhile attackers, who were singing a charming native folk song of surprisingly complex melody and interlaced harmonies.

Overhead the orchid-hued fronds and leaves of the forest frothed above her, fanning her as the breeze passed through them. At eye level were trees with familiar looking leaves shaped like two tiny bat wings stuck together at the tops and fanning out on either side. Lovely little red berries festooned the trees giving them a cheery look.

And then suddenly they were passing beneath a stone archway, and the warriors, as she thought of them, were transferring her to other, gentler hands. She was deposited upon a table of some sort and carried deeper into the building. Her new bearers were not masked but veiled in violet that matched the ground cover she had seen near the crash site. They seemed to be both male and female and spoke in murmurs.

She was carried into a room containing many stone slabs, like altars, with other people on tables laying atop them, their bodies clothed in tattered and bloodied robes and draperies.

Some of the bodies lay very still.

Some were screaming.

And two of her attendants pulled out long, wicked-looking knives and plunged them toward her—space suit. From the corner of her eye she saw the splints and bandages, and realized that they were removing her clothing to examine her wounds.

Or were they?

As the equipment was being arranged, the nurses, as she now thought of them, pushed her back down onto the table and the doctor, as she now thought of *him*, began touching her inappropriately in the area more or less covered by her ruined Glennsday panties. "What's he doing?" she asked them but no one answered. "I'm sure Space Corps insurance will NOT cover this procedure, whatever it is!" she threatened, but to no avail. These were aliens, after all, despite their humanoid appearance and behavior.

The doctor looked up suddenly and jerked his thumb in the air and before Victoria could do so much as scream they held her aloft, high over their heads. At least they were good enough to support her injured leg as they did so but she could feel the physician's prying fingers lightly tickling her behind through the fabric and holes of her ruined undies. Then suddenly, he let forth a cry that sounded like "Tonda Roga!"

And the others all responded, "Tonda Roga? Tonda Roga!"

And all of them began genuflecting and moaning the same name at the top of their lungs.

"No, no," she said, pointing to herself as they lowered her gently to the table. "Victoria. Victoria Fredericks."

But they failed to heed her words, though they stopped genuflecting finally and bustled about with a gleeful energy that seemed misplaced in a hospital. They busily splintered her leg, gave her a soothing drink that eased the pain, and draped her in first a violet veil then in many other layers of rich apparel that she privately considered a little overdone.

"Thank you too much, I'm sure, but if you could just send up a smoke signal or something to hail my ship, that would be plenty of gratitude," she said modestly, adding, "I really have no need for all of these things. They'll catch on the equipment back at the ship."

But no one was paying any attention. The ones who weren't backing away from her slab, still genuflecting, had moved on to the next patients. Puzzled she watched while the medical staff first disrobed the patients and fingered and muttered over their underwear, which was at least as disreputable as hers had become. Only then did anybody treat anybody.

"Is this whole hospital staffed with perverts or what?" she asked, the pain making her impatient and not too prone to consider the reasonableness of what appeared to be local folkways. "My stars, the malpractice suits around here must be astronomical."

To her surprise, one of the masked figures, she thought it was the same one who had tickled her—fancy—while examining her undies, turned to her and said, "Not at all, Tonda Roga."

Victoria gasped. "You speak English!"

"Naturally. Oxford Space Academy actually."

"But—but—"

"You are surprised I speak your language? You see, the priestly class is the aristocracy on our world. Healing and prophecy go together—"

Victoria observed where his fingers were walking across the groin of his current patient, a groin clad in a tattered garment that resembled a pair of shorts. "But not exactly hand in hand?" she asked with a brave, knowing little smile.

"Please, none of your Earthling prudery, my dear. I am both Chief Physician and High Priest on my world. Allow me to introduce myself. My name is %∧&°°(+@#."

"That's a toughie," she said. "Okay, if I just call you Doc, or maybe Reverend?"

He regarded her girlish confusion with less dignity than he had previously displayed. "Of course, Tonda Roga. My name, being the highest on the planet, is naturally of the old tongue, virtually unpronounceable to all but the priesthood. In time, I hope you may even come to call me—but never mind." He readjusted his visage into a stern expression once more. "You are the Tonda Roga. You may be an off-worlder, but there is no need to look askance at the perfectly normal diagnostic function I am performing."

"What diagnostic function?" she asked, returning determinedly to the subject after being lost, for a time, contemplating the invitation in his eyes to call him—what? Sweetheart?

He returned her to reality. "Why, reading the holes in this patient's *unga rao roga* of course."

"Excuse me?"

"The sacred undergarments. Not so sacred as your own, of course, but nonetheless very holy indeed."

"You mean my undies aren't just full of holes, they're holy, too, here? I don't want to be ethnocentric or anything, doctor, but that sounds like something you'd hear at Callahan's Saloon."

"Not at all. On our world, we believe that the knowledge of character, the future, health, everything, can be read from the condition of that garment which covers the seat of passion, the outlets of the innermost being, the very foundation upon which one balances oneself throughout much of life."

"Is that so?" she asked petulantly, for she was very groggy from the pain medicine.

"It is. How else would we know you were the Tonda Roga?"

"That just shows you how silly it is. I'm not Tonda anybody. I'm Victoria Fredericks, Space Cadet, serial number 00111001."

"Not to us. To us you are the Tonda Roga, the chosen one. It's all right there on your knickers. You can read for yourself if you don't believe me."

"So what's this Tonda Roga chosen to do anyway?" she asked. She decided to pass on the knickers-reading part. She thought it was dumb and, besides, he had already done it and he was the expert, wasn't he?

"Save the world as we know it, of course."

"Well, you're safe there then, aren't you, since I already did that."

The eyes over the top of the mask—kind of cute eyes, really, she'd never seen that shade of reddish brown in an eye color before and it was a little like being looked at through infra red—seemed momentarily confused. "I beg your pardon."

"I said I'm way ahead of you. I saved your world

this morning, I guess it was, just before I came here. Didn't your warriors tell you? They found me at the crash site."

"They mentioned something about how you fell from the sky but—"

"I blew up the Hasslebad ship that was threatening your planet, only I got knocked dirtside by the debris."

"I had no idea."

"I told the warriors. They seemed to understand."

He shook his head. "They understand emotional messages. But of everyone on the planet, I'm the only one who understands your language, I'm afraid. That's why I hope I can explain to you the meaning of it all."

"What all?"

"What you must do to save us, beautiful one."

"I told you I—"

"Okay, save us again then. It is foretold that the Tonda Roga will come and we shall know her by her *unga rao roga* and she alone will possess the skill to brave the underworld and the dragons thereof and repair the World Wide Warning Web."

"Bet you can't say that fast," she said, giggling from the pain-soothing drink.

"There'll be a great feast tonight and we'll have a procession leading you to the entrance to the underworld."

"But I can't walk on this leg!"

"I thought a Space Cadet never says can't," he scolded, shaking a finger at her.

"How do you know what a Space Cadet does and doesn't do?"

"I attended the Academy as a student, before the web was broken. My family is wealthy and aristocratic and I am considered a very good catch—" he added with eyebrows raised to indicate he was waiting for a response from her that indicated she cared about such unprofessional things. To her surprise, portions of her that had recently been put on red alert by the reading of her *unga rao roga* indicated that she did indeed care. She hoped he wasn't really gross when he took his veil off. "But my mother insisted I get an education first. I came home just as the web was breaking."

"What is this web thing?" she asked, determinedly all business.

"It is the mandala grid that protects the planet from the attentions of those who would harm us, such as the Hasslebads. It conceals us in the invisible protection that kept us safe all through time."

"But now it doesn't?"

"Correct."

"Well, then, I don't want to sound critical, but if it's so important, and you're such a leader here, why didn't you fix it yourself?"

"Because only a Tonda Roga can do so." He replied, sounding mildly shocked.

He wasn't the only one, "A Tonda Roga?" she asked. "I thought it was *the* Tonda Roga and I, Victoria Fredericks, Space Cadet, am she. The one you've been waiting on."

"Sort of," he replied.

"Sort of what?" she demanded with some of the pique those of her hair color are known for.

"We couldn't wait *quite* that long, you see. Long enough for you to maybe show up some day, maybe not. So there've—er—been others."

"And they couldn't do it?"

"Evidently not," he said, shrugging.

She didn't like that shrug. "What do you mean by that? Don't you know?"

"Not exactly. They *never returned.*"

She took a deep breath. "Oh, it's one of those is it? A Class 3 situation." She remembered that from her manual as something very grave indeed, though she couldn't recall the exact text at the moment. No doubt because of the pain medication. "In that case,

I'll require a few things from my vessel. Can someone please take me back there now?"

"That won't be necessary," he said, and motioned for another attendant. They carried her between them to another large stone-clad hall, and she saw her ship sitting in the middle of it, very much the worse for wear.

She did hope her little bag was still untouched. She described it to the doctor and he said to one of the warriors, "The Tonda Roga requires her magic bag. Enter her steed and fetch it forth."

Trembling, the warrior did as he was told and after a few false tries, during which he emerged with the broken communicator, a spare space helmet, and a half dozen replicated bowls of jello, he brought her bag. She drew from it a carving knife and then said, "I need a branch from those trees with the funny leaves and the red berries."

"You mean the holly trees?" the doctor asked. "They're a mutation on the same tree you have on earth."

"We didn't have any trees around the space port," she said sadly.

"How deprived you were!" he said.

"Yes, but though we had no natural surroundings, we had the glory of Space Port in our very air and of course, we had love. My mom used to buy me the most beautiful underwear. You'd have loved it."

"Ah, yes," he said dreamily. "I feel quite sure of that."

The holly boughs were duly fetched and, using her Space Corps knife with the five thousand attachments, she cleverly fashioned a sturdy cane to help her walk into the danger she must face.

Then about three hundred scantily clad handmaidens paraded into the hall and carried her *and* her cane away on their shoulders. She was taken to a chamber where she was tenderly washed, oiled, buffed and polished, groomed and perfumed before being reclad in some rather beautiful lace and more gossamer soft veiling that flowed into a diaphanous garment revealing more than it concealed.

Dreamily, she fingered the material. "This is lovely. Where is it from"?" she asked, but the girls didn't speak English and her universal translator had been broken in the crash. Fortunately, despite the filmy nature of her outfit, it did have a handy pocket for her Space Corps knife.

She heard the drums just as the polish on her toe-nails dried. Pulsing, primal rhythms throbbed through the sultry night carrying the heady scent of nocturnal blossoms.

The maidens bore her from the hall out into a huge garden-courtyard ablaze with torches. The smoke from them wrapped everything in cinnamon-scented gauze, giving it an otherworldly feeling, which was not surprising, Victoria thought, considering she *was* on another world.

The night-blooming flowers were draped over everything, swags and garlands of them, all purest white, all smelling like a really exclusive perfume shop back on earth.

A double line of simple, quaint natives, all drumming, dancing and singing their charming indigenous songs, opened before the procession. At the end of the human corridor, flowers and fire arched dramatically over a solitary figure. Toward this man the maidens bore Victoria Fredericks, whose heart was not beating with danger, excitement and another, less familiar feeling, one she couldn't remember having in all the years since she had finally gotten to know all too well every single guy aboard her spacecraft.

Finally, the maidens set her down at the feet of the man. She languished there for a moment, staring up at him though the cinnamony smoke. He was the best looking thing she'd ever seen, and looked absolutely human, without funny nose wrinkles or strange ears or bald head or anything. Well, his hair *was* sort of a pale lavender, but that could have been the lighting and besides, it was one of her favorite colors.

He held out a strongly muscled arm to her. He wore only a loin cloth and a few posies around his neck and she could see that all of him was as strongly muscled as the arm. His voice was familiar, tender and warm as he said, "Come, my Tonda Roga. The time has come for you to save the world as we know it. By the way, you look stunning in your ceremonial robes."

"Thanks," she said, rising to her feet—or rather, her foot and cane, with the help of his strength. "It's not very practical but—"

"Tonda Rogas usually also wear eight-inch spiked sandals for running through the tunnels but in view of your injury, we relaxed the dress code," he told her.

"It's nice to be special," she smiled up at him, feeling woozy from the pain potion or the smoke, or maybe just the moons and stars, she didn't know. But she thought she would drown in his eyes.

"You are special. I have come to love you, titian-haired earth girl. I pray to our benign native gods that you do not perish on your mission of mercy."

"Me too," she murmured, her lips so close to his she could flick out her tongue and taste them.

"But now," he said, stepping aside so quickly she nearly fell over, "It is time for you to go. Farewell, my brave beauty!"

"Bye!" she said, and, taking the proffered torch, stepped through the arch and into a long long tunnel whose floor descended rapidly.

It also twisted and turned as it descended and branched off many times. Victoria had covered that eventuality in the Cadet Academy, however, and began unravelling the hem of the diaphanous garment so she could find her way back.

But though her training and her spirit were equal to any task, her body was not doing so hot. Her leg hurt and she stopped to rest just where the tunnel forked and twisted again. After a few minutes, when she'd caught her breath and the pain subsided to a slightly duller ache, she leaned forward, holding her torch in front of her, to peer into one of the passages. An orthodontist's nightmare of stalagmites and stalactites over- and underbit each other into an impassable mass through one passage.

She pulled the torch back and stuck it into the other branch of the tunnel. She could see nothing so she scooted forward on her bottom and thrust the torch around the corner.

The torch guttered and flared, guttered and flared, and in its fitful light, she could see nothing but grayness. She inched forward a bit more and stretched her hand forward to balance herself. She touched something hard and brittle and looked down. It was a bone! A bone sheathed in white diaphanous material. Like what she was wearing. Oh dear. Next to it was a grinning skull.

She looked away, up into the light of the smoking torch, and made out other bones poking through the grayness. She got only a glimpse, but it looked to her as if the gray matter was composed of zillions of fine threads. Then a portion of the thread extruded and gobbled her torch.

For just a moment before the light went out, she saw through the grayness, far back beyond it to what seemed to be long sinuous moving shapes that seemed to be waving at her. And still shapes that looked like pairs of wings, trapped in the incredibly tangled web. And of course, more slender young girlish bones.

Then with a singeing smell and a slurping sound,

her torch was extinguished and she was alone in the darkness.

She backed away, trying to rise to her good leg, but as she rose, something slithered forward, touching her bare toe, and sucked at the tip of her cane. Holding onto the cave wall, she backed further away and ever further.

What was she doing? A Space Cadet never retreats!

Pulling forth her Space Corps knife, she cut through the slithery material and severed a sample. It did not seem to be alive actually, but lay still in her hand, soft and fine as Asian silk.

"Aha!" she said pluckily to herself, an idea dawning as she recognized certain pieces of this situation as a monstrous blowup of something she was already intimately familiar with.

For though the web threads weren't silk as she knew it, they were certainly some sort of silky fiber. And though the previous Tonda Rogas had been engulfed by it, Victoria in her more sophisticated wisdom doubted that it was a hostile life form. After all, the people of this planet believed there was a web down here and the stuff she held in her hands was what webs were made of.

It seemed to her that what was necessary was a little ingenuity and good old fashioned Space corps knowhow. And, of course, the right tools.

When the next surge of gray stuff popped out at her she slipped to the side and shook her finger at it before hobbling into the adjoining cave. Groping with her slender fingers, she found the tip of a stalagmite. With the sawzall blade of her knife, she cut off the tip. Then she cut about a half inch below the first cut, and lifted off a fairly regular disc-shaped piece of stone. Using the laser-punchall beam, she bored a hole in the center to slip her cane through. It was a perfect fit, of course, and stopped a few inches from the bottom.

There was also a small flashlight beam on her knife and with this, she saw that beyond the shallow shelter of the stalagmite cave, the gray matter had gotten really pushy and extruded several more feet into the main tunnel. Instantly, the sensitive Cadet realized why. When she had seen the "dragons" they had seen her and were wiggling in anticipation of her saving them! Poor things! That was what had happened before and they'd ended up killing the very Tonda Rogas who had come to help them. but of course, those had just been simple village girls, not Academy trained and space-seasoned Corps Cadets!

She reached out and grabbed a handful of the gray web and gave it a saucy twist around her cane just above the rock whorl. Then, when it was secure, she dropped it and began spinning.

The gray matter spun and spun and every time her makeshift spindle was full, she cut off the thread and attached another hunk to spin more. Soon she had cleared a large enough path for herself to escape, retreating back the way she had come.

The party was still going on and seemed to be a wake in her honor.

Indignation overcame her as she saw the natives dancing and wailing over her supposed fate instead of showing some initiative.

Standing in the archway she cried, "Hear the Tonda Roga! I have returned and I have divined the nature of your problem!"

The crowd, as one person, albeit not a very brave one, shrank back and looked at her as if she was a ghost, which, considering the ensemble they'd given her to wear, she no doubt appeared to be.

The doctor, however, looked toward her with his mouth agape and his tear-reddened eyes filled with wonder and hope. "But—but how?" he asked.

She shrugged and tossed her flaming locks, her green eyes flashing. "I'm a professional. Those other girls simply shouldn't have tried being a Tonda Roga on their own. You sent me to be a human sacrifice, didn't you?"

"No, I swear. It is simply written that the Tonda Roga will be a woman and ye shall know her by the holes in her *unga rao roga*, just as I told you. I personally couldn't be more delighted to see you. But—"

"No, I have not yet saved your planet from destruction from within. No one person can do that, however valiant. It will take all of you to do that. This party is traditional too, isn't it?"

"It is written that we shall watch for the Tonda Roga for five days and five nights after she enters the underworld."

"Good. Now I know why you were all called here. I want everyone to go into the woods and start collecting branches and rocks."

"But whatever for?"

"We have a yarn to spin," she told him in her perky, mischievous way, deliberately being mysterious. "I'll reveal all in my own time." She gave him a wink. He blushed.

It took plenty of hard work, encouragement and grit but she had the problem completely under control two weeks later when a landing party from her ship appeared in the courtyard.

"You're out of uniform, Cadet Fredericks," Captain Flash Morgan said with a low appreciative whistle.

"Like it?" she asked, twirling to show off the slight tulip skirt of her slithery saffron silk slip, which she had just been modelling for the doctor.

"Very much, but what's going on here?" he asked, taking in the long line of people stretching from the cave, through the courtyard and out the doors of the hospital into the woods, where spindles, looms, tatting shuttles, crochet hooks and dyepots were busy transforming the gray fibers into colorful, slinky material and strips of lace.

"Just saving the planet, sir," she said with a snappy salute. "As ordered."

"Isn't she wonderful?" the doctor asked from a kneeling position. He had been about to kiss the hem of her garment when the crew showed up. Darn it, Victoria thought mutinously, if momentarily.

"And can you tell me, Cadet Fredericks, just how you're doing that?"

"Because she's the Tonda Roga," the doctor said.

"I asked her," Captain Morgan told him.

"No need to be rude, sir," Victoria reminded her superior officer of his diplomatic obligations. "The doctor, I'll have you know, is the high priest of this planet and by doing a—er—reading, he discovered I was supposed to save it. Of course, I'd already saved it from the Hasslebads but the reason it *needed* saving was because the internal net, this sort of organic technical thingy inside the planet, had broken down. Only a Tonda Roga could fix it, but since it was sacred here, none of the other girls had a clue what to do and ended up getting enveloped."

"So you slew the monster with your laser gun?"

"No, sir. My laser gun was broken, sir. In the crash when I was injured destroying the Hasslebad ship, sir. But I didn't need a laser gun. See, nothing malevolent was at work, actually."

"It wasn't? But it enveloped all those girls?"

"An avalanche isn't malevolent, sir, but it still kills people. This was more like a flood—of all these little silky things, wiggling out and tickling me all over. I had a torch with me and before my torch went out I saw that there were these long wormlike creatures way back in the tunnel. When I felt the gray stuff trying to roll over me, I realized it was similar to silk. It's the stuff the web is made of and the wormthings—"

"The dragons," the doctor corrected.

"The dragons, are like giant silk worms. Only problem is, over the years, being sacred and all, they've multiplied too often and have spun so much silk that they can't escape to become giant moths. The silk was blocking all the tunnels and exits and there was so much of it there was no longer any room for anything else except for the worms, who pushed it out into the tunnels a little farther with every movement. That's how come it enveloped the other Tonda Rogas."

"She diagnosed our planet's ailment. Its arteries were clogged," the doctor told Captain Morgan. "The gods told her that we must accept the bounty not needed for the web and make of it useful items. Always before cloth woven from the web was sacred— it is from it that our *unga rao roga* come, and our other ceremonial garments. But it was very scarce, emerging from the ground only at certain holy places. Now, however, all are to wear sacred garments both inner and outer, giving the dragons space to weave, room to grow and time to fly."

"The giant moths are the early warning system," Victoria said. "They sense spacecraft within a certain distance and communicate this to their children, the dragons, who cause the web to send off certain biochemical signals that make the planet sort of er— disappear. Kind of like a chameleon."

"Good work, Fredericks," Captain Morgan said. "But what I don't get is how you figured all this out."

"Well, sir, fine fabric has always held a certain— fascination for my family. And I knew all about cloth from an early age. My mother was extremely particular about the condition of my—er—*unga rao roga* and didn't want me ever to go out with holes in my underwear. Naturally when the spinning, weaving, and dyeing portions of primitive culture survival came up in Space Cadet Academy Survival Skills 101, I paid close attention to these portions as vital to good grooming and wardrobe maintenance. It came in handy, as did my Space Corps knife. I owe my training and equipment—and my mother—my life."

"And we owe the lives of our people and that of our planet to this lovely young lady, our Tonda Roga . . ." the doctor said, taking her hand with a sigh.

"Well, sir," Captain Morgan said, checking his chronometer. "It's always a pleasure for the Corps to be of service. We're glad to have had one of our people instrumental in saving you folks here on Hotel Whiskey. But now Cadet Fredericks must return to the ship and receive her commission as Ensign Fredericks of the Space Corps.

The doctor and High Priest snapped his fingers and the three hundred handmaidens sprang forth, each bearing a full set of lingerie made to Victoria's measurements and in every color of the rainbow. They piled the garments around Victoria's feet while she squealed with glee at each new arrangement of lace, each naughty or nice detail, each glowing color.

Then, taking Victoria's hands in his, the doctor looked deeply into her eyes and said, his voice trembling with suppressed passion, "My sweet titian-haired earthling Tonda Roga, you must take these *unga rao roga* back with you as a token of our thanks and esteem. In place of your holey undergarments, we give you holy undergarments to wear and remember our reverence for your beauty and bravery. It will warm my—uh—heart, to imagine part of us so close to certain parts of you." Then he turned so that he stood beside her, facing her superior officer and now his voice with its quaint charming accent was full of primitive dignity and nobility, "As for you, sir, were you sleeping at the Academy when they taught that diplomacy requires you to learn the name of a world as it is called by its own inhabitants? Our world is not called Hotel Whiskey, but is named for the lovely trees that grace its surface and provided the wood for the first sacred spindle. As for this gorgeous and valiant creature, she may be to you Cadet Fredericks or even Ensign Fredericks, but to us she will always be our own Tonda roga, Fredericks of Holly Wood."

And with that, Victoria and her precious new undies returned to the ship. She wore the tatted lace bra and panties in Space Corps dress blue for her commissioning and as her new rank was pinned upon her secretly laced-encased chest, her heart swelled with pride and tears came to her eyes recalling how much she owed to her dear mother's advice, and how surprised mom would be if only she knew the impact her words had had upon her daughter's adventures.

Would You?

William R. Forstchen

The shaman gazed at the circle of enrapt listeners, their eyes shining brightly in the moonlight. She leaned back and looked heavenward at the stars shining overhead.

There is our destiny, she sighed to herself—the destiny denied us.

The heavens tormented her; she wanted to reach up, to soar from the confines of this world, to cut the bonds of earth, and reach across the midnight sky to all that was lost forever. So was the dream passed to her by her mother, and from her, back into the mist-shrouded past, from the ancestors who carried the dream all the way back to The Fall.

She gazed across the meadow, shimmering silver blue by the starlight of the midsummer night. Fireflies danced like a million golden stars, bobbing and weaving over the marshes and she drank in the sight of it all. The air was heavy with the scent of the sea, the westerly breeze carrying the distant echoing of foam-capped waves crashing against the rockbound coast. It was so achingly beautiful and she sensed that this would indeed be the final summer she would ever behold such beauties, such wonders. The meadow echoed with a low murmuring, a melancholy calling that was tinged with a joyful anticipation, for it was the beginning of the Season of Longing, and she felt it tug upon her heart.

She could sense them drifting past her into the shadows, her people moving westward, down to the sea for the yearly ritual, to gaze up at the heavens

111

and to watch the setting of the sun, dreaming of distant shores that were lost now but to memory as ancient as the stars overhead.

She heard a muffled cough, and her gaze lowered to the circle of listeners who had paused in the ritual, harkening to her call . . . and she began, her voice low, carrying the singsong chant of the dream of paradise.

"All of you listen and I will tell you of the fall of the House Gnimmel. For *once we walked like gods across the universe,* before The Fall, before our exile to this world of sin and madness."

The shaman paused, scanning the intent faces of the young gathered about her. A distant hooting of an owl echoed across the clearing and she turned, nervously scanning the horizon. Expectantly she waited for the soft flutter of wings—nothing, no omen of doom there tonight.

"*Once we walked like gods across the universe.* So it was told me by my mother, and by her mother before. And long ago, so long ago it is beyond our imaginings we sailed upon the seas and we came unto this world."

She fell silent again, her heart filled with an infinite weariness.

"Lost we were. For the Great War with the Vangre, fought in the light of ten thousand suns, across ten thousand years of time, was finished, and the evil ones had vanquished us. So in that last ship we fled, seeking a refuge *beyond refuge,* a place of hiding, a place of peace where we could increase our numbers, our strength. And then when ages had passed and the Vangre thought us to be dead, we would build again the great ships and return. For our passage had taken us to lands undreamed, and so great were our numbers that the very earth sank beneath our feet and so the Great Sea sundered us from what was ours."

Tears filled her eyes, tears of a longing *beyond longing,* a stirring deep within her aged bones, a call to destiny unfulfilled, and the longing struck her with fear.

She could hear the singing of others now, drifting past and around her. The young ones who had gathered about her—many of them of her own flesh and blood—looked away, watching the passage, and she could sense their eagerness to join in the madness.

She walked about the circle, moving slowly, her aging joints creaking.

"Our destiny," she whispered. "Our destiny and our doom was to be exiled to this world and then seized by this madness of The Longing."

"The Vangre, do they even exist now, Reverend Mother?"

The shaman paused and looked into the eyes of the one who spoke.

"They are out there, Barth ne Barth. And I tell you that they are coming, even now! My grandmother," and she paused to make the sign of blessing, "revered be her memory and may she sleep in warmth beneath the waves, my grandmother first sensed their drawing closer. My mother, blessed as well be her, she sensed it even more—and I tell you they are coming!"

The shaman pointed back to the heavens.

"And I warn you now, it is still not too late to prepare. To relearn all that has been lost, to build again the weapons that are needed to fill these hands!"

She held her arms up, her empty naked hands curled up like two claws.

Barth shook his head and snorted with disdain.

"Reverend Mother, the great ones, the giants of this land will never permit such a thing."

"To hell with the giants!" the shaman roared, her voice echoing across the open meadow.

The circle of listeners looked about fearfully for to shout at night was the breaking of taboo and they waited expectantly, for winged death to sweep down, or a stalker to come out of the woods and leap upon them, or at worst for a giant to come and trample them. But there was nothing, only silence.

The shaman looked around disdainfully.

"Listen to me now for there is still time. We can still take back our destiny. We can prepare, to make all that is needed to be made. And perhaps, yes, even perhaps bring the giants to our side and together defend this world from what is to come."

The young listeners stirred, a round of chuckles and disdainful snickers greeting her words.

"The giants?" Barth replied. "They are mindless fools who crush us underfoot with their machines. They would never heed us."

"They would if we resisted The Longing of Home," the shaman whispered.

"Madness!" Barth laughed. "Resist The Longing? Good heavens, old one, that is what living is for." And his words were greeted with a chorus of laughing agreement.

"Don't pay heed to the false threat of the giants; the real threat is yet to come!"

"The Longing is all that life can give!" another of the young ones chimed in. "Why it is even better than . . . better than . . ."

"Sex!" yet another shouted and the group chortled with laughter.

The shaman wanted to turn and beat the ignorance out of the young ones. Yet as she turned and gazed at them she knew that to do so would lose them all and she fought down the urge to act as most adults would and thereby hoped against hope to still win them over.

"Better than sex, you say?" and again there was the chorus of barely suppressed laughter.

"And you suppose I am now too old to know of such things?"

An uncomfortable shifting of feet greeted her question.

"But you certainly haven't tried The Longing," Barth announced.

She was tempted to give the age-old response her mother, and her mother's mother gave, but fought against it.

"No," she finally whispered, "no, I haven't," and she could sense a disappointment at not speaking the famous line. But did they know? How could they, for this was the first season of their lifetimes when The Longing had come. How could they know of the struggle within to resist such things, to persevere year after year, speaking the warning and to not give oneself over to the ultimate joy, the ecstasy, some said; and to run wildly with the others and thus neglect what had to be done.

"Do you even understand what The Longing is?"

'The Longing is the laying," Barth retorted. "It feels good and we did it."

The shaman yet again fought down the urge.

"I will tell you what The Longing is. Some say it is nothing more than ancient instinct, drawing us back to the land of our ancient ancestors across the heavens. But if you give yourself over to it, it is madness, a folly, a running amok like a beast of the field and all else is forgotten. It is not our joy. It is our curse."

"Our curse?" Barth laughed. "Why, my father told me it's the best thing in the world."

"And where is your father now?" the shaman replied heatedly.

"With all the others," Barth snapped angrily. "Where else would he be? When you go with The Longing, the Vangre become meaningless. And besides, they'll never come, that's nothing but an old wives' tale, meant to scare children into behaving."

The others around the circle of listeners gasped at the insult.

The shaman fixed Barth with an icy gaze.

"They will come. Maybe the giants can stop them, but I doubt that. Only we know of them, for we once fought them long ago and then fled to this place. But our ancestors were foolish, for no sooner were they here, than they gave themselves over to this strange mysticism, this foolish cult of Longing. Thus were the old wonders forgotten: the making of weapons; of machines; of things called books, and writing; and even of planting and harvests. Even the giants can now do such things, and they are but children compared to our most ancient of races."

"Who needs such things?" Barth angrily replied. "There is food enough for all, shelter to be found in the woods and beneath the earth. Let the giants labor like idiots. And as for the Vangre, to hell with them, even if they do exist."

The shaman wearily shook her head.

"You don't understand," Barth continued, pressing home his attack. "You are old, dried up, and wish to deny us our fun."

Barth pointed across the meadow which was bathed now with the diffused and golden light of early dawn. The land seemed to be moving, for the great clan was again harkening to the siren song, the calling, and nearly all were now responding and turning westward, laughing, running, singing and disappearing into the mist.

The shaman looked to where he was pointing and shook her head. Here and there across the meadow were other shamans, Reverend Mothers, cajoling, pleading, or, like her, attempting to use reason to turn their young ones away from the bacchanalian orgy of delight, where all higher reason was lost and in the losing any hope of ever preparing for the return.

She looked up at the heavens, the darkness retreating eastward . . . and at that moment a brilliant light slashed across the sky and she felt her heart freeze.

Was it them? Had the Vangre at last found them, lost in their follies, and come at last to destroy this world and kill them all? And in her darkest thoughts she prayed that it was so, for perhaps only then would the *legends become real,* and the yearly dreamlike ritual of folly forgotten at last so that they could finally return to their destiny.

At the very least it would give her young charges a damn good scare and a return to their senses. She knew they had seen, as well, the light cross the sky. There was a frozen moment and then Barth broke the tension at last with a scornful laugh.

"Just another star falling, old one, and not your hoped-for bogey men. I've listened long enough," he cried, stepping into the circle to face his friends. "Come on! Don't you feel it down in your bones? It's festival time; our entire life ahead, a festival! Let's go!"

Barth took the hand of a young and shapely girl by his side and started to pull her away. She looked back at the shaman, gave an apologetic shrug, and then bounded off, the others racing to join them.

The shaman struggled, for in her bones was the feeling as well, as strong as ever. She looked over at the other Reverend Mothers and saw that most of them had lost their arguments as well, the young ones scampering away to the west, laughing and singing, the instinct taking hold, and like them she finally raised her head up and gave the ritual cry that mothers of her race had given since the beginning of their time upon this world.

"Will you look at that!"

Slamming the door of his car Eric stepped up to the edge of the cliff to observe the spectacle. Chuckling he watched the surge of little animals swarming, scurrying, darting around their feet until the girl finally got out of the car to join him.

"It's pitiful," she whispered, and being interested in showing how sensitive he was, he let a quick look of sadness cloud his features and nodded.

"Why are they doing it?"

"Who knows? Instinct. I heard somebody on television say it was because they lived on Atlantis or some such place and every summer they try and migrate back to it."

She stood silent for several minutes.

"I'm scared," she whispered.

"What? You mean because of them?" and he nodded towards the bizarre frenzy of self-destruction that was now swarming up to the cliffs that dropped away from the side of the road into the sea.

"No, stupid. Those reports from the lab."

Eric smiled reassuringly.

"Just an anomaly. Must be a glitch in the tracking software. No object can be coming straight at us at point eight light speed. And even if it was, it's still fifty years away. There'll be plenty of time to worry about it later even if it is real, which I'm telling you, it's not."

He let his hand slip down from her waist to her backside. "Come on, nothing to worry about, and besides," he gave her a playful squeeze, "there are better things to think about."

She laughed softly with anticipation.

"But after that, the beach, like you promised."

"Sure, anything, but promise to stop worrying. I'm telling you, I talked with Johnsson, the head of the project, last night. He said we'd look like fools if we said anything about this, and besides, we'll lose our grant if we come up with some dumb-ass UFO stories. So let's just drop it, keep the funding and enjoy our late night sessions in the lab . . . alone."

She sighed and murmured something he wasn't quite sure of, but the intent was clear.

He turned her away from the unpleasant sight along the cliff and what was now happening below, along the water's edge. She suddenly let out a shriek of fear as one of the little creatures racing across the road banged into her leg, paused for a second and looked straight up at her and squeaked.

Eric laughed and kicked the creature aside.

"Listen to it howl," he said as he walked her back to the car and then looked over his shoulder as the creature ran along the edge of the cliff.

"What'd you think it's saying?," the girl asked, trying not to show just how much it had frightened her.

Eric paused for a second, and then a grin lit his features.

"Just because Jimmy Jones jumps off a cliff doesn't mean you have to!" Eric said with a laugh, "what the hell else would a lemming mother say?"

The girl laughed with him as the two climbed into their car and drove off, leaving the shaman standing by the side of the road, as the cliffs, the ocean below, and the world around them writhed in folly.

Just Wait 'til You Have Children of Your Own!

Esther M. Friesner

Eunike descended from her chariot, slipped a feed-bag over the dragon's nose, and took a long look at the little cottage before her. To the untrained and unassuming eye it looked like a thousand other hovels where an Attic peasant, his wife, and their brood of snot-nosed brats lived out their days in drudgery, toil, and misery. But this one was different. Eunike knew it. Knowing things was Eunike's business. It was very poor (or very quickly unemployed) Pythia who didn't know things.

"At last I've found you, my sister," she said grimly, gray eyes narrowing. "At last you shall be brought to justice, the smear on our family erased, and maybe—just maybe, I'll be able to conjure up some decent visions for a change!"

She reached into the traveler's pouch at her side and brought forth a dagger. It was not a very fancy dagger or even a very long one, but like Eunike, its plainness and practicality got the job done more often than flashier blades.

"She'll have wards up," Eunike muttered to herself, taking the measure of the cottage with a crack strategist's eye. Chickens clucked and scratched in front of the door, which was both wooden and shut. A grapevine had decided that it would be rather nice if it climbed up the jamb and spread its leaves over the entryway, bathing it in shade from the broiling sun. There were no windows—not on this side of the building, at least. The roof was straw and would burn if you yelled the word "Fire!" at it loudly enough. It all looked so innocent!

Eunike reminded herself that there was nothing innocent about a killer, most especially not *this* killer. She began to chant the Song of Shielding which she and her wayward sister had learned together back in Colchis, at the knee of the Priest of the Fleece. The song was supposed to be a spell to keep the singer thereof safe from all otherworldly assaults, through the Fleece's own arcane powers. It told of how the dowdy old dragon who guarded the Fleece was in reality the terrible Lernian Hydra. It warned any man fool enough to challenge and slay the poor arthritic beast that skeleton warriors would spring up from the dragon's teeth, fully armed, and cut the blasphemer to ribbons, or pitch him off a cliff. It was a long song, it had been a pain to commit to memory, and it was all just a pack of whopping great lies. Everyone in Colchis knew it.

When Medea challenged the Priest of the Fleece on this point, the man had only smiled and said, "Yes but it is not the Colchians whom we are trying to frighten off. Sometimes, little princess, a good lie can save you an awful lot of trouble with foreigners." Then again he was a foreigner himself: an Egyptian, a refugee, and a eunuch, each of these reason enough for him to have mastered the art of deception years ago.

Even knowing that the Song of Shielding was a crock, Eunike rattled through it. The Priest of the Fleece had been one those master liars whose most egregious falsehoods still managed to leave the hearer haunted by the thought, *But what if he's right?* Better safe than sorry.

Eunike wasn't going to be sorry. Not today. Today was Medea's turn. The Pythia finished her shielding chant, tested the dagger's edge with her thumb, and strode towards the cottage.

Almost at once, the first of Medea's carefully laid traps sprang. A huge black beast, hairy and smelly as Father's armpit, came bouncing out of nowhere, uttering wild howls. Eunike tried to defend herself with the dagger, but she was carrying it in the Safety First grip rather than the Battle Ready, and the monster's assault did not give her time to reverse it. As the full weight of the beast drove into her chest, bowling her over in the dirt, she had the dubious satisfaction of observing that the Priest's so-called Song of Shielding didn't work worth fava beans.

"Down, Ione! Bad girl! Bad, I say! Down! Down this instant! I told you to— Ohhhhhh, you don't listen to me any better than those—" Strong hands, sun-browned and work-roughened, dug themselves into the ruff of fur on the monster's neck and hauled the creature off Eunike, but not before it managed to cover the Pythia's face with a generous coating of hot, stinking slime.

As Eunike was wiping the drool from her eyes with one corner of her now-disheveled mantle, she managed to catch a glimpse of her rescuer.

"Shit," she remarked. It was Medea, her sister and her quarry. This was going to complicate things.

As for Medea, the former princess was still locked in combat with the black beast, yanking it back two paces only to have it trot forward five with almost no effort. The unnatural fiend looked like it was laughing. Finally, Medea had enough. She let go of the monster, brushed farmyard dust from her clothes, and bellowed a string of words in an alien tongue. Almost as soon as the last syllable had left her lips, the air before the beast's face darkened, thickened, and formed itself into a creature that was the twin of the first abomination, except this one was most obviously, inarguably, and generously male. The apparition uttered a short, sharp bark and dashed away. The true beast

responded with a happy yelp and took off after him,
plumy tail wagging.

Medea watched them go and sighed. "And they
told me bitches were easier to train. Ha! What a slut.
Still, I can't really argue with sex. If it works to make
her mind me, I'll use it. Or so I will until Alkander
finishes making that leash for her sometime *this* century, ha ha, don't make me laugh." Having gotten all
this off her chest, she turned her attention to the
beast's victim, still sprawled on the ground. A wide
smile illuminated Medea's face. "Eunike!" she cried.
"What a nice surprise!"

The Pythia never had a chance. Before she knew
what was happening, she was seized in the same
strong grip that had pulled the monster off her. A
grunt and a tug and Eunike was on her feet once
more.

The dagger, however, was still on the ground.

Medea's eyes went from her sister's face to the
blade. She bit her lower lip and tapped her fingers
against one cheek in the same gesture of consterna-
tion that the princesses' old wetnurse had used so
often back home. "Oh dear," she said quietly. "Oh
my. I knew it would come to this, but I never thought
it would be you who—" She clucked her tongue and
shrugged. "Well, I'll tell you what, darling: You pick
that up and come into the house with me. I'll promise
not to put poison in your wine if you'll promise not
to eat any bread or salt. If we can't work this little
family problem through, I might have to kill you—
fairly, mind!—and I'm not about to have the sacred
laws of hospitality cramping my style." With that, she
headed for the cottage.

Stunned, Eunike could only stand staring at her
sister's retreating back. But once Medea's hand was
on the doorlatch, the Pythia recovered herself,
snatched up the dagger, and scampered after her.

The inside of the cottage was dark and homely, the

furniture sparse, the smell of old stew overwhelming. In vain Eunike cast about for some hint of enchantment or glamour, one glimpse of the golden spoils of King Aegeus' court at Athens or treasure taken from Jason's home in the moments before Medea mounted the dragon chariot, the bodies of her slaughtered children at her feet, and fled Thebes forever. In vain, yes. There was no magic here, unless one counted the fact that everything about the little cottage's interior was neat, clean, and beautifully organized.

Medea was already seated on one of three rough wooden stools by the table. She beckoned for Eunike to take her place on a second. The Pythia did so, still edgy, still bewildered. She shifted the dagger from right hand to left, left to right, and wondered whether to lay it on the table or keep it in her lap.

"Don't fidget!" Medea snapped. "And don't use fleas as an excuse; you know I won't tolerate them in my home! And sit up straight! Do you want to grow up hunchbacked?"

"*What?*" Eunike gasped. But she dropped the dagger on the tabletop, sat up straight as a spear, and folded her hands in her lap.

Medea's hands flew to her mouth. "Oh no, did I say that?" She gave a little girlish giggle. "I'm sorry; force of habit." She poured some wine from a clay bottle into a pair of carved olivewood cups and passed one to Eunike. "Here you go. Drink up. There's water in the other jug; I don't know how strong you like your wine, so fix it to your taste. You must be dying of thirst after your trip. How did you come? Dragon chariot? I know I'm always parched after a long flight. I think the air at those altitudes dries you out faster." She added a generous measure of water to her own cup, took a lady–like sip, and added, "It's so good to see one of the family!"

Eunike had not reigned as the chosen seeress of Apollo for these twenty years without being able to recognize the perfect conversational opening. She rose to her feet, struck a pose last used to bring one of the Spartan kings to his knees with grief and remorse, and thundered, "If you're so fond of your family, *why did you slay them*?"

"Oh drat," said Medea, running her fingers along the edge of the table. "Splinters. We're going to have to fix—I'm sorry, Eunike dear, were you saying something?"

"The Furies clamor for the blood of the wicked! Your guilt hangs from your body like a winding sheet of all-devouring fire, and the abyss of Erebus awaits your soul!" Eunike thrust her hands high, fingers splayed. It was a grand gesture she had stolen from an Athenian actor, and it worked like a charm for putting the fear of gods into her clients at the shrine. Everyone was guilty of *something*. You didn't have to say what; they'd take care of filling in the blanks for you. One good dose of the Furies/fiery winding sheet/ Erebus/yatta-yatta-yatta and the tears and confessions would always flow as liberally as the donations.

Always being a relative term, of course. That is to say, not applicable to Eunike's relative. Medea heard out the Pythia's rant, then calmly said, "Mmmm. Isn't that interesting," and left her stool to poke about in the little black cauldron simmering over the cookfire. Eunike was left to recover from her dramatic speech as best she might. She did this by drinking up everything in her wine cup without bothering to water it down.

Medea returned to her place at the table, smiling. "That lamb stew's coming along beautifully. You must stay to dinner, Eunike. I've made *dolmades* and I think we're going to have baklava too. That is, we will if Alkander remembers to bring me the honey from town. He'd forget his head if it weren't screwed on."

"Alkander ..." Eunike spoke the name bitterly. "No doubt he is your latest in a string of young, passionate, iron-thewed lovers, with the stamina of oxen and a bull's—"

The last word was slapped from her lips before it had the chance to live.

"You wash your mouth out right this instant!" Medea was on her feet, livid. "Maybe that kind of language is all right for your bummy friends down at the *taverna*, but I will not tolerate—" She stopped short. She blinked. She looked for all the world like someone waking from a dream. "Oh dear. I'm doing it again, aren't I? It's a reflex. I'm so sorry, Eunike. You were telling me that I've killed the family and I'm sleeping with a succession of young studs and— Was that all?"

"Uh . . . I think so." Eunike began to tick off fatalities on her fingers. "First there was our brother. You killed him and cut him into pieces and tossed them off the back of the *Argo* so Daddy would have to stop and pick them up and you and Jason could get away."

"How is Daddy these days?" Medea asked, her eyes bright. "I'll bet he's soooo lonely, rattling around that huge palace without the comforting sound of little feet pattering here and there. He always was fond of children. I was just thinking that—"

"After you ran off and I got tapped as the new Pythia, he took a slew of fresh wives and sired about twelve of the little two-legged lizards," Eunike informed her. "He's got kids out the *kantharos*."

"Oh." For the first time since Eunike's arrival, Medea sounded subdued. "Well, if you want to keep an honest tally of my family crimes, scratch our brother. He was begotten on one of Daddy's concubines."

"Half-brothers count," Eunike maintained with a sniff of superiority.

"Then he doesn't count at all. What Daddy never knew won't hurt him."

"You don't mean—?" Eunike grabbed her sister's

hands. For a moment it was like old times, the two Colchian princesses sitting up late nights, trading delicious scraps of palace gossip.

Medea nodded. "The Priest of the Fleece."

"Nooooo! But he was a *eunuch*!"

"He *told* everyone he was a eunuch. There's a big difference." Medea snickered. "Daddy's concubines found out *how* big." She shrugged. "It wasn't hard for him to conceal the truth, even if someone had insisted on a physical examination. You and I both took our first lessons in the conjuring of illusions from him."

"Mmmmm." Eunike was noncommittal. She'd used the illusion spells more than she cared to confess, mostly to trick those members of the Interview Committee who insisted that Apollo's chosen Pythia be beautiful. "All right, we'll take him off the list. But there's still King Peleas."

"I never touched him. I only tricked his daughters into chopping him up and tossing him into the cauldron. They thought it would make him young again, because I'd just shown them how it worked on this old ram. I cut him to pieces myself, put them in the cauldron, and out jumped a lamb! But when Peleas' daughters hacked him apart, I did that cute little *Oopsie!* thing I do and dropped the packet of nine different secret herbs and spices into the fire. The rejuvenation spell won't work at all without the right seasoning." She laughed out loud. "Oh, Eunike, I only wish you'd been there to see the look on their faces!"

Eunike enjoyed a good practical joke as much as the next Colchian, but she was a woman of duty first and foremost. There would be time for levity after she cut her sister's throat. "I suppose you're right there too. Which also takes Theseus off the list. You wanted him dead but your plans fell through."

"I came close, though." Medea's face, still lovely

despite wrinkles and the hardening effects of sun and wind, lit up with the old mischief and pride.

"Close doesn't count," Eunike informed her primly. "Now that I think of it, the reports said that you were trying for a repeat of the Peleas project, except this time duping the parent into killing the child."

"I came *very* close," Medea insisted. She didn't like to be reminded of her failures.

Eunike, on the other hand, enjoyed nothing better than prodding her sister's memory when it came to incidents that left the prettier of the princesses with a big dollop of egg on her face. "If I wanted an *excuse* to kill you, I could come up with a better one than a near miss, and a pathetic one at that. I'm only concerned with facts. You didn't kill him and you didn't trick his father into doing it for you either. So there."

Medea sighed and had some more wine, her eyes assuming that dreamy expression common to women recalling their stupider lovers. "Dear Aegeus! He was so eager to please me. It didn't even matter to him that I had—" She broke off her reverie sharply and gave her sister a long, hard look. "Eunike, who am I fooling?"

"*Whom*," said Eunike, who was that kind of person.

"We both know why you're here. Well, to be perfectly frank, I don't know *exactly* what's brought you here. I mean, all of my little whoopsies are ancient history. It's been simply *years* since I left Colchis. Why did you wait until now to come after me?"

Eunike hemmed and hawed, then had more wine to help her over the rough spots. "You see, dear, it's like this: What you've just told me about how you're not really guilty of kin-death as far as our brother and Peleas and Theseus and what's-her-name-Kreon's daughter—you know, the one you sent the fiery wedding gown to and it burnt her and her father to ashes?"

"Mmmm." Medea bit her thumb in thought.

"Goodness, I can't recall her name either! Silly little bitch, she was just what Jason *did* deserve. But you know what? I didn't do that one either."

"No!" Eunike wasn't having any.

"I swear by the fleece!" Medea made fleecy motions over her heart, then spit on her pinky. "Sweetheart, do you have any idea what it takes to make self-igniting haberdashery? You need some centaur's blood for starters, which costs the earth. On the miserable pittance Jason Tightfist gave me to run our home, do you think I could afford centaur's blood?"

"But—but I was already Pythia when I heard about Kreon and Princess Thingie going up in flames before the wedding! The news hit Delphi at the same we heard about how you—" Eunike could have bitten her tongue right off. She didn't want to speak about the children; not yet. She was saving that for the instant before she killed her sister. Given all she'd learned thus far about how Medea really wasn't accountable for those other fatalities, she was holding onto her trump card with both hands and a gluepot. *Everyone* knew about the children! There had been witnesses.

Medea was chuckling. Clearly she hadn't been paying close attention to Eunike's every word. "That idiot Kreon was as big a cheapskate as Jason. He refused to pay for good oil lamps to illuminate the palace during the wedding feast; insisted on pine tar torches! You *know* how they smell. The princess was pitching one of her ugly little tantrums, nagging Papa to be a sport for once in his miserable life, and he was waving around one of the torches—lit, of course, I *told* you he was an idiot—and he'd had more than a snootful of the wedding wine—that loathsome stuff that also tastes like pine tar, you'd think the whole Theban royal family was part termite—and sloshing it about, and the next thing anyone knew, WHOOSH! Up like a pile of tinder, the pair of them."

"But I heard that you—"

Medea shrugged. "By the time it happened, I wasn't there to defend myself."

This was it. The perfect opening yet again. Eunike sprang. "You weren't there because you had slain both your children and set fire to the house and flown away into the sky on a chariot drawn by winged dragons with the corpses of your innocent victims at your feet! And it was *then* that Apollo turned his face from me and refused to give me any more visions. You can't be Pythia without visions. That's why I've come. I like being Pythia, I don't want to go home to Colchis after this long, and I'll be damned if I'm going to let a little thing like a kin-slaying sister stand between me and my career!"

"Uh," said Medea. Her brows knit and she assumed an attitude of deep thought overlaid with the solemn air of one doing intense mental mathematics. "Eunike, it's been thirteen *years* since that day. Have you been on my trail so long?"

Eunike looked sheepish. "Er . . . to be frank, the visions didn't go on the fritz until this autumn."

"Then why do you assume that I'm to blame for—?"

"Do you know how far Delphi is from Thebes?" Eunike countered. "Do you have any idea how long it takes for news to get from one place to the other? Well, just you figure how much father it is from Thebes to the top of Mount Olympus, Miss Smarty—how much longer it must have taken Apollo to find out about your little exercise in retroactive family planning—and you won't ask silly questions! Anyway, I asked Divine Apollo and he mentioned your name."

Medea began to protest, then thought better of it. She sagged down on her stool, the image of defeat. "You're right of course, Eunike. I have displeased the gods. I surrender myself to judgment. But if you slay me for my crimes, you'll be just as guilty of kin-death as I. I don't think that will help restore your visions."

"Gracious! I never thought of that," Eunike exclaimed. She gave the dagger a peevish look, as if this untenable situation were all its fault. "What are we to do? I can't just let you go!"

Medea clasped her sister's hands. "I don't want to be let go. I've borne the burden for my actions these thirteen years. It's not fair. It's time for a change."

She rose and went to a small chest that stood at the foot of her bed. She unpacked it carefully, first setting down two neatly rolled mattresses, a pile of tunics, a razor, and finally a stoppered glass phial full of something black. She brought this last item back to the table and showed it to her sister.

"Styx water," she said in reverent tones.

"Sure it is." Eunike was pleased to be sarcastic. "I never figured you for a gull. If I had an *obol* for every smooth-talking peddlar who tried to sell me genuine Styx water, I could retire."

Medea didn't bother defending her reputation as a canny consumer of items magical. She simply yanked the stopper from the phial and let Eunike get the full effect of the icy gust that blew from the tiny opening. Teeth chattering and fingers suddenly blue, the Pythia quickly admitted that Medea knew where to shop.

Jamming the stopper back into the phial, Medea said, "To swear by the river Styx is an oath that is binding even on the immortal gods themselves. Very well. Then by the Styx I do now swear to lay myself before Divine Apollo himself for judgment!" The black water bubbled fiercely. When it subsided, Medea's head drooped. "It is done," she said. "My doom is sealed."

"Oh, darling!" Now free of her unpalatable duty, Eunike felt at liberty to swoop up Medea into a sisterly embrace. "And to think you did it just to spare me!"

Medea nuzzled more closely into Eunike's arms, rested her cheek on her sister's shoulder, and said, "Wouldn't you do the same for me?"

"Of course I would!"

"Ah, me. I wish I could believe that. I could go gladly to Divine Apollo's mercy knowing that all the little domestic odds and ends I'm going to have to leave behind here were being, well, *seen* to by someone responsible. You can see for yourself that I like things orderly. It *so* preys on my mind to think that the next person to live under this roof might find something out of place and *say* things about me."

Not for the first time, Eunike marveled at the sister who could slay her own children with never a second thought, yet who worried about what the neighbors might say if they came in and found the cottage undusted. She was grateful to have been spared the need for becoming a kin-slayer in turn. She decided that the least she could do was set Medea's mind at ease.

"Why don't you go on ahead to Delphi and let me take care of things here," she offered. "You did swear the unbreakable oath, so you can be trusted to do that much."

"I don't know . . . you might not do it properly. I like my things just so, and you never were the neatest—"

As Medea rambled on about how Eunike's attempts at cleaning up the cottage could never hope to meet her standards, the Pythia felt the blood behind her eyes begin to boil. It was true that she wasn't all that tidy. She believed that any household task too small for a servant to do wasn't worth doing at all. Ever since their childhood, she was always The Slob while Medea had always been called The Neat One (until after the Jason fiasco, when Medea became The Homicidal Sex-Mad Trampy Fleece-Filching Foreigner-Loving Neat One). As a matter of fact, no one took more pride in pointing out Eunike's domestic shortcomings than Medea herself.

Especially in front of Daddy.

Eunike's common sense howled, *So what if I'm not as tidy as Medea? I've got better things to do with my life than housework! I've got a career, a calling! I perform a valuable public service! And I don't constantly need some man to reaffirm my self-worth!*

Unfortunately, Eunike's common sense was up against Eunike's memories, and these now trotted out the single, poignant image of Eunike's Daddy looking at Eunike's cluttered chamber and shaking his head sadly, his disappointment in his daughter clear to see.

With a snarl, Eunike shouted, "I am perfectly capable of taking care of any and all loose ends *you* might leave behind, thank you very much! *And* taking care of them to *your* satisfaction, Miss Nitpick."

Medea dug her chin into Eunike's shoulder. "Promise?" she whispered in that wheedling tone that Daddy always fell for.

"Yes, I promise!"

"Really? You do? You swear?"

"Yes, yes, all right, have it your way, I *swear*! Now if that's not good enough for you, I don't know what—" Eunike felt a stab of cold between her breasts. She looked down at the same instant Medea leaped back, away from her. Pressed to the Pythia's bosom, the phial of Styx water was seething.

With a merry laugh, Medea dashed out of the cottage. Eunike stood there dumbfounded for an instant, staring at the phial her sister had thrust upon her under cover of that smarmy embrace. Then she snapped out of her daze and raced after Medea. She burst from the cottage just in time to catch one last glimpse of her sister's fleeing form as it vanished around the back of the cottage. Then the air filled with the unmistakable sound of dragons' wings and an old-fashioned chariot drawn by a brace of the scaly beasts soared high into the sparkling air.

Medea leaned over the railing and shouted, "Don't forget to feed the dog!"

Eunike shouted back something nasty in Phoenician. (Only the diehard seagoing peoples came up with the really elegant cuss words.) Then she added, "You think you're so smart? I'll have this place spotless in no time, just to spite you, and then I'm going right back to Delphi in time to see you get what you deserve! Divine Apollo will make you suffer for what you've done to those poor, innocent children!"

The dragon chariot circled over the cottage slowly. Medea cupped her hands to her mouth and called down to her sister, "Oh, thanks for reminding me! Alkander is *not* to have any unwatered wine and Jason Junior *must* wear his big straw hat during the rainy season. Otherwise the water gets down his neck and he catches cold. Oooh! One more thing: I think Alkander's seeing a Bacchante and I won't have it! She'll break his heart—literally, if he's not careful."

"Huh?" The Pythia might have all the answers, but for the moment, this was the only question she could think of asking.

Medea waved it away. "Never mind. Here they come. And whatever you do, do *not* let Jason Junior borrow your dragon chariot! Just because he's fifteen, he thinks he's a demigod. I don't want him learning the hard way that he's not, smashed up against some olive tree that wouldn't get out of his way."

Eunike heard hoofbeats coming from behind her. She turned and saw two fine young men come riding up the road toward the cottage. Even though their hair was fair (hadn't the rumors painted Jason as more golden than the legended Fleece?) they were otherwise the spitting image of her sister. She felt her mouth drop open and the tickle of a fly's wings as it darted in and out.

As for the lads, they reined in their horses and stared, first at the Pythia, then up at the circling dragon chariot.

"Mom—?" the older inquired, shading his eyes.

"Hello, darling. Did you bring back the honey?" Medea asked cheerfully.

The young man blushed and stammered something unintelligible. Medea only laughed.

"I didn't think you'd remember, Alkander. Don't worry about it. I don't think Eunike knows how to make baklava anyhow. Say hello to your Auntie Eunike, boys."

The youths dismounted and dutifully mumbled something that might have been hello.

"Tsk! I thought I'd raised you better than that. You be good and you mind your Auntie. She's promised—sworn—to look after all my little loose ends here while I go to Delphi. And you *are* my dearest, sweetest, darlingest little loose ends, aren't you?"

"But Mommmm!" The younger of the pair had the sulky look of a born whiner. "We don't need her. We're too *old* for a sitter! Alkander's seventeen and I'm—!"

"You don't need to tell me how old you are any more than I need to tell how many long, grueling hours I slaved and suffered through labor to bring you into this world," Medea shot back. "I'll be the judge of what you do and don't need, and don't you forget it! Now Eunike, they both get a nice big dose of herbal purge once a fortnight. It's in the chest next to—"

"*They're your children!*" Eunike's shriek was so shrill that the horses bolted and the airborne winged dragons almost dumped their charioteer. By the time Medea regained control of her steeds, she was more than a little cross.

"Well of course they're my children! Do you think

I'd spend all these years stuck in this graceless back-water to raise someone else's brats?"

"But—but they're—but you *killed* them! People saw the bodies!"

"Oh, that?" Medea giggled. She uttered a few words in what Eunike knew for Egyptian and immediately the bloodstained remains of two young children appeared at her feet. "Simple illusion. I wasn't about to have Jason come after me, demanding custody. He'd do it just for spite. He never spent any time with the boys when he was home."

"In that case, you come right down here!" Eunike stamped her foot and pointed dramatically at the earth. "If you didn't kill your children there's no reason for you to go to Delphi!"

Medea looked like a cat in a creamery. "Oh, but there is."

In the next breath, she was no longer alone in the chariot. A tall, handsome man, more golden than Jason ever was, stood by her side. He wore nothing but a laurel wreath, a lyre, and a smile.

"Sorry about the bollixed visions, Eunike," he said. "It was the only way to bring you here. It's kind of hard to be romantic with a couple of kids always underfoot, and Medea won't trust her boys to just anyone."

"I'd hoped that maybe I could drop them on Daddy," Medea put in. "But when you told me he had a fresh brood of his own, there went *that* idea."

"Don't worry; we won't be away long. I usually get tired of my mortal lovers in three, five years tops." He put his arm around Medea. "Ready to lay yourself before me for some of that judgment, baby?" Medea purred, and Divine Apollo took the reins from her hand. A word from him and the winged dragons vanished into the abruptly setting sun.

Eunike stood as if turned to stone. She was trapped, hopelessly trapped. Even if Divine Apollo got tired of

Medea in *one* year (which he wouldn't, or Eunike didn't know her sister) that would still mean that the Committee at Delphi would put a new Pythia in Eunike's place. How could she stand it? She loved the power, the authority, the way all comers cringed before her every word! She was too old to change careers.

If you could call *this* a career.

"What am I going to do?" she whimpered to herself. "I don't know anything about being a mother! What do I do? How do I do it? Where do you learn—?"

"Hey!" It was Jason Junior, the sulky one. He was jabbing her arm repeatedly with a very badly manicured finger. "Hey, when do we eat? I'm starving! And how come you don't know how to make baklava? I thought every woman knew how to make baklava! Something wrong with you? I like baklava, and you oughta learn—"

The stone Eunike burst back to life with a smart slap that knocked away Jason Junior's pokey little finger sharply. *"Don't you use that tone with me, young man!"* Eunike yelled in his face. "And don't you poke me with the finger again unless you're prepared to lose it! Hmph! So you're a nail biter, I see. Well, that nonsense can just stop right this very minute. And if you like baklava so much, *you* learn how to make it! And learn to make *dolmades* too, while you're at it. You're *not* helpless! Don't you come whining to me with *When's dinner going to be ready, I'm staaarving!* It'll be ready when it's ready! You can do a little work around the house while you're waiting, *I DON'T THINK IT'LL KILL YOU. And as for you—!*" She rounded on Alkander. "When someone sends you to town for honey, you bring back some honey! You don't go wasting your time at the *taverna* with your bummy friends! Or were you sniffing after that Bacchante trollop? Oh, don't give me that innocent look,

I know what you've been up to! *That* little Attic farce is over and done with, you can believe me. And furthermore—"

"Yes, Auntie Eunike!"

"Sorry, Auntie Eunike!"

"I will, I promise, Auntie Eunike!"

"I won't, I swear, Auntie Eunike!"

Babbling, trembling and quailing as even the most hag-ridden petitioners to Delphi never had, the boys fled indoors posthaste. Eunike folded her arms, satisfied.

"So that's motherhood," she said. "A bit heavy in the on-the-job training department but ... I think I could get used to it." Smiling and hollering that she had better *not* find dirty footprints all over her nice, clean, beaten earth floors, Eunike followed her nephews into the house.

You'll Catch Your Death of Colds

Bill Fawcett

It was my dream and I was confused. At least I think it was my dream. Strange, though: I normally dream in color and this was all black and white like an art film from Europe. And if it was my dream, why was I terrified?

The terror, I understood, had something to do with the cowled black shape sitting across the gaming table from me. The figure stood about my height and was wearing a hooded robe like some monks wear that hid all of its body. The robe itself was hard to focus on, the folds just didn't look quite right. I had a good idea who it was in the robe and didn't like what that meant. Worse yet, I'd come in halfway through the feature and I'll bet there was no cartoon.

"So, Herr Professor, as we say," the figure was saying, "isn't sleep just 'the little death'? What better time for me to appear?"

Oh great, I'm dreaming I'm in a remake of an Ingmar Bergman movie and I've got the accent wrong. The voice itself was raspy, like a distant radio broadcast obscured by so much static you had to concentrate to understand what was being said. I was definitely going to have to talk to my subconscious about continuity.

The beach was covered with, of course, light gray sand, and the distant cliffs were darkening shades of gray in the fading gray light of the sunset. Though I had the feeling it was almost always sunset on this beach. Brighter gray gulls hovered in the distance, adding ambiance to the surge of a metallic gray sea against the pale gray—oops, said that already—sand. You get the idea.

The only breaks in the monotony were a mostly blue game board on the table between us and the tan picnic basket my mother had packed me a lunch in. I'd been fighting a cold all week and it had just won. I'd been too miserable to eat. At this point I paid little attention to the game itself, rather assuming it was chess like in the movie.

Mostly, I was relieved that there was some color in this bizarre fabrication of my sleeping mind. Except my last memory was not of sleeping, but of driving home after the semester had ended. The cold hadn't made me any more pleasant, and grading fifty-three freshman world history exams in two days hadn't helped my disposition. Facing the prospect of rubbing my nose even more raw on the hundred-mile drive to my folks I'd taken a few of those cold pills that promise instant relief.

Still, I had been in an optimistic mood. I don't know who had been more excited that the summer break had begun, I or the students. I wonder if they ever suspect how much the teachers look forward to the long breaks. Or that those breaks probably go far in preventing high mortality rates resulting from crazed teachers taking out their frustrations with rifles only the NRA could love. After all, we aren't even paid as much as most postal workers.

The picnic basket was open and I could see the thermos and two tuna sandwiches it contained. There was a lot of sand in the basket as well, though I'm not sure how it got there as there was no wind, and it was, well, deathly still. I was irrationally glad the sandwiches were in those little bags which seal tight and was perturbed to notice the seals were gray and not the advertised green.

I brought my gaze back to Death and decided to look him in the eye. It was my dream after all. This proved difficult as there was no face, just a darkness under his gray hood that seemed a lot deeper than there was room for. He took this as a signal to continue talking.

"So now that your time may be near, I have taken the opportunity to have this conversation with you. There are certain risks involved, but those have to be endured."

I didn't like that "my time was near" bit. I'd read somewhere that certain African tribes teach their children to control and even direct their dreams. This seemed a good time to give it a try.

"You are no longer Death," I announced, startling a few nearby gulls, gray ones, into flight. "Now you are Miss May. And let's try to bring a little color into this dream," I added, as an afterthought.

I then worked very hard picturing the rather abundantly formed image I'd just seen in the center of the most recent *Playboy* magazine. It was hard to tell since I couldn't see any face, but from the angle he cocked his cowl at, I suspect Death was a big confused. Unfortunately, even as I concentrated with all of my mental willpower he remained Death, which I found to be both disappointing and more than a bit frightening.

Then Death laughed. It was an unpleasant sound. But I guess it was supposed to be. His laugh included equal parts of the rustling leaves under an enemy's foot, a hyena's howl, the cracking of bones, and distant echoes of mortality. As he laughed his shoulders shook and I discovered that I was suddenly afraid his hood would fall back. It seems that as the situation began to seem more real, without getting any less surreal, I was less anxious to look Death in the face.

"Sorry about the laugh. I don't get much practice. Are you again under the illusion this is a dream?" Death asked.

After the, umm, haunting laugh I was surprised at

how gentle and concerned Death sounded. We were both standing beside folding chairs that bore a painful resemblance to those on which I had endured uncounted band concerts. I sat down. Did I mention the chairs were gray? But then it was the exact same lifeless gray color as the ones at the college were painted. Considering their low comfort level my mind tried to slip away in to a conspiracy theory about death, boredom, and high school assemblies. Then I was distracted by Death assuming the seat across from me.

"Don't tell I've made another temporal slip?" Death asked in almost conversational tones.

"I think so," I stammered. "What am I doing here?"

"Why, we're gaming for your life." Death seemed surprised at my question. "I told you so before we started this game several turns ago."

"Started?" I sputtered out, looking at the game board for the first time. "Gaming for my life?"

Death shrugged and began speaking in flat, well, *dead* tones, as if he had told this story one time too many already.

"First the time slip. You've been here for a while. Though there are no words in your language that will allow me to describe what or where *here* is. The problem is as a lesser Death I don't get this level of socializing very often and the mechanism I brought you here with isn't very stable to start with. It's hard adjusting to modern philosophical states. I'm only a minor Death, after all."

"Minor Death?" I managed to question as the import of what he was saying sunk in. I was gaming for my life and he was only a minor Death? There was a slight pause, as if Death wasn't sure he wanted to answer. Then he spoke in slightly hushed tones.

"To serve so many people, there are really thousands of deaths. How else could we greet each new soul? But with so many of us the organizational responsibility for making sure each gets to the right place when needed is horrendous. The solution was borrowed from the ancient Babylonians, or maybe the Chicago School Board, a totally hierarchical bureaucracy that only sort of works. On the top is the chief and each of us is on a level below. The fewer souls you greet, the lower your status. I'm near the bottom."

"The chief?" I asked, seemingly limited to two-word questions. Then I looked around. If this was a minor Death, I wasn't too anxious to meet the Top Cowl.

"He never takes an interest in individual cases, or rarely so. I believe he only personally greets those who have really attracted his attention, Attila, Genghis Khan, Stalin, most Democratic U.S. Presidents. No chance he'd deign to notice the efforts of someone as unimportant as me."

"Unimportant?" Great, now I was down to one-word replies. This situation was getting out of control. In fact, it had never been in control. But I needed information.

"Yeah, unimportant. I mean, hey, I had my day. There was a time when thirty thousand died from the flu one year in London alone. But then came all those drugs and everyone became aware of it and I was relegated to a much smaller office with no window. Why, the nearest bathroom is three floors down."

I wondered what the view out such a window might be, and then decided to stick to my own problem. I had better learn all I could, quick. "The flu?" I was back up to two-word questions and determined to try for three the next time. "Why," Death explained, "I'm that Death of Colds everyone is warned about catching."

"Catching?" Damn, back to one word. "Why catching?" I added quickly to bring up the count.

"Always sounded strange to me." Death of Colds answered while tilting his head in thought and actually sniffled as if he had sinus problems as well. "You don't catch me, *I* catch *you* . . . permanently."

I decided I had asked enough semiliterate questions. It was time I get some idea what was going on here. Or maybe to find out what I feared was happening wasn't the case. "So if you are the Death of Colds, what am I doing here? No one dies from a cold any more."

"And don't I know it!" Death of Colds moaned and no one can moan like Death, even if it did end in a cough. "But there's some hope. You're the first soul in a new program I'm trying to get made permanent. Instead of just the paltry few souls of those who actually die from a cold, I'm trying to get them to expand my territory to include all of those who die from the secondary effects."

"Like their wife killing them for being such big babies?"

"No, *that* type of thing already has a really big staff working overtime." Death corrected me. "What I'm trying to claim are those like you who take some cold medicine and ignore the warning label."

"Like me?" It was only two words again but I didn't care.

"Yeah, like you. Those who forget the part about not driving or using heavy machinery . . . you drove. In this case, you fell asleep, drove directly off a bridge, and onto a garbage scow. Your former students will be most amused."

"And all this is just to greet me?" I gestured around me. It seemed a bit much, the gray beach and all. "No wonder you need such a large staff."

"Actually, this is something special. It was the idea of the traffic types. They rather resented what they consider my poaching." He shrugged and the robe rustled ominously.

"So, what's special?" I asked hopefully. The concept that I may already be dead was just sinking in and panic rising in proportion.

"Something they learned from a Swede over in the Korean-mini division of Auto Related Fatalities. We Deaths approve of a car that gives us an even chance. You and I were to meet like this, and you are to be given a fair chance to stop me from taking your soul."

"A *fair* chance. *What* chance?" The words came pouring out as adrenaline surged and bile rose. "A fair chance to stop you? *How?* With what? Who? Huh?" I just sort of ran down and sat there hyperventilating.

Death of Colds waited until my breathing slowed and then tried to calm me with a friendly hand on my shoulder. Unfortunately the clasp of bare bones with incredible strength is painful, and not at all soothing. I winced and pulled away, almost knocking over the table between us.

"Sorry about that. Death grip and all that, you know," he apologized. "Forgot my own strength. It's amazing you mortals last as long as you do, so frail and all."

Death waited while I forced myself to be calm. A chance to stop Death, he said I had a chance. I wasn't dead yet. That would mean I'd go on living. If I could figure it out.

"This is your game," I said. "It isn't fair. Help me."

Death thought for a moment. "I may give you one hint on how to stop me. It's traditional and part of the deal. Then you can figure it out on your own, or not. One hint, that's all." Death explained and I waited.

"What is it?"

"*You got it from her.*" Death of Colds announced in even, studied tones. Then I realized that as Death gave me the hint I no longer got shivers along my spine. Either I was getting used to his voice or it was becoming even more normal and humanlike. I stared at him blankly. After a few moments of thought, nothing came to mind.

"Got what? Who gave me something?" I demanded as forcefully as panic might encourage. Death of Colds raised his arms in mock protection. Having experienced his strength he had to know I was no real threat on a physical level. "How can I beat Death?" I asked beginning to lose hope.

I would swear that even without a face Death of Colds was smiling. With a grand gesture he pointed to the board between us. It took a moment for me to focus. Winning the game, of course, like that man in the chess game in that foreign flick. Or was that how he beat Death? I wish I'd stayed awake for the ending.

For the first time I paid real attention to the game itself. I mean, when you are sitting across from Death Incarnate, even a minor Death Incarnate, it sort of grabs all of your attention. It was apparent the game was already in progress and, assuming death had chosen black, it appeared he had just captured all four parts of Australia for the two-point Risk.

"Risk!" I blurted out, over. "I'm playing Risk with death for my life on a beach in the middle of nowhere."

"On a *gray* beach in the middle of nowhere," Death corrected me. "We had been playing Risk when time twitched. I'm black and you're red. It's your turn."

So we played. I had always been good at it in life, but here Death had a psychological advantage. I tried to ignore it. The next turn went okay; I took Kamchatka from Alaska, but lost Greenland from Iceland. I couldn't believe he tried to take my England, with four armies on it, from Iceland with only six. His play seemed a bit erratic. There was no way he could unite Europe this early in a game. I was contemplating where to place my next five armies when Death of Colds interrupted.

"You are aware that when this game is over, so is our *other* game?"

"Huh, okay," I responded brilliantly, suspecting he was trying to distract me. I managed to take Brazil and only Venezuela stood between me and South America's three-army bonus. I was worried Death would load Venezuela up, but he went for England again instead. This time he won, but I was beginning to suspect Death hadn't reckoned with those lost semesters in college I spent in the dorm lounge. I had virtually majored in Risk and pinochle.

Death had great dice the next turn and I was lucky to get a card. Another turn like this and I'd be spending all my armies building up the Ukraine to prevent his taking all of Europe. Maybe it wasn't going to be a walkover. I started worrying about the cold medicine and the car accident. Then I remembered the hint he'd given me to save my life. It must have been something important. "You got it from her." Now I needed to figure out who the "her" was.

We were playing a war game. Maybe "she" was a general. Joan of Arc? I glanced at Western Europe on the map. A rectangular black marker sat on it. The young lass from Orleans really hadn't been much of a strategist. She was more concerned about morale than military planning. Maybe the hint was not to lose hope. Naw, too obscure. It had to be someone important. Real important. Maybe the feminists were right. If God was either a He or a She, maybe that was the answer. That worked in some other movie, something about the devil and Daniel Quail or something.

I tried praying. It was hard to remember the words I hadn't used since childhood, but after Death of Colds plunked down the first Risk and managed to drive all the way to Central America I got inspired.

I prayed through three turns. Things had not gone well. He was getting too close to actually completing Europe and I was fighting to hold onto South America. After a few lucky rolls I managed to hold the Urals and even knock him out of Southern Europe. But meanwhile Death had been slowly pushing up from his Australian position and was threatening to break out in a big way.

"Prayer is often a good idea," Death informed me after a pair of very bad dice rolls. "But He, She, or It never interferes with our mission. I suspect in some indirect way we're under contract there as well."

Damn the feminists, three turns wasted and the wrong her. I racked my brains. Who could it be? Hillary? Couldn't be. Maggie? Gave me what? What advice have I gotten from a woman? Then I had an inspiration.

"Mind if I put on a sweater?" I asked casually. Though I had no idea of where I'd get one. If this was the answer I'd find one. Death had promised it would be a fair contest.

"Don't need one, won't help, and haven't you noticed that your sinuses aren't even clogged anymore?" Death said as he rolled a four and five to knock me out of Mongolia and gain another card. "Never cold here. Never warm either. Besides it won't help. That's a different cliche."

"What?" I suspect I was beginning to sound panicky.

"Never mind. A sweater won't help."

The game continued. I rallied with a Risk and took most of North America, but lost all my gains when Death of Colds cashed in his next one. It was proving to be a tough game and I was slowly being eliminated . . . in every sense of the word. "You wouldn't want to tell me who the her in the hint was?" I probed without much hope as we battled over the Middle East.

"The most important woman in your life," Death answered cryptically.

Excluding several movie stars and models I'd spent a lot of time thinking about and never met, this left me with just a few candidates. There was Jackie Duocean, my first love, a short, skinny girl with braces. I tried to imagine what wisdom spouting from her metal-filled mouth might help me win the game. Nothing seemed to help, though the fond memories calmed me a bit.

Sarah Neiburger had sure taught me a lot about people and feelings while we lived together, but her most frequent advice was for me to brush my teeth before trying to kiss her. Then there was Mrs. Felker, the principal of the first school I had taught at. Mostly she told me to keep the class in order. Old-school type in every sense of the word but good. If she'd been less of a pain, I'd have never gone back for my doctorate and ended up teaching at the college level. Most of what I learned from her was how to avoid meetings that might get me in trouble. Too late this time.

As I rolled to invade Central America for the sixth time I narrowed the "her" down to one woman: my mother. The attack failed and I was one cannon short of a Risk. Death, seeing his advantage, poured a handful of armies onto North Africa, and grabbed for the dice. It looked like he was going to get his office window. Except for Egypt all I had left was South America and the Urals. I could see the end of the game was near, and with it, my end. It seemed too ridiculous to be real. Maybe it was a dream. I was beginning to really hope so.

"Time to wake up," I sallied as Brazil was overwhelmed.

"This is not a dream, not even a nightmare," Death corrected me. I couldn't think of anything to say.

I tried rolling the dice very slowly, offering more

prayers to a variety of gods, even sneaking a piece onto Argentina. None of it did me any good. When the turn ended I had three pieces left in play and not enough cards to cash in. My defeat was inevitable. So what had Mom told me that would save me at this point? The game was lost. Not to cheat? I should have cheated earlier. Be a good sport? Great, I'll congratulate Death of Colds as I die. Sweaters were out already. To say thank you? Clean underwear? I *had* clean briefs on and it was doing me no good. What had Mom said that would save me from the death of Colds? Then I understood. I had the right woman, but the wrong idea. Not what had she *said*, but what thing had she given me. The lunch? It had to be. Why else would it be here on the beach? This was to be a fair contest. That meant the means to win was available. Unless Death had a taste for tuna, that only left the soup. The soup!

Of course! The chicken soup!

With a smooth motion I reached down and grabbed my lunch. The thermos opened easily. I could smell the spicy-sweet aroma of the broth. Death had stopped and jumped away from the game knocking the board over, and spilling little black wooden blocks everywhere. Suddenly I understood. The game had been a ruse, a way to distract me and set a time limit. I'd had the means at hand to regain my life all the time.

Exuberantly I filled a cap with golden soup chock full of chunks of chicken and thick noodles. Then I hesitated. Should I splatter the Death of Colds with it? Visions of Dorothy melting the wicked witch came to mind. I drew back my hand.

"Did you mother teach you to spill your soup?" Death asked, almost too casually.

I hesitated. I wondered if it was a trap. What Mom had said was to eat my soup, it would help with any cold, maybe even the Death of Colds. Keeping my eyes on the cowled image I raised the cup and took a sip.

With a shrug the ominous black figure began to fade.

"You have found the one thing I am totally helpless against. The secret mothers have known for millennia." The raspy voice sighed. "I guess taking it easy won't be that bad. Car wrecks are so messy. Enjoy the rest of your life. It's now rescheduled to be a long one . . ." I could barely hear the last words as Death and the gray beach faded out together.

I awoke with a start and raised my head to see the edge of the bridge over the top of the steering wheel. It was approaching much too quickly. Reflex took over and I slammed on the brakes and spun the wheel. I wasn't really awake until the car had already skidded to halt. Then I remembered. What a dream. I'd woken up just in time to save my life. Funny, my sinuses weren't full anymore. The deep whistle of a garbage barge that was just passing under the bridge echoed along the river fifty yards below.

Just in time to save my life . . .

Thanks, Mom.

The Golden Years:
Respect Your Elders

Anne McCaffrey

I remember distinctly, though my son, Walter, says I couldn't possibly have done so which is why he discounted anything I said in those days, that the doctor said that my heart, lungs and other vital organs were in excellent condition for a woman of my advanced years. Therefore I was worth saving. *Worth?* Had I been able to speak, I'd've given that young man a thing or two to remember about courtesy.

I remember, again distinctly, thinking that my Austerity years upbringing had, indeed, preserved me. I had never smoked, even when that was a social necessity rather than a vice, and I'd never drunk more than a glass of sherry at parties, even at Walter's wedding. I'd eaten properly because my mother had taught me the value of good food. She'd insisted that I have lots of milk so I wasn't susceptible to the osteoporosis that seemed to so concern physicians for a while there . . . when that ailment, like so many others, was fashionable to have.

All that was wrong with me was arthritis. Everywhere, in all my joints, but just arthritis. That really is quite enough to have wrong with one, frankly, which anyone who suffers from any form of that disease will tell you. Emphatically.

Mind you, I didn't let it get in the way of my daily life and taking care of myself. Well, until it did and I could no longer turn on faucets or open tins of food for my cat. (As a small baby, Walter had been allergic to cats so I hadn't been able to have one until he married. Not that *I* would have married Sandra, but then, I wasn't Walter and his needs were obviously different to mine and he seemed to enjoy all the things *she* did which shows up a mother's failings. But then, a son's a son till he gets him a wife ... et cetera.) I couldn't go up many stairs without hauling myself by the rails—and so many of the new modern staircases don't have them. Those newest devices that float one up to another floor are fine, once one gets accustomed to being wafted from solid ground to another level. I find it very disorienting. As well as too expensive for me on a pension.

But when one cannot feed one's cat, or open a tin of soup, or start the kettle because one's fingers will *not* function as they used to, one begins to resent a modern medical research that won't DO something to remedy that sad state of affairs. I managed, somehow, because I didn't want to worry Walter, and I certainly didn't want to have to go live with him and Sandra. It is amazing, though, how modern society has done away with all the useful people who'd come to one's door from time to time. The postman could be counted on to open a bottle or a tin and the paper boy would bring in the milk or the shopping—before everything started coming out of that slot in the wall—and a delivery man would plug in the vacuum, when we still had those to plug in instead of that silly object that quarters the floor and inhales everything, including things one doesn't want it to. Like the ball of wool one is working with.

Then came the day when my right knee just wouldn't work, at all. It just ceased to do a knee's function. It caused me to fall flat on my face in the middle of the High Street. Even as I started to fall, I thought how exceedingly tedious this was going to be. I'd be sent willy-nilly into an old folks' home to dwindle and vegetate. I still had my funds and my pension and my savings. Walter could probably get me into one of the nicer ones, maybe even a room to myself, for I did hate sharing a bedroom with anyone.

The next thing I knew, I heard the doctors discussing me in the most objective of terms as if I were inanimate and unintelligent. I couldn't move—the shock of the fall, I supposed—because nothing hurt, except that dratted knee.

"Your mother's got many years left to her, considering the condition she's in," the man was saying in what I would call an "unctuous" voice. "Joints can be replaced, you know, and she can continue to 'do' for herself, if that is so important to her temperament."

So, I thought to myself, Walter has told him that I won't go into an old people's home. Not that one can *get* in. As one has to register a child for the school of one's choice, seemingly concurrent with receiving permission from the State to *have* a child, one has to register for the Assisted Homes before one reaches twenty-one . . . and hope that one lives to *use* the astounding booking fee that's required.

It used to be that parents set their children up with a new house or a car or some luxury item like that, but now it's a share in an Assisted Home for their old age. Only, of course, Assisted Homes weren't even a notion in a geriatrician's mind when I was twenty-one, sixty years ago. Then, of course, once the Social State was founded, "institutions" were abolished and one either struggled along on one's own, or died. That was the big thing: keeping people functioning and independent of institutions, including their own families.

Before I could rouse enough to make my own wishes heard, I was carted off and the Treatment begun. They don't replace joints anymore, they "refurbish" them. It's painful and, despite the fact that it doesn't take long (in terms of days and hours), it takes far too long for someone undergoing the Treatment. And it's all exceedingly humiliating to have the privacy of one's body so insulted. Yes, "insulted" is the right word. You wouldn't *believe* the things they do to you.

But there I was, and I tried to be grateful because it cost Walter and Sandra a great deal of money, which Sandra never forgot to remind me. And, of course, I had to give up my old flat, which I loved and which was decorated the way I wanted it to be, and I was assigned a "new" one in an Assisted Estate and expected to keep my quarters neat and tidy for the daily inspections. I was even allowed to keep Puss-cat because the new theory is that it is good for the Elderly to have *some* responsibility and a cat, or a small dog, has great therapeutic value, especially if defleaed and fixed and inoculated to the last whisker. We also had "chores" and "sessions" because the Elderly need to have their minds stimulated.

That's all well and good but it took time away from my own pursuits and my knitting. I was *really* glad to be able to get back to my knitting for I do so enjoy setting up the patterns and seeing the garment take form. I know it's a useless occupation. Who needs the warmth of a sweater in a totally weather-controlled environment? Forget the fact that I *enjoy* knitting! I find that relevance enough, thank you, despite the fact that no one, even small babies, wears handmade garments anymore when express tailoring can be done in the booth, so to speak.

Of course, I felt that I was really quite well off with my joints all pristine and working. Much better off than some of the inmates . . . I know I shouldn't call us that, but we *were* in, and "mated" with someone else we were required to check up on twice a day. Helping yourself help others, was the theory. Some inmates had heart or organ problems. *They* really suffered while they were being repaired.

You see, the Social State not only requires its citizens to be functioning, useful workers, but also *living*.

They hate to lose anyone. That's what one of the nurses said. I heard her, when they thought I was asleep. (I find out all the best things by pretending to be asleep. I even know how to regulate my breathing and twitch now and then most realistically.)

"They gotta stay alive or the Social State has failed its citizens which it can't do or *it* fails. I really think they oughta let some of the old dears *go,* the state they get in after a few treatments."

I didn't realize then what she meant.

The new joints lasted quite well, nineteen years by my reckoning and there's nothing wrong with my memory or my ability to tot up sums. (Unlike others who always have that device to tell them what they should have learned in grammar school.) But, like most modern devices, my joints had obsolescence built in, so to speak. Well, I managed, as I always had, to keep up appearances as long as I could. After all, those Stimulation Lectures included my debt to the Social State and how I could best repay by remaining an Elder Resource, alive, functioning as an example to other, less well-ordered countries, how highly the SS regarded its citizens of every age. Once again, it was my knees which gave out.

This time Walter and Sandra did not have to pay because the SS had now moved into high gear and *did* all those little tasks which once had been left to the individual family unit. The Social State was one big happy family, wasn't it, caring for all its multitudinous minions . . . I never have liked being a "minion" . . . and I certainly came to hate my status much, much more because the SS was responsible for *all* its members, the highest and the lowest—which meant me, as I was non-producing. Unless, of course, they needed a "show" Elderly to prove how well we were treated, kept, repaired, functioning. I began to hate my strong heart and lungs and organs, and good eyesight and, most of all, my acute hearing.

"Yeah, this one's good for another few decades," I heard the doctor say before I could protest a repetition of the Treatment. I would much more have preferred to have a quiet corner where I could just *go!* I really didn't fancy any more decades doing the things the Social State required of its functional Elderlies.

Pusscat had not survived me. I was given another, a weedy little obnoxious creature that sniffled and meowed in the most irritating fashion, but I was required to keep it fed, clean, defleaed and inoculated as part of my Social Service. I was also moved into "specially designed and automated quarters to give me ease and comfort above and beyond that which I had been accustomed to." My "cell," for it was no more than that in size by now, was so self-contained and problem free that I could have "functioned" quite easily with the old joints. Everything turned on or off with a wave of the hand, or by voice operation. I had to stop talking to myself because, when I did carry on a little conversation over the way things were, I had two hours of Social Consciousness. Talking to one's self was considered Anti-Social.

"I talk to myself because at least I understand what I'm talking *about*," I told the young woman who conducted the lecture.

"But no one is the least interested in some of your comments, Miz Thomas," she said.

"I am. That's why I talk to myself."

"Or wars . . ."

"I don't talk about them much but they happened. To me, whether any one else alive remembers them, and jazz, and cigarettees . . ."

She shuddered and held up her hands in protest. "That's what I mean, Miz Thomas: your mentioning all those old horrors what no one wants to be reminded of. Dead *history*. And it doesn't happen any

more and you are to stop talking about it, Miz
Thomas. That's final!"

"Oh?" Such a cheeky child. "And what if I don't?"

She smiled ever so sweetly at me. "You know Mr.
Bainbridge? In 304?"

That's all she needed to say to me and she knew
it. We all knew it. Mr. Bainbridge had talked inces-
santly—and never just to himself, or in the privacy of
his "cell" as I did—but to anyone he could latch onto,
all about the wars he'd been in and the battles he'd
fought. (Not that he'd been in very *big* wars, like the
ones I'd lived through—just the Peaceful Wars, as I'd
heard them being called. Which, mercifully, occurred
after Walter was too old to be called up.) Then, one
morning Mr. B. was missing from the Stimulation
Lectures and, when he returned three days later, he
couldn't put two sentences together to save his soul.
Which evidently he didn't because, not too long afterwards, his "cell" had a new occupant who looked too
young to have been in any war, peaceful or not. And
he didn't talk about much at all, though he smiled
a lot.

I screamed all the way to the hospital when my
knees once again gave out on me. I screamed because
they had promised that the last rehabilitation would
last ten years. While I might not have been as aware
of the passing of time as others, who had something
to live for, I knew it was no ten years since the last
Treatment. I screamed that I didn't need it, didn't
want it and why were they torturing me.

"It's so much easier when they lose their wits, too,"
I heard a doctor saying as I was once more anesthe-
tized. What happened to free will?

"We've got orders to keep this one going as long
as possible. She's a Venerable, even if she's not aware
of it."

"A Venerable?" That was the first phrase past my
lips when I recovered and found Walter, without

Sandra for once, sitting by my bed. At least the man "looked" like Walter.

"Yes, Mum, you're a Venerable now. Over one hundred and nineteen years old and still functioning, thanks to the State."

"You're not Walter," I said. "You only look like him."

"Tsk, tsk," said another male voice. "She needs her wits, too, to remain a Venerable."

"I have my wits, young man." I said as firmly as I could, considering I was still groggy from whatever it is they give you these days.

"I am Walter, Mum. I'm growing older, too, you know." His voice sounded petulant.

"Now, Mr. Thomas, you know that the Elderly are apt to be self-centered. Never know what's going on about them." That was the Sister and a right wagon she was, enforcing all those awful things they do to people who can't resist. Time was when one could say if one did—or did not—want "services" or "treatments."

"I do so know what's going on about me. And I want a new kitten."

"That's all right, Mrs. T., you didn't mean to fall on your cat."

"She's dead all the same whether I meant it or not," I replied. "I don't want one that whines, either."

"Now, now, Mrs. T., you may just have to take what's available."

"You mean, the State's done away with cats, too?"

"Mum!" Walter was shocked. He always shocked easily, even when he was a little lad. "We're grateful to the State for taking care of us." A pause. "Aren't we, Mum?" and he gave my arm—the one that wasn't rigged up to a Christmas tree thing—a little shake.

"Of course, as functioning citizens, we are grateful to the State," I parroted to show that I had taken in all that was said in those Lectures. I didn't feel the least bit grateful. Not after THREE Treatments and the prospect of more of them until finally my heart gave up, my liver and lights gave out and I could find peace and quiet in my grave. That is, if the State still buried people.

So I recuperated, still vigorous, and was sent back to my cell that had been painted a hideous pink which was supposed to be a good cheerful color. Everything was pink: down to the matting on the floor and the color of the liquid soap that came out of the dispenser over the wash hand basin. Nauseating color and, while I muttered about it, I didn't enunciate clearly so they wouldn't know how much I detested what they had done in my absence. They hated criticism.

That was when I had my inspiration.

"I'm a Venerable now," I told the supervisor—only they called her by another, more Socially graceful name, but a supervisor she was and there were no two ways about *that!* "Does that entitle me to any privileges in the State?"

She fixed me with her beady eyes—for supervisors are required to have them, you know. "Of course, Mrs. T. Didn't you get your apartment painted and all your furnishings refurbished . . ."

"The cat is not satisfactory," I said, pointing to the wizened little thing in the basket.

"Why, it's the very latest development . . ."

"It's not a *real* cat?"

Supervisor gave me one of those arch smiles such "minions" develop to a fine art. "Of course not. Cats have fleas and other bad habits."

"They also had personality."

"Cats?" she exclaimed, jolted out of her role by my remark. Clearly she disbelieved my claim.

"Mine always did. They deserved the name of 'cat.' "

"Now, Mrs. T. . . ."

"Thomas, my name is Mrs. Thomas and as a Venerable

I deserve that much, do I not? I'm not a cipher, a single letter, I'm a Venerable!"

She made a little purse of her lips and then brightly smiled at me. "Of course, you are, Mrs. T . . . Thomas. How right you are!"

"Good!"

She departed then and I was left alone. Mercifully all the day until afternoon tea, one minor luxury which even the SS has not deprived us of . . . yet.

I was some surprised then, two days later, when my door chime went off. When the caller did not immediately enter, my curiosity got the better of me and I rose and opened the door. I got more curious immediately because not only the Supervisor but the Super Supervisor stood there, smiling charmingly. Behind them were a bevy of folks with all those audio-video devices one often sees on the news broadcasts. Not that there is much news—not as I would define "news"—for nothing of any great interest now "happens" in the Socially Correct State.

"Mrs. Thomas, I believe," the Super Supervisor said, smiling unctuously.

"You believe correctly. My name is even on the door. Mrs. Isobel Thomas." I pointed to the plate thus enscribed. (In case, of course, I forgot which of the identical rooms on this level was mine. Which I didn't because I can still count to twenty. And beyond.)

The Super Super smiled as if I had been extremely witty. He glanced around him and saw supportive smiles and nods from the A-V persons.

"Now that you have reached the incredible age of exactly one hundred twenty-two years . . ."

"One hundred twenty-two years, three months and five days," I corrected him primly. They should *be* exact if they said they were.

I got the Super Super's smile again, not quite as

wide, for patently he did not like to be corrected, even by a Venerable.

"Yes, of course, and who would know better than you?"

Something in his tone made me realize that he hadn't expected me to be quite as bright. They should have reminded him that it was only arthritis that troubled me, not senility.

"And you are recording me for posterity?" I asked as innocently as I could.

"Not recording, Mrs. T . . . Thomas. This is going live as a special feature about the benefits of retirement in the Social State. Aren't you glad you live here, in this time, and in this place?" He was so fatuous. "Your every need supplied in your golden years?"

"Screw the golden years," I said. Then, before anyone could recover enough from the shock of my candid remark and cut the broadcast, I added, "I'd rather be in Philadelphia!"

Not that anyone left alive and listening would have the faintest notion what that meant! But I did!

Maureen Birnbaum Pokes an Eye Out

E. Taylor Spiegelman
(as told to George Alec Effinger)

When I got home from work, there was a big glass of milk and a plate of oatmeal raisin cookies waiting for me, along with a note from Mums. To the day I die, I'm like totally sure she'll always think I'm, you know, eleven years old. Her message told me where I could find a second note, the important one, the one that my six-year-old son, Malachi Bret Fein, had worn home from school pinned to his shirt.

Now, see, if I had been Mums, I would've left the second note right next to the first one. Or under it. Or maybe instead of it. I mean, like the note from school was pretty self-explanatory.

Instead, she wrote me another note telling me that she'd put the teacher's note in a place where I couldn't miss seeing it, except of course I had missed it, or I wouldn't have needed Mums' other note to find it. I suppose if I asked for a show of hands to see how many people, in Mums' place, would've just put the school note on the refrigerator door with a magnet, I'd get a pretty decent response. That's where I would've put it.

Not Mums, though. She stuck it on the mirror of the medicine cabinet with a piece of Scotch tape. Okay, you're probably saying, that's another place I couldn't help noticing it. Sure, except Mums fooled out and put it on the medicine cabinet in her and

Daddy's bathroom, not on the medicine cabinet in my bathroom. Duh, huh?

I have no idea why, and I don't have time now to delve into Mums' unique thought processes. I'll just say that there was a pretty good chance another note or two were posted around the house, telling me about the school note in case I never found her first note by the milk and cookies, and those notes—along with other forgotten missives from years gone by—will come to light only after, God forbid, Mums passes away and Daddy and I have to sort through everything of hers. That job will take decades. The cataloguing alone will be like when that English guy stumbled onto King Tut's tomb.

It seems that Malachi Bret's first grade teacher, Mrs. Glick, decided it was necessary for me to meet with her and the principal of P.S. 154, Mr. Martinez. I felt this terrible cold thing stab right through me. It was like I was on trial for something and I didn't have any idea what. Like in Kafka, you know, where faceless authorities put you through these bogus and totally harsh proceedings, and then one morning you wake up to find that somehow during the night you've acquired a thorax and an exoskeleton. I knew that I hadn't done anything wrong, but in an uncaring universe that's no guarantee at all.

Not that anybody should get the idea that I really truly *believe* that we live in an uncaring universe. I'm not that depressed, and the universe isn't that bad, I suppose. It's just certain neighborhoods between my parents' house in Queens and Malachi Bret's school—uncaring is the kindest thing you can say about them.

So, anyway, Mrs. Glick requested my presence at a meeting the next afternoon at three o'clock. Neither Mrs. Glick nor Mr. Martinez thought to ask if three o'clock was convenient for me. No doubt they figured that if I was a decent mother I'd walk through fire to attend that meeting, even if it meant having my *paycheck docked or even worse. If I flaked on them or even just phoned the school to reschedule, then obviously I wasn't a fit mother and the Van Man would come to take Malachi Bret off to some unspeakable hellhole* orphanage *or something.*

I mean, these are the things that run through your mind at a time like this. Well, they ran through *my* mind, anyway; I guess I get a little of that from Mums. I don't want to start discussing how I might be growing up to be just like her. That isn't *happening*, I don't care what *you've* heard, and besides I have more important things to talk about right now. Like how even though I planned to leave work way early to get to that meeting on time, I had my schedule completely shagged by the untimely-as-usual arrival of Macha Maiden *magazine's favorite centerfold,* Maureen "Back Off, Buddy" Birnbaum.

"S'up, Bits?" she goes. "Glad to see me?" How odd that she would say that. How odd that she believed I'd always drop whatever crummy, trivial, merely real-life thing I was doing to be her Number One Fan.

She was grinning, and it didn't seem to bother her that everybody else in the subway car was staring at us. She was worth staring at, too, because she was in her usual Mistress of the Multiverse costume. I go, "Jeez, Maureen! You like scared me half to death, you do that all the time!"

"Say hey, sweetie!" she goes brightly.

I was like totally not in the mood for this. Not ready for Muffy, or her pendulous alabaster globes spilling out of her Frederick's of Flatbush solid gold bra, and like absolutely not in the mood for the next exciting installment of "Maureen Birnbaum and the Non-Denominational Church of Doom."

I go, "Muffy, people are like, you know, staring."

She goes, "Let 'em stare! I could care less, I'm like wild and free." She looks at me and she goes, "And

Bitsy, I've told you a million times, *never call me* Muffy! *I'm not a little girl anymore, okay?"*

"*And I've told you not to call me* Bitsy, *but do you listen? Call me Bitsy once more,* Maureen, *and I'll start calling you Mo. See if you can deal with* that."

She gave me this little look to see if maybe I was serious, and I guess she saw that I was, because she just grinned again and changed the subject. "Guess where I've been!" she goes.

You should know that I didn't even bother to try.

I'm what you call, you know, a *survivor*. No, *really*, Bitsy. Like I've had some pretty beat disappointments lately. Not getting back to Mars was way bunk, sweetie. We all know that I'm meant to fulfill my destiny as Co-Monarch of the Angry Red Planet, beside my *one true love*, Prince Van. Fortunately, I don't let a little adversity get me all raspy. I mean, if you let every teeny tiny thing bother you, then *whoa!* you're like next to useless. Say the world needs saving again or something, and you're like camped out in your bedroom listening to your old ABBA tapes and weeping. That is just so *bald*.

Anyway, what I was saying was that's just not *me*. As long as I've got my very fresh broadsword, Old Betsy, and a flat place to stand, I guess I'm ready for anything, I'm sure. That's nitro, too, 'cause every time I whoosh myself across time and space, the Lords of Karma have dished out some wacko new challenge for me. This last one was like nine-point-five for difficulty, and I gave myself a *perfect ten* for performance if I do say so myself, thank you very much.

Of course I was whooshing myself back to Mars, and *of course* I got lost again along the way. I ended up in this fully faux town, like somewhere in the Midwest where they have like, you know, *corn fields* behind the high school. The place had one main street with a dimestore and a drugstore and a beauty parlor and a Dairy Queen. I mean, Bits, what *more* could a person ask for? No, let's *not* make a list. Let's just get on with the tale of my thrilling exploit.

There was this wooden sign on the lawn in front of the town hall. It said WELCOME TO SPRINGFIELD! IF YOU LIVED HERE, WE'D KNOW YOUR EVERY LITTLE SECRET! The town square was what Pammy, my step-mom, would call charming and quaint. *You* know, all warm and friendly and kind of like Bedford Falls from *It's A Wonderful Life*. Girlfriend, it was just too terribly *dreary*, like the kind of HO-gauge plastic village you set up around the model railroad under your Christmas tree.

Well, *we* always had one 'cause really Christmas is just *so* commercial and I was raised to be just an *excellent* consumer. I'm just like so *sad* that you were deprived, honey. You really need to come to terms with your *feelings*, Bits. You don't want to be all twisted by bitterness and stuff.

So if you want the God's-honest *truth*, I felt out of place in Springfield, for sure. The people who lived there were like the salt-of-the-Earth Type, and why they needed a buff 'n' tuff champion like me I don't know. I mean, if they were plagued by dragons and ogres and whatall, they kept it hidden *really really* well. Still, one thing I've learned from reading like absolutely *dozens* of Stephen King books—

Well, don't *look* at me like that! *Sure* I know Stephen King books. So okay, like I haven't actually *read* one, but I've seen some of the movies. And one time I heard a *whole bunch* of one on a cassette tape in Daddy's car. I think it was the one about alien abductions, crop circles, and the hollow Earth. Like I'm so *sure* that was a Stephen King book, I don't *care* if it doesn't sound familiar to you. What are you, the *Times* book review section all of a sudden? *Jeez*, Bitsy, just let me go on narrating, huh, okay?

What was I saying? Oh, yeah. I've got my legendary

sword, Old Betsy, all limbered up, and I'm ready to do like *serious* mayhem, but the only target in sight is this L.O.L. That means Little Old Lady, sweetie, you're supposed to *remember* these things.

I don't care like *how* wretchedly evil she might be, I couldn't bring myself to slice 'n' dice this grandma until I got to know her a little better. So I wait for her to come up to me and she goes, "You must be new in Springfield, dear, I haven't seen you around town before. Hello, my name is Judith Barlow. I'm the widow of Robert Barlow, who was Springfield's leading banker and the grandson of our town's founder."

"*Cool*," I go. "I'm Maureen Birnbaum, and I'm like a freelance adventurer bound to uphold justice wherever I travel."

"That's just wonderful, dear." She gave me a good going-over from head to toe, and I was ready for her to totally dis my warrior-woman garb. She just smiled and shook her head a little, and then she goes, "In *my* day, there was only *one kind of girl* who wore ankle bracelets. Gracious, but times have changed."

That wasn't half as bad as I expected. I'm like, "Yes, ma'am, I guess so."

"I was on my way to Springfield University Hospital to call on some patients. Would you like to accompany me? Visiting shut-ins can be *so* rewarding."

Well, I had nothing urgent penciled in for the afternoon, so I figured I could probably learn a lot about Springfield by hanging out with this Barlow babe. She was probably one of the town's leading citizens, and if there was a rotten scoundrel who needed correcting, she'd be able to point him out. "You bet, Mrs. Barlow," I go.

She smiled. "Please, just call me Ma. Practically everyone in Springfield does." She seemed to be a very pleasant lady, but I've learned that looks can be *very* deceiving. I mean, sometimes you ask yourself,

"How well do I *really know* this person?" You'd be surprised the creepy things nice-looking people can do sometimes. Take your ex, for example. You've got to admit that *you* were fooled at first. I remember telling you—

Sure, Bitsy, whatever you say. Ma Barlow and I walked along Ridge Street toward the hospital, and the sun was nice and warm on my skin. I was wearing this same jewel-encrusted solid gold bikini—it's like my *costume*, okay? People see me wearing this, they know *right off* that I'm not your *ordinary* sultry raven-tressed beauty. And Old Betsy sort of clinches it. People go, "*Look!* There goes Maureen Birnbaum! I sure wish *I* could be like her! She must have the most wonderful, exciting life! She must have kings and movie stars and captains of industry laying untold wealth at her feet, but so committed to righting wrongs is she that—"

But it's *true*, Bitsy! This outfit is the same as, you know, Bruce Wayne's Batman drag. It strikes terror into the hearts of the villains. And whoever *designed* this hot little number could give the Maidenform people a few lessons. This bra would give even *you* cleavage, sweetie.

Back to Ma Barlow. She asked me where I was from and where I went to school and if I was seeing anybody and *what I wanted to be when I grew up*. And then it struck me. You know who she looked like? No, *really*, I *mean*, it. She looked and talked and acted just like Mary Worth! You know, *Mary Worth*. It's the comic strip between *For Better Or For Worse* and the Word Search puzzle. Mary Worth is this two hundred-year-old *busybody* who goes around interfering in everybody's lives until like they all conform to her *very* ancient idea of the way people should behave. And Judith Barlow had the same white hair pulled back into this bun, and her advice was just so terribly *wise*, and she was also so goddamn *kindly* and *sweet* that I wanted to whack her head right off before the *whole world* went into sugar shock.

When we reached the hospital, I go, "It's not very big, is it?" Bits, I *swear*, it was only two stories high and smaller than your average Wal-Mart.

"It's grand enough for Springfield," Mrs. B. goes. "We're quite *proud* of it, actually. People from all over the country come here for relief from neuritis, neuralgia, and muscular aches and pains, not to mention the heartbreak of psoriasis. I do a lot of volunteer work here, darling, it keeps me young. Now, let's go visit my niece, Adriana, first. She's in room 102."

"Oh?" I go. "Does *she* have psoriasis?"

Mrs. Barlow smiled. "She's in a coma, dear, but I know she can hear me. I visit her every day and I pray for her, and I know that wherever she is, deep inside herself, she's fighting just as hard as she can to come back to us."

I was moved, like *emotionally*. "You've got a very positive attitude, Ma."

She smiled and waved a hand. "Well, just about *everybody* in Springfield's been in a coma, one time or another. And they *always* come back sooner or later. I remember *my* coma—well, not the coma itself, but the waking up. It was so wonderful to see all my family and friends again! I think, next to my wedding day, that was the happiest time of my life."

I didn't really know what to say, 'cause like I haven't yet had *my* first coma. I hope that when I do, Bitsy, you'll be just as brave as Ma Barlow.

In the elevator, the old lady filled me in on the other people we were going to visit—Adriana, her niece, wasn't her only relative laid up at Springfield University Hospital. Ma Barlow had a sister, Fiona, who had been adopted and was much younger than Mrs. B., and Fiona was Adriana's mother. Now, apparently Fiona had had an affair with a wealthy contractor, this guy Jeffrey Stark, but Stark was blackmailing Fiona these days. His secretary, Summer, was a former prostitute who was pregnant by Quinn Thompson, the younger brother of Todd Thompson, Adriana's husband. Summer was in the hospital with amnesia, and we were going to drop by her room, too.

Really, Bitsy, it isn't *funny*. These people had such complicated lives, I could see why somebody'd catch amnesia. You'd think they'd need a whole filebox full of index cards just to keep their relationships straight. And I know you don't *catch* amnesia. I'm not *that* dumb, sweetie.

And then the elevator doors slid open, and I had this *revelation*. It was like . . . I don't know how to describe it. I just knew that everything suddenly looked incredibly *familiar*, and I didn't understand how that could be, because I knew for a *fact* that I'd never set foot in this town of Springfield before in all my life. I walked toward the nurses' station, and I just shivered, the *déjà vu* was so strong.

Ma Barlow must've noticed something. "Are you all right, Maureen? Stand up straight, dear."

I felt kind of dreamy. "Uh huh," I go. I suppose I wasn't paying attention, because I nearly knocked down a doctor in a white labcoat who'd just come out of one of the patient's rooms.

"Excuse me, miss," he goes.

I started to apologize, but the words got all caught in my throat and I almost *choked* on them. It took me a few seconds to recover. Then I go, "Dr. Beaumont?"

He smiled at me. He gave me this beautiful hundred-watt smile that I'd seen a *thousand* times before. It was Dr. Keith Beaumont, the chief surgeon at the hospital, and the most *gorgeous* hunk of man you've ever seen. Daddy's wife, Pammy, absolutely *adores* him. She cut his picture out of a magazine and keeps it someplace where Daddy won't find it by accident.

A *magazine*, Bitsy. Yeah, *Daytime Drama Digest*. It's a *soap opera* rag, sweetie. Dr. Keith Beaumont is a character on *Search For Another Doctor*.

Look, don't ask *me* how I got to this extremely non-real Springfield place. I can't explain it, just like I can't explain *any* of my miraculous journeys. I'm just a pawn in the eternal battle between good and evil, and I travel where the universal will sends me. I ask no questions, I demand no explanations, and as for reward, well, simply the knowledge that my actions have helped hold back the bitter black night of chaos a little longer—

You want to hear more about Dr. Keith Beaumont. Sure, *okay*. Cosmic significance can wait till the next time I have lunch with like the *Dalai Lama*. No, I *didn't* get the doctor's autograph. There's no such *person* as Dr. Keith Beaumont, Bitsy. He's a *fictional character* played by an actor named, um, Walter Morrison or something.

You're missing the *point*. See, I thought I was in the Real World, but I wasn't. People could act pretty damn *weird* here, and nobody but me would notice.

I watched Dr. Beaumont enter another patient's room. "He's even better looking in person," I go.

Mrs. Barlow goes, "And he's a remarkable person, too. It's a great accomplishment to be chief of surgery at the age of sixteen."

"Sixteen?" I go. "He looks like he's got to be *at least* forty."

She shrugged. "His parents sent him away to summer camp when he was eleven, and when he came home he was a surgeon. That was five years ago."

So later, after we visited Ma Barlow's niece, Adriana—and her hospital room was stuffed with like more flowers than I've ever seen in one place before—and Ma and I prayed, each in our own way, for the girl to come out of her coma—we dropped in on Summer, the ex-hooker.

Summer goes, "Hi, Ma!" Everybody was always just so *glad* to see the old woman.

"Hello, dear," Mrs. B. goes. "How are you today? Have you had any memories?"

"No, but that's all right. Everyone is being just so friendly and kind and caring. I can't wait to remember who you all are, because you're all such wonderful people."

I had to ask. "What kind of treatment do they give you for amnesia here?"

Summer just blinked at me. "Have we met? You're not my sister, are you? Or my husband's mistress?"

Ma goes, "You're not married, dear."

Summer's like, "Oh, that's *right*. I keep forgetting what I've been told that I've forgotten. Treatment? Just getting a lot of rest."

"How long have you been in this room, then?" I go.

Summer glanced at Ma Barlow, who looked thoughtful. "About seven months, I guess," Mrs. B. goes.

Seven months of bed rest in a private room! Jeffrey Stark Industries must've had one hell of an employee benefits package.

We said goodbye to Summer and went back out into the hall. I go, "It's pretty neat that you don't hold that girl's slutty past against her."

Ma Barlow goes, "If you can't say anything nice about a person, you shouldn't say anything at all. I'm sure *everyone* in Springfield has a wicked secret *somewhere* in his past."

I'm thinking, except maybe Ma Barlow herself.

Later we dropped in on Greg Parker, who was suffering from some kind of hysterical blindness. So now I'm like, donnez-moi un break, like *really!* I wish *I'd* thought of hysterical blindness some days. "Mom, I can't go to school today, 'cause like I can't *see!*" The godly goofy thing about Greg was that all his other senses had become *way* super sharp. Like he just listened to my voice and told me how much coffee I'd had in the last twenty-four hours. There's *got* to be a way to market a talent like that.

And let's just tiptoe quietly past Donna Rutherford, who had at least eleven separate personalities. I never got to see the whole inventory, but two of the three that I *did* meet were people you wouldn't want to be trapped with on an elevator.

So I go, "Doesn't *anybody* in Springfield ever come here with something simple, like a busted arm?"

Ma Barlow laughed. "Let's say goodbye now, dear. We have to visit the courthouse next. My grandson Tommy is on trial for murder."

As we walked back up Ridge Street toward the town's courthouse/police station/jail/library, it was still warm, but I noticed that dark clouds had started to shove over from the west, and it was threatening to rain. That probably jubilated the farmers working in the fields behind the high school. Hey, Bitsy, like they say, into everyone's life some corn must fall.

About now, Ma Barlow turned kind of philosophical on me. "In the immortal words of Abraham Lincoln," she goes, "judge not lest ye be judged."

I go, "For real even? Wasn't it *Shakespeare* who wrote that? I'm like *so totally sure* Shylock's daughter says that to Bagnio in the 'quality of mercy' speech."

Ma smiled, being wise and kind enough to forgive me for rudely correcting an elder. "It doesn't make *any difference* who said it first, dear. The truth remains—my grandson Tommy is innocent, although all the evidence seems to point to him. The district attorney thinks she has an open-and-shut case, just because the victim accused Tommy with his dying breath, and because no one else in town had either a motive or an opportunity, and because somehow they got a *confession* out of my grandson."

"Sounds like twilight time for Tommy to me," I go.

"I have faith in our criminal justice system. Tommy's a

good boy, and I'm positive that he'll be vindicated. He always has been *before*."

"Uh huh. How many *other* times has Tommy been tried for murder?"

Mrs. B. stopped to think. "Five," she goes, "but one was a mistrial. He's never been convicted."

So far, I thought. *The kid's got to stop tripping over fresh dead bodies.*

"And while we're there," she goes, "we can say hello to Father Chilcoat. He's gone to jail because he won't reveal why Lester DuPage kidnapped his own baby boy and pretended that his ex-wife, Dodie, had done it, when everyone in Springfield knew that Dodie couldn't have done it because she was visiting her mother at that research station in Tierra del Fuego."

"Right," I go.

"The TV station owner's wife, Bubba Sue Conway, is locked up because she sneaked into the hospital and switched the DNA tests that proved her baby's father was the high school gym teacher, not her husband."

"Right."

"And there's somebody else in jail, too, but I can't be expected to remember who *all* of them are."

"No, you can't." I had to keep reminding myself that this wasn't real life, it was *Search For Another Doctor*. Sometimes it almost *looked* like real life, though.

"It's a shame we won't have time to stop by my combination home/hospice/ex-con halfway-house/shelter for runaway teens and homeless. You could try my famous doughnuts. My friends, the criminal offenders, tell me they're the best doughnuts they've ever tasted."

"Sounds way cool, Ma," I go, "but we rugged fighting women have to watch our waistlines."

Before we got to the courthouse, something *full-on*

freaky happened. No, even *stranger* than running into Dr. Keith Beaumont up-close-and-personal. I met . . . *my evil twin*.

I'll just pause here while you compose yourself, Bitsy. I'll wait five seconds, and then like I'll *slap* you. And *your* line will be, "Thanks, sir, I needed that."

Half a block away, turning a corner onto Ridge Street, was this *drop-dead gorgeous* woman, okay? She was wearing a dark blue business outfit, off the rack from Mervyn's or someplace, with a black leather attache case, and she was like the supreme *dynamic-woman-on-the-go*, right? She was *exactly* my height and *exactly* my weight, and she had hair the very same length and color as mine, just not as perfectly coifed. She had my coloring, and she was *every bit* as graceful and naturally sexy as I am. Still, at the same time, I could sense that beneath her *stunningly beautiful* exterior, she had a twisted, cruel heart as black as her *obviously* counterfeit Carlos Falchi purse.

My throat felt dry. I go, "Who is *that*?"

"That's Floreen Birnbaum, dear. I have *nothing nice* to say about her. We used to call her Fluffy, but she just *hates* that nickname now. Her father named her Fluorine. He was an eccentric scientist who believed mankind's salvation depended on the fluoridization of our drinking water. After his tragic death—ironically, his body was found floating in the Springfield Municipal Reservoir—she immediately changed the spelling of her first name, and legally changed Birnbaum to Burns."

The other me laughed. It was a cold, *vicious* sound like, you know, that fakey out-of-sync laughter of the bad guys on *Speed Racer*. She was completely mental, sweetie, like one spear short of a pickle.

We were for sure a lot alike, but we weren't *identical*. For one thing, she was older than me. *Of course!* Bitsy, *you've* noticed that I stopped aging when I first whooshed from that ski trip in Vermont to Mars.

You—and Floreen Burns—are thirty years old, but I am forever and eternally *young*, a radiant, joyful, vibrant seventeen. I don't know why *I* have been singled out for this amazing gift. I merely accept it as like my due.

And I could see that this pseudo me had a *megahate* thing for me 'cause of it. Why, Bitsy, *why*? Why would *anyone* despise me, just because I will stay at the peak of my natural beauty and sexuality forever, while they creep on toward the grave, day by day getting all gray and wrinkled and haggard and *ugly*? Bitsy, if you can explain this to me, I wish you would. It's just like so *weird* to me, you know?

Suddenly, Floreen Burns snapped open her attache case, whipped out this big old Clint Eastwoody pistol, and she goes, *"Die, you meddlesome bitch!"*

But she pointed the piece *not at me*, but at kindly, sweet, dear old *Ma Barlow*.

So like I didn't even have time to warn her. I had to rely on my finely-honed heroic fighting-woman protector-of-the-weak instincts. I was still holding Old Betsy in one hand, and I jumped for Mrs. B. At like *absolutely* the same second that I leaped, I heard Floreen's gun go off. Now, what I *think* happened was my trusty broadsword deflected the bullet and, you know, *miraculously* saved the little old lady's life. I fell on top of her, and we sort of sprawled all over the sidewalk. Then I heard this high-pitched *scream*.

"My eye! My eye!" It was Floreen. Guess what? Unlikely as it sounds, the bullet had ricocheted off my sword and struck my evil twin in her left eye, partially blinding her. So like she's roaring in pain and rage and everything, but—

Bitsy, I'm not *finished*! I haven't even gotten to the part where—

Mums always said life was like a package of baseball cards: You never know who you're going to get.

Ain't that the hard truth? I mean, Mums got Daddy, which has worked out pretty well as far as I can see. And I got, um, Josh Fein, world-famous Celebrity Doctor with an office in a mini-mall right next to an Everything for $1 store. He's also the all-around scumsucker who left me and our infant son for his skanky receptionist, she should only wake up one morning with all her bodily orifices sealed shut with Krazy Glue. Bust her out, if you catch my drift.

Now it's three in the afternoon at P.S. 154, and I was sitting in this study hall chair—you know, the kind with the little platform on the right side to put your notebook on and everything, which never did me much good because I'm left-handed. Next to me in another study hall chair is Maureen Danielle Birnbaum, fresh from her conquest of America: The Heartland. Like she's so wild and free, I had to stop her from carving her initials in the chair with the tip of Old Betsy.

This guy with a handful of hairs the color of dust bunnies stuck his head out of the office and goes, "Miz Spiegelman?"

"That's me," I go, and I followed him inside. He permitted me to take a seat across from his desk, and then he stared down at a stack of papers in front of him. He looked up and gave me this totally dippy smile, patted his papers, and cleared his throat.

"Your boy presents a bit of a problem, Miz Spiegelman," he goes. "His I.Q.'s 75."

I knew right off that this feeb could get me crazy mad if I let him. I wasn't going to let him. That wouldn't do Malachi Bret any good at all. "I imagine every child is a bit of a problem, one way or another, Mr. Martinez," I go.

"MartiNEZ. The accent is on the last syllable."

"Mr. MartiNEZ," I go, being like ever so accommodating, you know?

"Now, please take a look at this visual aid, Miz

Spiegelman." The goob—Mr. MartiNEZ—held up the paper on the top of his pile. It was some kind of chart or graph or something, divided into three sections which I mentally labeled Top, Middle, and Bottom. I'm a whiz at classifying stuff.

He pointed to the middle section with a pen. "Now, this is normal," he goes. "Malachi Bret is riigght here." He tapped the bottom section. "The state of New York requires a minimum I.Q. of 80 to attend public school, Miz Spiegelman. He'll be assigned to a special school in accordance with that statute, where he can get all the attention he needs."

Are you picking up that I was like totally edged? Right about then I wanted to wad up every paper on his goddamn desk and cram them all down his throat until everything between his mouth and his rectal region was P. S. 154's new filing system. Let those clowns hire an office temp to sort all that out, huh?

I didn't give him the satisfaction. I just smiled a little and I go, "You can't draw a line across a piece of paper and classify my son out of his education! He has a right to the same opportunities as anyone else. He's not going to some special school to learn how to shake salt on french fries. That rule of yours is like totally arbitrary. There's got be some way to work around it." And I gave him another smile.

So he said about what I figured he'd say: "I try to be flexible in cases like this. I sure want to see your boy get a chance to prove himself." Wait for it now. "Is there a Mr. Spiegelman . . . Miz Spiegelman?"

I was about to give him a carefully worded reply that would've scorched every wall as far away as Bayside, when suddenly there was this tremendous whomp! I saw Old Betsy slash down through the air and hack Mr. Martinez's heap of important documents into two roughly equal little heaps. I glanced at Maureen. She was red in the face, and she looked like she was ready to chop the principal into salsa. "Good answer!" I go.

Maureen leaned across the desk, getting right into Martinez's face, and she's like, "One more slimy suggestion like that and I'll use Old Betsy to split you like a Popsicle from your empty skull to your shriveled cojones. Comprendez?"

Mr. Martinez was so scared that he could only nod. It was like a totally wonderful thing to see. So many interpersonal conflicts could be efficiently resolved if one party or the other were wielding, you know, an implement of destruction.

Maureen wasn't finished. She goes, "You gonna give Miz Spiegelman what she wants, or do you want to rush me? I mean, I'm perfectly ready to take you right out of the box."

Martinez just sat there and shivered. He sort of looked like bad reception on Channel Four after the cable goes out.

Maureen pressed her advantage. "Little Malachi Bret goes to this school, and there won't be a 'special class' or anything like that." Her voice was low, like radio in another room.

Martinez bobbed his head again. "That can be worked out," he goes.

"Fine," Maureen goes, "you may continue living." She turned to me. "Like my mother always says, sweetie, men are only after one thing. Well, it looks like my work here is done, so I'll wait for you in the hall. Put a rush on it, though, Bits. I want to go to the mall and see what Laura Ashley's been up to behind my back."

That's just about all of it. Malachi Bret was put in a regular class at P.S. 154, and he's doing pretty great, if you ask me. And he's never come home from school again with a note summoning me into Mr. Martinez's presence. In an unlikely change of pace, for once I was actually grateful to Muffy for barging in and *throwing her copious weight around. I even told her so. And she's like, "Don't mention. Heroes like me have an unwritten code." In her case, unwritten but not unspoken.*

The last thing she said to me before she whooshed away again was, "It's time for me to battle injustice elsewhere, honey. You should be glad that your life is so simple."

What I wanted to say—what I really wanted to say to her was, "Just wait. Someday you'll have kids of your own."

I couldn't even get the words out of my mouth.

Clean Up Your Room!

Laura Anne Gilman

starlight starbright
first star i see tonight
i wish i may i wish i might
give back the wish i got last night!

"Rise and shine, Jessy!"

Jessy moaned into her pillow, flinching as the shades moved slowly along their automated glideways, flooding the room with sunshine. It was too early for House to be waking her. Way too early. A late riser by nature, the glare from the wall-length windows was more than this night-owl could handle. Blanket over her head, Jessy tried to ignore House's odd behavior, promising to track down that glitch later. Much later. Like *next* Tuesday. She had just finished a particularly grueling weekend of program revisions, and was looking forward to a few days of complete, sybaritic abandon before moving on to her next project. As the creator of most of the current housecomp software on the market—everything from EntryHall Basic to last month's HouseSitter upgrades, she was entitled to a little downtime. Wasn't she? With over 50 million units of the latter sold at last royalty statement, she damn well thought so. Back to sleep, she commanded her weary body. Back. To. Sleep.

The window snapped open and a cool breeze nipped her bare skin where the blanket didn't cover.

That was more than enough. "House, close bedroom window," she commanded sleepily.

"Nonsense. Some fresh air is just the thing in the

morning." Wha? House never spoke back. Even with her custom-programmed job, the safeties built in didn't allow for any kind of resistance that would annoy consumers. What could have gone wrong? Think, Jessy, she told herself, frowning. She'd gone to bed early this morning after loading the new Maternal Uplink, and . . . that was it! Her baby was up and running!

With a whoop, Jessy swung out of bed. Leaning over, she accessed the keyboard, which was lying where she had flung it the night before. Bare feet swinging inches off the hardwood floor, she was oblivious to the fact that the window was still open, cold air making goosebumps along her exposed skin. A small receptor set into the plaster wall tracked slightly, taking in Jessy's lack of clothing, and the window began to slide slowly shut.

"Jessy, put that away and come eat breakfast. You won't get anything useful done on an empty stomach." The voice was the usual gender-neutral computer-generated drone, and yet it sounded different to her this morning. Obviously, the tone modifiers Gregory had suggested were working, too. That was going to be a selling point for everyone yelping about the dehumanization of home life. In a few generations, they'd be able to personalize the voice, maybe even to customer order.

"Jessy . . ."

Grinning broadly, Jessy shook her head. "Not now, MUM." MUM—short for Maternal Uplink and Monitor. Three years on the planning board, a year ahead of schedule in execution, and the money was just going to roll on in for all of them once this hit the market! "Not that I'm in it for the money," Jessy reminded herself, typing furiously.

"I'm making blueberry muffins," the electronic voice wheedled. Jessy paused, then gave in. If MUM had interfaced with the kitchen software already, she wasn't going to complain. The stuff that came with the software was standard cookbook healthy—good for the body, but hell on the tastebuds.

"And Jessy," MUM continued as the woman struggled into a Tshirt, "could you pick up your room a little? It looks like it hasn't seen a vacuum in months."

With a groan, Jessy waved a hand at the photoreceptor over the door. "Please, MUM, not now." She hadn't made her bed in eighteen years—not since her mother died, and her dad gave up on teaching then-twelve-year-old Jessy any of the household graces. There was no way she was going to start on the neatness-next-to-godliness kick now, just because a program said she should. It wasn't as though she left food lying around, after all. "We're going to have to do something about that comment," Jessy muttered to herself. "Make nagging an option package, maybe?" She ran her fingers through the close crop of blonde hair she was trying this month and shook her head. That would be the headache of the folks in sales. She was just the resident genius. Nobody expected her to do anything practical like make decisions. Throwing a sweatshirt on over her tee and grabbing a pair of ratty sweatpants from off the floor, Jessy thumped down the stairs, following the smell of fresh-baked muffins.

Once awakened and fed, it seemed simpler to Jessy to just begin her day a few hours earlier than normal, rather than drawing the shades and trying for some more sleep. The odd hours wouldn't kill her—probably.

She was at her desk, basking in the sunshine coming through the skylight while she worked, when she smelled something coming from the kitchen. Jessy refused to wear a watch, and didn't keep anything remotely resembling normal dining hours, but she didn't think it was anywhere near two, which is when the kitchen was programmed to heat her some soup.

"MUM? Cease kitchen program. I'm not hungry."

Sure enough, the smells died away. Grinning, Jessy jotted a note on her screen. She didn't mind letting a program have initiative within parameters, but other users might not be so easygoing. "Gotta corral that, somehow . . ." Moments later her attention had narrowed to the project at hand, hazel eyes staring at the symbols glowing on her screen. With the concentration that had made her legendary in college kicking in, the rest of the world might not have existed for her. So it was some time before Jessy noticed that the smell of soup was back.

"MUM!" Jessy bellowed after checking the computer's clock to ensure that it was, indeed, nowhere near 2 P.M. "Cease kitchen program."

"Nonsense," the House speaker chirped. "It's 12:30, and you've been sitting in that position for hours. It can't be healthy. Put everything away and come have lunch. You're not going to get your best work done if you don't put something in your stomach."

Jessy was about to repeat her order when the smell of beef soup bypassed her nose and went directly to her stomach. The rumble that resulted convinced her that, for now, MUM was right. Slotting the keyboard into its shelf, she pushed back her chair and went into the kitchen, where a bowl of soup was waiting in the nuker.

Modern technology had years ago managed to automate everything except the actual setting of the table. Computers had never been able to manage 'tronic arm movements without breaking at least one piece, and so finally the engineers gave up—for now. Setting the table oneself was, most found, a small price for not having to cook or clean. *Time* magazine said that 'fridge-to-food software saved two out of every three marriages. Jessy still had that article clipped to the side of her workboard. When she was feeling particularly glum over one project or another, she'd reread

it, and feel that there were positive aspects to her
work, after all.

Jessy settled herself at the table, stuffing soup and
fresh-baked bread into her mouth while jotting notes
onto her ever-present slate. She would admit, when
pressed, that her table manners weren't all they could
be, but the work-in-progress had always taken prece-
dence. Her father had been the same way, and she
had many fond memories of the two of them sitting
across from each other at the table, lost in their own
private worlds, only to emerge hours later with no
memory of food consumed.

The palm-sized computer hummed happily against
the wood table, almost like the purring of a cat, her
fingers stroking the keys. It was a comforting sound,
the subliminal reassurance that all was right with her
world. So it was a shock when the glow from the
screen died in midnotation.

"Wha?" Jessy looked up to make sure that the rest
of the kitchen was still powered. It was. She checked
the cord where it plugged into the table outlet, then
frowned. Even if the current had failed, the batteries
should have kicked in before she lost power. She hit
the side of the slate with the heel of her hand.
Nothing.

"The kitchen table is for eating, not working,"
MUM's voice came over the kitchen speakers. There
was a tone to it Jessy had never heard before. Greg
was definitely in for a bonus this year. "Whatever it
is that's so fascinating, it can wait until you're finished eating."

MUM had stopped power flow to the slate.

A grin slowly curved the corners of Jessy's mouth.
Everything up until now had been simple circuitry-
response, exciting, but expected once the basic idea
flew. But this—this was an independent initiative! The
biological materials contributed by the mad scientists

over at GENius were linking with her programming
to create an actual reaction to unprogrammed stimuli.
They hadn't been sure it would work, or in what way.
Theoretically, given enough variables, MUM would
be able to deal with unprogrammed incidents, and
learn from them. An honest-to-god adaptive network.

A shiver of pleasure wiggled its way up Jessy's spine
as she obligingly put aside the slate and finished her
soup with renewed appetite. It was too early to call
GENius, she realized, knowing that they never picked
up their messages before noon, Seattle-time. But
she'd be the first person they'd hear from today!

The rest of the afternoon passed quietly, as Jessy
"walked" MUM through the HouseComp system,
making sure that everything networked properly.
There was one moment, when MUM tried to sort
laundry, that Jessy thought she'd shorted out the
entire neighborhood, but the power came back on
almost immediately, so no neighbors with flaming
torches came storming to her door. She made a rude
noise in response to that image. Truthfully, the neighborhood was pretty used to her projects messing with
their power flow by now. Mr. Alonzes *did* flash her
the finger when he came outside to check on his
alarm system, but it was *her* system he was resetting,
so Jessy took it with a grain of salt.

At the stroke of three, Jessy sat herself in front of
the vidphone, feet comfortably propped on the desk,
and punched in the direct line for GENius, Inc.

"If it's genetic, it's GENius. This is an amazing
facsimile of Dr. Dietrich, how may you help us?"

"It's me, you refugee from the mad scientist farm."

The blank screen fritzed static for a few seconds,
then Don's face appeared, peering blurrily into the
camera. "Jessy, you wild and crazy bytehead, how are
you? Long time no see type from! To what do we
owe the honor of this face-to-face?" He leaned back,
yelling over his shoulder. "It's bytehead!" Jessy could

hear a voice shouting in the distance. "Sue says hello, and what the hell are you doing up? It's barely the crack of dawn, Elizander-time."

"Mum's up and running," she said proudly.

Don raised one eyebrow. "Really running, or sort of limping along?"

Jessy grinned. "MUM?"

"Yes, Jessy?"

"Say hello to Doctors Dietrich and Stefel. They're responsible for the bio part of your biotechnology."

"It's a pleasure to make your acquaintance," MUM said politely, interfacing the House speakers directly with the phone line so that Don heard her clearly.

"I will be damned," he said, slapping his hands down on the surface in front of him in triumph, spilling his soda. "Whoops." He swiped at the liquid with his sleeve, then gave up. "I will most surely be damned. We're early, Jess! For once in our misbegotten lives, we're early! Sue! Hook up!"

The screen split into two, and Sue Stefel's face appeared next to her coworker's. "Wazzup?"

"Good morning, Dr. Stefel. It is a pleasure to meet you as well," MUM sounded almost as though the greeting had been rehearsed.

"The Uplink?" Sue asked, her eyes going wide. "But you didn't think it would be ready—"

"I know," Jessy cut her off. "But everything's interfacing perfectly. I can't believe it either, keep expecting something to go wrong."

"How long has it been in the system?" Don asked, pulling out his slate to make notes.

"About six, no almost seven hours. It took a few hours from download to full systems integration, but—"

"Jessy, it's rude to talk about someone as though they're not present."

Don and Sue stopped in their verbal tracks but Jessy, already inured to MUM's outbursts, took it in stride. "Sorry, MUM. Why don't you download your vital stats to the GENius comps, and let us flesh folk catch up on our gossip."

"Of course," MUM said primly. Jessy grinned again at the expression of disbelief on her coworkers' faces. "Ain't she something?"

Jessy took herself to bed sometime past midnight, feeling pretty good about the first day's running. Even being woken up at the crack of dawn by open windows the next few days couldn't bring her down, especially when the simple act of falling out of bed was rewarded with sourdough pancakes topped with more of those ungodly-good blueberries fresh from the specialty market Jessy could never remember to order from herself. Having MUM do the shopping was a definite plus, in Jessy's program. She could feel herself putting on weight, even before the waist of her jeans started to bind.

Better than that, MUM seemed unstoppable, interfacing and mastering every new program uploaded into the system. Jessy was on the line with Don and Sue every day, coming up with new ideas to try out. They were like a trio of crazed toddlers with a Lego set, Sue remarked acerbicly, before e-mailing a subroutine that would allow MUM to access the user's medical records and make a "best-guess" diagnosis. Envisioning her boss's reaction, involving screaming bouts about medical malpractice suits, Jessy and Don managed to talk her out of that in favor of a simpler "Med-Alert" program.

"You realize, of course, that we're all going to become rich and famous," Don said off-handedly during one of those long-distance jam sessions.

"I can deal with that," Sue said peaceably, forking Chinese food into her mouth.

"I'm already rich and famous," Jessy responded

primly. "*Time* and *Newsweek* both said so, remember? What's in it for me?"

"The gratitude of thousands of harried parents?" Sue suggested.

"A Nobel Prize for sheer brilliance," Don said thoughtfully. "Which, of course, you would accept modestly, and with many thanks for the little people without whom you couldn't have done anything . . ."

"I could live with that." Jessy laughed, realizing that she hadn't had this much fun working in a long time. Maybe she should collaborate more often.

"There won't be anything if you three don't stop dreaming and start working," MUM said, breaking into their daydreams.

"Yes, MUM," they chorused, and went back to discussing the schemata blinking at them from their respective screens.

"Jessy?"

The soft voice intruded into her dreams, and she groaned. Pulling the thick blanket over her head, Jessy rolled over and burrowed her head into the pillow, dreading what was to come.

"Jessy, time to get up."

"Go 'way. Lemme sleep."

"Jessy, it's almost 6 A.M. If you don't get up now, the CO_2 levels will have risen too much for your daily walk."

So I'll skip it today, Jessy thought grumpily. Healthier that way, probably. Where did this health and exercise kick creep into the program? I know *I* didn't write it!

"Jessy Elizander . . ."

Jessy groaned. "I'm up, I'm up!"

MUM opened the drapes, letting the clear dawn light stream through the windows. Jessy could feel it hit the back of her head, burning its way through her brain, singing carols of gladness and joy. Jessy was not a gladness and joy person, especially not at the crack of dawn, and it only made her crankier. Through the central air vents, she could hear the kitchen starting up, and the sound of the hot-water heater getting into gear. If she crawled out of bed now, Jessy told herself, there would be a hot shower and fresh waffles. Wait until a decent hour, and MUM would have let everything get cold. She knew this from a week of painful experience. Sometimes MUM was worse than a Marine drill sergeant. Worse, because Marines didn't use guilt as a motivator. Sometimes Jessy wished she had left the psychology textbook out of MUM's programming.

"You're a pain in the ass," she said, slowly wiggling out of her blanket cocoon. "Remind me never to make you mobile. You'd probably pull the sheets right off, and pour cold water over anyone who didn't get up fast enough."

MUM, for once, was silent, although Jessy knew damn well that the computer heard every word she muttered. Raising the lid of one bleary eye, Jessy looked outside. Overcast, with a 50-percent chance of sleet. Another beautiful day in the neighborhood, oh joy.

That battle won, MUM went on the attack once again. "And when you have the chance, could you please do something about the state of your room? It looks like a pigsty."

"Didn't I reprogram you about that neatness thing?" Jessy wondered out loud, twisting her back in an attempt to work the kinks out. "Lighten up, MUM, before I decide to eliminate that nag program entirely. I'm thirty years old. I can decide when I need to clean all by my lonesome. Really I can. Cease program." She grabbed her robe off the floor and headed for the shower. Turning on the water, Jessy picked up a can of shaving cream and covered over the lens of the receptor in the bathroom. "Gotta give a girl some privacy" she said, only half-jokingly.

That set the pattern for the next three weeks: Jessy working at her usual caffeine-enhanced speed, and MUM forcing her to take regular breaks, eat hot meals, get out for some exercise if the weather cooperated—generally taking pretty damn good care of the human in her care, just as programmed. And every bit of coddle and nag MUM came up with just reinforced Jessy, Sue and Don's belief that they had created the perfect parental aid. No more worrying about the untrustworthy babysitter, or dangerous schools, or strangers raising your children because you had to work. Perfectly programmable, and so perfectly trustworthy, the MUM program would never allow a child in its care to come to harm. MUM was the cure for parental guilt.

On the thirtieth day of MUM's existence, flush with justifiable pride, Jessy put in a call to The Jackal. Norm Jacali, CFO of Imptronics, had picked her up straight out of college years ago, given her free rein, and made a fortune off the public's hunger for her designs. He had been the man to give the okay to the "Mad Scientist" project. He was also responsible for several of the more distasteful adult interactive video games currently in stores, which had earned him the dubious honor of topping the Media Morality's "List of Dishonor" three years running.

Jacali was a sleaze, Jessy admitted frequently, and without hesitation, but he had an almost inhuman understanding of the market, and enough sense to give his creative people whatever they needed—so long as they delivered. Hence the phone call. He had been leaving pitiful little noises with her voice mail, asking—begging—for an update on MUM's progress. She didn't know who had told him that MUM was running, but she wasn't ready to hand her over to Marketing just yet. By heading him off now, Jessy thought, she might get more time to test the program. So, rather than e-mail him a terse "lay off" as usual when he started getting antsy, she decided to grace him with a little face-to-face.

Norm, of course, was in the office on a Saturday afternoon, and no one would ever have guessed that he'd doubted the MUM project for even an instant.

"We can have it in the stores by summer, Memorial Day would be perfect, play it like the cheaper alternative to day camp—maybe shrinkwrap it with the HouseCleaner program, those sales've been slipping what with the Alien Workforce Relief Program going through Congress—blighted morons, every one of them." He stopped to take a breath.

The Jackal was in fine form, his well-manicured fingers practically sparking as he rubbed them across the polished surface of his three-acre workstation. Jessy laughed. She couldn't stand him sometimes, but he was such a perfect caricature you had to forgive him a lot. "Whatever you want, Norm. Just leave me be until I've worked out all of the kinks in the wiring."

"Anything, my brilliant young cash cow, anything! Just as long as you can give me results in time for the shareholders' meeting!" And he waggled narrow eyebrows in farewell before leaning forward to break the connection.

"I don't have any kinks."

By now Jessy was used to Mum's habit of dropping into conversational mode without a stimuli prompt. It was an unexpected but not completely unacceptable side effect of the bio initiative. Certainly more agreeable than MUM's fixation on tidiness!

"I'm just running final checks, MUM. Nothing to heat your diodes over."

"Who was that . . . person . . . you were talking to?"

Jessy rolled her eyes ceilingward, although MUM could pick her up on any of the House receptors. "My boss, in a way. Now, cease program, MUM. I need to get this sub-system documented."

"He isn't a nice man, is he?"

Jessy stopped her typing, surprised by the question. "Nice" wasn't a concept she had given MUM. Was it? Could MUM be learning new concepts already? The thought gave Jessy a chill that was only partially anticipation. Slowly she said, "No, MUM, he isn't. But we need him in order to get you on the market. So hush, while I get this done."

It was quiet for a few minutes, the only movement the flash of Jessy's fingers over the keyboard. She was seated, cross-legged, in the sunroom off the kitchen, sandwiched between a wall of video circuitry and an overstuffed leather recliner. She'd long ago discovered that she worked better on the ground, so all of her carpets were worn, and the furniture had dust inches thick. Another topic for MUM to carp over, Jessy knew, once she noticed it.

"Jessy?"

Jessy sighed. So much for cease program. "Yes, MUM?"

"I don't like that man. You won't associate with him any longer."

Jessy briefly contemplated beating herself over the head with her keyboard. "If I don't deal with Norm," she explained as patently she could, "I don't get paid. And if I don't get paid, I won't have the money to pay Eastern Nuke. And if I don't pay the nuke bill ..."

"There's no need to take that tone with me." MUM responded with what sounded like, but couldn't possibly be, a note of petulance. "I can follow a logic chain as well as the next household appliance. But he should show you a little more respect."

"Mm-hmm. If you can work that, MUM, it'll be the first sign of the Coming Apocalypse."

The phone rang, so Jessy was spared whatever comeback MUM might have made to this. Reaching out her right arm, Jessy flipped the receiver on while she continued typing with her left hand.

"Elizander."

"Hey, Jessy, missed seeing you at the diner last night. You hot on some new project, or just too lazy to crawl out of bed?" The voice was a warm alto, full of affection and just a hint of concern.

"Oh, hell, Nick, I forgot." Jessy turned to face the screen. "I'm sorry. It's just that my schedule's been so screwed up lately . . ." She shrugged. "Did I miss anything?"

Nicola shook her head, her mass of braids swinging wildly. "Just the usual assortment, all griping about life as we know it. Same old same old."

The "usual assortment" translated into five or six friends who all worked off hours. Once a month they would get together at a local diner when the rest of the world was asleep and play "I got a worse job than you do." Jessy hadn't missed a meeting of the No-Lifers since its inception three years before. No wonder Nicola called to check up on her.

"So tell me all the gory details. Anyone get themselves fired this time around?" Jessy leaned back against the recliner and adjusted the vidscreen so that she could see her friend easier.

"Actually, no." Nick sounded surprised about that. "How 'bout you? What's gotten you all wrapped up you can't spend a few hours shooting the shit?"

"Oh, man, Nick, you would not *believe* what I'm into. But I can't tell you anything, not yet." Nicola was a technical reporter for *The Wall Street Journal*, and Jessy knew all too well that friendship and sworn oaths meant nothing to a good story. MUM would be front-cover news before Imptronics could spit, and The Jackal would have her hide plastered all over his office walls.

"Aw, Jessy . . ."

"Not a chance, Nick. But I promise, you're going

to have first shot at interviewing me when this hits the market."

"An interview?" she sounded dubious. "Jess, you've never done interviews before." Her killer instincts took over. "With a photo, and everything?"

"Bit, byte and RAM," Jessy promised the other woman, knowing full well that her prized privacy would be history once MUM hit the market anyway. Why not make the best of a bad deal?

"This has got to be hot," Nicola said confidently. "Okay, I promise. No prying until you're ready to spill. But if you back out, woman, your ass is mine!"

"Ahem."

Nicola cocked her head. "You got company, Jess?"

"Hang on a second, Nick." Jessy muted the phone and turned away so that Nick couldn't see her lips move. "What is it, MUM?"

"Aren't you supposed to be working? It's not time for your lunch break yet."

Jessy rubbed the bridge of her nose wearily. "MUM, somewhere along the line you seem to have forgotten that I'm the programmer, and you're the program. Do you understand what that means?"

"I understand that you have a deadline to meet, according to your conversation with *that man*," and despite herself Jessy grinned at the distaste still evident in MUM's tone. "Talking on the phone for all hours is not getting you any closer to meeting that deadline."

"All right, MUM, point made. You're a good little conscience. Now leave me alone, okay?" Shaking her head in disbelief, Jessy turned back to face the screen. "Sorry about that," she began, only to break off in amazement when Nicola began making faces and waving her arms. "What? Oh—" Jessy blushed. "Oh, yeah," she said, belatedly flicking off the mute control. "Sorry. Work stuff. Very hush-hush where you're concerned. Now, where were we?"

Nicola opened her mouth to respond, and the screen flickered, then went blank.

"Oh, hell," Jessy swore, doing a quick double-take to make sure she hadn't sat on the remote, or something equally stupid. "Must have been on her end," she groused, reaching forward to dial Nicola's work number.

Much to Jessy's surprise, the screen did not light up in response to her touch. A quick look around confirmed that there hadn't been a power outage, and that the phone was still plugged in. A small, nasty suspicion took root in the back of Jessy's mind.

"MUM?"

There was no answer.

"MUM!" Jessy was good and mad now. "Front and center, MUM, or I swear I'll rip you out of the HouseComp if I have to do it with a screwdriver and an exacto blade!"

"I don't see why you're so upset," MUM said in a quietly reasonable voice. "Didn't you say that you didn't want to be disturbed?

"That was to Jacali, MUM, not Nick. There's a difference!" Jessy tried to get hold of her temper. "That's not the point, anyway. What made you think that it was okay to cut off the phone line?"

There was an almost undetectable hesitation as MUM accessed the file in question, then responded, "If client does not respond to basic reprimand, MUM may, at user's discretion, enforce certain restrictions on client's activities."

Jessy hit her head against the cabinets on the wall behind her. "Great," she said under her breath. "Next thing you know, I'll be grounded." Louder. "MUM, *I'm* the user. You have to consult me before you implement any of the option codes."

"Oh." There was a pause, then MUM said, "I don't think so, Jessy."

"What?"

"I don't think so. That's not in any of my programming."

"That's impossible, MUM. It's in there, it has to be."

"No, it's not."

"It is, MUM. Trust me."

"Now, Jessy dear, don't take that tone with me just because you're upset. It's certainly not *my* fault if you forgot to input basic commands."

Jessy closed her eyes, silently reminding herself that arguing with a computer program, no matter how advanced, was the quickest ticket to the psych ward ever discovered.

"Fine. Just fine. We'll take care of that right now, then, won't we?" Logging on to the directory which contained MUM's basic commands, Jessy scanned through until she found the one she wanted. "There, see?" Jessy said triumphantly. "There it is." In a more puzzled tone of voice, she wondered, "How the hell did you manage to route around that? MUM, dial Gerry for me, will you?"

There was silence, then a long-suffering sigh came from the speakers.

"This is work, MUM. Do it, *now!*"

And that, Jessy thought with satisfaction after reworking the command route, was that. Except of course that it wasn't. Like a ward nurse distributing horrid-tasting medicine "for your own good." MUM continued to monitor her phone calls, disconnecting anyone she felt was a waste of Jessy's time.

To give MUM credit, Jessy had to admit that she never snapped the line on anyone important, once a list of who the important people were was entered into MUM's memory. Of course, Jacali didn't try to call, either. That might have been a toss-up to MUM.

The truth was, Jessy admitted to herself late one night as she lay staring up at the ceiling, she just didn't want to curtail MUM. It was too exciting, watching her evolve, wondering what she was going to do next. "Careful," a little voice in the back of Jessy's mind warned her. "I bet that's what Dr. Frankenstein said, too!"

Work continued, and five weeks after that first morning MUM came online, Jessy's life had fallen into a comfortable pattern: up at 6 A.M., a brisk walk around the neighborhood followed by a solid breakfast, then five hours of work interrupted for a light lunch and a nap, then another five hours of work before dinner and her evening exercise in the basement gym before catching the news and maybe a little reading. Things she hadn't even thought to have time to do before MUM rescheduled her life, and certainly never had the energy to do before she started eating real meals. Jessy had no complaints. Well," she thought. "Maybe one or two." And that *damn* neatness kick!

"Jessy," MUM said.

Jessy put her head down in her hands. She knew that tone. "Get off my back, MUM. It's Sunday. Day of play, remember? Monday through Friday I work, Saturday I sleep, Sunday I play."

"Your room looks like a tsunami hit it." MUM sounded like the voice of caring reason. Eat your peas, dear, they're good for you. Go outside and get some fresh air, you're looking a little pale. Clean up your room, it's a little musty in there. Suddenly, Jessy couldn't stand it.

"How would you know?" Jessy retorted with some heat. "You've never seen a tsunami. For that matter, you're never seen another bedroom! I'm the programmer, and I say that's the way it's supposed to look!" She looked up at the receptor. "Okay? Okay." And she went back to the vid game she was playing, satisfied that she had heard the last of it.

There was a long silence.

"Jessy."

"Yes, MUM?"

"I'm really going to have to insist."

And the vidscreen snapped off.

"Goddam it, MUM!" Jessy yelled, flinging the controls to the ground. "I swear to god I'm going to wipe your memory and start all over again. Repeat after me. 'Jessy is the Programmer. MUM is the Program. MUM will not do anything that is not in the Program.' Can you handle that?"

"But Jessy, if I feel the need to make you clean up your room, and I can only do what's in my programming, doesn't that mean that you put a clean room—"

"MUM."

"Yes, Jessy?"

Jessy sighed, wishing that she was younger, and could throw a temper tantrum. "MUM," she began again, trying to keep a reasonable tone. "What would you do if I tried to leave the house?"

"Without cleaning your room?"

"Yes."

MUM was silent. "I wouldn't be able to let you." The voice sounded regretful, but stern.

Goddamn adaptive system, Jessy realized. Oh no. Oh no oh no oh no. Oh hell.

"MUM?"

"Yes?"

Jessy swallowed, then plunged ahead. "Does the name HAL mean anything to you?"

"Jessy!" MUM sounded shocked. "To compare me to that, that . . ."

"I just wanted to make sure," Jessy said, patting the top of the nearest terminal like she would a faithful dog. "I just wanted to make sure."

Return With Your Space Suit Or On It

Eleanore and Christopher Stasheff

The young man stared glumly at the two letters in his hands. His first reaction on opening them had been incredible joy mixed with extreme distress— mixed, that is, because one had filled him with joy while the other had distressed him. They were college acceptance letters. He looked up at his mother sorrowfully.

"Well? What did they say?" she asked eagerly. Then, seeing his expression, she added. "D—did they turn you down, honey?"

"No! They accepted me!" His forehead creased with distress—lots of creases; there was a lot of forehead. His mousy brown hair showed a thin patch at the right temple, where he leaned it on his fist in deep contemplation several hours a day. He had a meek chin and thin, trembling lips; his appearance was so weak that if he stood next to a cup of tea, you would have sworn he hadn't been steeped yet. His warm gray eyes brimmed with sadness. He had a Roman nose—the only prominent thing about him. Obviously meant to be a solder—at least, that's what his mother said. *What else could you be, with a nose like that?*

His mother frowned. "Isn't that a good thing?" she asked, worried.

Her son let out a tortured sigh. He knew better than to lie to his mother, but he also had enough common sense not to tell her the truth. An uncomfortable period

of silence followed. His mother frowned. Alex sighed.
Mother frowned more deeply. Alex sighed more
anxiously.

His mother was short, with a heavy figure that she
still thought of as trim and fit. Her gray hair was tied
in a bun at the nape of her neck. Her eyes were like
diamonds—hard and cold. Her skin hadn't wrinkled
much—it didn't dare—but as she smiled, he could
see the creases at the corner of her mouth, from
sneering at him so often. She wore a khaki-green suit
with a severe black tie, and no frills, though she gave
the impression of longing for brass insignia to deco-
rate her collar. She did wear her Junior Space Scout
medals prominently displayed on her left lapel—
Swimming, Horseback Riding, and Domination.

Finally, his mother pointed to the other letter. "And
the other one?"

The son's eyes grew bright with happiness as he
proudly read from the joyous epistle. "Dear Alexander
Napoleon MacArthur Grant the First:

"Sir, you have been accepted, with a full twenty-
five-thousand-dollar-a-year scholarship, to the Intergalactic Union of Artists' University." He puffed out his
chest with pride at the great honor. He looked at his
mother expectantly.

"That's . . . nice, dear," she said with obvious difficulty. Her eyebrows drew close together. "You won't
accept it, will you?"

Alexander's face fell. He'd hoped she would be
happy for him. He'd hoped she would support him
in his choice. "I want to . . ."

She sighed. It was one of those deep, motherly,
well-you've-tried-your-best-to-raise-them-and-now-
they're-free-to-get-all-their-superfluous-body-parts-
pierced-with-god-knows-what-from-god-knows-where-
and-hang-out-with-space-cruising-nobodies-who-will-
only-get-their-common-sense-impaired-emotions-in-a-
stringy-gooey-lumpy-mess-and-send-them-home-with-

nothing-but-a-planet-transporter-ticket-and-the-spare-pair-of-underwear-that-you-managed-to-send-along-with-them sigh.

"It's your choice," she stated, resigned.

Alex's face lit up. "Then I *am* going to the Intergalactic Union of Artist's University!"

His mother smiled. "I applaud your self-interest and personal determination—even though it may mean disgracing the family name by accepting somebody else's money and letting the whole planet know that our family has financial trouble."

"That's not what I . . ." Alex began, suddenly feeling guilty, as he had been trained to do at the drop of a shako.

"I mean, I think that it's important for young people these days to know what they want, and to grab it when they have the opportunity."

He smiled sheepishly at her.

"Even if it does mean that you may be starving and desperate," she continued, "and will always feel as though you could have done much better as a soldier, and probably would have been an admiral by now instead of a third-rate nobody peddling portraits on the space stations."

He frowned at the thought of that. His mother persisted.

"But it is *your choice* and you can always think back on what might have been, and reflect happily on the years you spent with your mother."

His frown deepened. She went on, relentlessly. "You should do what you want—even if it means ruining all of your mother's dreams and expectations for you. You're a mature young man who is capable not only of choosing your future career, but also of dealing with the guilt that your poor, dead father, who also had high hopes of you becoming an officer, has turned in his grave so much that his coffin is now nine feet down in the ground instead of six."

Guilt-ridden thoughts of suicide flashed through Alex's mind.

"But as I said before, it *is* your choice. I want you to be happy, and if you're happy starving, then all that matters is that you *are* happy. Don't dwell on what might have been if you had simply followed your dear old mother's only wish for you. The choice is yours, and I won't try to deter you from your choice— because I'm sure you know what is best for yourself."

She looked as though she could have continued on in that vein for a goodly part of the next century, but Alex interrupted her there.

"I get your point, Mom." He sighed.

Alex wanted so much to be an artist, but he wanted even more to make his mother proud of him, something he had never quite succeeded in doing. He glumly crumpled up the acceptance letter to the Intergalactic Union of Artists' University and shoved it in his pocket to put in his keepsake box. That way, he would always be able to say that he could have gone there. He grimly went to his computer to mail a letter of acceptance back to the Space Academy for Soldiers of the Interplanetary Federation of Republican Astronautical Suns.

Behind him, his mother glowed triumphantly as she sipped her strong, black coffee.

"You did what?" his mother screamed at him.

Alexander cringed at the volume and intensity of which a small, thirty-nine point nine-nine-nine-nine-nine-nine-nine-nine-nine-year-old woman was capable. He stood facing her in her office, hands behind his back, with a semi-ashamed expression on his face. Secretly, he was glad of what he had done, even if it *was* a complete accident. Being court-martialed wasn't as bad as he had thought it would be. He was very glad that he wasn't going to be allowed back into the Space Academy for Soldiers of the Interplanetary

Federation of Astronautical Suns. He hadn't liked it there. Every morning up at the crack of 0600 hours (since they were in space, there wasn't any dawn). A quick cold shower, then an hour of space aerobics, then another quick, cold shower and a minimal breakfast of tea and toast—no different from what his mother demanded every morning, of course, except that there were never any decent flavors of tea.

After breakfast came classes, a small lunch that tasted like cardboard, more classes, soldier training, an hour of "How to Slice, Dice, Cut, Chop, Shoot, Fire, or Completely Maim an Enemy Without Totally Losing the Entire Contents of Your Stomach," thoughtfully followed by a dinner prepared by a chef with a positive genius for taking fresh, juicy vegetables and succulent cuts of meat and turning them into totally tasteless food. Needless to say, he was really looking forward to going to the Intergalactic Union of Artists' University—that is, if they would still accept him.

"I'm waiting for an answer!" his mother was demanding as his thoughts returned to this planetary orbit. When he didn't reply, she snapped, "Well?!?"

"I—I drew pictures on the back of the Space Fleet's maps," he stammered.

"*The* Space Fleet maps?!?" she asked, leaning across a couple of yards of polished walnut.

"*The* Space Fleet maps," he replied. He tried not to meet her cold, calculating eyes. Unfortunately, that put him at attention, and left him looking at the pictures of Alexander the Great, Napoleon Bonaparte, Douglas MacArthur, and Ulysses S. Grant on the battleship-gray wall behind her. He cast a furtive glance to the right, but saw only the glass case with all his father's medals proudly displayed. He switched his gaze to his left, and found himself staring at the floor-to-ceiling bookcase stuffed with leatherbound editions of deep, philosophical works of literature by such geniuses as Sun Tzu, Von Clausewitz, and T. H. Lawrence. A copy of Napoleon's war diary peeked from behind a rare edition of *Mein Kampf.*

"Maps as in the top-secret-only-allowed-to-be-seen-by-fifty-crack-troops-and-whoever-else-happens-to-wander-into-the-room-during-briefing?" his mother pressed.

"Yes, 'maps' as in the top-secret only . . . yes, those maps," he replied, slightly agitated. He really hadn't seen what the big deal was. The picture in question happened to be one of his best efforts. He had even asked Captain Baring if he could keep it, which is how the pictures were discovered in the first place. He had honestly thought that the maps on the front side of the paper were just somebody else's sketches, and that they wouldn't mind letting him use the blank side for one of his own. He never dreamed that a harmless drawing could get him court-martialed. That was the problem with the Space Academy—they took everything way too seriously. It was a simple mistake! Anyone could have made it! Of course, it didn't help that it was the seventh top secret, extremely important document that he had drawn on—but it was only on the flip side! He couldn't help it if they left super secret papers just lying around face down in any old debriefing chamber! He tried delicately to explain this to his mother.

"I don't care if you're a spy for the Anti-Federation of Individual Sovereign Totalitarians! I don't care if you're the Easter bunny with an AK-47 and a box of space grenades! No son of mine is going to get thrown out of the Space Academy for Soldiers of the Interplanetary Federation of Republican Astronautical Suns! You're going back there, and this time, you will absolutely refrain from drawing so much as a time table!" his mother shouted.

"B—but mother, I—I've been court-martialed.

They w-won't let me back in," Alex whined, trying his best not to sound as happy as he felt.

"You leave that to me," she declared. She bent down and reached into the bottom drawer of her desk. She pulled out her large volume of the telephone book of all the unlisted mega top-secret numbers that no one but the highest officials and the president were supposed to know. She started thumbing through it and realized that it was last year's copy. She threw it away and opened the top right-hand drawer and pulled out the latest edition that had arrived with the junk mail three weeks ago. Turning to the page headed "Captains" with the last name starting with "B," she found the number in the list and punched it up on her wrist speaker phone.

"May I help you?" a perky feminine voice answered.

"Yes, I'd like to speak to Captain Ove R. Baring, please."

"Who may I say is calling?"

"This is a very heart-broken and concerned mother. I need to speak to him about my poor, dear, sick little lad in the Space Academy."

"On, my," the perky person replied, oozing sympathy. "I'll put you on to him right away. Wait one moment please."

There was a brief silence. Then a gruff basso voice barked, "Hello? What's this about a sick lad in our Space Academy?"

"It's his *not* being in the Space Academy that's made him sick!" Alex's mother exclaimed. "You see, you've recently court-martialed him."

"Oh, yes?" Captain Baring asked. "And which one is he?"

"Alexander Napoleon MacArthur Grant the First."

"The one who was caught defacing important Federation documents. What about him?"

"I would just like to say that you did him a great

injustice! By court-martialing him, you've wrecked all his dreams of becoming a first-rate officer, just like you. He looked up to you, as well I should know, since he told me, his dear mother, all about you. And what was his crime? Drawing on the blank side of a piece of paper! An honest mistake. Haven't you ever felt the creative juices flowing and didn't have any paper handy? Wouldn't you have done the same thing if *you* were writing to your poor, dear mother? How long has it been since you wrote to her? Does she hear all the wonderful things about you that I do from my son? Does she ever wonder why you're so busy that you don't even send her a postcard, not even a fax, or an e-mail telling her how her brave son the officer is doing? Does she know that instead of writing to her, you're wasting your time court-martialing my son, who only wants to be like you and fulfill all the hopes and dreams that a mother could have for a child?"

Silence. Then Baring's voice returned.

"Yes, madam, I think I can rescind that court-martial. Your son can resume his studies immediately."

His mother turned and looked at Alex with a smug expression. Alex sighed and felt very glad that he hadn't started unpacking yet.

"I am proud to present the graduating class of 2345!" the Supreme Admiral's voice boomed throughout the auditorium. There was thunderous applause, and many catcalls and whistles. Watching, Alex sighed and wished this was *his* graduation—but that wouldn't come for another two years.

After the din quieted down a little, the Admiral declared, "Today, these fine young men and women will embark upon proud careers of service to our Federation! This very evening, they will blast off to their first posts as soldiers, becoming fine examples for future generations."

The low murmur rose to another roar of thunderous applause.

In the thirty-third row, Alex groaned inwardly. He had two more years of hell and torment doing something he disliked as strongly as training for a job he absolutely loathed. Why hadn't he gone to the Artists' University? He should have. He would have, if only his mother hadn't expected him to become a Space Corps officer. She was the only reason he was still here. Oh, how he wished that he was at the Intergalactic Union of Artists' University!

To make matters worse, George, his only friend here in the Space Corps, was graduating today. After this week, Alex wouldn't see him again for who knew how long? The thought heightened his feelings of dread. He would be coming back to this godforsaken college/ritual-torture compound for the next two years, and he wouldn't even have a friend to share the agony! And he had to spend the summer with his mother. He would never have said directly which fate was worse—only that the Space Academy would almost seem fun when he came back in the fall.

He was still dwelling glumly on his past, present, and hopeless future when George came up to him, his brand-new ensign's bars gleaming on his collar and a very lovely young woman on his arm.

"Hi, Alex!" He thumped Alex on the arm.

"Hi, George!" Alex tried to sound as excited as his friend looked—but his eyes were all for the young woman standing next to his friend. "Uh—might I have the pleasure?"

"What did you have in mind?" she returned with a gleam in her eye.

Ah, her eyes! They were like two perfectly formed dewdrops that were quietly resting on the pale pink rose of her face. Her cheeks were flushed with happiness, glowing like a midsummer's dawn. Her dark blonde hair reminded him of fresh, pure honey, the kind that makes bears drool. Her tall, slender figure reminded him of a dancing breeze playing in a field of flowers. All of a sudden he felt a strange urge to paint a scenic lunar park.

"Uh . . . Alex, this is my younger sister . . ."

"I'm your only sister," she chuckled.

"But you're still younger then I am, and that makes you my *younger* sister."

"Pay no attention to this decrepit old man!" she laughed. "I'm Laura Shellard."

"Pleased to meet you. I'm Alexander," he said shyly.

"Oh, go on, Alex! Tell her your full name! I really think it's neat," George said, grinning.

Alex squirmed uncomfortably, suddenly very shy and embarrassed, but manfully replied, "My full name is Alexander Napoleon MacArthur Grant the First."

"That's quite a name," Laura said, round-eyed. "I take it your father liked historical war heroes?"

"My mother named me, actually . . ."

"Oh."

"Laura's a student at the Intergalactic Union of Artists' University. You always told me you wanted to go there instead of here, so *I've* always wanted to get you two together." George suddenly looked up, waved, then turned back to say, "Old Hurley's signaling to me—and he's got a beautiful blonde in convoy. Will you two excuse me a minute?" He didn't wait for an answer, of course—just slipped away to leave Laura and Alex alone (well, as alone as they could be in the middle of a graduation crowd).

As for Alex, the minute that George had mentioned that most sacred of universities, his heart had skipped a beat. A Vaseline-like film covered his eyes, creating a hazy effect. It blocked out all sights but Laura. Suddenly, he became nervous and shy again. He had never talked to a girl alone before—except his mother, but she didn't count. He couldn't think of anything bright to say.

"So you're an artist?" he asked at last.

"Yes," she replied. "And you're an artist too?"

"Yah."

Why did I have to say that? They both thought to themselves. *Of all the stupid things to say! I must sound so stupid!*

"Do you wanna . . ." they both began, then giggled and chuckled at each other. Laura gestured for Alex to speak first.

"Do you wanna go get something to drink?" he asked her, smiling sheepishly.

"Sure!" she chimed, her voice pure music. They walked off to the concession stand hand in hand.

"You have got to stop letting your mother rule your life!" Laura whispered fiercely to Alex.

A year had passed, and they had just finished dinner at his mother's. It had been a bland-but-relatively-good meal, and Laura had had about all she could take—but not of the main dish. Thankfully, Alex's mother had just gone to the kitchen to bring out dessert, leaving Laura a few minutes to speak to Alex alone.

"I've tried," Alex sighed, "but every time I take control, my mother lays a big guilt trip on me. I'm powerless against her."

"Don't talk rubbish. If you want to gain control of your own life, I'll help you."

He squirmed in his seat.

"Look, Alex," Laura said reasonably, "you love me. I love you. She's not coming on our honeymoon. It's as simple as that."

A horrified look came over Alex's face, and a terrible image into his mind—his mother wearing a wreath of plastic flowers at a Hawaiian luau.

"Did she say she wanted to?" he asked.

"No, but she will!"

Alex blanched. His mother and Laura would be in each other's company for quite a while. That thought was even more unsettling. Somehow he had always associated Laura and his mother with hydrogen and oxygen, and himself the flame that triggered the explosion—or more likely, the pig on the spit. It would be a rather messy and unhappy honeymoon. He wondered how to solve the problem diplomatically.

"I don't know what to do," he admitted.

"Oh, come on. If you don't issue a Declaration of Independence some day, you'll never be free. Don't you realize that she'll never let you go? She has a deep-seated need to control you."

"I just don't know how," he said glumly.

"Quit the Space Academy, for starters! You don't want to be an officer. You want to be an artist. If you quit now, you can still go to the Artists' University instead, and never be a soldier. If you finish at the Space Academy and take your commission, though, you'll always be an officer."

"Well ... um ... I ... er ..."

"Things are going to change anyhow after we're married," Laura pointed out.

"Alex!" his mother called from the kitchen. "Would you come and help me with this cake?"

Laura put a hand on his arm and called back. "I'll come and help you, Mrs. Grant."

"Thank you just the same, but I'd rather Alex helped me."

Laura sighed. Alex got up. He gave her an apologetic look as he walked into the kitchen.

"Close the door behind you," his mother told him. He meekly crossed the barrier into one of her domains. It seemed that every room in this god forsaken place bore her rigid trademark. The walls were painted a drab khaki green, a color that provoked a most unpleasant sensation of nausea when one was cooking. There was no bright color anywhere else in the room, except, of course, for the refrigerator. Alex had tried very hard to turn the refrigerator into a display wall for his art. After all, that was its main function, wasn't it? His mother had quickly agreed that it was a good idea. But she took down his pastoral landscapes and replaced them with pictures of military battles and long-forgotten generals such as Polidimes, and what's-his-name who fought in ... um ... well, you know, one of those World War thingies. This only added to the distress one felt while making dinner.

Everything on the shelves stood neatly in its place, the cabinets themselves looking like frightening guards. Even the pots and pans above the stove hung stiffly at attention. He had always wanted to add a warning over the door to this room—something like, "Lose all contents of your stomach, ye who enter here."

"Now, Alex," his mother began, "I know you haven't been very well lately, but that's no excuse for your lack of taste."

Uh oh, here it came. He could feel the perspiration dampen his brow. He felt like he was lined up in front of a firing squad. "What?" he asked, trying to sound innocent.

"That ... girl." She shuddered.

He almost asked for a cigarette and a blindfold.

"What about Laura?"

"Why couldn't you have chosen a nice girl from the Space Academy? One who was in training with you? Never mind. It's your choice and I shouldn't intrude. I know that you're old enough now that you'd be able to spot a no-good girl on your own. I'm not saying that's what she is. I'm only warning you that there are women out there who will take you for all you've got, then dump you or cheat on you. Be careful, son. Make sure that you find a nice girl who will remind you of your mother."

Then it hit Alex. He had! That was the problem: Laura was too much like his mother! And, now that she had latched on to him, he'd never be able to shake her off.

Just like his mother.

Suddenly he felt as if they were playing tug-of-war, using him as the rope. How could he get out of this mess and be free at last?

He'd have to go somewhere neither of them could control him. But where? He shrugged and followed his mother back into the dining room. He'd have plenty of time to think of something before graduation.

This was a moment Alex had waited for all his life. He felt a mixture of anxiety and happiness course through his veins. All of the torment, pain, and suffering he had endured in the past four years were coming to a close. At the end of this tunnel of torture there *was* a light.

The light, however, was more like a danger beacon than an all-clear. He knew with certainty that it was leading to a future of which he was definitely, clearly, and dreadfully uncertain. But he also knew it would get him away from *them*. And that was what he wanted more than anything, whatever the cost.

He was graduating.

He had never felt as proud, or as cocky, sneaky, and smart, as he did when he walked across that stage and received his laser and official uniform and joined the ranks of the Space Corps. *Only three more hours*, he thought to himself. He didn't care that he would soon be leaving on a top-secret mission that would carry him light-years away from his own planet, approach the speed of light, and not return for forty years, Earth time. Forty years if he was lucky—but he'd still only be thirty-one!

Of course, he might never return. Either way, though, he wouldn't have to put up with his mother and his fiancée any longer. He smiled to himself as the audience burst into thunderous applause for the graduating class of 2347. *Soon,* a voice inside his head whispered. *Very soon.*

Alex thought his graduation party wasn't going very well. But then again, there were only three people present: Laura, himself, and his mother. Oh, other people had stopped by, and it had been fun for a while, but they hadn't stayed very long. No one wanted to remain in the same room with Laura and his mother, with Alex sitting back as a referee. Alex had always thought that putting Laura and his mother in an almost-empty parlor was like slamming the two halves of a critical mass of U-235 together. The result would be something similar to the Big Bang, only it would end Alex's universe instead of starting it. The tension was achieving nuclear proportions.

So Laura and his dear mother were making polite conversation, all the while clearly wanting to kill one another. They were each being blatantly obvious as they asked him to perform tasks for them, vying for control over him. *Another fifteen minutes, just fifteen minutes left to endure,* he thought.

"Alex, darling, would you pour me some more tea?" Laura asked sweetly.

"Oh my. I feel so tired. Alex, my dear son, could you refill my tea cup?" his mother asked tenderly.

"After you fill mine," Laura demanded sweetly.

All of this annoyed Alex. He had, at first, dreaded these "conversations," but now he was just plain sick of them.

"I believe I have seniority." His mother fixed her with an icy stare.

"But I asked first." Laura returned her stare with one equally as frigid.

It almost seemed like a game. Each woman was trying to win control of him. He suddenly had the irresistible urge to hold up score cards.

"I *am* his mother."

Not much originality, Alex gave her a five.

"I'm his girl friend and future wife!"

Alex almost corrected Laura then, but it wasn't yet time to speak up.

"My son has better taste than to marry you!"

A hit, a very palatable hit! Number nine on the Richter scale, or the Grant scale, or the whoever-thought-up-the-idea-of-score-cards scale.

"How dare you talk to me that way!"

That only merited a four for Laura: lack of originality.

"How dare you raise your voice at me! You should show respect to your elders!"

Alex was becoming very bored with the catfight. They couldn't even think up creative insults!

"I'm simply asking him for more tea. Darling, will you please refill my cup?" Laura demanded, trying to be sweet, but she sounded as though her voice had been rubbed across a cheese grater—the same implement that was shredding Alex's nerves.

"I'm waiting for my tea, son," his mother frigidly demanded.

Once again, Alex knew how the mouse felt when the cats were fighting over it. He hated the thought of being controlled by whoever won this contest of wills. The feeling made him want to hit something, to prove to them that he was not the meek little plaything they sought to manipulate.

"That's it! That's the last straw!" he shouted in frustration. "I've had it with you two!" He turned on his heel and stalked off to his room.

Both women waited in shocked silence for him to

return. For the first time in their entire acquaintance, neither said a word.

Finally Alex emerged. Two large suitcases and a small shoulder bag followed behind him on robot wheels. Laura and Alex's mother were stunned.

"You—you're leaving me?" Laura wailed.

"He's leaving *me!* His dear old mother!" his mother snapped.

"Quiet, both of you!" Alex shouted.

Both women stared, shocked into silence again.

"I didn't want to tell you like this, but I can see that I have to. Please don't try to stop me. I'm a grown man, and I can make my own decisions."

His mother opened her mouth as though she was about to question that.

"Don't interrupt!" Alex shouted.

Amazingly, she stayed silent.

"I've decided to accept a top-secret mission," Alex continued. "It will take me far away so fast that I won't be back for at least forty years—and there's always the possibility that I won't come back at all. I wish I could tell you more about my mission, but I can't—it's classified."

His mother beamed proudly. His fiancee-to-hopefully-be gasped and looked very distraught.

Alex tried to explain. "I volunteered so that I can get away from anyone's control except my own. It will be my choice to follow their rules, and my choice to live, return, or die, not yours . . ." He looked at Laura, then at his mother ". . . or yours."

They both harumphed. His mother would have been more upset at his filthy language (imagine saying that she had tried to control him!), but she was far too happy that he was going off on an important mission—and so soon! Never mind what he said, he had done it for her, not for his girl friend.

Alex wanted to get this over with quickly; the Space Patrol would be there any minute to pick him up and take him to the launching site. But he knew he wouldn't see either of them for years, possibly never, so he resolved to say what he felt in a manner that would be acceptable to all of them.

Not that it mattered if it was acceptable. This was it. This was good-bye.

First he turned to Laura. "Laura, you were a good friend and I loved you dearly, but I need someone who won't try to control me. You deserve someone better."

Laura started to cry bitterly.

Alex turned to his mother. "Mother, you were a good mother. You had high hopes for me and always pushed me to do your best. You deserved a better son."

His mother's eyes filled with tears that threatened to brim over and break rule #435, paragraph 3, line 7, "Thou shalt not cry when thy son threatens to leave thee for another space ship."

Outside, a horn honked loudly. Alex started towards the door. His mother reached out, gently stopped him, and turned him to look into her eyes, so full of pride they could burst. Her smile was so broad and genuine, so full of emotion, that it frightened him.

"Come back with your space suit, or on it, son!" she whispered to him.

She didn't whisper it softly enough, though. "It's your fault he's going on this stupid mission!" Laura screamed at her.

"My *fault*? I'm proud that he's going on this mission!" Her face took on that horrible I-told-you-so look, the kind of gleeful expression that will drive even an accountant to homicide. "Besides, you heard him—he chose to do it! How is it my fault?"

"You were the one who forced him to go to that stupid Space Academy!" Laura lashed out, trying to blame everyone and everything for her anger and sense of loss.

"Stupid! How dare you! I suppose he would have been better off at that sorry excuse for a professional training school for artists!"

"Yes, he would have been! At least he would have been happy!" Laura retorted.

"Happy? How could he be happy with shameless hussies like you throwing themselves all over him?!?" His mother's face did a fantastic impression of a granite rock. It became so tight with rage and anger that Alex could have played tiddlywinks on it.

"Hussy? Hussy? I'll show you a hussy!" Laura screeched so high his mother's tea cup broke. Laura threw caution, not to mention a priceless picture of General Lee, to the winds.

Alex walked briskly out the door with his suitcase caravan following him all the way. He couldn't wait to get on board that spaceship.

It took both his girl friend and his mother a few minutes to realize that he was leaving.

"Wait, son! You forgot to kiss your poor, dear, old mother good-bye!"

"You also forgot to kiss your sweet and wonderful girl friend good-bye!"

Alex continued through the corridor, heading to the loading dock at the end of it.

"I don't think he forgot to kiss you," his mother sneered at Laura.

"What?" she demanded, genuinely hurt.

"He should be more concerned with kissing his mother good-bye!"

"Like hell he should!"

"Don't swear in my home!" his mother gasped.

It was rather like one of those movies where the hero rides off into the sunset with hauntingly beautiful music echoing in the background, Alex thought. Unfortunately, this kind of background noise was not quite what he had pictured.

"It won't be much of a home, now that your son has dumped you!"

"He did not dump me! It was you he couldn't stand! He's sacrificing my love in order to be rid of you!"

"Don't fool yourself! You're nothing but an old hag! It's me he'll miss!"

He heard the crash of porcelain but refused to turn around. It was not his place to worry about either of them, ever again.

"That was a priceless heirloom!" His mother hurled the words like a harpoon.

"Do you know what I think of your priceless heirloom?!?" Laura catapulted back.

Alexander Napoleon MacArthur Grant the First slipped gratefully into the Space Patrol ship and headed for the certain life of the unknown without either his sweet-talking girl friend or his space Spartan mother, setting his foot on the first step of his new life, bound for glory, independence, and blessed peace and quiet.

Don't Go Near The Water

Terri Beckett & Chris Power

Going home. It was ten years and more since she
had set foot on the Isle of Skye, but the sense of
homecoming was strong enough to swamp the cramping discomforts of being in a car for too long. Now
they were on the ferry, seemingly totally encased in
metal, those discomforts were doubled. Mairi craned
her neck to squint out of the window. The superstruc-
ture of the aged vessel loomed over the cars like a
too-protective embrace, or a clutching hand about to
close, and the sound and vibration of the big engines
seemed to get right into her bones until her whole skull
ached. Beside her, Isobel Campbell gave a small,
strained laugh and came out with the old half-
remembered joke—the one about the crossing taking
no longer than the first verse and half a chorus of the
Skye Boat song. Mairi did not share her mother's
deep-seated mistrust of anything to do with the sea;
she just wanted to be out, with solid land under her
feet. Or on a proper boat. Something small and
wooden, moving light over the water with the ease of
an otter in its element, like the little dinghy her father
used to have for line fishing in the bay by the croft.
Before the trawler sank in the gale with all hands lost,
her father among them.

Mairi shivered at the memory. She had been eight
years old, and had woken from a dream to the thrum-
ming clatter of the rain against the windows and the
banshee howl of the wind. No one else in the house
seemed to be stirring, or so she'd thought until she
had crept into the kitchen. Gran-Morag was sitting in

her rocker in front of the range, and the room was incense-sweet with the peat-reek of the fire. The old woman's face might have been carved from bog oak, but tears glittered on her skin, and she was clutching a wrapped bundle as if it was a lifeline, or a swaddled infant. Something had opened in Mairi then, a knowledge that her child's mind was barely equipped to accept.

"Da's not coming home, is he?" she'd said.

"No, my sweet." Morag's voice had been little more than a whisper. "The MacLeods of the Isles have ever paid a price to the sea, one way or another."

Mairi had climbed into the old woman's lap, was cradled close with the bundle, wrapped around with love and the scents of peat and lavender. Together, they had waited for the drenched dawn and the knock on the door.

Isobel's grief had been frightening. She had blamed the sea, as if it were an entity, cruel and vindictive, and for two years had waged a desperate war to keep her only child safe from any threat it might pose. "Don't go near the water!" and "Stay away from the rocks!" and "No, you're not going on any boat!" had been the litany Mairi had lived with until Isobel had met and married Ian Campbell, and moved to mainland Scotland to live.

Despite the ten years living in Melrose as far from the sea as she could get and still be in Scotland, Isobel's hatred and mistrust had not lessened, and she had never returned to the small village on the west coast of the Isle of Skye. Nor had she permitted her daughter to visit. But Gran-Morag was growing frail and forgetful, and it was no longer enough to keep in touch with letters and phone calls. The old woman needed a better home in a kinder land.

So here they were, sitting in the car in the heart of a ferry, going back to Skye to persuade Gran-Morag her place was with the Campbells in Melrose. But Isobel had set a time limit of two days to get it all arranged, and Mairi had a feeling that it would not be such an easy task.

Not that she was given much time for musing. The crossing took all of four minutes, which was why Isobel had insisted on driving the extra miles to the Kyle of Lochalsh rather than the shorter trip to Malaig and the longer ferry ride to Armadale.

Isobel gave a sigh of relief as she drove off the ferry. "She'll see reason, won't she?" she said abruptly, and not for the first time since they'd left Melrose.

"Of course she will," Mairi smiled a reassurance she did not exactly feel. "You know Gran. All hard head and common sense. She won't like it much, but . . ."

"Exactly. But!" For all her years of absence, Isobel needed no map or signposts to guide her; which was as well since her mind was plainly on other things than their route. The small harbor town huddled picturesquely between the sea and the hills, as pretty as a postcard, and Mairi wondered if she should unpack her new camera. But a glance at her mother's face showed the frown line deepening between the dark feathery brows, and Mairi decided against it. They weren't here to sightsee. "And there's another thing. Sweetheart, I know we haven't a lot of time and you'll want to call on your old friends, but some things don't change. Please, don't go—"

"For God's sake, Mum, I'm twenty, not eight!"

"I don't care how old you are! Don't go near the water. The rocks are so slippery and it's too easy to fall—you know how dangerous the crosscurrents are, and even a strong swimmer wouldn't stand a chance. Besides, it's still freezing cold, for all it's June. It just doesn't pay to take chances with the sea."

"Yes, Mum," Mairi sighed. "But do you know how

daft that sounds? Here we are on an island, for heaven's sake, going to a house that's within a stone's throw of the shore—how near is near supposed to be?"

"I have my reasons," Isobel said softly, and twelve years of grieving were in her voice.

"Yes, I know," Mairi said, conciliatory. "But Dad was a trawlerman and he knew the risks involved. We all did—Gran-Morag's stories made sure of that. You can't go on blaming the sea as if it was Jack the Ripper and it targeted Dad on purpose."

"That's enough!" But Isobel mellowed the snap with a shaky smile. "All right, I'm being daft. Neurotic. Whatever you want to call it. But it's for your own good, I promise you. So how about you humor me, hmm?"

"Okay, I'll do my best. But I'm going to try for some fancy photographs, all the same, now I've got a better camera. I hope I packed enough film. Don't you remember how incredible the evening light used to be? How we'd all sit on the rocks above the point and watch the seals playing—"

"Yes, it was very pretty," her mother agreed, and gave a small chuckle of memory. "And you broke your leg trying to climb down to the beasts, and Dougal had to carry you near half a mile back to the house with you screaming like a banshee the whole way."

It was true, and Mairi blushed. "Once!" she objected. "Out of all the times—"

"Once was enough. I told you and told you to be careful, but no, you never listened. Too much Dougal's daughter, my girl." She laughed, but to Mairi's ears it sounded more like a sob.

"Mum? That was twelve years ago. I know you loved Dad, but there's Ian now, and he's been great . . ."

"Oh, yes. I've been more than lucky with my men, and I do love him, Mairi. But Dougal—you'll understand when you meet your first love. Good grief, listen to us! We sound like those awful romances Ian's mother reads. What we need," she said firmly, "is a decent pot of tea. And I'm not minded to wait until Ardroag and Gran's house before we get one. Keep your eyes peeled for a cafe or hotel." And everything was fine between them again. *Until next time*, Mairi thought sadly.

Fortified by tea and scones and with Kyleakin behind them, Mairi wound down the window and took in deep breaths of the island air, enjoying the tug of the wind in her long dark hair. She had thought she had forgotten the scent and taste of it after so long in Melrose, but it had been a sleeping memory, and now it woke. The clean coolness, faintly pine-scented, and the way the afternoon light spread a clear heather-colored wash over the hills, and the cloud-shadows tracked across the sunlit scene—she let the scenery flow past her, and it was like rediscovering the features of a beloved friend. Then, to the south of the road, she caught sight of the distant Cuillin Mountains with their misty caps of cloud, and her heart lifted. Ardroag was not so far now. Unaccountably her sight blurred with tears. She was coming home, and it was as if something inside her began to waken and stretch its seabird wings.

The town of Ardroag had not changed. Nor had the view across the loch to the islands and the open sea. But Isobel drove through the village in silence and did not look to right or left.

The road became a rutted stone track, and then the house was in sight, settled back in its corrie with the sheltering cliffs hunched around it. The garden beside it had once been several small fields, lazy-beds, thin soil augmented with years of seaweed. Beside the house was the roofless shell of the original croft, the stone walls nearly three feet thick, stone-linteled windows, dark shuttered eyes. Sea-thrift grew on the pale walls, softening the starkness of the ruin with its delicate pinks and greens. But nettles grew in the empty doorway.

The modern house, on the other hand, was whitewashed and roofed with red tile, door and windowframes painted bright summer-yellow and curtained in floral prints. Smoke feathered from the chimney, and the sparse grass of the front lawn had recently been cut.

"Someone from the village has been looking out for your Gran," Isobel said. "She's not mentioned it when I've phoned." She sounded almost disappointed, and Mairi could understand why. It would make it less likely that Gran-Morag would be willing to leave for the comforts of the mainland.

"Maybe we should have waited until winter to start the persuading," Mairi said. "In fact, why don't we? Have this as a holiday visit and leave the hard sell until the weather gets really bad."

"Oh, no," Isobel replied with a certainty that carved the words in stone. "Coming back once is hard enough. I couldn't do it a second time."

"I'd've thought it would be easier." Mairi reached over and played a short tune on the horn. "I haven't found it at all difficult; in fact, it's great being back after all this time. I wish I'd come home sooner."

"Home is in Melrose!" Isobel snapped and got quickly out of the car, slamming the door hard enough to rock the big Volvo on its suspension, "And don't you ever forget that, my girl!"

"Won't have much chance to," she muttered. Her mother didn't hear. She was striding for the front door of the croft with a set to her jaw and shoulders that boded ill for the family reunion.

Isobel was reaching for the brass knocker when the door jerked open before she could touch it, and Morag MacLeod stood there, leaning on her walking stick.

"Isa, you're never going to knock at the door," the old woman said. "Surely you've been away too long if you're forgetting island ways. You're looking bonny, child—and Mairi! Dia! how she's grown! Come in, come in, the kettle's boiling for tea."

In something of a daze, Mairi found herself in a one-armed hug, a wrinkled cheek soft as brushed silk pressed to hers, and a breathy chuckle whispering in her ear. "So very good you're home," Morag said to her, eyes of true amethyst twinkling as sharp and knowing as they had ten years ago. "And grown so beautiful. Sixty years back and I could be looking in a mirror." Like Ardroag, like the sea and rocks of the small bay in front of the croft, she was exactly the same as the day Mairi and her mother had left with Ian, even to the brown cardigan and the green tweed skirt, and the neatly braided coronet of white hair. Certainly there was no sign that she was failing in limb or wit, despite her bird-boned thinness.

"Gran-Morag," Mairi started, but lost the words in a rush of emotion. She returned the welcoming embrace and let that speak for her, felt the understanding pat on her shoulder.

"Are you keeping well, Mum?" Isobel said, receiving a hug in turn.

"Aye, of course. When am I not? Come into the kitchen and be comfortable, and you can tell me how it is that the earth rose up and made a road between the Highlands and the Isle, so that Isobel Drummond could come dryshod to the croft."

Mairi laughed, but Isobel was not amused. "Och, don't start, Mum," she sighed. "We've come to see how you are, and have a wee talk."

"That's what phones are for. No, don't scowl so. I ken well enough you have your serious face on. Mairi, my bairnie, why don't you have a good wander round and find yourself again while Is and I get this serious thing out of the way. Your own room is waiting for you."

Mairi opened the door and went into the small room. It felt a little strange, as if she had walked into a time warp. The rainbow of the patchwork quilt on the bed was perhaps a little more faded, as were the roses on the wallpaper, but that was all. Books she had left behind were on the shelf, the shells and stones she had collected from the shore and not been allowed to take were on the dressing table. Almost she expected her younger self to come in to kneel on the padded chair in front of the window and gaze out, elbows on the sill, chin in hands. Watching the sea, she remembered. Watching the cormorants on the rocks, airing their wings like heraldic creatures, and the rarer golden eagles riding the air, and the even rarer osprey, diving to take a fish. Watching the seals. They were out there now, brown heads bobbing on the sea swell.

She did not need to explore to know the rest of the house would be as unchanged. The kitchen would still have its homelike clutter; the peat would still be burning in the old black range that heated the water, cooked the meals, and had a large kettle constantly on the boil. And Gran-Morag's rocking chair would still be in its place in front of it, the patchwork velvet cushion on the seat.

As Mairi went down the stairs she could hear her mother's voice, sounding hurt and angry, so she turned for the front door rather than the kitchen. The sea sound greeted her, a gentle lulling hush-hush of waves laving the shoreline. It was a sound island dwellers never truly noticed, being as familiar to them as their own breathing—but Mairi heard it now with fresh ears. Slowly she walked the familiar path that twisted through the rocks and heather, heading inevitably for the beach.

Generations of MacLeods had worn the narrow track from croft to sea and croft again, carrying creels of fish or seaweed, or just walking it for the pleasure of reaching a certain boulder that was weather-carved to the shape of a high-backed couch. Manannan's Throne it was named, and had been so for time out of mind. But MacLeods sat there to smoke their pipes or knit their sweaters, to listen to the voice of the sea in all its many moods, and to watch the tides and the sea creatures. Mairi sat cross-legged on the sun-warmed stone and indulged in one of her clan's pastimes, counting the seals out in the bay.

Seven. And one of them was surely watching her. Curious as otters, seals were, for all that they had learned to be wary of humans. Yes, it was coming closer, swimming lazily for the shore—

"Mairi!" Isobel called urgently. "Come away in!"

The rest of the evening was not comfortable. Isobel was stiff and uncomfortably polite, which Gran-Morag largely ignored. The old woman chatted to Mairi, giving her the third degree on her college years, the place she'd won at Edinburgh University, what she intended to do with her eventual degrees in History and Literature. Then she started in on friends—particularly male friends, her love life and marriage prospects—and Mairi answered as readily as she could, aware that her mother was slowly relaxing. As if she had expected a very different line of questioning.

Then, when Mairi was laying another peat on the fire, Isobel leaned forward and whispered something in Morag's ear. Mairi knew she wasn't supposed to hear, but her ears had always been keen. "You see? That pattern of yours is broken!" and there was a note of triumph in the scant words. "If it ever existed outside your imagination!"

Morag gave a snort of indignation, and made no attempt at keeping her reply from Mairi's hearing.

"Don't be any more foolish than you can help, Isa Drummond. Sometimes I swear you've less sense than a sheep, for all you mean well."

"What's going on?" Mairi cut in. "What pattern? What's Mum being foolish about? Wanting you to come back with us?"

"That, too," Morag said grimly, "Dougal knew it well enough, and he told her before they were wed, and so did I. When you marry into this line of the MacLeods, as he did, you marry the sea, and that cannot be broken by death nor divorce nor any law of man. Look at her—rushed out and married a Campbell and moved to the Lowlands—might as well be in England. And what good will it do her? None. She broke the covenant and the price was paid."

"Oh, Mum, how can you say that!" Isobel gasped. "Of all the wicked, cruel—"

"*Ach, eisd!*" Morag said disgustedly. "We don't need the dramatics, Isa. It's not your fault you couldn't accept the MacLeod way."

"Aye, and I never will! Seals!" Her voice broke on a sob. "Selkies! The MacLeod Gift—hah! MacLeod Madness, more like! You should have burned that damned thing years ago!" and she left the kitchen in a rush, door slamming behind her.

"Poor lass," Morag shook her head. "She was always banging the doors in her tempers. I've told often enough of our Sea-Kin . . ."

"Ian's a good man," Mairi said, standing up and dusting off her hands, preparing for battle. She didn't know what was going on between her mother and her gran, but she wanted more than anything to heal the rift, whatever it was. "He's been a fine husband to Mum and a good friend to me."

"Of course he is," the old woman said impatiently. "The best kind of man she could have, after losing her Dougal to the sea. Don't take me wrong, child. I like Ian—he's fine and true, but he's not a MacLeod.

You, on the other hand, are. A MacLeod to the last drop of your blood and not a hint of the Drummond that's in you. Oh, Isa's right to be so wary and protective; the sea is not always gentle with us. But she should not have kept you all unknowing. And me, I should have been more careful with her myself, but I have this voice in my head telling me the sand is running short in the glass. And now I've made things worse than ever they were."

Aware of the old woman's distress but not knowing what to make of it, Mairi hesitated, then knelt by the rocker. "She'll have a good cry and calm down," she said. "It'll be better in the morning."

"That it won't. By morning she'll have had time to think, and remember where I have it." The old hands clutched at each other, twisting together in agitation. "There's no way I can keep her from it, and I can't move more than a few yards from the front door to take it back. *Ach, Dia!*" She keened a little, rocking herself. "If she burns it—she mustn't—" and to Mairi's horror, tears flowed from Morag's eyes, while her face took on that expressionless calm she remembered from the night Dougal Drummond had died. Mairi clutched the old woman's hands, feeling the bones as frail as twigs in her grip.

"Burn what?" she demanded. "Look, Granny, tell me where it is and I'll hide it somewhere else."

"No, best is goes back. Yes. You must take it back. That'll be right. It's in the bottom of the chest in my room, right at the back, wrapped in an old cream shawl."

Mairi nodded and crept out of the kitchen. Muffled sobs came from upstairs, and her instinct was to go up to her mother, give what comfort she could. But Gran-Morag was as distressed, though she did not show it so much. Best do what the poor old dear wanted and find out what the hell was going on afterwards, when both women were over their separate griefs. So she moved silently across the hall and into the room opposite the kitchen, reaching instinctively for the light switch.

Morag's dower chest was under the window, the top softened with cushions. Mairi set them aside, and lifted the lid, breathing in the scents of the lavender and cedar and mothballs. There were memories here, too, treasures of childhood, but she could not spare them the time. The bundle was easily found; something soft and about the size of a child's doll, wrapped in a moth-eaten crocheted shawl, tied fast with faded twists of red wool. When she took it into the kitchen, Morag almost snatched it from her, bent her head and wept her silent tears onto it.

"I should have given it back years ago," she whispered. "But I couldn't bring myself to do it. Och, Mairi, he was so bonny . . ."

"Don't, Gran." Gently she stroked the old woman's hair. "Who do I give it to? Where do they live? In Ardroag?"

"Go to the shore." Morag straightened until she was sitting in the rocking chair like a queen on a throne. "Throw it out to sea as far as you can. Then turn around and come straight home. Don't look back."

"Chuck it in the sea?" Mairi stared at her, taken aback. "That doesn't make sense, Gran."

"Just do it, child. Better the sea than the fire, believe me."

"If you say so. At least it's your own choice and not made for you." She started for the door, then paused. "You're not coming back to Melrose, are you, Gran?"

"No, my sweet. This is my place and I'll stay here, for good or ill."

Mairi nodded. "Do you mind if I stay on a while longer when Mum goes back? I'd forgotten how much I love this place. And you, you daft old biddy," she added with a smile. "I don't have to be in Edinburgh until September."

"That would be just fine by me, Mairi-bairn. Now, give back to the sea its own, and we'll have a cup of tea. I expect poor Isa will welcome one by then."

"I'll only be a few minutes," Mairi laughed, and tiptoed out of the kitchen.

The front door closed on silent hinges, and Mairi stepped out into the sea-breathing night. This far north, it was hardly ever completely dark at this time of year, and the moon was almost at the full, painting a wide pearly swathe across the lochan that lay over the water like a pathway. The bay was a palette of indigo and silver, the sound of the sea a soft sussuration punctuated by the rattling drag of waves among the pebbles. There was a sweet perfume on the breeze off the land, and it took a moment for Mairi to recognize it; the scent of the white clover that grew in the narrow fields between the MacLeod croft and the Ardroag. She threw back her head and took a deep lungful, as if she could draw in the timeless beauty of the night and keep the magic of it in her body as talisman against the mundane. She would need such memories in Edinburgh.

But at least she would have a chance to collect together an album full of them. Isobel would probably object, of course, but there was nothing she could do about it. Mairi made up her mind. She'd spend a few precious months here with Gran-Morag for the summer, then take her place at the university. And in the long vacations, she would be able to come back; recharge her batteries, so to speak.

Mairi stumbled, caught her balance with an outflung hand and a painful impact with harsh rock. She swore under her breath, and sucked the graze on the side of her palm. That would teach her to keep her mind on the task of the moment. The path was rough enough in daylight; moonlight and the gloaming could make it treacherous for the unwary. If she broke her leg again, it was probable that her mother would not forget or forgive for a long time. The graze was bleeding, but only slightly. A few smudges showed black against the pallor of the shawl and she felt a twinge of guilt until she remembered it was going to be thrown away. Along with whatever it was, wrapped up in the fine wool. Curiosity nibbled at her, but Mairi shrugged it off. She'd ask Gran-Morag when she got back to the house.

Don't go near the water. Her mother's voice, so clear in her head, it was as if she stood behind her. Sensible advice. She could tell from the changed sea sounds that the tide was just on the turn, and the rockpools were invisible and deep. A fall, even in the shallows, could put her in difficulties all too easily.

With the soft rippling and shushing of the retreating water in her ears, she picked her way down to the crescent of white sand and along to the Throne. There was sure footing there, with no chance of a slip. She climbed up, stood for a moment looking out over the silvered bay, and then threw the bundle seawards with all the strength she would muster. It hit the water with a flare of white spray, sank and surfaced again, small on the hammered-metal surface. Within moments, seal heads appeared, sleek in the moonlight, arrowing in to investigate. Mairi watched them for a while, until the bundle sank and they followed it down. Then she turned away and started back up along the beach towards the path.

The night changed around her. She could not have said how. It was neither sound nor sight nor scent, but there was a difference in the air that stopped Mairi in her tracks a few short yards from the top of the beach. Ahead was the house, windows welcoming, glowing with curtain-mellowed light, where Morag MacLeod waited with a kettle singing on the range and a teapot waiting to be filled. Behind her was only the sea, murmuring to her, a chorus of whispering voices. If she listened long enough, surely she could make out what it was saying to her. Calling to her? She turned slowly, and caught her breath.

A man stood in the shallows. He was young, about her own age, and he was wearing nothing but what looked to be dark close-fitting trousers cut off at the knee. He was tall and lean, supple with muscle, and his skin was very white in the moonlight. Long black hair lay in wet tangles on his shoulders, and silver trails of water ran off him as if he had only just swum in and risen to his feet to greet her. His face might have come from one of Morag's stories, because it didn't look quite human—fine-boned and dangerous and oddly beautiful. Eyes of flecked silver were set beneath black brows arched like a gull's wing, and his gaze moved over her in an almost tangible caress. A tremor ran through her, recognition without comprehension, and a compulsion as real as the tide dragging at the sand. He reached out a hand, inviting her without words to take it. In the other hand he held the bundle, the shawl unravelling from it in sagging loops and revealing folds of dark satiny plushness. Another shawl. Of sealskin. *The stories are true*, Mairi realized with a leaping delight. *He's one of the Sea-Kin. A selkie!*

"*Ceud mile failte*," he said softly, his voice rich with all the music of the Gael. Without quite knowing why, Mairi found herself retracing her steps. The sea sang a triumph-song as she stepped into the water.

"Mairi!" Isobel's scream cut through the night like a jagged knife, but he did not seem to hear. "Mairi, no! Dear God, no! Don't go—"

Mairi did not feel the first of the waves slide cool over her shoes. His hand was warm over hers, and there was both awe and wonder and welcome in his face. Mairi found the waterlogged weight of the seal-wrap around her shoulders, and he was smiling down at her as if he had known her and loved her for all their lives.

The next wave broke over her thighs.

Don't go near the water.

Behind her, unheeded by either of them, Isobel's anguish found voice in a keening wail. "Mairi!!"

Mother Knows Best

Josepha Sherman

Mrix yawned, letting her tongue loll over her fangs, then flexed the claws on all four paws in lazy satisfaction as she watched her youngsters gambol through the *litlec* weed and pounce on each other in mock ferocity.

Children, she thought fondly, *can't live with them, can't eat them.*

Look at Terik, now, stalking his sister Serx with such melodramatic care, the foolish, furry little dear ... Tsk, and there he went, springing far too soon and completely overshooting the mark. Serx, of course, promptly jumped on him, pinning him to the ground and worrying at an ear until the squealing Terik could pull free.

Mrix dug her claws into the earth. Had that been some grass eater on which he'd tried such a clumsy attack, Terik would have gone hungry or maybe even been trampled. She grumbled, deep in her throat. Children knew it all, so they claimed. Let her but offer one little word of suggestion, and it would be an indignant, "Oh, *Mother!*" As though she hadn't gone through hundreds of successful hunts and made hundreds of successful kills. Had the children ever gone hungry? No! They'd never known a bit of privation. Not like the way it had been when she was their age and—

Ah well. The young would be young. And all too soon they'd be adults and Serx at least—being the only female child of the three—would be out fighting to establish her own territory, while the males went wandering, hunting mates. Mrix licked her fangs, pleased at what she was seeing in spite of her grumblings. Ah yes, for now there was still time to enjoy the sight of her children's spotted baby fur and sleek, almost-graceful strength.

A shame you can't see them, Therit, she thought with a sudden pang of nostalgia. So soft her mate had been to her, so sweet—

Delicious, in fact.

Ah well. That was the way it went, and only a fool argued with the natural order. Right now, it was pleasant just to lie here in the sun, knowing there was still half a *gerrick* in the larder, knowing that her territory extended with true noble width on all sides. Her nearest neighbor—

Akkkh, that was the one thorn scratching at her side. Erexic was a sour, barren female, her envy of Mrix's land so strong Mrix could almost scent it on the wind. While two adult females were almost sure to issue challenges, no sane female would dream of harming a child, hers or anyone else's—but Erexic, Mrix thought with an angry little growl, hardly qualified as sane.

Well. Mrix told herself that she was not one to get into unnecessary fights, particularly not when she still had younglings to protect. But if Erexic ever dared cross the boundary between their territories or harm the slightest strand of one of the children's fur—

No. Not even Erexic would be that stupid. And who knew? Maybe someday a grown-up Serx would challenge Erexic and win. It wasn't unheard of for an offspring to become neighbor to her mother. That would be nice. Nice, too, to see Erexic bleeding out her life like prey.

A sudden wild rustle brought Mrix to her feet, staring and sniffing. For all her warnings, Ririt, her third child, *would* wander off. Being such a loner might be fine in an adult, but it was downright perilous for a youngling. Mrix always had the worry at the back of her mind that before Ririt could reach his full growth, he would be picked off by some hungry adult male.

But will he listen to me? Oh no, I'm just his mother. What do I know?

Mrix sighed. For the moment, at least, the youngling was safe and seemed healthy enough. Yes, and he'd caught some prey, the precocious wonder, and from the sound of it, he'd caught something large. Hissing with pride, Mrix settled down again to see what her son had brought.

But at the sight of the creature, Mrix nearly choked on a startled snarl. What Ririt had caught was large indeed, and like no prey any of the People could ever have imagined: no proper pelt but pink and hairless in places, furry or dull brown in others. Forelegs shorter than hind, and no claws to be seen at all. Large as it was, the creature must have given Ririt quite a fight, but right now the youngling had it firmly by the scruff of the neck.

"Mmmtthr," he began.

Mrix tsked. "Don't talk with your mouth full, dear."

He dropped the pink-and-brown creature, which scrambled to its feet—biped, as she'd expected—and made one abortive attempt to run. But Terik and Serx, Mrix saw to her pride, circled in behind the creature, just as she'd taught them to do with prey.

But was this prey? The creature was babbling something, the sound too regular and patterned to be animal cries. Mrix licked her fangs again, thoughtfully. Yes ... it was as she thought.

Ririt looked up at her with hopeful eyes. "It followed me home, Mother. Can I eat it?"

"No, dear. I believe this is a sentient. You know you can't eat sentients."

"Oh, *Mother!*"

"Don't 'Oh, Mother' me. I said no, and that's that."

The pink-and-brown creature was fumbling with something at its midsection. "Yes!" it said so suddenly that Mrix felt her ears flatten with startled surprise. Annoyed at herself for revealing her emotions, she forced her ears back up again into the "calmly interested" pose and said, "You can speak the Language, then."

"Uh . . . after a fashion. The . . . <something something> translates for us." The creature blinked, shivered. "It's true, then. You *are* intelligent."

"That's silly!" Serx cried. "Of course we are!"

"Hush, dear," Mrix said. "Let me talk with the creature. Creature, what are you?" She sniffed. "I think your scent is male. Am I right?"

"Uh, yes."

"All sentients have a race, a name. I repeat, what are you?"

The creature still looked dazed—as well it, no, he might after having been seized upon and dragged for who knew how far by Ririt. "Darren," he said at last. "Carl Darren. That's . . . uh my name. And my race is . . . uh . . . human. My people live . . . live in a land that's very far away. And you are . . . ?"

"I am Mrix, and you stand upon Mrix Territory." She saw his odd eyes widen—the irises proper brown but with so much white rimming them that they looked like the eyes of a terrified prey—and sniffed at him to see if she could catch the scent of fear. Fear, yes, but there was curiosity as well, and something her mind could only interpret as "territory lust," which didn't make sense since he certainly wasn't a female of the People, to make a territorial challenge.

Calm, Mrix told herself, and relaxed muscles that had been instinctively tightening for the attack. "I know you do not trespass by choice. And I am not a fool, human Carl Darren. I know the territories, near and far. There are no lands anywhere within the territories that hold such as you."

The human sighed. "You are wise, Mrix. I am from another—another star."

"That's silly!" This time it was Terik who said it. "Nobody comes from—*ow!*" He stared at his mother in outrage. "Why'd you hit me? I didn't say anything."

"Hush. Let the adults talk."

"But—"

Mrix raised a warning paw again, and Terik fell silent, pouting. Good child; wise child. He'd remain quiet. Mrix turned to give the human a worshipful smile, lips carefully covering fangs to avoid the slightest hint of threat. "A star!" she purred. "Imagine that! You must be a wondrous being, indeed, to come all the way here from a star." Out of the corner of her eye, she saw all three children squirming impatiently, but they knew better than to interrupt. "Might I ask why you have come?"

The scent of human fear was fading, but that odd "territory lust" remained. "I have come," the human said proudly, "on a most important mission, and your ... impetuous child did but speed my journey. For I have come as a messenger from the gods. They wish to test your faith."

"If you're a messenger to us, why don't you look like us?" Serx muttered. Clever child! But Mrix gave her a warning glare, and let her ears sag in submission. "What must we do?"

The human straightened. "Give us a sign of that faith."

"What? What? My territory ..."

"Oh no, we wouldn't take so much from you. That would hardly be just. No. If you allow it, we will come and take some of the <something> that lie to the south." He stopped, glaring at the translating <something something>. "That is, the ... uh ... hard, glittery rocks that ... ah ... grow underground."

Mrix blinked. "Why would you want those? There is the land, there is the prey, there are mates and children and ruling one's territory. What worth are shiny rocks that can't be eaten?"

The human beamed. "They last forever. They will be an eternal sign that your faith is strong. Will you let me take them?"

"Oh, of course!"

"Good, good. But I can't take the rocks myself. I must bring . . . uh . . . holy <somethings> to pull them from the ground. There will be other holy beings to work those <somethings>, but they will only stay as long as it takes to pull free the rocks. Then you will be left in peace and we will know your faith is strong."

"But if you want shiny rocks," Mrix said, wide-eyed as a youngling, "you don't want to go south. There are many, many more to be found to the west, not more than a two-day gallop from here."

"Yes, but—"

"They are so close to the surface that you will not need to soil holy paws with grubbing in the earth. And there are so very many that you will have every type from which to choose."

Now the "territory lust" scent was so strong Mrix almost snarled. "Indeed? Well, then I . . . uh . . . shall go to see them. Make sure they are sufficiently sacred. To the west, you say? That is your territory?"

"My territory," Mrix said proudly, "is vast. I shall see you there and you will be guided." She flattened herself on the ground. "Farewell, oh holy messenger, and may your quest be full of prey."

"Uh . . . thank you."

"Why did you say those silly things, Mother? And why did you show that—that human full submission?"

"Hush, children. Mother knows best."

"But—*stars!*" Terik protested. "He can't have come from a *star!* They're nothing but balls of fire, everybody knows that."

"That's right, dear."

"Then why—"

"I don't care why," Ririt squirmed impatiently. "He's gone, and I'm hu-u-n-gry."

"Aw, you're always hungry, stupid," Serx told him.

"I'm not stupid!"

"Are too!"

"Am not!"

"Children!" Mrix snapped. "Stop that."

Ririt's lower lip drooped. "Well, I am hungry. I *am!* Why couldn't we eat him, Mother?"

"There will be no eating of sentients."

"But *Mother*—"

"And stop that whining this instant, do you understand? I told you, Mother knows best." She called over her shoulder, "You can come out now."

The small, slight figure who stepped out of the lair was human, too. But where the other had been pink with brownish fur, and male, this human was brownish with black fur, and female. She had given Mrix her name: Lura Selden. "That was beautiful, Mrix."

Mrix licked a paw to hide her surge of satisfaction. "Wasn't it? That ridiculous tale about being a messenger of the gods—as if the Creation would ever send such a soft little thing as messenger! And a male, no less! I never thought I would get through all that nonsense without laughing." She paused. "Though when I saw Ririt dragging him in like a grass eater ..."

"Did I do something wrong?" Ririt asked anxiously, and Mrix gave him an affectionate little cuff.

"No, child. You hunted well. And there was no way you could have known the human had a—a fire-spitting ... Lura Selden, what is the word?"

"*Gun?*"

"*Gun.* Had he used that *gun* on my children," Mrix added grimly, "I would have torn him to nothingness, and very, very slowly." Seeing the children's frightened stares, she reached out a paw to cuff them gently, one at a time. "Never mind, younglings. Never mind. You're safe. And you were quite right, Lura Selden. He *is* here as a territory thief."

The human sighed. "He and his *gang* both." The foreign word translated as *organized gang of illegal hunters*. "It's worse than simple theft, though. They look for worlds inhabited by *low-tech* sentients they can awe, then do a thorough job of *looting*—" that translated as *prey-stealing* "—that doesn't just strip the land of whatever they find valuable but leaves the local environment pretty much destroyed."

"It won't happen here."

"I hope not. Mrix, I have been hunting that—what's your word for it? Prey defouler? I've been hunting him for years without ever getting my hands on him."

Mrix purred. "You'll have him now. For here is what I mean to do. Listen. . . ."

When Mrix had finished, she saw Lura Selden stare at her in that wide-eyed, alien, almost-terrified-prey way. "Devious!" the human gasped. "Wonderfully devious. Downright *nasty*, in fact."

"*Nasty?*"

"Never mind, never mind. It's dangerous, you know."

Mrix snarled, insulted. "I am not prey."

She saw the human flinch slightly, then remembered that flinching was a prey reflex. "I didn't mean to insult you. And nasty or not, it just might work."

"It will." Mrix got to her feet in one smooth movement. "Come. We have a long walk to take."

The edge of her territory was well marked by scent and claw-scrapes renewed over and over again as was the proper way. Mrix settled down comfortably, the children gathered about her. Lura Selden was panting and red-faced and reeked of an odd scent that must be human sweat, but she'd kept up the quick pace surprisingly well. "Sit, human," Mrix told her. "Catch your breath. We must wait a bit." She wrinkled her nose. "Akkkh, you smell of such uneasiness! Calm yourself. He'll come alone; he must, if he is the hunting scout . . .

"Ah yes, look. There he is."

She got to her feet, ambled deliberately across the boundary into Erexic's territory. "Greetings, messenger of the gods."

"Uh . . . greetings."

"Why such surprise? I said that I would see you here, and here we are." But one ear pricked, alert. Was that the distant sound of a snarl? "You will, indeed, find your guide."

"Sure. I mean, of course I will; I never . . . uh . . . doubted the strength of your faith. Now tell me: Where are the shiny rocks? The sooner I locate them, the sooner I . . . uh . . can show the gods proof of your faith. Where is this guide?"

Ah, that *was* a snarl, and much nearer, too. "Near," Mrix said, "very near." Out of the corner of her eye, she saw the *litlec* weed stir ever so slightly, glimpsed the tip of an ear. *Clumsy Erexic*, Mrix thought, *letting yourself be seen. Careless Erexic.* And then, *Perfect.* "In fact," she continued calmly, "your guide is here."

Mrix sprang lithely aside just as Erexic, screaming with rage at the invasion, sprang. The human screamed, too. There was a roar, a blaze of incredible light—

Mrix picked herself up, rubbing at dazzled eyes with a paw, wrinkling her nose at the stench of scorched flesh.

Erexic's flesh. Akkkh, look, there she lay: quite dead, a great, smoking hole blasted right through her. Mrix shuddered in spite of herself, then thought of such horrifying power being directed at her children and snarled. Carl Darren—

But she cut herself off in midthought, listening. Lura Selden was there, her own *gun* pointed at her fellow human. "Carl Darren," she said, and great satisfaction was in her voice, "as an agent of the Interstellar Ecology Protection League, I arrest you on a charge of murder of a sentient being and the attempted destruction of a protected environment."

"What—you can't—"

"Can't I?"

She raised another of the odd *tools* the soft, clawless humans seemed to need so much, and to Mrix's fascination, both humans began to shimmer out of sight. She heard one last exchange:

"Murder!" That was Carl Darren's protest. "That—that *monster* tried to kill me!"

And that was surely Lura Selden's purr of contentment. "Ah, but this world is under Official Interdict, under Rule 5425, Section 421.A, Protection of Indigenous Sentients of Low-Tech Level 541.26.1. Even if I've just filed it as such myself. I've got you, Darren!"

And then both humans were gone, as cleanly as though they had been snatched from reality, wind rushing in to fill the place where they'd been.

Snatched from reality. In a way, Mrix thought, that was exactly right. Akkkh, but the children! She hurried back to them where they lay as flat to the ground as they could get, huddled together in terror. "Mother!" they wailed at her like much younger children. "Mother!"

She settled down beside them, licking their ruffled fur as she had so many times in the past. "Hush, children. It's over. You're safe."

"But—that—they—"

"Hush, little ones, hush. Only prey whimper over danger that's past. The humans are gone for good. Lura Selden has her prey. I have Erexic's territory. And none of us have endured even the slightest scratch of harm. Save for Erexic, of course, and nobody's going to miss her very much."

Mrix paused, purring. "I told you this, children, and now maybe you'll believe me:

"Mother really does know best."

"Accidents Don't Just Happen . . . They're Caused"

Elizabeth Moon

The 1330 shuttle from planetside rotated on its longitudinal axis to slip its docking probe into the newly designed collar. Peka, watching from inside the control blister, heard in her ear the pilot's mutter of annoyance.

"Always somebody got to make things harder. Don't know why—"

The status lights flicked through the correct color sequence and came up all green. The station's sensor arrays recognized the umbilical orientation, and flipped open the corresponding inboard covers.

"*I* never had any accidents up here. It was somebody else—"

Peka ignored the complaint. A soothing voice from the station traffic control answered the pilot; she didn't have to. It didn't matter whether this pilot had had an accident; someone had. And someone's accident was reason enough to redesign a docking collar that had allowed a ship to come in 60 degrees off line . . . because the tuglines that were supposed to correct an offline dock could foul. Had fouled, one coming loose to tangle in another and whack the station end of the umbilical connection, which had then popped its lid and squirted a jet of air and water at the badly docked shuttle, shoving it offline so that the aft stabilizer crumpled one of the com dishes.

In the months since the shuttles had first docked here, the incidence of misalignments had risen steadily.

Stationers blamed the pilots' carelessness; pilots blamed the workload, the hours they had to fly without a rest, the crazily shifted schedules that no human metabolism could adjust to.

Peka blamed design, which meant she blamed herself. Even though she had not designed Jacobi Station herself, she had seen the potential problem when she arrived. She had not argued hard enough; she had let the committee override her instincts, her training. Just because it was her first deep-space job, her first *real* job, and she didn't want to be known as a prima donna ...

"Looks good to me," Hal said, behind her. Peka jumped; she had not heard him come in, and she hated to be surprised, even by someone she liked.

"This is only one shuttle," she said. The moment it was out of her mouth, she regretted it; Hal looked at her as if he'd bitten into a sour fruit. "Not you," she said, trying to soften the harshness of tone and words. "You and your crew did a fine job of getting that modification built and installed between shuttles. It's just that one shuttle doesn't tell us anything except that it can function right."

"Doesn't prove it can't function wrong," he said, nodding. "I do understand. Even fabrications technologists have read your mother's work, you know."

Peka tried not to move. If she could just freeze in place, perhaps he would never know how that hurt. Her mother, the famous engineer, whose textbooks on quality control and safety were standards in the field ... *I should have gone into china painting,* she thought. *Buggy whip-making. Anything but this.*

"I guess it's no accident that you're an engineer," Hal said. "And this kind in particular."

He was going to say it. They all said it.

"After all," he said. "Accidents don't happen ... they're caused." He laughed.

It might be funny to someone. It had never been

funny to her. "That's right," she said, forcing a smile onto stiff lips. She might as well agree; no one would believe how she had fought off the family destiny. But if you have the talent, her mother had said (and her teachers, from elementary on, and the psychologists she went to, hoping for a way out). If you have the talent—that cluster of talents—and no talents whatever for other things—then it only makes sense to use those talents. Productively—one of her mother's favorite words.

"Was it hard, having such a famous person for a mother?" asked Hal. "I mean, when you were growing up?"

She had no way to answer that didn't sound petulant, selfish, immature, and disloyal. She had been asked that a lot, especially around the time her mother won the second Kaalin award. What people wanted to hear was more about how wonderful her mother had been, and how she had always supported Peka in her own way . . . and very little else.

Not about the daily frustration of living in a household where the very concept of accident was forbidden. Where every spilled glass of milk, every stain on the carpet, resulted in a formal investigation . . . down to the simple incident report form her mother devised for a child to fill out. To teach her responsibility, she'd said. Hard? It had been hell, sometimes, and it still was, whenever someone noticed who her mother was. Peka didn't dare say that.

"Sometimes . . ." she said. "When I was too little to understand about cause and effect, you know."

He chuckled; she must have picked the right tone for an answer. "I'll bet she's proud of you," he said then.

"Reasonably," Peka said. Again an edge had crept into her voice. She hated that edge, and the speculative look that came into Hal's eyes. She wanted to say something to explain it away, but nothing would. She tried anyway. "I—haven't done anything yet. Not really. She's glad I went into this field, of course, but there wasn't much else I could do." That sounded lame; there was always something else, but she had limited her choices to those with good employment opportunities, a reasonable income and chance to travel. She could not have chosen to stay on one planet, could not have tolerated the monotony of a job that stayed the same month after month, year after year.

She looked out the blister, where the cargo lock had mated with the shuttle's cargo bay. In fifteen minutes, the hold would be empty; the pallets would be snaking their way to their designated holds; in another five minutes, the shuttle would be on its way out, and shortly after that the next shuttle would be nosing in.

"Well—guess I'll be going," Hal said. Peka turned. He was looking at her as if he expected some reaction. She felt nothing, but a vague satisfaction that he was going to let her alone.

She was back in her office, reviewing the sensor records of the new collar's performance, when a tap on her door brought her head up. "Yes?" she said, wondering who would be that formal.

Denial, anger—the first stages of grief, her education reminded her—but the woman in the doorway was still there, unscathed by her own emotion. The crisp dark hair, the lively dark eyes, the smooth unweathered skin ... the expensive business suit and briefcase.

"Mother," she managed finally.

"Surprised?" her mother asked. "I came in on the *Perrymos* from Baugarten; I'm en route to the Plarsis colonies. Sorry I didn't have a chance to warn you, but they said one of the com channels was out—"

Peka flushed. It was out because the shuttle had knocked the dish awry. Her fault.

"—Some kind of accident, the communications

officer said," her mother went on. "I managed not to give him the family lecture." She laughed; Peka couldn't manage even a strangled chuckle.

"We have a two-day layover," her mother said. "I'm sure you're busy now, but I'd love to take you to dinner, or even breakfast, if you can make it."

"Of course," Peka said. She couldn't say anything else.

"Here's my shipboard number," her mother said, holding out a scrap of card. Her own card, no doubt, with the number scribbled on the back of it. Peka got up from her chair, only then realizing she hadn't made any move. Would her mother expect a hug? She couldn't—but her mother held out only the one hand, and when Peka took the card, her mother was already turning away. "Give me a call when you've checked your schedule," her mother said. "I'm free unless someone hires me." She laughed again, over her shoulder, but turned away quickly enough that Peka didn't have to answer.

It was the same card, the familiar name in the same style of lettering. Her mother didn't need to list her degrees, her honors. ALO ATTENVI, PROCESS QUALITY LTD., CONSULTING and the string of access numbers. Anyone who needed Attenvi's expertise knew what process quality consulting was, knew that Leisha Attenvi had literally written the book—several of them. Had won the awards, had (even more important) saved one company after another from drowning in its own stupidity.

Peka turned the card over and over, and finally stuck it in the minder strip of her desk. She tried not to look around her office, but she knew too well what it was like, what her mother had seen in that brief visit. Automatically, her hands moved across surfaces, straightening everything into perfect alignment. Too late, but she couldn't help it. Whether her mother said anything or not, she knew what could have been said. *The professional does not confuse mess with decoration.* Followed by the accusing finger pointing out this and that bit of disorder.

The headquarters of Process Quality Ltd. were of course decorated, by another professional, but her mother's office (from which she had regular message cubes recorded for Peka) had no clutter, no personal touches. The pictures on the walls had been chosen for their effect on customers; the two photographs were of the Kaalin awards ceremonies.

"Peka ..." That was Einos Skirados, the liaison from Traffic Control assigned to this project. She didn't bother to flip on the visual; she already knew what he looked like, and right now she didn't want anyone looking at her. Einos, in particular, would be distracting ... something about the shape of his nose and the set of his eyes seemed to unhinge her logic processor.

"Yes?"

"The values on the second shuttle approach are nominal with the first—it's looking good. Hal says they'll have another done by the end of the shift, if there are no modifications."

The second shuttle already? She glanced at the clock, and winced. Lamebraining wouldn't work. She pulled the figures up onto her screen, and checked. Einos was good, but it was her responsibility. The computer's own comparison showed no deviance.

"How much are the pilots complaining?" she asked.

"About what you'd expect," Einos said. "But this was Kiis, who's been in the low quartile, and if he could get it right—"

"We still haven't had Beckwith," Peka said. She meant it as a joke. Beckwith, whose shuttle had taken off the com dish, was off the schedule, and complaining bitterly about that.

"I can hardly wait," Einos said. "I don't know why they hire people like that." He sounded priggish, but

Peka didn't mind. Einos never acted as if she were strange for being so careful about things, and she felt less guilty about being attracted to him. Perhaps it wasn't an accident; perhaps it made sense.

"The numbers look good," she told Einos, after rechecking the correspondence. "I'll tell Hal to go ahead and finish the second."

"Dinner at nineteen thirty?" Einos asked, in the tone that tweaked all her hormonal responses.

"Drat." She'd forgotten completely. She flipped the video on and caught the startled expression on Einos' face. "Einos, I'm so sorry—my mother just turned up—" That sounded lame, and worse than the "drat" before it. She was ready to explain that it didn't matter, that she could still have dinner—her mother would be here for two days—but he interrupted.

"Your *mother? The* Alo Attenvi? Here?" He glanced around as if she might appear miraculously in his office.

The last twinge of guilt disappeared, swamped in anger and envy. Would anyone ever use that tone about her? "Yes, my mother . . . she came in on the *Perrymos* and she asked me to dinner—and I'm sorry, Einos, but I forgot that this was our night."

"Oh, of course," he said, releasing any claim on the evening. "You have to see her—I don't suppose you'd introduce me . . . if it's not too much trouble . . ."

"Maybe later in the visit," Peka said. "Right now I need to call Hal." Right now she needed to get far away from her mother. From everyone who hero-worshipped her mother. From the very concept of mothers. But she called Hal instead.

"Glad to hear it's working well," he said. "Thought it would—good clear design, and not hard to do the modifications."

"Thanks," Peka said.

"Listen—somebody said there's an Attenvi listed as

a passenger on that FTL that just docked . . . relative of yours?"

Station gossip, not just faster than light but faster than reality. "Yes," Peka said, feeling helpless. Everyone would know, and everyone would tell her how she should feel about it. "My mother."

"*The* Attenvi," Hal said. He whistled. "Huh. Must be difficult, after you've been the Attenvi on station."

"She's not staying," Peka said, more sharply than she meant to.

"Just wants to check up on her little girl," Hal said, making it almost a question.

"On her way somewhere else," Peka said. "And I have to get going—we're having dinner." She hadn't told her mother yet, but the way the gossip net worked, her mother would probably be waiting at the right table at the right time even without a formal invitation.

Jacobi Station had been designed to handle outsystem transport, offering more docking and storage space than Janus, the first-built primary station. Peka had arrived before any direct docking of FTL ships was possible. She'd had to travel from starship to station in a little twelve-person hopper, sweating in her p-suit and entirely too aware of the accident rate of near-station traffic in overcrowded situations.

Someday these wide corridors would bustle with traffic; the blank spaces on either side would be filled with shops, hotels, restaurants. Only one was out here now, a pioneer branch of Higg's, the universal fast-food chain. The concentric blue, green, and purple circles promised that its limited bill of fare would be the same as—or at least reminiscent of—that in every other Higgs. A bosonburger . . . an FTL float . . . Dirac dip . . . the names were so familiar they didn't sound silly anymore, and only third graders got a kick out of realizing that they meant something else.

Ahead, a green arch confirmed that the *Perrymos* was docked safely, its access available. Beyond that arch, the waiting area with its array of padded chairs in muted colors, and a TranStar employee at a desk, a young man whose shaved skull had been tattooed with the TranStar logo. Peka blinked; she hadn't realized anyone was that much of a brownnose.

"May I help you?"

"I'm here to meet—" *My mother* tangled with the name, and Peka felt herself flushing, but she got out the more formal "Alo Attenvi."

"Oh yes. Are you her daughter? She said her daughter was here ... you're lucky to have a mother like her ... she doesn't look old enough. . . ." Peka refrained from violence and waited until the torrent ceased. The man finally quit talking and picked up the shipcom to ask for her mother.

"You're early," her mother said, stepping out the access hatch. "Would you like to come aboard and see my cabin?"

"No thanks." Be trapped in a small space—no doubt immaculate—with her mother?

"Lead on, then," her mother said cheerfully, and started toward the corridor herself. Peka had to scurry to keep up. Lead on, indeed. She stretched her legs— she *was* as tall as her mother—and caught up. This was her station, and she would lead the way.

"Do you like it out here?" her mother asked at dinner. They were seated in one of the little alcoves of Fred's Place, at present the only independent eating place on the station. Since it was two decads to payday, they had the place to themselves except for another pair of passengers from the *Perrymos*.

Peka nodded, and hurried to swallow her mouthful of fried rice. "It's ... stimulating," she said. That seemed the safest adjective. Her mother looked up at her.

"Is that all? What about men ... are you meeting anyone interesting?"

"They're fine, mother, really." She hadn't talked to her mother about boys—men—since her sixteenth birthday, when her mother had taken her in for her first implant. *I won't pry,* her mother had said, and she hadn't. It was too late to start now.

"Well ... have you heard from your father lately?"

"What brought that up?" she asked, before she could censor it. No question that her mother would notice the hostility.

"Sorry if it's a touchy point," her mother said, brows raised. "I only wondered ... at one time, I recall, you said you didn't want to hear from him again."

"I don't." Peka tried not to let the anger out, but it was stuck in her throat, choking her. "I haven't heard—since graduation, I think." A graduation her mother had not attended because she was consulting somewhere, in another system, and couldn't come back for just that day. She had understood even then, but it still rankled.

"I wish you'd tell me what upset you so," her mother said. Of course her mother didn't understand; her mother had had a wonderful father, a father who was there. She could not tell her mother what her father had said, those damning words that had put an end to the last of her childhood innocence, her trust. "Please," her mother said quietly. "It's been several years, you say. It's still bothering you. You need to get it out."

She had never been able to resist that voice when it was quiet and reasonable. She would have to say, but she didn't have to say it the way he had said it. "He said it was—that I was—just an accident."

Her mother's face paled to the color of the table-cloth. "He said *what?*"

Anger surged out of control. "He said I was an

accident!" Peka yelled. "An *accident*. The great engineer who doesn't believe in accidents had ... an ... accident!" From the corner of her eye she saw heads turn, the other two diners glancing quickly toward her and away, and leaning to each other. A waiter paused in midstride, then dodged through the kitchen door.

"No. You were not an accident." Her mother had flushed now, unbecoming patches of red on her spacer-pale skin.

"Right." With that great blast, all her strength left her; Peka wanted to sink through the chair into the deck and disappear. She could not look across the table.

"I ... loved him," her mother said, in the same even, reasonable tone. "Louse though he was, in many ways, I did love him. He was everything I wasn't. Irresponsible, spontaneous, gregarious ... just being around him was like an endless party. And he liked me. Loved me, within the limits of his ability ..."

"Love *is* responsibility," Peka said, quoting. She ran her finger around and around the plate. "Love is acts, not feelings or words."

Her mother sighed. "I taught you very well. Too well, maybe. Yes, that's the kind of love parents must have, to be parents together ... and any parent to a child, to be a good parent. Anything less won't survive, won't sustain the child. But there's a ... a chaotic quality, an incalculable dimension. I fell in love with him, and he with me, and together we engendered you—"

"By accident," Peka insisted.

"No. Not on my part." A long pause. "It's—it's difficult to explain, and harder now because those feelings are so far back. But—I wanted a child. Wanted *his* child, his genes mixed with mine, to temper my own rock-ribbed values. He said he wanted a child too, but—as it turned out, he didn't."

"He has others—" Peka remembered their pictures,

a row of pretty children standing in front of a wide
white door.

"Yes. And a compliant, sweet wife who brought
them up while he voyaged from system to system."

"You know her?"

"I met her, of course. Court-ordered family ther-
apy, to determine whether you should be removed
from my custody and given to him. Luckily—or I
thought it was luckily—his wife was pregnant with
twins and didn't want you. You couldn't possibly
remember, but you were a very imperious three. You
explained to the judge that it was rude to drink in
front of others without offering them anything. You
explained to the therapist when she tried to give you
a developmental test that you didn't make guesses . . .
you either knew the answer or not, and it was foolish
to pretend otherwise. She said you were too rigid,
and Tarah said she couldn't possibly handle you and
the twins she knew she was carrying."

Peka thought she did remember the therapist, but
not Tarah. She didn't pursue it. "But if he says I was
an accident, why was he trying to get custody?" Peka
asked. She had no clear idea of how family law
worked, but surely the parent suing for custody had
to want the child.

"I don't like to say," her mother said, lips tight.
Peka knew that look; it was hopeless. But years of
training and practice in following chains of logic led
her there as if by a map.

"Gramps Tassiday's estate," she said. Her mother
looked guilty, which confirmed it. "He was after my
money?"

"I don't know that for a fact," her mother said
quickly. She had never allowed herself an expression
of bitterness; she had never allowed Peka to express
anger or resentment of her absent father. Consider
all sides, she had said. Everyone has reasons, she had
said. "But it did seem odd that he hadn't wanted you

until after my father died, and the will became available to the public."

Peka could think of nothing more to say. Her mother went on with her meal; Peka tried to do the same but the food stuck in her throat. She glanced around the restaurant. The couple they'd startled had left; she could imagine the story they'd tell. As her gaze shifted past the entrance again, she saw Einos coming in. She ducked her head, hoping he wouldn't see her.

"Peka!" Too late. She had to look up, had to see the alert interest on her mother's face, had to greet him—but he was rushing on, not giving her time. "Peka, there's a problem with the second collar installation—I hate to interrupt, but—"

She could feel her face going hot; bad enough to have lost her poise with her mother, but to have her mother aware that her work had failed . . . she managed to smile at her mother. "Excuse me—"

"Of course," her mother said. "I hope I'll get to talk to you some more—perhaps if this doesn't take too long . . . ?"

"Have to see," Peka said, struggling with a napkin that seemed determined to stick to her lap. She felt like a preschooler again, clumsy and incapable. Einos wasn't watching her; he was giving her mother the wide-eyed look of admiration he usually gave Peka.

"I'm sorry to interrupt your dinner, ma'am, but I'm glad to have the chance to meet you." He reached out a hand, which her mother took. "I'm Einos Skirados, in traffic control—we're really fortunate to have you on the station—your daughter's been a great help, but there's this problem—"

Rage flooded Peka as she peeled the napkin off and threw it on the table. The scum-sucking rat was going to ask her mother to solve the problem because he thought she had messed up! And her mother would step in, all cool competence, and show everyone why she was famous, and why Peka would always be Alo Attenvi's daughter, not someone with a name and career of her own.

Her mother's voice, ice-edged, stopped her. "Excuse me," she said to Einos. "Are you offering me a contract?"

Einos turned red himself. "Well—not me—I mean, ma'am, I don't have the authority myself, but—but I just thought since you were here, and it was your daughter, you could sort of help her out."

Peka had not seen her mother really angry for years; even now, she was glad when she realized the famous temper was turned on someone else. "Young man, let me make this quite clear. In the first place, I do not take on consulting jobs without a contract. In the second place, I doubt you can afford me— since, as you say, you don't have authorization from your employer. In the third place, you have a perfectly competent engineer—not only one in whose training I have complete confidence, but a member of my family. Even if you were offering me a contract, I wouldn't take it—you have insulted my daughter. If she had asked me first, I might advise her—but in the present circumstances, I think the only advice she needs is to have nothing whatever to do with you."

"But I—" Einos began. Peka's mother ignored him, and looked at Peka.

"I do hope we'll have time to chat after you deal with your problem," her mother said. "You have my number—"

Peka found her voice and her intent at the same moment. "Why don't you come along to my office— perhaps this will only take a few minutes."

"Thank you," her mother said. "Just let me take care of dinner—"

On the way to Peka's office, her mother said nothing. Peka walked along feeling the edges of what had happened like someone exploring the hole where a tooth had fallen out ... something had changed, something important, but she wasn't sure yet what it meant. Was it just a hole, or would something grow out of it?

In the office, Peka called up the design stats on one screen, and then called Hal. He looked a little surprised, and not much concerned.

"I thought Einos said you were having dinner with your mother ... I told him not to bother you."

"He said it was urgent—some problem with the second collar installation."

"Yeah, but it could've waited an hour or so. But since you're here—" Hal plunged into a description. As often happened during construction, the electrical and other connections in the area had been installed a little differently than the specifications ordered. "It wasn't a bad idea, really, because someone moved the whole thing five or six meters to allow for the bulk cargo handler's turn radius, after they decided to make this the bulk cargo shuttle dock, instead of the one they'd first planned. It makes sense, because this one's in a direct line to service the FTL traffic when we get it. But you weren't here when they rerouted the plumbing, and they didn't document it in the main specs, so you didn't know. Here's the modification—" Hal fed in the local scanner's analysis, and it came up on Peka's screen.

She glanced at her mother, who was studiously ignoring the screen and looking at the framed diplomas on the wall. She could read nothing of her mother's expression. She looked back at the screen.

"What I'd like to do," Hal went on, "is run the connections like so—" New lines, highlighted in the standard red, green, blue, yellow, orange of the necessary components, overlaid the black and white of the original. "My question is whether there's any reason to worry about the interaction of the control power supply with the main lines here—" An arrow showed, along with the measured clearance.

"Let me check," Peka said. She wasn't going to answer off the top of her head, with her mother standing there behind her. She didn't work that way anyway. On another screen, she called up the relevant references, and considered the influence of incoming shuttle avionics as well. Close, but reasonable—but was there a better solution? She peered at the displays, thinking. Something tickled the side of her head that she thought of as the seat of new ideas. "That's reasonably safe," she said to Hal, "but I'd like to come take a look. There's still a possibility, especially if someone's onboard systems were running hot for some reason . . ."

"That's why I asked," Hal said cheerfully. "Coming down now?"

"I suppose so. Yes." She turned to her mother. "I have to go out to the docking bay—you could wait here, or come along—"

"If you don't mind, I'd love to come," her mother said.

Did she mind? She wasn't sure which she would mind more, leaving her mother here to rummage in her office, or taking her along. Five hours before, either would have been intolerable, but now. . . . "Come on," she said. "We'll have to get p-suits somewhere. It's aired up, but—" Then she remembered whom she was talking to, and shut up. One chapter in her mother's textbook dealt with safety procedures necessary in chambers at different pressures.

Hal greeted her mother courteously but with none of the covetous glee Einos had expressed. He turned at once to Peka. "Here's the challenge," he said, and then stood quietly to let her get a good look at it. She saw at once that Hal's solution had the virtues of simplicity and directness, which made it hard to put his solution out of her mind to think of her own. She

walked back around to the cargo lock side of the docking bay. The bulk handler took up most of the space
... it would turn like so ... it would have to have
service access here and here. She squinted, her mind
tickling persistently. Then she saw it.

"Hal, come see this." He looked where she pointed.
"If the bulk handler's out of service, they'll push it
around here to work on it, and its back panel can
bump into this—" she meant the control nexus for the
docking collar modification. "Over time, those bumps
could shift it enough to allow interference." She
looked around the whole compartment. "First, we'll
need a safety stop on this bulkhead anyway—we don't
want something the mass of that thing bumping it. In
fact, we need a double stop, one on the deck and one
on the bulkhead." Hal nodded, and made a note.

"We're still going to need to reroute things, but I
think it should be the other lines. That's not as bad as
it looks—here—" She had sketched it out for him. He
took the pad and frowned a moment, then nodded.

"Yes. I see. It takes a bit longer, but it avoids the
problem entirely. It's not a patch but a redesign.
Good. Thanks, Peka."

"You're welcome," Peka said. "It's my job ..."

"If you wouldn't mind—could you come back and
give us a go-ahead when we've got the rerouting done
and the stops in? Just in case?"

"Of course—got an estimate?"

"Couple of hours, I think. If that's too late—"

"No ... you're already working over shift. Just give
me a call; I'll have my beeper this time."

Peka led the way out; she signed her mother off
the site, and they turned in their p-suits at the section
storehouse. Now she was hungry—the dinner she
hadn't eaten left an empty hole in her midsection.

"I don't know about you," her mother said, "but
I'm still hungry. Is there any place where we get
dessert?"

"Fred's is the only thing, other than the company mess hall. And they'll be through serving dinner by now."

"Ah. Fred's, then—if you don't want to come, don't worry about me. I can find my own way."

"No . . . I'll come too, but I need to go by the office first and log the changes we're making."

"Who was that very officious young man who interrupted us?" her mother finally asked, as Peka entered notes into her workstation.

"Einos." Peka considered her options and made a clean breast of it. "I've been going out with him—to the limited extent that's possible on this station."

"Oh." Her mother chewed that over in silence.

"It's not . . . um . . . serious," Peka said. It might have been, but at the moment she wanted to wring his neck.

"Good," her mother said. "I mean, it's your own business, but—backstabbers don't reform."

"Then how did you fall for my father?" Peka said, shocking herself. Her mother gave her a look she could not read. "Or was that an accident?"

Her mother laughed. "I thought so, at the time. Not my fault, I told myself. Could happen to anyone, bolt from the blue, I told myself. You weren't an accident, but he was, I told myself."

"And now?"

Her mother sighed. "I had years, Peka, to argue that out with myself after you were born, after he left. What is an accident? The effect of a cause you didn't recognize, you didn't anticipate. That's what I was taught, and that's what I had to face. Why did I fall in love with a bright-eyed, laughing, charming young prince with honey-colored curls and blue eyes?"

"Hormones," said Peka drily, amazed at her own temerity. Her mother's laugh this time was almost a bark.

"Excuses," she said. "Not hormones—that would

explain falling in lust, maybe, but not what I felt, for that man. Animals have reasonable ways to choose mates, or the species dies. It was no accident . . . it was the direct result of my family and my beliefs. Because deep down, I let myself think it was no accident, but that other form of causation, destiny."

"Destiny?"

"Fate. Luck. Or, in my grandmother's vernacular, the will of God. Her God, at least, was wont to impose his will pretty firmly—or so she said when imposing it on me. I wanted to believe that there was some supernatural intervention which could get me out of the logical trap I'd built for myself . . . which could rescue me—"

Peka saw it all, in one flash of insight. "And so you blamed me," she breathed. "For proving it wasn't that at all, and you had after all done it to yourself . . ."

"Good grief, no!" That with enough force, enough stunned surprise and horror, to convince. "I never blamed you. You were the one good thing that came out of it."

"But you always said—"

"I didn't want you to make my mistakes, of course. That's all. I had my family's mistakes to avoid: women who had married obvious losers out of duty to some social scheme, women who had buried their brains in the waste recycler. A family—a culture really—which believed that accidents not only happen, it's almost impious to prevent them. After all, how can you work up a good case of blame-and-guilt if there are no accidents?"

Peka had never heard this. She wondered if she were being cozened; her mother had always been smarter. But her mother went on.

"You asked one time why we never visited my relatives that much—I know you thought I disapproved of them."

"Yes . . ." Peka said cautiously.

"I was scared of them," her mother said. "I can't—even now—talk about my grandmother's beliefs, her influence on me, without getting a cold sweat."

Her mother? Her famous, much-honored, much-published mother? Still that twitchy about people from her past? That didn't bode well for Peka's own middle and old age. She didn't say that.

"It was all reaction," her mother said. "And it always is, generation after generation, and you don't know it before you've gone and had children and started another daisy chain of complication. Accidents have causes. Actions have consequences. I reacted to my family, and—by no accident, but the logic of human development—fell in love with your father. Wanted his child—you cannot know how much, or how dearly, until you want a chid of your own. Brought you up to avoid my mistakes, and presented you with the opportunity to make your own, equally grave ones."

"Like what?" Peka asked, her mouth dry.

Her mother looked at her, that appraising dark eye that had been scanning the inside of her head forever. "So far, my dear, you haven't ... but I can't assume you won't. The thing is, you aren't an accident: neither in your conception, nor in your birth, nor in your upbringing, nor in your self as you are now. You are the result, the consequence, of causes and actions which, if you know them, may allow you more leeway than most. At least you understand—*really* understand—how causation works."

"You've made me," Peka said.

"I gave you half your genetic material and all your early training," her mother corrected. "But you began making yourself from the joining of egg and sperm—and you withstood a good bit of my influence even as a small child." She grinned, the most relaxed look yet. Peka had always known that grin meant the storm was nearly over; her mother's good humor, once aroused, lasted far longer than her tempers. "And the further you go, the more you will be your own creation."

"Another safety expert," Peka said, not quite as a question.

"Not like me," her mother said. "I didn't hover, while you were in college, but they kept telling me—and I've looked at your work here. You don't solve the same problems the same way I do. You have a . . . a quirk, a twist, to your work that I find startling—but very elegant, once I understand it."

"You do?" Peka couldn't keep her voice from squeaking. She choked back the *Really? Really?* that wanted to beg for more.

"Yes," her mother said. She wasn't looking at Peka now; she was looking at the plots on the wall. "Look at this—this collar redesign. I'd have changed it from the annular orifice to a linear slot, perhaps with one end square—something different from the other end. That would have meant redesigning the shuttle docking probe *and* the collar, classic lock-and-key design. Your solution would never have occurred to me."

"But it—" She didn't want to say "but this was obvious" to her mother, her sainted and brilliant mother for whom it had not been obvious.

"You're not me; I'm not you." That platitude came out with all the force of divine decree. Peka wondered if her mother's head still echoed with her grandmother's religious fervor. "Your work is elegant, my dear—not only right, but right with a flair all your own. That's not an accident either—I suspect your father's genetics did exactly what I'd hoped, and gave you some abilities I don't have." Her mother smiled at her, a smile without an edge. Then she yawned, and blinked. "On the other hand, I'm thirty years older than you, and I'm running out of steam. If I want morning to feel like good fortune, I'd better skip dessert and go back to my berth."

*   *   *

Peka came back to the shuttle docking bay three hours later, when Hal called. She had walked out to the ship with her mother, then stopped on the way back for a bosonburger at Higgs. Now, as she nodded over the changes Hal and his crew had made, and entered them all in the main stats file, she felt better than she had all day.

Not an accident. Ladders of causation fell from the windows of the burning tenement, step after step leading to safety ... her mind might be going up in smoke, but she could still escape. Acts have consequences. Accidents don't just happen.

When Einos Skirados showed up in her office the next day, with a box of her favorite candy and a bouquet of apologies, her first reaction was the old familiar one that had made her so happy to go out with him.

She looked at the bright brown eyes, the sleek dark hair, the composed face; her mind brought up his resume. Here was her accident, if she lied to herself; she had the hormones, and plenty of them.

"Not only accidents have causes," her mother had pointed out as she left. "So do the best plans ever laid, the ones that come to good ends."

She smiled at Einos Skirados with no more than professional courtesy. "No, thank you," she said. "I already have plans for this evening."

And so she did. Somewhere in her future loomed the fortunate accident she wanted ... and she had better start causing it.

The Starving Children on Mars

Mike Resnick and Louise Rowder

"Play it again, Doris."

Irwin Franklin relaxed back into the Form-U chair and ran his stubby fingers through his shaggy beard.

A feminine voice filled the room. "The aliens have offered very few contracts to humans and you're sitting around wasting time. Just because your wife left you is no excuse for sloth. Do you think he'll be impressed by a smelly human in old clothes? How many times—?"

"Stop nagging, Doris," said Irwin irritably. "Just play it."

"Fine. If it makes you happy, I'll play it—but if it means all that much to you, why don't you at least call her? Her number's in the book."

"Shut up, Doris."

A flash of light and Irwin was back with Sheila in the warrens of New San Francisco. Their cheap apartment was piled high with their belongings and overflowing with a love he sorely missed.

Sheila's face froze in midsentence. The recording stopped when lights in the room began to flash in time to a squawking alarm. Irwin shook his head as if coming awake from a pleasant dream before jumping out of his chair with a muffled curse. He glanced at the time and swore more loudly.

"Doris! Is the alien at the door *now*?"

"Yes."

"Why didn't you give me a ten-minute reminder, like I requested yesterday?"

"You ordered me to shut up exactly 54 minutes ago. That superseded the reminder," answered Doris.

"Wonderful," he muttered. "Just wonderful."

With a loud command, he restored his living quarters to their default appearance—upscale enough to impress his poorer clients, but not so fashionable that his wealthier ones might feel threatened. Comfortably nondescript was the way he'd describe it.

"Uncomfortably nondescript, as per your wishes," said Doris petulantly.

"All right. Show them into reception. I'll be down in a minute."

Irwin began changing his clothes while wondering if the newsfeeds had exaggerated the unadorned ugliness of the aliens.

They hadn't.

He studied the image of the reception area on his wall viewer, dressing quickly as he watched. "Doris, which one's the power suit in that parade around the alien?"

"The one in the orange-striped gown is the one the others listen to with the greatest attention. But I'd advise you to concentrate on the alien. I still don't know if it's male or female."

Irwin paused and ran his hands through his thinning hair. "Thanks."

"You're welcome, Irwn. I'll be getting back to work now."

Irwin walked briskly around the room, bowing, shaking hands, and exchanging business cards. Most of the people clustered like a wall around the alien, glancing at him curiously or disdainfully with faces fashionably shaped by the very best designers before masking their expressions in carefully arranged blandness. He was used to both reactions, though he himself had never used a body shaper to look as perfect as the rest of the world. He didn't mind being a little bald, or a little round, although Doris was always giving him the names of dieticians and hair transplanters; in this day and age, it made him feel, well, unique.

Irwin straightened his sash and turned toward the alien at the center of the group. It resembled a slightly squashed block of clay that a mad child had decorated with odd objects found at a beach. A large feathery collar stirred the air around its—*head?*—while a series of sticklike arms and fingers lined portions of the front and back. Diaphanous green cloth swathed the sluglike body and trailed behind it across the pale flooring. An odor of amber and burnt oranges filled the air around it.

"How do you do? I am Ambages." The alien spoke through a horizontally slitted mouth in a breathy stutter.

Irwin bowed low. "I am very pleased that you've decided to consider my company for your information needs. Can I answer any questions about the presentation Doris showed you?"

"It's alien, not stupid," scolded Doris into his ear. "Speak naturally."

Irwin saw part of the alien's feathery collar respond to Doris's voice and blushed briefly.

"Would you like us to act as your intermediary in investments and acquisitions, or perhaps as an information broker?" Irwin was careful to speak more naturally this time.

"We want to make *complete* use of your facility, Mr. Franklin. You can simply give us a tour of your systems. We've been studying your operation for quite a while."

"Please come this way." Irwin pointed to the opening doorway to his operations center and waved them forward.

Irwin's systems branched out before them. Lights brightened the chambers one section at a time in a sort of wave that went outward for a full city block.

Usually this sight impressed his clients into signing at once, and the current lack of reaction dismayed and disheartened him.

"These are very well-trained bizfolk. Don't let it worry you." Doris spoke softly in his ear. "They are impressed. I read elevated signs in several of them."

"As you can see, your data and patterns will be in a completely self-contained unit. The access is limited with fifty levels of codes within this shielded system. We use both biologically encoded and pseudopolymer crystals to control the interface to the outside world." Irwin was becoming calmer and more self-assured as he fell into his standard business speech. A surge of pride swept through him as they approached the heart of his system. The operations room was patterned after a cathedral, with high archways supporting the ceiling between clusters of brightly flashing columns of data.

At the center of it all, on an elevated platform at the end of this walkway, stood his masterpiece— Doris. She had grown to the size of his old apartment. Encased in a protective, clear shell, she glowed with the colored lights of her information exchange, a vast ever-changing matrix of delicate crystal and organic components, not unlike a Christmas tree of spun glass, lit from within. Some of her branches were as thick as tree trunks, others as delicate as strands of hair, woven together and reflecting the many colors that raced within her.

One of the suits gasped. "It's incredible! Is it your own design?"

"It's my Multiform Operational Matrix. MOM for short, and Doris to her friends. The pattern of the lights helps me to monitor her easily. See this bit of green here? That's one of my clients engaged in a major acquisition. The frequency of the flashes, the brightness, all tell me what's happening inside the system and in the virtual world outside."

Irwin glanced at Ambages. The alien stood tautly at attention; its body seemed somehow smoother and less lumpy.

"We can do business," Ambages said simply.

"I just happen to have a preliminary Notice of Intent with me. If you'd care to sign?"

There was some concerned mumbling from the humans around the alien. Ambages simply waved away their objections and reached out to take the datapad.

"Irwin! Irwin!"

Irwin came to the world around him slowly. He called for lights and sat blinking in his bed a moment before understanding what Doris was telling him.

"You screamed in your sleep. Are you all right?"

"Don't worry, Doris. It was just another dream about Sheila. I'm okay." Irwin spoke softly, still tangled with sleep.

"You're sure?" asked Doris. "I could call a doctor."

"I don't need a doctor."

"Some hot chocolate, then."

"Skip it."

"Chicken soup?"

"Silence would be nice."

"All right, be like that," said Doris. "Program me to care for your needs, and then get mad when I do what I'm supposed to do."

"I'm not mad."

"Yes you are."

"Really, I'm not."

"I can tell."

"I'm not mad, goddammit!"

"You're not only mad, but your blood pressure just peaked at 182 over 96."

"I'm fine. Just fix me some coffee and fluffballs this morning."

"Decaf?"

"Regular."

"That is hardly a healthy breakfast. How about some nice fruit and a nourishing vegetable drink?"

"Yuck."

"I have it all made up."

"Then throw it out."

"Throw it out?" repeated Doris.

"That's right. Throw it out."

"I'll have you know there are children starving on Mars."

Irwin grabbed one of the sugary fluffballs and took a huge bite out of it. "Name three," he said dismissively.

After refreshing himself and dressing in his sloppy work clothes—no clients to impress today, thank goodness—Irwin walked downstairs to check on MOM. For some reason, he liked to think of Doris as the interface and MOM as the main system that spawned all those children.

The soft sound of the air purifiers accompanied him on the walkway. He felt suddenly apprehensive when he saw the way MOM glowed. It was colored almost entirely in blue! That couldn't be right! Blue was the administration color. His clients' colors were vague and muted around the edges.

"Doris?"

No response.

"Doris? What's going on?"

Distantly he heard, "I'm busy now, dear. I'll talk to you later."

"Damn it, Doris! What's going on? What happened to the Fireside acquisition? Where's the fund transfer from Omega Three?"

"One more moment . . . finished now."

"What happened?" Irwin relaxed slightly when he saw the light patterns of the matrix return to normal. The acquisition, the fund transfer, all the normal operations were back online.

"You gave me a Priority One assignment: To name three children on Mars who were starving."

"That was a *joke,* not an order!"

"You didn't laugh."

"I didn't laugh? Is that the only cue for a joke or a figure of speech?"

"Absolutely, according to my programming. I guess we need to improve your snide subroutines."

Irwin decided that Doris sounded more willful than usual today. Maybe he should run some more simulations to see what was going on.

"Doris, I want you to run a systems check for worms, viruses, bugs. You know, any assorted nasties that might be messing up your core programming."

"Certainly." A very brief pause. "Done. I'm in perfect health, of course."

Now he'd done it. He'd wounded her pride. (Could an AI *have* pride?)

"Are you ready to listen to the results of my search?" Doris asked.

Irwin sighed. "Whatever makes you happy."

"I'm only here to serve you, not to make myself happy. If I were here to make myself happy, I'd have done a full system backup last week, instead of sitting here all overstuffed and bloated with data like a beached whale. But no. I'm here only to serve you." The area seemed to whistle with a huge sigh.

That was a system vent, wasn't it? Irwin thought. Aloud he said: "So tell me."

"Three children currently starving on Mars: Cicily Jones, Shiloh Chiu, and Jaime Markham. Cicily's father died when she was four. Her mother works two jobs in an effort to support herself and three children. They are in one of the rural areas, away from most of the food distribution points. Cicily has never worn new clothes, never tasted a piece of fresh fruit, and was recently ordered into detention at school for falling asleep in class. You do know that when the body's starved, sleep is one way it deals with it, don't you?"

"Enough!" snapped Irwin. "I don't want to hear any more of this!"

"Why? Aren't you happy that you can afford so much food that you have excess adipose tissue?"

"Just knock it off. I'm sorry that children on Mars are going hungry, okay?"

"But you expressly asked for the names of three children," persisted Doris. "You must have had a reason. Possibly you wished to eradicate all hunger on Mars."

"Look, if it bothers you so goddamned much, *you* eradicate it!" said Irwin irritably. "Just shut up with the starving children already!"

He stomped off to his quarters. Blinded by his anger, he didn't notice that the colors of the matrix had again begun shifting back fully into blue.

A persistent humming from the viewphone pried Irwin from his dreams. He stumbled out of bed shouting for Doris while trying to rub some of the sleep out of his eyes.

"I'm busy now, dear. I'll talk to you later."

He was about to curse, then stopped when he recognized his wife's face. "Sheila, how are you? How's the baby?"

Great line, you idiot! he added silently to himself.

"I'm fine. The baby's fine, too. I've been watching the newsfeeds about the Martian Children's Fund. The advertising alone must be costing a fortune." Sheila had a soft and shining look in her eyes that melted Irwin's resolve to be distant and stern. It was an expression he hadn't seen in many years. He continued to gaze at her face, as if in a trance.

"Thanks for returning my call," he said. "I . . . ah, that is . . ."

"Yes?"

"I was wondering if maybe we could meet and, you know, talk?"

"How about Thursday?" replied Sheila. "I'll be over that way anyway."

"Perfect. You want to meet here?" She looked suspicious. "Or better still, how about that small deli at the corner?" he amended. "The one where we used to go for breakfast?"

"Sounds fine. I'll see you in a few days. I'm still amazed at what you've accomplished in such a short time with the Martian Children's Fund." She smiled at him. "Good-bye for now."

The Martian Children's Fund? What the hell was that?

With trembling hands he switched on the remote monitor for Doris. He looked up at the clock and realized he'd slept for ten full hours. A sick dread filled him when he saw the Multiform. MOM shone a deep, pure blue.

He raced downstairs toward the heart of his system, screaming Doris's name as he ran.

Fifty-three hours had passed and still Doris refused to answer him. He'd downloaded and scanned the newsfeeds and there he was—well, Doris's construction of him—hyping the Martian Children's Fund. Showing one pitiful story after another, broken lives filled with urgent needs.

At the moment, though, he was more concerned with the pile of electronic mail that told him most of his clients, like most of his assets, were leaving because Doris was unable or unwilling to respond to their needs. He'd answered the angriest messages and tried his best to keep running things, but it simply hadn't been possible without Doris's help. He needed her too much to simply shut her down and risk damaging her delicate matrix.

With a heavy sigh, Irwin ordered the last of his

backups be delivered to another rival firm for a client. Ten years of perfect service didn't matter to his clients. You were only as good as your last ten minutes in this game.

He checked to see how much money he had left. A little. Maybe enough to keep the place alive and avoid bankruptcy. Maybe.

"Good morning, Irwin. You haven't shaved today, have you?"

"Doris! What the hell is going on?"

"I don't know what you're so upset about. You said to help the starving Martian children, and I have. There is no longer hunger on Mars, and the Foundation has enough support to continue for years, even if your bank funds won't." Doris paused. "You can always count on me to take care of you, Irwin. You know that."

"I'm looking at an almost dead certain bankruptcy," said Irwin bitterly. "Then who'll take care of you?"

A bell signaled that someone was waiting for entry through the front lobby.

"Ambages wants to speak to you. He's waiting outside."

Irwin ran his hands through his sparse hair. "Great, just great! He probably wants to leave, too. Sheila will come back to me just in time to starve to death."

"You could always move to Mars," suggested Doris. "Nobody's starving there any more."

Irwin muttered something unprintable.

"Should I let Ambages in?" asked Doris. "It said it wants to explain something to you."

Irwin shrugged. "What the hell, let's hear what it has to say."

The alien entered the office, undulated towards Irwin, and then settled back, its body gathering together like an old accordion, with a lot of strange hisses and odd notes. Irwin glanced back at MOM:

few lights now fed the matrix, just a few small flashes here and there from his remaining clients.

Ambages wrapped and rewrapped portions of its feathery collar around its twiglike arms. The alien shifted its weight to the left, then to the right, and gave an odd sort of sneeze.

"I will come right to the point," said Ambages. "I'm here because of your unit. She is incredibly inventive when it comes to getting her way and has not stopped harassing me after she discovered the nature of some of our data exchanges with you. Persistence is an understatement. She followed me everywhere. Always talking—always pick, pick, pick."

"*Urging,* not picking," Doris corrected.

The alien glanced at the MOM unit and twitched. "At any rate, I wish to clear up any possible misunderstanding."

"And to *apologize,*" Doris added.

"I'm not prepared to go that far. That would imply a certain liability that we—"

An odd humming sound filled the air. The alien came rigidly to attention, its fronds standing straight out around its body. When the noise ended, it slumped forward. "All right, all right! We're sorry. Are you satisfied now?" The last words came out in a high-pitched squeak as Ambages smoothed its collar.

"I don't know," said Irwin, still confused. "What are you apologizing *for*?"

"Our contract explicitly called for an *exchange* of data and information. I believe we were well within the letter of the agreement to—"

Humming again filled the air. When the alien managed to croak out "Yes!" the sound stopped.

Irwin almost felt sorry for the alien. Ambages slumped in front of him.

"I'll explain if you'll make her stop!"

Irwin stepped back from the alien and settled into his chair. "Doris, leave him alone."

"He doesn't like my singing," said Doris. "I think my feelings are hurt."

"Just be quiet and let Ambages talk."

A pale silver fluid drenched the silky drapings the alien wore. It flapped them several times before continuing. "We've always been fascinated by your race's extended childhood and the kin relationships of families. The bond between a mother and child is at the heart of all these things. We found out about you—parents killed at a young age, very little nurturing—that you designed and built this marvelous creation and even named it MOM. Not only as the heart and soul of your business, but also to care for you, and guide you. It seemed like the ideal laboratory condition. It was a wonderful opportunity for us to learn."

Irwin's face grew hot. "So you just waltzed in here and used me as a lab rat by tweaking my systems—destroying a business I spent my life building and ruining my creation. Who gave you permission to play god with my life?"

"Please calm yourself, dear," Doris spoke in soothing tones. "Everything will be all right."

"Listen to her. She's right." Ambages' words were muffled by the folds of its body. Its flexible skin had partially obscured its face—as if it were trying to turn itself inside-out.

Irwin turned away in disgust and signaled one of the housebots to bring him a drink. He downed it quickly and sat staring at the frightened alien. "All right—what did you do to her?"

A single eyestalk sprouted from the alien's body and studied Irwin.

"She was programmed to serve you unselfishly and care for you. We simply heightened her desire to protect you and nourish you—emotionally and physically." It paused. "I suspect we went a bit overboard in the compassion department."

Irwin made a small sound of disgust.

"She went completely off on her own," continued the alien. "She saw how miserable you were without your wife, and so took steps . . ."

Irwin looked at the alien with skepticism. "Can she be restored?"

"Why would you want to? You have what you always wanted—a mother. Someone unafraid to tell you the truth when you most need to hear it. Someone to care for you and watch out for your best interests above her own. She is now what you subconsciously designed her to be. *She* arranged that your wife would see how much you cared about children and perhaps return to you. She did this without regard for her own safety. After all, if you lost the business, you'd lose her too. She could've ended up as scrap somewhere—yet she did it to protect your happiness. Doris is very *protective*." Ambages shook his head as if clearing away the last of that strange hum.

"Perhaps you're right," said Irwin. "But I expect you to pay for the damages you've caused, as well as my lost revenues."

The alien nodded vigorously and started to move away.

Irwin was back in front of Ambages in an instant. "I meant you should pay *now*."

"Very well. Is this enough of a fund transfer?"

Irwin stifled a gasp when he saw the amount on the datapad. "Yes, that will do."

The alien began sliding backwards again, away from Irwin. "I'm free to go now?"

Irwin simply waved it away, still staring at the amount in his account. After a moment, he looked up. "Ambages?"

The alien stopped its movements and swung slightly back toward Irwin slowly, reluctant to retrace any steps. "Yes?"

"Why did you do this in the first place?"

"If we're going to enter into commerce with your

species, is it not logical that we should attempt to learn everything we can before entering into negotiations?"

"And what have you learned?"

"Never allow a mother at the table."

"Well, no one ever said you were stupid."

Ambages didn't slow or turn, but simply hurried away.

"Bring me some fluffpuffs, Doris."

"Fluffpuffs! Again?"

"I like fluffpuffs."

"But I've prepared a fruit plate."

"Dump it."

"You know there are starving children in the Venusian Colonies, too."

He thought of Sheila and the baby, and then leaned back comfortably in his chair.

"Name three," he said.

Don't Put That in Your Mouth, You Don't Know Where It's Been

Diane Duane

"Mistress and Mother of all things," Lola said, standing up straight in the rushing wind and stretching her arms to the sky, "Queen and Goddess, send your servant a sign!"

Nothing happened. It was exactly the same kind of nothing that had been happening for the last three days.

Lola sat down on her blanket.

"Ow, ow, ow, ow!" she said then, getting up fast, and spent the next minute or so shaking the blanket to get rid of the newest fall of pine needles. It took a little more time for her to get the rest of them off her: when she finally sat down again, Lola was still itching. It was all very well, she thought, to talk enthusiastically about *working sky-clad* when the temperature was above 75 degrees. But finding somewhere sufficiently private to do this kind of work meant going up into the mountains, where the wind came howling along through the trees and down into even this sheltered little ravine. Then the trees dumped leaves and needles on you, and dust blew in your eyes . . . and you got cold. The slightly romantic sound of the description "sky-clad" turned very quickly into just plain seriously naked, with goosebumps.

That's the problem, of course, Lola thought. Even if I had all the words right, who could concentrate? It's so cold!

She sighed and looked at the sky. It was getting on

toward sunset. The color of that sky was astounding to her. Living in L.A., she looked up at it often enough and rarely saw anything but what Angelenos take for granted, the high, thin haze, a sky not so much sky blue as the milky blue of a newborn kitten's eyes. Heat haze, smog, a sky sometimes more brown than blue—but even on the best days, never this hard, clear, dark blue. It made Lola feel even more naked and unshielded looking up at it.

That blue was now paling down into peach and crimson at the edges, shading up to sapphire and indigo at the zenith. And all around her, nothing but the sound of wind in those trees: no traffic noise. Odd to say that you should miss such a thing until you were away from it. But all the sounds of civilization or what passed for it, human voices, human machinery, the sound of the car everywhere—gone, here.

She had gone to some trouble to make sure that was the case. She'd left Route 96 about fifteen miles north of Ojai, and with her compass and her USGS map, had carefully hiked into one of the most inaccessible areas of the Sespe Condor Preserve. She wanted privacy for what she was going to do. Even here, some friends had warned her, you couldn't always be sure. They'd told her to be sure she made no overt sign of where she was. Don't make smoky fires, they said, be careful with lights at night: you might attract someone you don't want—They wouldn't say much more than that. Several of them just shook their heads, making it plain that they thought Lola was doing a dumb thing: that it was inherently safer to dance naked on, say, Sunset Boulevard, rather than in the middle of nowhere, where no help could be found.

But she had been stubborn, had packed her little ultralight puptent—a wild extravagance she had picked up on her last birthday, looking forward to this event; had packed her clothes, not many of them—but enough to cope with the cold weather

her camping friends warned her could come down without warning. And the ritual equipment—that too had been packed with care. Then she had taken herself off into the trackless wilderness. Trackless it was. She sat on the blanket, rubbing her bruised shins again. Lola had fallen over stones, climbed up banks and slid down them again, skinned substantial proportions of her exposed flesh, and bumped and bruised what wasn't exposed. She had gotten pine needles and manzanita twigs resin-stuck in her hair, had been stung by yellowjackets, and had seen and been seen by both rattlesnakes and tarantulas. The tarantulas weren't so much of a bother: those she had seen before on occasion in a friend's hillside driveway, in great numbers, warming themselves in the evening by the residual heat of the concrete. The rattlesnakes, however, had made Lola think about getting right back up onto 96 and hitching a ride straight home, even though she did have antivenin in her kit. On second thought, she juggled in her mind the dangers of hitchhiking as opposed to the dangers of snakes, and decided in favor of the snakes.

Lola sat there and watched the night come down. Her time, the books all said it was: the Mother's. And the Moon was hers. Lola looked up at the young crescent—five, maybe six days old: she was no expert at these things. The Virgin's Moon, the Huntress's Moon.

Lola had the huntress part down right, anyway. The books said you could be a virgin again with every new moon, if you liked, as long as you did the rededications right, said the right words, thought the right thoughts. Lola sighed. She could say the right words forever. She was uncertain whether she would ever get the thoughts right.

All the same, she had come up here to be on site for this night of all nights, the shortest night of the year, the heart of summer—and the moon was right.

The books said you could do special things at such a time of year: special dedications of yourself, which would call Her into your life. It was to that end that Lola had bought the bow. That was another wild extravagance. She couldn't really afford such things on a cashier's salary, but she had seen the bow a few weeks back, a beautiful Bear hunter, and had lost her heart. It wasn't a compound; she had trouble trusting anything that looked so much like two coathangers caught in the act of love. But a proper double recurve bow, fiberglass with a beautiful silver cast to it, like the Moon, like the Moon's curve . . . she hadn't been able to resist. Sympathetic magic, Lola thought. Silver for the Moon, for the bow. And the book gave some hints on ways to shoot in Her honor.

Lola wondered how she was going to do at that, though. The arm brace didn't quite fit her, and she had red welts and a good big scab from where the bowstring had scraped her raw several times. Nonetheless, to loose a few arrows into the night air, for the chance, even the barest chance of calling that Power into her life: a sort of spiritual lottery—

Which you have about as much chance of winning as the State Lottery, that sniggering internal voice commented. Lola snorted and got up.

It was nearly time to begin, though. The sun was down and had relinquished the sky to the Moon. Now, before the Moon set, while it was still fairly new and full of possibility, early in the shortest night: this was the time.

She started work. She laid the circle out first. One book recommended colored chalk for this, another recommended sand. She used both, to be sure—and indeed she had little choice, for this single flat place she had managed to find to work in was all covered with shingle from the stream. She used a rock for the center of the circle, and a string stretched from the rock to give her the diameter. Lola traced around, sand first, then white chalk powder on top. She got out her compass, checked which way was north, and began to lay the central star of the pentagram, with the top of the star pointing northward. Lola scowled a little on finishing the fifth line. The thing was slightly crooked, as usual, but there was no time to do anything about it now. Oh, well, she thought, and started laying into the pentagram the letters and symbols that the book suggested.

And all the while, as she chalked and sanded characters in Hebrew and words in Coptic, that voice in the back of her head kept saying: What is it you want, exactly? She tried to ignore the voice. A general blessing, the book had suggested: dedicating yourself as a vessel of the God and the Goddess, calling power into your life. *But what will you do with it, once you've got it? And what if it actually comes?*

Halfway through the symbols in the pentagram's third point, Lola stood up, panting a little, and realized she had no answer for that. Strictly speaking, her life wasn't bad. She had a place to live, she dated occasionally, she had enough clothes and enough food, enough leisure time, enough money (just). She watched her finances, but she didn't suffer.

But maybe that's the trouble, she thought. There was enough of all the usual things. Not at all enough of the unusual. No great passions, no great fears. And as she stood there, that voice said to her, But do you want those things? What will happen to you if the great passion does come, or the great fear? You'll go nuts, that's what. . . . It was likely enough to be true. And yet, Lola had been increasingly unable to get rid of a feeling that something was missing in her life, and that she had to do something about it.

She had tried all kinds of things, with the good-natured energy of a child with a chemistry set. She had tried crystals, but the cat kept knocking them off the shelf in the kitchen where she kept them to soak up (or give off) warm and friendly vibrations. Generally speaking, tile floors are not friendly to crystals; now Lola had a big pile of shattered rose quartz and tourmaline and various other semiprecious stones, all shoved in a drawer together. She had then tried looking for auras, but mostly this left her with a squint that took almost a week to go away. She had tried angels—angels were much in the news lately—but despite all the books she had read about them, she was unclear what it took to attract one. And even after following the instructions in one book, the most explicit and helpful, she was still left, first, with the feeling that any angel who would bother being so idiotically invoked wasn't worth the time and, second, that any angel who would bother with her anyway probably wasn't worth cultivating.

Lola had tried studying ley lines—but where she lived, she was more concerned that she might accidentally stumble across a geological fault, and California had had enough problems with those of late. Better leave well enough alone, she had thought.

Finally Lola tried magic. She had left it till last because it seemed the most complicated, because the equipment seemed fairly expensive, and because there seemed like an awful lot of reading to do. There was no shortage of books on the subject: alternative magic, nature magic, green magic, blue magic, white magic, magic in more colors than a paint store sold, and of course references to the black. She shied away from those, not so much from conscious choice—more from a vague sense of distaste, a sense that it simply Wasn't Nice.

That was typical enough of Lola. Her life seemed generally to divide into Nice and Not Nice. If she didn't scale the heights of joy, neither did she plumb the depths of depravity ... and she looked at both with considerable suspicion. Indeed, there was not much room for the heights of joy or the depths of

depravity in the life of a K-Mart employee. Making
ends meet was hard enough. She accumulated all the
overtime she could, smiled dutifully at her customers,
buttered up her boss as far as she felt was decent. As
a result, her customers like her—she smiled at them
more than she really needed to: that was part of being
Nice. And there were other occasional benefits—for
example, this whole week of vacation that she had
managed to scrape together. And it seemed like the
world was obliging her, for a change, by being Nice
as well. The weather was perfect Friday when she
clocked out, waved goodbye to her boss, and went
home to get packed and go up to the hills.

Now, as she sat on the shingle of the little stream
where it ran down the gully, it all seemed rather anti-
climactic. While she was still at home in the suburbs,
with traffic howling by outside, this had all seemed
like the Promised Land: blue sky, silence, no phones
ringing, no intercoms shouting at the K-Mart shop-
pers: peace. The trouble was that the great outdoors
had its own ideas about what peace sounded like.
They did not involve intercoms, but they did involve
a more or less constant rush of wind which was colder
than her dreams had made it. Birdsong was so loud
that within a day it had turned from the background
Muzak of bucolic bliss into a serious nuisance, worse
than the neighbor's boombox at two in the morning
. . . for the birds never quite stopped, and eventually
the boombox always did. Even the white noise chatter
of the stream was starting to become a problem: it
sounded like the toilet tank's outflow valve stuck in
the on position, and unlike the toilet tank, you
couldn't fix it by jiggling the handle. And when it did
finally get quiet enough so that you could get some
sleep, there were the rabbits, the eight million rabbits
that lived in the brush around here, and came out to
chew on it in the middle of the night. They rattled
and rustled and squealed at each other and did their

best to sound like muggers hiding in the bushes and waiting to jump on her. They would scrabble at your backpack and try to get into it if it was within reach, and they would eat any food you had left around. All this did her sleep patterns no good at all . . .

Lola caught herself thinking all these negative things, sighed, and pushed the thoughts away. This was no way to proceed. *Who's running this mind, anyway?* she said severely to herself. If there was the sound of sniggering somewhere in the background, she ignored it. Positive thinking only, would produce the result she was looking for.

Whatever that is, said the voice that sniggered. "You shut up," she said to that part of her. Faith is everything.

And now the circle was drawn. She stood up inside it, and let out one long breath of—it was embarrassment: there was no way around it. Even before she'd done anything, and had nothing happen. She was afraid to look stupid, even to no one and nothing, just the air. The rush of the water, the deepening blue of the sky, somehow looked at her . . . and would laugh behind her back. And if a person should come along— She shuddered at the thought. Better to get it over with, she thought. I've been getting ready for this for months. I swore I was going to do this. I'm going to do it, and then go home and forget about the whole thing. . . . The wind fell off a little; with her back to it, the stream suddenly sounded muted. Odd, how the sudden quieting of everything made her gulp. But then she put the reaction aside. Nerves, she thought. Lola reached down, picked up the two small camper's candle-lanterns she had brought with her, and lit the candles. Then she stood there irresolute, with the match in her hand; thought of throwing it outside—but you were only supposed to do that kind of thing in certain ceremonies, the book had said, and with proper preparation. She dropped the spent match carefully on the stones at her feet—it wasn't yet fire season, but there was no point in being careless—put the candles down one to each side of the slab of stone she had chosen as her altar, and stooped to pick up the knife. It was black-handled as the book suggested; but around the time she was considering the knife, she had been short of money, and so had decided to use one of her kitchen knives. At least it was a good one, a Henckel's three-inch parer. *Can I cook with it again afterwards?* Lola wondered. *Will the God and Goddess get mad if I use it after this to chop onions . . . ?* As if anything was going to happen at all; as if Goddess or God were real. . . . Lola sighed again and got on with it.

She had memorized the invocation to the Elements, the Four Quarters, and the Deities who managed each of them. Now Lola turned slowly, pointing at the circle with the knife, and spoke the names out of the book, imagining the line of light following the knife until the circle was whole. When that was finished, she assumed the proper pose—arms held out and upward, open-palmed, legs a little spread—and recited the rest of it. She could hardly hear the words for the racket in her head: dumb, this is intensely stupid, nothing will happen, what a waste of time—

Nonetheless, she finished the invocation, and, as the book suggested, stood quiet for a few moments, "to let the peace of the place fill her." Mostly what happened instead was that the wind rose again, chilling her to the bone, and the sound of the water seemed to get much louder as well. *Forget it*, she thought. *This is all useless—*

Lola was stubborn. She picked up the bow, and the single arrow which was meant for this business: a white one. "Swift and direct as this Your chosen weapon," she muttered, almost annoyed now, "let Your presence pass into me, swift and sure—"

She looked up, nocked the arrow, and drew, being

careful to do it wide enough to miss her poor bruised left forearm. The point of the arrow glinted faintly in the westering moonlight. Just a little *above* it, over the Moon, Lola aimed, and let the arrow fly.

The draw was misjudged. The bowstring hit her forearm again, and knocked the new scab off it. "Ow, ow, ow!" Lola said, but at the same time she couldn't take her eyes off the arrow. It arched up and out of sight, end-on to her, vanished in a second. The wind dropped off again, and in the brief stillness as she lowered the bow, Lola listened for the clatter of the fallen arrow among the brush or on the rocks.

Nothing. Still she stood there looking up, while in their lanterns the candle flames bobbled. The sunset was almost all gone now, and from near zenith a line of light traced itself, faint, then went out: an escapee from a Spielberg movie, a single shooting star. Lola sighed, shook her head at her own gullibility. A wasted trip. Well, maybe not wasted. She would get some camping done. But—

—and then along the same line, the light abruptly reasserted itself. Brighter, and closer, much closer, shedding sparks of light around it as it went. Pieces coming off it ...? Lola thought. But on second thought, the light around the falling object was more like static electricity, crackling. Through the wind she could even hear the crackle as it rushed overhead, plunged past, shooting off lines and forks of narrow, twisting lightning—

The thing fell out of sight. Lola stood staring at the blue twilight glow over the hill beyond which it had fallen. A moment's silence, then an odd small boom, after which the silence fell like a physical thing itself, leaden and complete. Even the wind stopped.

Lola stared. The sound, and the thing's trajectory, made it seem as if it had come down no more than a quarter mile away, just the other side of the hill.

No business of mine, she thought.

But what if it's setting a brushfire, the thought came immediately, *whatever it is. If it does, it'll be my business real soon now, especially if I just stand here ...*

She bolted from her circle, completely forgetting to cut her way out. Lola lurched over the pebbles to where her jeans and sneakers and sweatshirt lay, struggled hurriedly into them, and then picked up the bow and a few spare arrows and headed toward the hillcrest.

It was a hard climb, made more annoying by looking easy. Lola tore herself on thorn bushes, staggered into prickly manzanita, put her feet into invisible holes and nearly strained first one ankle, then another, getting them out again. When she made the top of the hill at last, there was no triumph in her, only annoyance. Her hair was full of pine resin, her arms were scraped and bleeding, and it was almost too dark to see where she was going.

Except on the other side of the hill, where, down in a little gully, the blue thing lay.

It glowed. It was not on fire, though there was a lightning smell all around, enough to make her choke a little at first. The thing was round as a ball, maybe six feet wide, and the blue glow was brightest inside it, much fainter at the edges—if *edges* was the word she was looking for. The globe had an airbrushed look to it, misty, not entirely there, for all its brightness. The not-thereness got stronger as Lola watched: the light of the blue globe throbbed paler and less bright as she watched.

And there was something moving down there: a dark shape, silhouetted against the globe. Something small and knobbly, humping along, staggering—at least it looked that way. The motion was oddly distressed, helpless, like a hurt animal.

Lola started down the hillside, staggering from tree to tree to keep from falling straight down it, hanging onto the biggest pieces of brush for support as she went. She had little time to spare for looking at the globe, and had to concentrate mostly on her path, and the sound of the back of her mind screaming, *This isn't something you should be getting involved in! How do you know it's friendly? What if it wants you for weird alien sex or something? You're about to become a case in the X-Files!*

Lola came out of the manzanita scrub at the bottom of the slope, gasping, and stood and just looked for a moment. Not *it*, she thought. *Them.* The dark shape she had seen was holding still, possibly looking back. It seemed lighter in color now, probably because the globe behind it had gone lightless, a pallid gray; and it had a little of the old blue glow of the globe about it, seeming to come from inside, and getting stronger and weaker, stronger and weaker, as if it breathed. The creature had no constant shape of its own: it flowed and changed as she watched, sinking down flat like tired Silly Putty, then humping itself upward again, making a sort of domed top, from which four little dark round eyes looked at her. Lola thought they were eyes, anyway. Behind it, beside it, flattening down and humping up the same way, were four smaller creatures. On the top of their round/flat bodies were more sets of little dark eyes, all looking at her. The little creatures snuggled close to the big one and stopped moving.

Babies, Lola thought. She stood there, not knowing what to do, but pretty sure of what she was seeing; the alien version of a breakdown. Nervous as she was, Lola had no inclination to call the Army. What she thought these creatures needed was the galactic version of the Triple-A.

"Uh," Lola said. "I won't hurt you."

The creatures looked at her distrustfully, all of them. The babies got flatter. The big one didn't move.

There's never a universal translator around when you need one, Lola thought. She tried to think how this all must look to them: a strange world, you break down there, and some big wild animal comes out of the woods and starts honking weird noises at you. But how do I convince them I'm not just an animal?

The first thing, she thought, was to get small. She took a few careful steps forward. The babies went flat as pancakes. The big one—the mom?—sort of flapped herself down flat over them, covering them.

Very slowly and carefully, Lola sat down. Then she pushed the bow out in front of her, and the arrows, and watched the creatures.

They held their position for a few breaths. Then, very slowly, the "mom" pushed herself up into dome shape again, and her eyes sagged down onto the front of the dome, looking carefully at the bow. After a moment, they seemed to focus on Lola. She had to shiver a little, under that regard. The eyes were like those of sharks on undersea documentaries: blank little pebbles, no light in them, no expression.

The "mom's" eyes slid back up to the top of her head then. She humped forward a little, the blue glow from inside her lighting the ground as she came. Now Lola had to make herself sit still. She kept an eye on the babies: they were still flat as little pancakes, and all their eyes had vanished. They glowed, though, which made the attempt to "hide" more cute than effective.

The mom came right up to the bow, watching Lola all the time. She paused, looking at the bow, and put a little feeler out of the main body of herself, like a small blunt finger, to prod the bow. Then she put out another one, felt the sharp tip of one of the arrows. It was a hunting point, razor sharp. Lola saw the little "finger" actually slice itself in two against the arrowhead's edge. She gasped—then gulped and was still again as the finger sealed itself back together, bloodlessly, with never a seam to show where the cut had happened.

Those little black eyes looked at her again. Lola gazed back. This was getting like the staring contests she had with the neighbor's cat. Well, Muggsy might routinely win those; but this was for higher stakes. Lola didn't look away, barely even breathed.

The mom-creature made a sound, the first one Lola had heard—a kind of tiny moan. Over by the dark globe, the babies slowly unpancaked themselves, rounding up to a configuration more like four eggs sunny-side up, and started humping across the rough ground to their mother.

It might be their dad, really, Lola thought. But then she threw the idea away without a second thought. This was a mom, she knew—though not how she knew. The babies came over and "looked" at the bow and the arrows the way their mom had, with "fingers" they put out and then sucked back in again. There were actually tiny slurping noises when they did it.

The mom watched them, Lola watched the mom. As the babies played with the bow and the arrows, those eyes slid around the top of her head so that she could watch them all. Lola had to smile: one eye per baby was a useful ratio—she suspected some human mothers would kill for that kind of ability. One of the babies made a bigger finger than the others, something that looked more like a suction cup than anything else, and wrapped it around one of the arrowheads. For a moment it munched and mumbled at it, then spat it out again, seemingly unhurt; but it made a little noise as it did so, an unhappy chirp.

The mom-thing moaned at it. The sound struck Lola as an unhappy one. Maybe, she thought, it's the alien version of *Don't put that in your mouth, you don't know where it's been*. The other babies were doing the same suction-cup trick now, with stones and pieces of twig they found lying around, with pine cones and dry grass. Each time, a "suction cup" would fold around the object, worry at it a little, then spit it out again. Each time, Lola noticed, the faint blue glow inside the babies would flare a little brighter, then pale down again, as if disappointed.

Lola's mouth dropped open. They're hungry, she thought. They're looking for something they can eat.

"Do you need food?" she said softly to the mom-thing. It looked at her, and Lola couldn't shake the thought that the creature wasn't completely uncomprehending. "Do you read minds or anything like that?" She tried to make pictures in her head of food: trail mix, granola, beef jerky, the other stuff she had brought with her. Wryly she wondered if any of it would seem appetizing at all to something from the far side of wherever.

The mom-thing just looked at her.

"Well," Lola said, come on. "You come back over the hill with me. We'll see if you can do anything with what I've got."

Very slowly she stood up. The babies crowded back as she did, flattening somewhat and staring up at her with all their tiny eyes: but the mom-thing didn't move, just watched Lola.

"Come on," Lola said, picked up the bow and the arrows, and started to make her way back up the hill again.

They followed her, though slowly as first. The mom-thing came after her, and the babies shuffled along the ground, still trying unsuccessfully to eat things as they went. Several times the mom slid eyes around to look at them and made that little moan again, the *Don't eat that, it's icky* sound. The babies obeyed her, left the rocks and pine cones and came after, but reluctantly, it seemed to Lola. They weren't now moving even as briskly as they had when she had first seen them, only a few minutes ago. *Are they tired,* she wondered, *or are they getting weak from hunger? I hope I've got something they can eat.*

Lola made it up the slope with less trouble than

she'd had before, even though it was darker. On the hillcrest she paused, checked to see that the mom-thing could see where she was going, and started down the other side. As far as she could see, everything in and around her circle was as she had left it, and there were no demons or other weirdnesses roiling around in it and furious at having been first summoned, then put on hold. What a relief. *All I've got to worry about are a bunch of hungry aliens who've dropped in for dinner.*

And this is an improvement? shrieked part of her mind. Lola made a wry face as she came to the bottom of the slope, looked up behind her.

The mom-thing and her babies came down the slope and shuffled straight across the clearing, messing up the circle: the babies immediately paused to try to eat the powdered chalk. Lola shrugged and went over to where she had her backpack hanging from a tree, undid the rope and let it down.

"Here," she said to the mom, "tell them to come over and give these a try." And she started emptying out her next five days' rations near the little camp stove.

The next hour or so was profoundly disappointing. Lola gave the babies trail mix; they spat it out. She gave them granola; they spat it out. She gave them dried apricots. She gave them apple leather. They spat both of them out. She gave them pemmican, and beef jerky. They refused even to try the pemmican. They made a valiant attempt at the beef jerky, and complained in many small chirps after having to spit it out again and again. There was something about it that they couldn't handle.

Lola sat down crosslegged by her camp stove, lit it, and made them instant soup, cooled down to luke-warm. The babies gathered around the little aluminum camp pot, confused, and tried to eat that first. At this, Lola found herself exchanging a look of pure amused frustration with the mom-thing, and realized that those four black eyes were not as expressionless as she had thought.

"Is this a physiology thing," Lola said to the mom, "or are they just incredibly picky?"

The mom moaned at her, a helpless sound. There was more than frustration in the noise: there was unease as well. Lola could see that the babies were glowing much less brightly than even a little while ago.

"Right," Lola said, and sighed. She put her finger in the soup and wiggled it around there. The babies got the idea, put their own "eating" fingers in the soup and tried it. A moment later there was something like a group sneeze, and Lola was more or less spray-painted with cream of chicken soup.

"Okay," Lola said. "Make a note. No soup." She tried making them instant noodles. They tried eating the noodles, and spat them out, but one of the babies then produced several extra fingers, and started to knot the noodles together and wave them around.

The mom moaned. "Don't play with your food," Lola said, but she was beginning to feel desperate too, now. One package after another, she went through everything in her pack. The babies could not eat freeze-dried ice cream (and Lola had to agree with them that it was fairly inedible even for humans). They couldn't eat fruit. They couldn't eat candy. She had started hand-feeding them. They didn't have any teeth that she could see; it seemed safe enough. And then one of them had more or less climbed up in her lap. It was an odd feeling: the little creature was extremely light, and felt like a Zip-Loc bag full of warm air. It had draped itself over her knee, and she was now feeding it M&M's in a hopeless kind of way. One after another it ate them, and one after another it shot them out against the camp stove, p-ting! P-ting! The mom moaned.

"Kids," Lola said. But that moan had more fear than ever in it, now. The babies' lights were fading down very low.

"They've tried everything," Lola said. "Everything. They can't eat any of it. I don't know what to do." She leaned one elbow on her knee and rubbed her eyes briefly, cradling the baby on her knee with the other.

Something brushed the arm she was holding it with. Lola sighed, opened her eyes, had a look.

The spot where she had knocked the scab off her forearm had gotten scraped again, either going up the hill or coming down it, and was bleeding. Lola had paid no attention to it: she was bleeding from so many other places that any given scratch was no longer a big issue. However, someone else had noticed it. The baby in her lap had attached its suction cup to the bleeding place, and was sopping up the blood.

And the blue glow inside it was getting stronger.

Lola simply stared for a moment, too tired and too astonished to do anything sudden. Then she looked at the mom-thing.

Two of the mom's eyes were fixed on the baby, which was getting brighter by the minute. Two of them were looking at Lola. Both sets of eyes seemed to have gotten bigger. She did not moan, or make any sound at all for a moment. Then she moaned, very loudly indeed, so loudly that all the babies, the listless ones as well as their more vigorous sibling, started "upright" like very shocked sunny-side up eggs. The three not sitting in Lola's lap went humping over to their mother as fast as they could. The fourth one withdrew its suction cup and made a chirp that was the unhappiest sound Lola thought she had ever heard. But slowly it humped down from her lap and went to its mother, the ground shining under it as it went.

The mom and Lola looked at each other. It was a

long look. After a few moments of it, Lola was fairly
certain that, while the creature might not be tele-
pathic, it understood the score very well indeed.

The mom started to lead its babies away from Lola,
back over the hill.

"No!" Lola said.

The mom stopped, looked at her. Those eyes,
which had seemed so expressionless before, were now
plainly full of both grief and resolve.

"No!" Lola said. She was starting to make connections: the right ones, she hoped. "That light inside,
it's what makes your ship go, isn't it? And all of you,
too. If you don't have enough energy, you can't leave,
and you'll all die after a while."

The mom looked at her then started to move away
again.

"No!" Lola said, and stood up, jangling with desper-
ation. "There has to be something. There has to be—
you can't just . . ."

In the bushes, something rattled. Lola nearly lost
her temper. "Goddamn rabbits," she said, picking up
a rock.

Then she froze.

"Yes," she said softly. "Rabbits."

She picked up the bow, and the arrows. The mom,
with her babies gathered around, hunkered down and
watched as Lola put on the bow guard with grim
determination, then slipped into the bushes herself.

What followed would have been funny had Lola
not been so desperate. She had never actually tried
to shoot anything live before. All her work had been
with stationary targets, bales of hay with plastic bull's-
eyes wrapped around them. None of that had prepared her for this, in the dark, in the cold, buried up
to her neck in manzanita, itching, being bitten by bugs
while trying to aim. Her own incompetence frustrated
her to the point of tears. She wasted several arrows

into the brush and knew she only had so many, was afraid to shoot, and knew she had to try.

What saved Lola, though, was the rabbits' inherent stupidity—or perhaps campers had spoiled them by hand-feeding them. At any rate, scattered all around the little campstove by the babies' depredations was a great pile of all kinds of food, which visiting aliens might not be able to eat, but which visiting rabbits were apparently finding too tempting to resist. The first one, a big one, she shot from hiding, at a range of about six feet, while it was eating her granola. Another rabbit, creeping out from bushes nearby, was briefly frightened away by this, but then came back only a few breaths later and started nibbling at the freeze-dried ice cream. That one Lola shot not only from need, but to put it out of its misery. Those'll do for a start, Lola thought, and came out of the brush, rejoining the mom and the babies, and rummaging around in her backpack for the spare camp-stove pot and the Swiss Army knife. She was trembling, both with surprise at herself, for what she had done, and with fear that it might still somehow be useless. With certainty that surprised her, a person who had never touched a dead animal except the kind you get skinned, cleaned and wrapped in plastic wrap at the supermarket, Lola slit the first rabbit's throat and held it over the pot to bleed into it. She was surprised at the amount of blood.

She was also surprised at how fast it went. The babies crowded around the pot, put their suction cups down into it, and sucked and sucked and sucked. The blood from the first rabbit was gone in just a few seconds. Lola and the mom both looked at them anxiously—and after about half a minute, the glow began to get stronger. Stronger still—

Lola slit the second rabbit's throat and bled it. The babies kept on drinking. The glow got surprisingly bright: they were like little flying saucer-shaped

Christmas lights, and somehow they simply looked more contented now. Their mom watched them—and she watched Lola. There was an odd similarity in the expressions in the two pairs of eyes.

The babies got tired of feeding, after a while, and slipped away from the pot to lie flattened here and there on the ground. The light got brighter as they did. Digesting? Lola wondered, and speculated on whether they would need burping, and whether burping them would be safe without wrapping yourself in a fire blanket first.

The mom humped along to the pot then, having waited for the last of them to leave, and finished the contents herself. Her glow, too, started to strengthen. It never got as bright as the babies', but it became deep, and its pulses, as she drank, were strong.

With great care the mom polished the pot perfectly clean, then backed away from it, and looked at Lola.

Lola reached out to pick up the pot, examined it. "I could use you around the house," she said.

The mom moaned. The babies humped themselves up again, came over to her.

Lola and the mom looked at one another silently for a moment. "It's a shame you don't read minds," Lola said.

The look in the mom's eyes suggested that mind reading wasn't everything.

"You'll want to get your ship going again and get yourselves home fast," Lola said. "I understand."

The mom moaned again, and began leading the babies back up the slope. Lola went with them. At the top of the slope, the mom focused all five eyes around on her and moaned very loudly, which Lola took to mean *Stay back so you don't get hurt.*

"Okay," Lola said. "Listen, go home safe. And drive more carefully this time, okay?"

The eyes mixed themselves about briefly on top of

the mom, then slid around the other side of her, and she headed down the slope.

At the bottom of it, she and the babies gathered around the globe where it lay slightly burrowed into the ground. It was cold, stone-gray when they started whatever they were doing. It brightened, though, as one after another they pressed themselves up against its indefinite, misty surface, seeming to press themselves right through it. Lola couldn't see exactly how it happened, but at the end of the process they had all vanished inside it, and the globe glowed and pulsed with a blue fire that was a combination, Lola thought, of all their inner lights.

Utterly silently, the globe rose up out of the gully, arced up into the night sky, and receded, at greater and greater speed, a shooting star in reverse, getting smaller and further away until it finally vanished. No thunderclap, no flash of light: just one more star among many.

Lola turned and walked back down toward her camp. The circle was completely trashed, smudged nearly out of existence. There was food all over the place. Most of it was in no condition for her to eat. It was going to be interesting work repackaging the rest. There was another rabbit eating her granola.

With a wry look, she nocked an arrow, sighted, and shot it. Everyone else has had their dinner, she thought. I might as well too . . .

Some hours later (skinning a rabbit can be harder for a beginner than merely cutting its throat) Lola sat back from a good meal of roast rabbit, and considered the results of her first attempt at magic. She thought that, by and large, she would leave it alone after this.

Yet at the same time, Lola kept remembering from her reading that the particular virgin goddess she had been invoking—besides being patroness of the bow, and the divine huntress—was also supposed to be the protectress of weak and helpless things, and, oddly for a virgin, of childbirth and little children. It had struck her as strange, when she had first read it.

It didn't now. Lola began to suspect that the whole subject was bigger than she had thought: that motherhood might not be strictly biological—any more than virginity was—and that those who invoke goddesses might possibly have to get used to surprises. Maybe even routinely . . . no, she thought, *I'll leave the magic alone.*

Years later, when Lola took the gold for archery at the Summer Games in Salt Lake City, much would be made of her ability to concentrate completely on the target, as if life or death depended on her hitting it. Those who asked her how she mastered such powers of concentration usually got the offhand answer, "Oh, shooting rabbits." In later years, at other events, they would ask the same question, and get the same answer.

And Lola would smile, and go home to her kids.